Charles Boner

Chamois Hunting In The Mountains Of Bavaria And In Tyrol

Charles Boner

Chamois Hunting In The Mountains Of Bavaria And In Tyrol

ISBN/EAN: 9783741149313

Manufactured in Europe, USA, Canada, Australia, Japa

Cover: Foto ©Andreas Hilbeck / pixelio.de

Manufactured and distributed by brebook publishing software
(www.brebook.com)

Charles Boner

Chamois Hunting In The Mountains Of Bavaria And In Tyrol

CHAMOIS HUNTING

IN

THE MOUNTAINS OF BAVARIA

AND IN THE TYROL.

BY

CHARLES BONER.

𝔚ith Ellustrations

BY THEODORE HORSCHELT, OF MUNICH.

A NEW EDITION.

LONDON:
CHAPMAN AND HALL, 193, PICCADILLY.
1860.

PRINTED BY

JOHN EDWARD TAYLOR, LITTLE QUEEN STREET,

LINCOLN'S INN FIELDS, LONDON.

PREFACE

———◆———

In this new edition of 'Chamois Hunting' some Chapters have been added containing the experience gained during several years' shooting in the Tyrol.

Interspersed through the book will also be found various additional information respecting the habits of Chamois, as well as many new incidents, which may amuse those who took an interest in my former adventures. In "Pepi's Cottage" some very strange and peculiar local customs are described, and a Chapter that could well be dispensed with has been removed to make way for it.

For the Frontispiece I have to thank Mr. Karl Haag, who kindly permitted a copy to be taken of his admirable water-colour drawing.

An account of the curious habit of "Arsenic Eating" has also been thrown into a Note at the end of the Volume.

CHARLES BONER.

Munich,
September, 1860.

PREFACE

TO THE FIRST EDITION.

— ◆ —

IN the following pages will be found several German words often repeated; for, much as I dislike the admixture of one language with another, the present case left me without an alternative, the words in question not having an equivalent in my own tongue. I have therefore employed "Laane," "Latschen," etc., each time any mention is made of these objects, thinking it was better to do so than adhere pedantically to some English explicative, which would fail, after all, in conveying the exact meaning.

The compositions from the pencil of Mr. Horschelt need no praise of mine. The happy arrangement of each small picture speaks for itself; and we both may esteem ourselves fortunate in having found so skilful a hand as Mr. Hohe's to transfer them to the stone.

With regard to the scenes represented, I would observe, that they were chosen as giving a *general* notion of the mountains, rather than of the difficult and dangerous places met with by the chamois-hunter. Indeed not one of the views shows a position of any peril.   I was anxious to avoid everything that might appear like exaggeration; and for this reason a sketch (" Descending the Mountain") which Mr. Horschelt had made was omitted, lest the daring hardihood displayed therein might excite doubts as to its truth.

In the descriptions, also, it was equally my aim to keep rather *within* the limits to which I might have gone.   Some forms, perhaps, appeared to me more grand, and certain bright effects more beautiful, than they might have done to another: however, I am not aware of having given to either an undue importance or a too heightened colouring.   What I saw is described as *I* saw it.   My wish has been to reflect back on the page those pictures which, as they passed, my memory had retained; to impart to others the same vivid impressions which my own mind had received.

CHARLES BONER.

St. Emeram, Ratisbon,
  January 10, 1852.

CONTENTS.

— ◆ --

Part the First.

Part the Second.

— - —

Part the Third.

Notes.

xiii

List of Illustrations.

CHAMOIS HUNTING

IN

THE MOUNTAINS OF BAVARIA

AND THE TYROL.

INTRODUCTORY CHAPTER.

ABOUT twelve years ago I went out for the first time in my life to shoot deer. It was winter, and every attendant circumstance had the delightful excitement of novelty. As the woods whither we were going were some distance off, the whole party assembled betimes to a substantial breakfast. Then came the departure in the light sledges, each of us packing himself up in furs, and his feet and legs in coverings of sheepskin, to bid defiance to the sharp dry air, that was piercing enough to penetrate through every covering. Once off, the merry jingle of the bells on the horses' heads, the flying snowflakes as the light-limbed Hungarian horses dashed on over the smooth frozen surface—the benumbed passers through the streets shuffling along still half asleep, stopping however as we swept by—the partly hidden faces peeping from the windows, as the mingled melody of the many bells told what was coming—all afforded me amusement and gave me intense pleasure. There

B

was then the arrival at the place of our destination, the forester's house, where all his men and under-game-keepers drawn up in order were awaiting our arrival—the troop of beaters, uncouth, wild-looking peasants, clothed in every description of dress it is possible to imagine—the conversation with the head-keeper about the game, and the questions as to the day's sport—anxious inquiries too from one of the party, whether a deer that he had wounded some days before had been found or not—in short, the whole scene in which I had become an actor was totally new and strange to me, and I looked on, curious to see what novelty would happen next.

Each little incident that has so often since seemed like an every-day occurrence, was full of interest then We went out at last into the forest, where all was frost-bound, and every branch and twig enclosed in a crystal covering; where not a sound was heard, except the distant tramp of the beaters on the crackling snow, as they wound upwards through a hollow. Presently I was left alone at my appointed stand. By-and-by the sharp sound of a rifle came tingling through the clear air, and soon after a troop of deer would come stepping along quite scared and wondering over the snow. It was a new world to me, all this, and every incident gave me fresh delight. Later came the chace of the boar; and in summer-time I was on the hills, or moving amid the deep stillness of the woods at noon after the majestic stag. *That*, I thought, surpassed everything in enjoyment: the beautiful scenes into which it led me, the exciting circumstances that were constantly occurring, the gallant bearing of the magnificent creature that my rifle had at last brought down—all this caused my whole being to thrill with longing and with joy. After such a day in the forest, there was the sweet pleasure of going over every incident again in thought; I saw the mighty stag as he moved over the green sward in stately pride, I felt anew the hope and the fear and the breathless longing, and I once more stood over him as his vast form lay stretched upon the earth in the sunny beech-forest. At that time I lived in such sweet absorbing memories, or in anticipation of what was to come. For a day in the woods, with my rifle over my shoulder and the hope of meeting the red deer, I should have given up anything.

At last, however, as a matter of course, I grew somewhat calmer. My delight was not diminished—it was as great as ever; but the flutter, and the palpitation, and the burning impatience, were subdued. And indeed there was much need they should be. Then too I became initiated in the mysteries of the noble art, and by degrees learned to look on what belonged to it with a more tranquil eye. And when I thought how new and strange all had once appeared to me, how delighted I had been on first stalking through the forest, and how many there were in England to whom such exquisite pastime was quite unknown, it seemed that if I attempted to describe what had afforded me so much pleasure, the subject was one that could not fail to interest others also. I carried this idea long about with me, indolently delaying to execute what I had planned, when behold! another did what I had only thought of doing, and Mr. Scrope's book on Deer Stalking appeared. At the moment I was about to preach myself a sermon for my indolence, with a wise moral about the evils of delay, etc., but after a time I began to think the evil was not so great after all, and that it was very well as it was; much better indeed than had two works on the same subject appeared simultaneously.

Year after year passed away thus, and, thanks to the great kindness of the noble possessor of the extensive forests where I shot my first red deer, I afterwards enjoyed the privilege of always joining his party when the season began. Overlooking the Danube, the woods through which we ranged extended on every side for many miles. Right pleasant days were those, when we were met in the morning by the young foresters bringing their report of where the deer were to be found. The young fellows had been abroad since the dawn, and had crossed the furthest hill-top and skirted many a wood to be ready by the time of our arrival. They now came pouring in from all sides to the trysting-place, bringing with them the expected intelligence. In Stein Scigen were two stags, one of ten and the other of twelve;* indeed he might have fourteen, so large was his slot. Another had been round Hell Berg and Schopf Loh, but had seen nothing. He had seen tracks of deer, it is true, but they were old ones; and where they had gone to he could not think. They must have been disturbed, for " he had had them there" for four successive days, and they were there yesterday. Suddenly perhaps a messenger would arrive, all breathless with haste, with such speed had he come down the steep path that leads through the forest to the village. He brought the news that *the* stag which had disappeared so suddenly was come back again. " The same that Count H. missed lately?" " Yes, the very same :" he was now in a small wood on the hill-side in the next forest, and a young peasant who

---

* An expression made use of above may need explanation. The points on the antlers of a stag increase in number with his years ; to them therefore reference is always made when denoting the age and size of the animal. " A stag of twelve" is one with twelve points or branches to his antlers.

was quick of foot had been despatched immediately to inform his Highness of the event. Such was the information contained in the head-forester's hastily written note. What excitement was there then, and what hopes and questionings! As I look back on those days, I can hardly believe that all is now over, that the forests are as deserts, no longer peopled by their red inhabitants— that these, like the Red Indian of the prairie, have been hunted down and exterminated, and their haunts, once so full of life, become silent and lonely.

I think it would be quite impossible for me to describe the sensations, the exquisite delight of that delicious time. The freshness of the morning, the deep stillness of the woods at noon, the green and golden pageantry as the sunbeams pierced through a thousand crevices in the leafy roof, the breathless expectation when a light footfall told me the forest king was approaching—everything, in short, that belonged to the hunter's life was full of pleasurable sensations. But soon even these delights were to give way to others still more exciting. Our party during the shooting season was usually joined by two gentlemen who went regularly to the mountains to hunt chamois. Often of an evening, after a day in the forest, and while we all were sitting over our coffee after dinner, they would relate some adventure that had befallen them while watching for a strong buck high up among the snowy fastnesses of Berchtesgaden, or tell of the merry life they led on the less formidable mountains and in the *Senn Hütten** of Baierisch Zell; while on another occasion our very blood would almost curdle, as we listened and heard how one of them had crept along the narrow

* *Senn Hütte*, the same as "Chalet." The hut inhabited by the herdsmen and the dairymaids during their summer sojourn on the mountain.

ridge of a precipice near the Ober See, to fetch a chamois he had shot; and how, had his foot slipped or his head grown dizzy, he must have dropped perpendicularly through the air into the lake far, far below him. And to these tales of adventure I listened with as much eagerness and curiosity as I had done, when a boy, to tales of shipwreck and of sailor life; and with the same feeling too,—an ardent longing to share in such adventurous pastime. The other, more susceptible perhaps than his companion to the glories around him, would describe the scene that presented itself to his astonished gaze, when, having gained the summit of the mountain, the mists suddenly parting let in the golden light of the rising sun, and showed huge rocks and precipices, and green herbage, and high-up valleys all lying close before him at his feet. There was genuine enthusiasm in all these descriptions, and, like all genuine feeling, it did not fail of its effect. I could no longer resist the desire to move with rifle at my back amid such scenes; to step along those narrow ledges of rock, or creep up through the steep ravines which had become almost like well-known places to me, so much had I heard about them, and so particular had been my questionings; and at last the wish I had cherished for years was realized, and I stood upon the mountain-top and saw the chamois among the rocks.

Deer-stalking in the forest, with all its pleasures and excitement, was but tame sport to this. I could now well understand how with some it might become a passion so strong and irresistible, that not even all the hazards of a poacher's life prevented its gratification. The magnificent scenery, the daring and the danger, the vigour and elasticity of limb which the pure mountain air imparted, the glorious sunrise overflooding gradually the plains of snow, the loud cry of joy of the peasant-girl ringing upwards to the very sky,—all this sent a thrill through my whole frame, and my blood seemed to feel the thrill and tingled with exultation.

What would I not have often given could hearty old Christopher North have been with me to enjoy the sight, —to have watched the driving mists coming upwards from the valley, and have listened for a second amid that silence and solitude? He rather paints than describes; his words are colour, with which he fills a canvas, and so presents you with a picture of the scene. And then, too, that other master of his art, Edwin Landseer,—what a new field was here for his truthful pencil! Hardly a day ever passed but some good effect, some picturesque group, or some striking incident reminded me of him, and made me wish that he could be there, to catch the happy moment and give it a permanent existence. The peculiar tone of that mountain scenery, the expressive features and bold characteristic bearing of the chamois, the occasionally perilous positions of the hunter,—all this, and much more beside, would, with his poetic mind and wonderfully skilful handling, afford such pictures as even his hand has not yet produced.

I had given up my intention of describing the red deer and the forest as soon as Mr. Scrope's book appeared; but when the new world that mountain life presents opened upon me, the former wish arose again, and I determined that chamois-hunting should now be my theme. It was a subject of which nothing was known in England, and I felt sure that if I were able to impart to what I wrote but a tithe of the charm which the scenes described really possess, it could not fail to interest. Should it not do so, the fault is solely mine.

CHAPTER II.

APPROACHING THE MOUNTAINS.

He only who has dwelt in the mountains, or has wandered for a time over their sides, and through their valleys,—who has entered the simple but comfortable cottages, and chatted familiarly with the peasantry in their own peculiar dialect about their occupations and their pastimes;—such a one only can form a notion of the feeling of delight which is experienced when at length a sudden turn in the road shows him the mighty forms striving upwards to the sky, their peaks, may be, gleaming brightly with a covering of snow, or, if the air be clear and it still be summer weather, appearing with that beautiful deep blue tint which forms the distance in the South. There is something so cheering and gladdening in the sight! It calls to mind familiar greetings and rough but hearty welcomings,—pleasant returnings homeward from the chase, and song and the merry dance. Already with the mind's eye is seen the wide view from the mountain-top; you again snuff the pure bracing air; and the shout and the *Jodler** of the shepherd-boy or *Sennerinn†* already resound in your ears.

* *Jodler.* The peculiar song of all mountaineers, the high notes being always a falsetto. The Brothers Rainer, formerly in England, sing it in perfection.

† *Senner—Sennerinn.* Dairyman—dairymaid.

As we approach the now near horizon all wears a different character. The houses are built otherwise, and have altogether another look than those we passed before; the roofs project over the sides and are bordered with some simple ornaments; a light wooden balcony is before the windows of the first story, and the walls are of snowy whiteness, and the trelliswork and doors and shutters are neatly and even tastefully painted. It looks gay, and green, and cheerful. And on the roofs we now see a bell, which, swinging between its cross-beams, calls home those who are in the fields to dinner or to supper. It is a sign that the wealth of the peasant here consists in pasture-land; and indeed no corn is seen, but the slopes and plain are covered with rich grass and with lowing kine. And then, too, the passers-by! The green pointed hat, worn alike by both sexes, with its golden tassel and gay flowers on the brim; the grey *joppe** and short leathern breeches of the men; the gold-embroidered boddice and striped petticoat of the women are now not only more frequent, but are almost exclusively seen; and if we stop at a village, all that meets the eye tells us at once we are among another race than those we left behind in the flat country. It sounds pleasantly too —gratefully falling on the heart rather than on the ear— that friendly " *Grüss di Gott!* " (God greet ye!) with which each one salutes you as he enters the inn or place where you may be. There is a heartiness and simplicity, an absence of all conventional formality in the salutation and the manner of it, very characteristic of, and according well with, a mountain people. And how clean the village looks, how neat and healthy its inhabitants! They live better and work less hard than the peasantry of the

* *Joppe* is the loose short coat worn by the mountaineer of Bavaria, and by the Tyrolese peasantry.

more northern provinces; they are not exposed to a burning sun during the harvest season, nor to the wet and cold attendant on field labour. They are up on the mountain pasturages in summer, and in autumn and winter are comfortably housed in their snug cottages in the valley. Their corn they buy, and from their herds on the mountain they derive milk and butter and cheese in abundance ; and thus may be said to live literally on . the very fat of the land.

But how distinct the blue peaks become! We shall soon be at their base, nor will it be very long, we hope, before we are mounting their sides, and stepping carefully along yonder ridge that cuts the sky so sharply ! For that is the Plau Berg, and some chamois are still there, and it is the place where we hope, with the forester's permission, to get a few days' stalking. How clear the air is ! The outline of every distant object is seen with wonderful distinctness : there is not a cloud in the sky, and the sun lights up the woodland slopes, and makes their sober brown and gold look quite gay and festal on this lovely autumnal morning.

And there is Tegernsee, its broad expanse of water as waveless as the air, and as clear and lucid too. A single boat is moving lazily across from a cottage on the opposite shore, and you wonder how so young a girl as she who is rowing can get such a cumbrous craft to move along even thus quickly. The broad brim of her green hat shades the upper part of her face; but that only makes the brightness of her black eyes the more apparent, and round her head are twined the braids of her long thick hair, just as it is worn by the women of the Tyrol. The silken kerchief crossed over her full bosom is tucked in her boddice ; and if the *mieder** does seem too tight,

* *Mieder* is the stiff boddice of silk or velvet worn by the women. It

it is rather from the swelling luxuriance of eighteen summers, than from any effort made in plying her rude pair of oars. She always had a friendly smile for you on entering her boat; though, as it seemed, she was not without her little stock of sorrow; for as I one day rowed by a country-house whose garden was reflected in the lake, she looked up wistfully at the closed windows; and I learned afterwards that the Jäger of the family, who had now left their villa for the town, was her lover, and that he had not yet written to her since they parted. " He has not forgotten me, I know," said Marie, with her usual pretty smile; " I shall soon get a letter, I am sure." And I am sure I hope with all my heart she may, for it were a pity so young a face should wear a look of sorrow. And were no letter to arrive, how oppressively sad to have that deserted house constantly before her as she rowed daily across the lake !

But I have forgotten the mountains and the autumnal morning, with talking of the pretty maiden of the ferry; however, she and her skiff, with its train of dancing light behind it, belong to the scene, and form a pleasing and even necessary feature in the landscape. As if all was to be festive on this exquisite October morning, here comes a gay procession. What a noise of deep, hollow-

---

is either richly embroidered, or in some parts a silver chain is passed like a lace from one side to the other, and fastened with hooks of silver. Indeed much luxury is often displayed in the dress of these country lasses. The cap (*Riegel Haube*) of the Munich girls, for example, contains a considerable quantity of the precious metal. The men too, in the lowlands especially, are given to display in their buttons. A rich peasant may often be seen with a long row of these down the front of his coat, one overlapping the other, each being formed of a broad silver coin of two groats value; on his waistcoat the same. On the frieze *joppe* of the mountaineer, however, there is no opportunity for such display.

sounding bells is heard coming up the road that winds along the lake! There in front a stately cow advances, her horns adorned with a large wreath of beautiful flowers,—roses, dahlias, erica, and evergreens. Above her head towers a pile of festoons and garlands; and within an arch of flowers and foliage is a bright crown of tinsel, and below it in the same shining material a large C. It is the cattle of his Royal Highness Prince Charles of Bavaria returning for the winter from the mountain pasturage. They are splendid animals of the Altgau breed; short-legged, full-uddered, and with dewlaps like the Colchian bulls. Many are the bells they wear,—long broad bells, of sweetly sonorous metal, fastened round their strong necks by a thick strap of leather. But the foremost one has alone the coronal: she is to walk first, nor would she let one of the others pass her on any account whatever. She maintains her place in front as resolutely as I have known *une Dame du palais* insist upon having the *pas* when other ladies were present; and she heads the procession with a sturdy air, and a look of ineffable contempt for all going on around. Nor is it mere fancy that she is proud of her pre-eminence; she knows as well as you do that she is to be first; and she deserves her rank, for in truth she is a splendid creature. And behind comes the tall herdsman, his hat more than usually gay with flowers, and with a tuft of fine yellow feathery grass, that looks not unlike the plumage of the bird of paradise. How proudly he walks behind his troop, while the gardens that border the road are filled with gazers; and further on, the Queen and her ladies are waiting to see the cattle returning home to the valley. He looks calmly about him, but greets no one: he feels that today *he* is the principal personage; he is celebrating his triumph. I would fain wager though, when he sees

the sweet friendly face of the young Queen yonder, his
countenance will relax somewhat, and that it will soften
and suddenly grow bright like a cloud when a sunbeam
falls upon it. Following him is a troop of goats, all un-
adorned save one in front; and after them comes the
maiden who tends them, smart in her holiday attire.
Bringing up the rear, like the baggage-train of an army,
a waggon is lumbering on with household necessaries
piled high upon it, and drawn by two sturdy oxen, whom
a little peasant-boy, with a face as cheerful as the morn,
guides along. The merry scene pleases him; he does
not regret to leave the mountain, for what child ever yet
grieved at change of place? But gay and festal as "the
return from the Alm" always is, it is by far not so pleasing an event to the Senner and Sennerinn as the departure for "the mountain" in spring. Then, as the forester's young wife told me, who stood looking at them with
her baby laughing on her arm, then if you meet them,
and, wishing them good day, ask whither they are going,
the reply, "Auf die Alm!"* is quite musical with pleasure, and their faces radiant with thoughts of the life
awaiting them on the green mountain slopes. But when
meeting them in autumn, on their downward path, you
put the same question, the answer, "Home!" tells at
once by its tone how reluctant they are to leave their
summer dwelling-place.

And indeed it is not to be wondered at. On some elevated spot, sheltered perhaps by perpendicular walls of
rock a thousand feet high, closed in, in a sort of "happy
valley" up among the mountains, or else may be on a
verdant piece of table-land, free and unbounded on every
side, are built the rough wooden habitations—mere log-
houses—of the Sennerinnen. Far, far below them the

* "To the pastures on the mountain!"

world lies extended. With the sun they rise, and are on
the mountain-tops watching the brightness as it gradually
diffuses itself over earth and sky. There, with the dawn,
while the day is bursting forth in magnificent array,
stands the peasant-girl all radiant and effulgent on some
peak, the sun's rays glowing around her. Above her, in
the distance, the snowy summits are growing rosy with
the light; while the lesser mountains and the valleys
below her have not yet seen the sun. And soon the
whole face of the stupendous wall of grey rock is flushing
in gratulation; all is teeming with sunbeams and brilliancy; the haze over the lake and river divides and
evaporates; and shore and village, upland and hamlet
lie before her eyes clear and distinct in the dewy
freshness of an early summer morning. All is still on
the mountain.   She gazes on the coming glory, and is
silent; she watches the gradual development in mute delight; but when the sun himself has at length come
forth the spell is broken, and as she turns to look after
her herd, proclaims her sense of freedom by a loud burst
of song; and if ever content, joy, and light-heartedness
were expressed in sounds, they are to be found in the
simple melody of such mountain carol. What a jubilant
outcry ! I know nothing like it.   How loud, how high,
some of the notes ! how rapidly they change ! what gladness is in that *jodler*, and how boundingly the song returns from the high shrill tone, descending note by note
to the more sober ones, as though the heart were gradually recovering from its sudden fit of ecstasy.   But it
is only for a moment; and again it is heard mounting
higher, heard louder than before, and faintly echoed back
from the opposite mountain.   No, that was not an echo,
—it was a Sennerinn from those distant huts yonder an-
swering the other.

It may be thought that the rough uncultivated nature of these peasants, placed as they are year after year amid the same scenes, and following the same unvarying occupations, will not be much influenced by the appearances of external nature; and that to suppose them to be so is rather a poetic fancy than plain sober fact. But I am not of this opinion: I believe that, unconsciously, they are impressed by the sublime scenery around them: they enjoy it differently from the man of more refined mind, but the result is perhaps nearly the same, only different in degree and quality; in both the principal feature being enjoyment, though more sensuous in the one than in the other. And that they do enjoy it to the full—to the full according to their capacity—is evident from their manner, their looks, and their conversation. They live surrounded by grandeur, and glory, and magnificence. Wonders happen around them; nor do they pass unheeded, for it is these that break the monotony of their life. We too are encompassed by wonders, but in the strife and turmoil we have no time to stop and marvel; while they, separated for months from the world and its wearing cares, keep their minds fresher and more susceptible to outward impressions. Knowing nothing of conventions, nor hardened or pressed down by want, they are, both mentally and bodily, more healthy and more vigorous. The purity of the air gives elasticity to the heart as well as to the limbs, and their simple diet is most surely not without a happy influence. Meat they never taste, and their sole drink is milk or water. Their pleasures are of the simplest kind: song is for them at once an occupation and a pastime, and when on the mountains, you are sure to hear some solitary watcher over his herd beguiling the lonesome hours with a mouth-harmonicon, or filling the air with one of their happy

songs, quite as full of happiness in its way as the carol-
ling of the lark.   Occasionally the chamois-hunter descends to their dwelling, to cook a warm meal or to pass
the night under shelter of their roof.   From him they
get the latest news of what is going on in the vale; they
give him a hearty welcome, and the evening is passed
merrily, and concluded, may be, with a dance; for the
Jäger is sure to find favour with the sex, and no young
knight-errant was ever better received by the fair dames
of a castle where he craved hospitality, than the trim
and merry young hunter by the Sennerinn on the mountain.

But to return to the high-road.   There was no boat
to be had at the moment to take me across the lake to
the little village of Egern; so, putting my portmanteau
on the cart of a young peasant who was just driving by,
with rifle in hand up I jumped, and in less than a quarter of an hour we were at Rottach, five minutes' walk
from the place of my destination. A little urchin offered
to "*radeln*"* (trundle) my things to the inn; so helping the little fellow to put the luggage on his barrow, off
we set together.   But he soon stopped to rest, and when
he saw me waiting for him, he told me "to go on: there
was no need whatever for me to stay, he would be sure
and come;" and as I saw he wished to have the glory

---

* The sight of the green fields and hedgerows is not more pleasant
to him who has been " long in populous cities pent," than is to my ear
the sound of a genuine provincialism, uttered in a broad dialect, giving
earnest as it does of being really beyond the influence of the town.   Once
in Somersetshire I remember a peasant pointing out to me a place in the
distance, and telling me it was near where yonder " housen " were ;
giving the word " house" its old Saxon plural.   That one word seemed
at once to remove me from the haunts of over-civilization, and I felt
sure I had really got into the country.   It was the same with the
"*radeln*" of my little peasant-boy, and I welcomed it accordingly.

of performing his piece of work quite alone, I left him to follow at his leisure.

I am always glad to employ a child when circumstances make it possible; first, because I like children's company and to hear their talk, and also because I wish that they should know how comely a thing it is to be employed usefully, and how sweet the earnings of one's own labour are. I have a habit, when walking, of scattering crumbs for the birds, who are almost sure to find them; and just so, I fancy, a chance incentive to industry, or a little reward for some kindly meant attention, may not be wholly lost, but, being remembered long afterwards, may incite to a love of occupation, and encourage to acts of friendliness and to good behaviour. Most children are delighted to be employed, and the consciousness that they are *of use* makes them quite elate : it is the germ of a feeling which, if properly nurtured, ripens into self-respect.

Having made my arrangements at the village inn overlooking the lake, I went to the forester's house to present my credentials. Ha ! there are the antlers over the gable, denoting who is the inmate. Eight—ten—twelve ! a good stag must he have been that once bore them. It always gives me pleasure to see this trophy over the doorway or on the pointed roof, for it is a sign of freemasonry, and tells me that, in case of need, there is a comrade near. The letter presented, and my story told, I heard exactly what I was prepared for. " Things look very bad just now, Sir; I fear there is not much to be done. The chamois have no peace—the peasants are always out in the mountains, and what they do not shoot they scare away. However, if I can oblige you, I shall be very happy to do so. I'll speak to the under-keeper, and hear if he has seen any chamois lately."

c

When he came up, " Well, Meier," inquired the forester, " what chance is there, think you, of doing something on the mountains? All looks very bad, I fear. Do you think you might get a shot or two ?"

Meier's countenance wore no encouraging look, and he only repeated what I had already heard, of the scarcity of the chamois, and of the depredations the poachers were constantly committing. " All about here, as you know," the forester added, " were chamois and red-deer in abundance, and now it is a chance if a single head of game is seen in a day's stalking. However," turning to Meier, " the Peissenberg would be the likeliest place —there perhaps might be a chance."

" It is the only place where there are any now," Meier said. " Chamois *are* there, but the mountain is large, and there being so few perhaps we might not see them. And then too a single gun only! with two persons it were easier. However we can try. I will place you," he said, turning to me, " where the chamois are most likely to pass, and then I will go through the wood and drive them out. But I cannot promise you will get a shot."

" Never mind," I answered, " let us try; if we see nothing it cannot be helped."

So it was arranged that on the day after the morrow we should try our luck on the Peissenberg. I was just going away when the forester said, " There is a good stag on the Ring Berg; Meier has heard him for some days past, if you would like to try for him."

A stag in the rutting season ! I pricked my ears at the announcement. " A *good* stag ?" I asked.

" Oh yes, a very good one."

" Of how many, think you ?"

" Of twelve certainly. Meier saw him yesterday,

about two hundred yards off, but the ground was unfavourable, and he did not fire."

" Yes," said Meier, " he is a capital stag. I have often heard him of a morning, but not till yesterday was I able to get near enough to see him. He is worth going after, I assure you."

" But," said the forester, " delay in this case is not advisable, for at the top of the mountain is the boundary line between the royal chase and that which the peasants now have. At this season the stag will be always on the move, and as the limits are so near, he might very likely cross over into that part which is not ours; if so, we can do nothing."

" Has he any hinds with him ? " I asked.

" No; but there must be a few on the mountain."

" Well, that's the grand thing; if that is the case he will hardly go away. However we'll try for him tomorrow. Can you go, Meier ? "

" The best way," said the forester, " would be to start this afternoon, and sleep at a farm-house at the foot of the mountain. They can perhaps make you up a bed; and something to eat and drink you are sure to get. Then start the next morning early, so as to be on the mountain when day breaks. By leaving about half-past three today, you will get to the farm in good time this evening, and can sit out a little and listen if you hear the stag. And take the shell with you," he said, turning to Meier; " perhaps you may want it, if you hear him near." And so matters were settled.

At the appointed time I saw Meier from my window coming to fetch me, and we presently set off for the hills. It was a delicious afternoon. We ascended by a path which had been made for the cattle; and as it had been raining lately, and the cows had just been driven down, the road was none of the best. The scene below was very lovely, as seen from our gentle eminence. Repose, and peace, and calm, were impressed on the landscape. The bright quiet afternoon was just fitted for the placid lake and the undulating woodland. There are some spots with which only certain effects accord, which demand a particular sky to suit their marked character. Now to me Tegernsee seems one of these. Sun and gladness belong to it, nor would grand masses of shade and a strong effect become it so well. Art would no doubt make even such appearances harmonize with the scene, for what cannot Art accomplish? But what I mean is, its features being of a placid stamp, a stern expression would be more difficult for us to reconcile with it. With the human countenance it is the same.

We came at last to a spot surrounded by high woods, and here we seated ourselves to listen for the stag. The evening was calm, and all was very still, yet we listened in vain for the much wished-for voice from the woods above. After waiting some time we were about to go, when from a turn in the road before us three men emerged. Quick as lightnig out flew Meier's telescope, as he said, "They all have guns!" He looked at them for awhile, and muttering, "The rascals!" put up his glass, but still continued watching them till they were out of sight behind the rising ground where we stood. As we rose to go we saw them again among the bushes: they now perceived us too; and, as if to show that they did not care for having been seen, began whistling and making all sorts of jeering noises till we were out of sight. "They will be out betimes tomorrow, no doubt," said Meier; "they will try for the stag, too, I dare say."

We came to the farm. It was a large building on a pleasant meadow, surrounded by the mountains. On en-

tering, the cheerful blaze of a fire burst upon us, at which
the supper for the maids and labourers was being prepared. Now a cowherd, now a dairymaid dropped in,
and exchanged a word with my companion, or stopped
and chatted with us both and asked about our plans for
the morrow. A savoury omelet was soon frying on the
kitchen-fire, and this, with a slice of bread and a glass or
two of beer, formed an excellent supper. We chatted
around the fire for a time, and then went upstairs to rest,
where to my surprise I found two excellent beds in readiness, instead of clean hay, as I had expected. One look
at the night, to see what promise for the morning, and
then to sleep.

CHAPTER III.

AFTER THE GOOD STAG.

THE next morning we were up and ready by four o'clock. The moon and stars were still shining brightly; the air was fresh, but not cold. I went to the door of the house and looked out into the night. Nothing stirred: there was no sign of a single living creature being abroad: not even the murmur of a rivulet was to be heard, descending from the mountains to the plain,—a sound which among the hills seldom fails to greet the ear, either near or in the distance. But there rose around me that low hum, that indescribable rustle, which is never heard but in the silence of the night, and which seems to make the stillness palpable. From the depth of the forests before, behind me, and on every side, came that low, deep murmur *tingling* on the ear, as when the myriad buzzings of the invisible insect world in summer unite in one drowsy, hollow tone at noon. It was not loud, but it was distinct and very audible, even to an ear not quickly sensitive: it came from out of the earth, and from the woods, and from the sides of the mountains, and rising upwards filled all the air, even up to the very hill-tops lying in the cold light of the stars. Was this low sound perchance the breathing of Nature in her trance-like sleep?

We took our rifles and set out. Until we came to the

woods it was easy enough to proceed ; but here, it being
steep and slippery, and as we were unable to see the path
and the obstacles it presented, our progress was rather
slow. This however I should say of myself only ; for my
companion was always in advance, nimbly mounting before me, and waiting till I reached him. The logs of
wood left to rot on the ground are sadly inconvenient on
such occasions : you knock your shins almost to pieces
against them, or treading on the slippery surface of the
humid branches, go down earthwards with your nose as
pioneer. We presently came to a clearing, where we
stopped and seated ourselves on a felled tree to listen for
the stag. Twice we had heard his hoarse rumbling roar
from afar, as we ascended the hill-side, but now again all
was hushed, and we listened and listened in vain. Taking
a large sea-shell out of his *rücksack*,* Meier put it to his
mouth, and began to imitate that peculiar sound betoken-
ing ardour, impatience, and anger, which the stag makes
at this season when seeking the hind. It was really a
pretty sight ; it had even something classical in it. There
the young fellow lay, reclining on the fallen trunk, his
hat off, his throat bare, and the coming light playing
about the upturned shell, as, Triton-like, he blew into
his ocean-horn, and made the air vibrate with the hoarse
bellowing. Below, in a vast chasm, were floating thin
mists, gently rising upwards to meet and to be dispersed
by the sun. On they came like waves ; and it needed
no very brilliant imagination to behold an ocean before
you, and he with the spotted shell lying on its shore.

But no answer came. Once before we had heard, just

---

* *Rücksack.* A square bag or sack of coarse green canvas, used as a
knapsack by the peasant generally, and by the hunter to carry his game.
A cord runs round the mouth or opening, by which it can be drawn together. From this part a strap passes over each shoulder, and is at-

as the shadows were beginning to leave the top of the opposite mountain, a hollow sound come murmuring across the valley before us. It was scarcely audible; it was a low muttering, as though it proceeded from out of the mountain itself.

"Did you hear it?" exclaimed Meier. "That's the stag, but he is a great way off. He will go, I am afraid, on the other side of the mountain, and then we may not follow him, for there the royal forests end."

"How vexatious! he probably has no deer with him, or he would hardly go away."

And again through his shell sounded the deep hoarse tones; but it was all in vain. "He must be far off, quite out of hearing, or he would come for certain; he would be sure to answer the challenge. But since we heard him last, he has gone no doubt over the brow of the mountain, on the other side where the sound cannot reach him. It is of no use to wait any longer."

So up we got and went further. We stopped at a spot that overlooked the whole dell and gave a good view of the steep mountain-side facing us. "We may perhaps see a roebuck—it is not at all unlikely—the underwood there is a good covert for them," said Meier; and jumping on the stump of a felled tree, which overhung the precipitous declivity, he gazed carefully around and below. But nothing was to be seen. The new laws which had been in force since the Revolution effectually prevented the chance of our seeing any game whatever: all was destroyed or driven away. Some goats only with tinkling bells round their necks were browsing here, and came near to look at us; then on a sudden they sprang away, with a troop of white kids after them.

tached to the corners below. The capaciousness of such a rücksack is something quite marvellous; there is really no end to what may be stuffed into it.

As the young Jäger stood on that block, leaning on
his staff, I could not but think how picturesque a group
he and his dog made. The mountain stick was thrust
forwards, forming one leg of a triangle, and his body the
other; and on the top of it both hands were crossed, on
which his chin rested. The grey *joppe* hung loosely
about him, his bare knees showed beneath the short leathern breeches, the rifle was slung at his back, and his
dog sat at his feet watching as steadily as he. As he
leaned forward, supported by the firmly-planted pole, he
was quite hanging over the depth below. The whole
figure was motionless; the eyes only turned from side
to side, exploring every bush and prying into each sha-
dowy nook, or running over those green patches among
the trees where it was likely a roe might come to graze.
I remember to have seen, when a child, a print in the
Bible, of Jacob thus leaning on his staff; and I quite
well remember too how much the figure pleased me, and
how in the attitude there was for me a charm which I
could not then account for.*   And in some strange wise
or other this picture was always associated in my mind
with a sentence in 'Murray's Exercises:' "And Jacob
worshiped his Creator leaning on the top of his staff."
The Bible picture and the well-known words recurred at
once to my mind; and here I saw before me what my
childish imagination had often dwelt on with indefinable,
inexplicable delight.   Since those days of childhood the
boy had himself leant upon his staff just as Jacob had

---

* Nor am I much better able to do so now.   In a figure thus leaning
there is an air of perfect repose, united however with power and strength;
for you see the whole man before you standing at nearly full height; and
though the attitude impresses one with rest, it indicates at the same time
a readiness for action, which takes from it all appearance of slothful ease
or of fatigue.

done; and thus too had, like him, worshiped his Creator amid the mighty works of His hands.

We now went to the top of the hill. Below us was
the lake, in all the freshness and brightness of early
morning, and behind rose the rocky ridge of the Plau
Berg, and behind this again other peaks covered with
eternal snow. A look round, and then downwards, and
home. After having reported ourselves to the forester,
it was arranged that on Monday we should start at five
and try for a chamois. However, on Monday the weather was unfavourable, and other circumstances also prevented me from stalking on that day. So packing a few
things in my rücksack, I set off across the mountains for
Fischbachau.

CHAPTER IV.

HAVING alluded to the stag during the rutting season, it is as well perhaps to add a few words on this subject for the information of those uninitiated in the mysteries of woodcraft.

On the feast of St. Egidius, 1st of September, the rutting season is said to begin. Thus it is, at least, according to the old sayings of those practised in the noble art of Venerie. The stag leaves the deep recesses of the forest and comes forth to the skirts of the woods, and is seen even by day in the glades and coppices. The good pasture of the summer months has made him sleek, and the blood begins to flow through his full veins with a more impetuous current. Like the youth who has bloomed into manhood, and who looks around him with a brighter eye than heretofore, the stag now gazes dauntlessly in all the pride of vigorous strength, and his bold front seems almost to challenge to the attack. He who ere this has dwelt like a recluse in the forest solitudes, now comes forth into the noonday world; away he bounds, and before the morning dawns he is in another territory; he has traversed the valleys and has toiled up the steep mountain-sides, and, bearing away for the well-known open glade in the beech-forest, has reached it before the hinds have brushed the dew from the grass in retreating to their covert.*

And thus, year after year perhaps, will a stag be seen at a certain spot at this particular season, although he is absent the whole year beside. Not only is the distance he travels, but the speed also with which he traverses the ground, astonishing. His pace is a sort of ambling trot, nor does he skim over the ground at full speed except when the foe is nigh; indeed at this season a stag could not maintain such pace long, he being too well-conditioned, and his broad back and sides too heavy, for the exertion of a stride like the courser's when careering over the plain; and though the poet may, with undisputed license, describe him as *galloping* along, he never does so except when suddenly scared and when *hotly* pursued. And indeed in his other pace there is beauty too, and more of majesty. Though retreating before some danger, there is no ignoble haste or precipitancy in his flight. With front erect and steady eye he moves over the ground seeming hardly to touch the earth, so lightly does he step along; and in his whole mien and bearing he is " every inch a king."

At the usual time he suddenly appears amid his old haunts and his former loves. Until now a troop of hinds only were to be seen by the hunter who watched for them at morning or at evening, with the calves of this, and the

* Since these words were written I have met with a very graceful allusion to the deer being out at early morning, in the poems of M. Casimir Sarbievius, translated by R. C. Coxe.

> " Friendly dews! with faithful guiding
> 　　Show where roving, feeding, loving,
> Sought the stag at last his hiding,
> 　　Cautious through the covert moving!
> Show your king the cloven horn,
> Gentle dews of early morn!"

fawns of last year; but now on the skirts of the herd he
sees—or at first thinks he sees—a pair of branching antlers towering in the air; and behold! the monarch is
indeed returned. He has added another embattlement
to his crown since he was last seen; in stature too he is
changed, and well indeed may he claim, irrespective of
his diadem, to be called " a royal hart." But how different now his look from that time when he disappeared
in the wilderness; like the prodigal, who, with wasted
strength and but a wreck of his former self, skulks away
that he may be seen by none. How worn and broken
down did he leave the scenes of all his pleasures, and how
vigorous and in what gallant trim does he return! Should
a rival dare to loiter about the spot, he goes forth to
meet him, to do battle for his rights; to maintain them
or be vanquished in the encounter. No knight, burning
to achieve a deed of chivalry, ever charged down upon a
foe with more valiant daring than will he, when he sees
approaching the antlers of some new wooer tossing in the
air and seeming to defy him to combat. Nor does the
challenge remain unanswered: with his brow-antlers
lowered like a lance in the rest, he rushes on the foe,
and lucky is the intruder if he can ward the thrust;
for should it penetrate his ribs or shoulders he would
most surely pay for his temerity with his life.*

---

* It is not more than three weeks since the day on which I write this
(December 5th), that a young stag, one of six only, rushed upon another,
and striking his brow-antlers into his side killed him on the spot. It
was a strange occurrence, on account of its being late in the season; had
it been a month earlier there would have been nothing surprising in it.
During the rutting season however the weaker stags are kept away from
the herd by the stronger ones; and when these go, the younger ones
then take their place, and are in their turn as fierce and as jealous of an
intruder as their more potent rivals were before them.

. The poet Thompson errs greatly as to the stag at this season :—

> " When in *kind* contest with his butting friends,
> He wont to struggle, or his loves enjoy."*

There is no kindness here. These tournays are of the most deadly description, and again and again each returns to the fight with that burning rage and quenchless animosity which drive two creatures to mortal combat.

As a proof of the terrific shock which is occasioned when one stag bravely meets the impetuous charge of his adversary, I would state that I have seen the bleached skull of a stag, found in the forest, on one side of which the very frontal bone itself had been fractured, the antler on that side having been literally wrenched from its shivered socket in such a struggle. The animal had dropped from the frightful injury ; and his remains were found as here described, one antler being still left.

The following account of a stalking adventure in the highlands of Styria, affords an astounding example of the blind rage by which the stag is animated at this particular season, as well as of the extraordinary vitality with which he then seems to be endued.

The story is here related as it was told me shortly after the occurrence ; and exciting as the details cannot fail to be for the sportsman, the lover of natural history will also find in them much to interest him.

" Well," continued C—— D——, after telling me the result of his three preceeding days' stalking in the mountains at Steyer, " I left the forester in the hut and went to Lany Thal,—a good place, as I well knew, and where the game from the hills on both sides were constantly passing. There was a pool here where at the season the stags used to come incessantly ; and, on looking at the ground, I

* ' The Seasons '—Autumn.

saw it was all trampled on, the mud and earth pawed up
and scattered in all directions. So here I sat, and taking
out my shell began to have a little talk with whatever
stag might be in the neighbourhood. But before proceeding farther, I should tell you something of the aspect
of the country, and what this Lany Thal was like. You
must know then, it is a long, narrow valley, and on one
side are hills sloping gradually away upwards, to no very
great height, with trees and underwood here and there,
while occasionally a large open clearing enabled you to
see what was going on, and whatever game might be
moving about there. Well, it was this hill-side I had
opposite me, as I sat waiting near the pool. But at my
back the ground was different. There the mountains rose
more abruptly, and to a greater height: it was rocky and
wilder—in short, more of a chamois country than the
other side.

"So, as I said, I was bellowing away with my shell, and
it was not long before a young stag answered my call.
But just afterwards I heard a capital stag roaring furiously; and presently, right away up the slope, about
five hundred paces off, some deer began to show themselves moving about. I looked and peered between bush
and tree in every direction to find the stag, when suddenly
I heard just above me from behind a sharp, long-drawn
'Pis-sch!' and a couple of chamois, who had been startled
by my presence, dashed away upwards. Hardly were
they off when down comes a stag from the mountain at
my back, and makes straight for the pool. Here was a
dilemma! I knew a good stag was before me though I
had not seen him, and felt sure I should be able to
entice him near enough to get a shot. And just at this
moment comes the insignificant fellow right in my way!
Were I to fire at him, the other good stag would be off:

and if I let him reach the pool unmolested, he will at
last be sure to see me, and will dart across and scare the
deer, and they and the other stag will then be all off
together. The thing, therefore, was not to let him
come far down, but to make him return the way he came.
So bending forward, and taking off my hat, I waved it
before me, muttering between my teeth in anger at the
intruder, ' Get back, you rascal, will you, what the deuce
do you do here?' He stared surprised for a moment,
and then, as I suspected, was off up the mountain. So
now all was right. But still no stag appeared."

"Had he been scared away by the other stag, do you
think?" asked I.

"No; he was there still; that I was certain of; and
as the ground was broken and favourable for stalking, I
longed to be after him, and see if it were not possible to
get near enough for a shot. But it was too early yet; so
I resolved to wait till the wind should blow downwards
from the mountain-tops, and then to try my luck. Well,
by-and-by, I heard a strange noise : groans, and a clattering and low smothered sounds. Two stags were fighting, and the noises were caused by their antlers as they
clashed together, and by the intensity and desperation
of the struggle. I was off in an instant, and approached
the spot where they were, carefully looking round, however, lest by chance I might come upon some outlying
deer, or any of the herd that would be standing about
while the combat was going on. At last, I see the two
in deadly fight : two good stags both, though one had
more points to his antlers than the other. They were
evidently old stags. There they were on the open space
as in the lists for a tournament—their heads low on the
ground—and with forehead to forehead bearing down on
each other, and going round and round without either

being able to obtain an advantage over his adversary. I
had noted which was the better one of the two, and
determined to wait my time till an opportunity should
present itself for getting a shot at him I had marked.
But still with antlers interlaced, on they yet kept struggling; and round and round they turned, but never was
the better stag so exposed as to enable me to get a fair
chance. For you know, it would be a pity to have given
such a stag as that a bad shot—in the haunch, or the
flanks, or in the neck perhaps. Strangely enough the lesser
one I could have shot capitally over and over again; but
I had made up my mind what to do, and determined to
abide by it, and not let my impatience entice me to fire
too soon. While thus anxiously watching the battle, all
of a sudden they disappear. They both are off. But it
was not long before the noise of the struggle could be
heard, and off I was at once after them again. This
time I got closer than before; but still I never could get
a fair shot at the larger animal. I was waiting all the
time with my rifle to my shoulder, ready to fire, when,
for a moment only, the one with the spreading antlers
turned his broadside towards me; the trigger is touched,
and down he rolls in front of his opponent. He tries to
rise, and struggles on the earth, but is unable to get up.
All this time, the other, instead of running off at the
noise of the rifle, stands before his fallen foe, and then
charges down again upon him as before. In the madness of his rage, he had evidently not heard the shot. As
you may suppose, my thought was now centred in him;
for to get both the stags, that would indeed be a triumph.
So I crept up still closer to the group, and fire. I think
he is hit; I feel sure of it: I tell myself he *must* be hit.
But while thus re-assuring myself, he whom I had hoped
was wounded mortally, rears in the air as if to give more

D

impetus to the blow and butts with all the weight of his body and with all the intensity of fury upon the wounded stag struggling on the ground. When I saw this, I assure you I was quite overcome. 'And so I have missed him after all,' thought I. You know what a feeling that is, and how at the moment one would give anything in the whole world for but a single shot more to retrieve the misfortune. Had I only the forester with me, with my second rifle! And so I stood helpless, looking at the stag and waiting to see what would happen next. There were two pines on the spot, opposite each other, and against one I was leaning with my back. Close behind it too were rocks, so that in this direction I could not retrograde a step.

"Now while standing thus, the stag at which I had fired gazed at me as if he had now only perceived me for the first time; and with head low on the ground, rushes upon me between the two trees, as glad to find a near object on which to wreak his vengeance. I thought it was all over with me now, for step back further I could not; but though I expected the next moment to be flying on his pointed antlers up in the air, I still, as you may suppose, made myself as thin as possible while flattening myself against the pine. On he came, and passed so near, that had I stretched out my foot, I could have given him a kick. He went on, and rushed down the slope; and though I could hear him as he broke away, he was soon out of sight."

"And how many points had the other stag?" I asked.

"It was a capital stag of twelve; he was an old fellow, and had, no doubt, had more in former years. But as he was still attempting to rise, and not knowing where my shot had struck him, and whether he might not get up at last and be off, as is not seldom the case when wounded high up, I ran to him, and tried to get to his side, which however was not so easy, for he turned towards me as I approached, keeping me off with his formidable antlers. At last I managed to dig my long knife twice in his side; and now, even should he rise, he would leave such traces behind as would enable me to follow. This done, I quickly loaded one barrel of my rifle, not taking time to use a patch, but only ramming down some dry moss on the powder, and then shot him through the head."

"And where had your first shot struck him? And could you find no traces of blood on the track of the other stag?" I asked, impatiently.

"My first shot had hit him in the very best place right in the middle of the shoulder, which accounted for his being unable to rise. As to the other, I followed him some little distance and could find nothing. You may fancy how vexed I was. At any other time such a stag as I had shot would have delighted me; but now, as I had not the other too, I felt as if I did not care about him. What an opportunity it was, and how unfortunately it had turned out! So I went back to my stag, and then to the spot where I had been standing, and thought the whole affair over again in my mind. And I remembered exactly how well I had him at the moment I aimed, and at the very second my finger touched the trigger, and it seemed as if he *must* be hit: but then again I could not help saying to myself it was not so positive either; for if he were, is it likely or possible he would, without taking the least notice of the shot, have charged down three times on his fallen enemy, and have butted him as he had done?

"So with a heavy heart I gave the matter up, seeing clearly enough that the second stag was missed. As it was getting dark, it was useless to attempt to follow the track of the stag. And in a state of mind which only a person who has been in a like situation can understand, vexed and dissatisfied with myself, I set off towards the hut. Here the matter was thought and talked over again and again.

"Well, being moonlight, at two o'clock in the morning I started again to try and get a shot at the stags that were belling on all sides, and when it was day, went with the forester to show him where the stag lay, that he might have it fetched and carried down.

"You know the feeling when you think it is not possible to have missed, and how you still keep on looking for a drop of blood, and still hope on against hope. And so it was with me now; and I could not help going again, though of course it seemed useless, to follow the track of the second stag. But nothing was to be seen more than on the day before. Not a blade of grass, not a stone that my eyes did not carefully examine. And so I went on peering and peering, when only think, suddenly I see a drop of blood on the ground. It seemed to be too much good fortune to be real, and I therefore did not halloo to the foresters, but still went on step by step, looking carefully on the earth. Now another red drop is seen, and on the same side; and presently traces of the blood having spirted out on *both* sides, showing clearly that the bullet had gone right through him.

"I was just on the point of turning back to communicate the glad intelligence to the foresters, when the voices of persons approaching from below reached me, causing me to look round to see who was coming. I at once recognized them: they were the men I had ordered when in the hut, to wait at a certain spot to fetch away my first stag. I could not see them, but I heard one

shout to the other, ' *Da liegt er schon!* ' ' Why there he
lies!' On hearing this, as you may suppose, I was all
excitement, and cried out to ask *what* it was lying there.
' Why the stag, to be sure,' was the answer. For they
thought this was the stag they had been ordered to come
for. At these words down I rushed to the spot, almost
mad with expectation; and there indeed lay the second
stag, with a shot that had gone right through his lungs,
the bullet passing out on the other side."

"And was he a good stag?" I inquired; "as good as
the other? What did his antlers mark?"

"He only had eight points; but he was a splendid fellow, and hardly less in size than the other. His whole
body bore traces of the late battle. Everywhere were
long furrows in his coat, where the terrible antlers of the
other had scraped away the hair, as they were thrust
forwards with deadly intent; and as to his head, it was
scarred and torn and marked all over, bearing proof of
the intensity of this as well as former battles.

"The body of the one I shot first had some terrible
wounds in the neck, caused no doubt by the thrust of
those fearful pointed brow-antlers, which his foe brought
to bear on him with such fury as he lay helpless on the
ground. Near the fresh bullet-wound was an old wound
also, received evidently in some former similar encounter. Both, as I said, were old stags, and had measured their strength with many a mighty foe. The one
shot last, however, was evidently accustomed to lord it
over all the others in his domain; and, though no doubt
a bully, possessed notwithstanding a courage which no
attack ever daunted. The shot he received from me he
certainly believed to have been inflicted by the other
stag; hence his rage, and furious attack on his enemy
as he lay prostrate on the ground."

" On what day was it that it happened ?"

" On the 17th of October. I had, as you know, shot four stags already ; but to have witnessed this desperate battle, and to have shot both the combatants, attended, too, as the circumstance was, with such peculiar incidents,—*that* was the crowning piece of good fortune."

When once the stag has joined the hinds he does not quit them. He walks continually round and round the herd, keeping them together and preventing even a single one from leaving him. A stag will sometimes have twelve, fifteen, twenty, or even more hinds with him, and proudly but despotically he moves among them, like a sultan in his serail. His blood is boiling in his full veins; his passion consumes him, and he flies to the pool, not to assuage his thirst, but to cool the fire that is burning within him. He rolls in the shallow water and lays himself in the slimy bed ; and when he rises recking from the mire, his back and sides and throat are covered with it, and the long hair of his neck is matted together like a thick and tangled mane. He eats little or nothing now. Ever and anon he stands still, and by a low, deep, hollow sound, that seems to come from his very inmost being, and tells of consuming pain and longing, will he give vent to the feelings that goad and torture him. I know no sound to which I could liken it. It is not a roar, nor a bellowing, but a *rumbling* sound, approaching perhaps nearer to a deep, long-drawn-out groan than aught else, which at last is, as it were, hurled forth two or three times, in a short, quick, impatient manner. At early morning, while the stars are still watching, you may hear the hollow tone from the hill-side, and, if you do not know what it is, might perchance fancy it came from the bowels of the earth, and that the mountain was inwardly convulsed by elements at strife with each other.

Indeed I imagine that an incipient volcano would make some such noise.

The throat of the stag swells now to an unusual size. Week after week goes by, and his appearance at last gives token of his spendthrift waste of strength and of wild excess. His once sleek sides are sunken in, his broad back has dwindled into narrowness, and a sharp ridge is visible along its length. The haunches that were so full and rounded have hollows in them, the head is no longer stately and erect, nor in the creature's whole mien and bearing is there more of pride and majesty. The voice has grown thick and husky, and a hoarse sound, void of strength or fullness, is uttered at distant intervals. Senility has taken the place of youth; and of strength, decrepitude. At such time it is comparatively easy to get near the stag, for he sees and hears nothing, and, if I may use the expression, is reduced almost to a state of imbecility. I have myself crept along the ground, and got from bush to bush until I was near enough to have brought him down with a pistol-shot.

It is in truth astonishing that the stag should be so long-lived as he is; for the whole year through, with the exception of at most two months, he is either taxing his nature to the utmost, or striving to recruit his strength through an inclement and unpropitious season. The rutting is over; and now, with lantern body and but the ghost of his former self, he has the raw winter months before him. There is no green pasturage where he may appease the cravings of hunger; the ground is covered with deep snow; nor can he get at the young corn, which, were it not thus hidden, would furnish a most dainty banquet. He is obliged to have recourse to the rind of the young trees, and to nibble the tips of the last shoots and twigs. Poor nourishment this for a famished worn-out

creature! yet till the spring-time comes it is all he has
to feed on. And hardly has he recovered himself a little,
when nature demands of him an immense exertion : his
antlers fall off close to his head, and another pair, even
higher and stronger than those just lost, are to supply
their place. And this operation is not a work of time,
proceeding slowly and with gradual development; but,
by a strong effort, of rapid, nay almost sudden, growth.
In three months the stag has put forth his branching
antlers again; and this time too the stems are thicker
than before, and on each is one point more than the preceding year. When we think of the comparatively slow
rate at which a hothouse plant, with all possible care and
forcing, expands in growth, or a child or other young
animal increases in stature, we can hardly comprehend
the productive power that, in so short a time, should be
able to force into existence an excrescence of such size
and weight, demanding too for its nourishment the
noblest juices—the sap and very marrow of the body.
Yet so it is. From the stag's head, " shorn of his beam,"
the young shoot springs up, and like a sapling, buds and
puts forth a branch, and then another and another. Upwards still it rises ; and the thick stem divides on high
into more taper branchings, forming as they cluster together a rude mural crown. ' At the extremities all is
soft and tender, porous, and with much blood. Over the
whole, to preserve it from injury until it has grown firm
and hard, is a thick velvet covering; and not until all
beneath can bear exposure to the air does this fall off.
When first got rid of, the antlers are as white as ivory,
but they soon acquire their usual darker hue.

It is now summer, and the stag revels in abundance.
He roams through the woods and enjoys the glorious
time in quiet luxury. But, as was said before, this is of

short duration: the Feast of St. Egidius is at hand, and his life of slothful ease is at an end.

CHAPTER V.

A WALK TO FISCHBACHAU.

THE young forester Meier was going to see his father, who lived at the foot of the Peissenberg; and as my road over the Kühzagel Alp passed his house, we set off together.

"Well, Meier," I asked at parting, "are you sure I shall find the way?"

"You can't miss it. To the top of the mountain goes a road; a little way up is a bridge; do not cross it, but keep straight on. Higher up you will come to a place where there are three roads—take the middle one, it leads downwards, and then you have the mountain stream beside you all the way."

"Well, adieu! and by the time I come back look out for the chamois."

Now it is a very easy matter for one who knows a road by heart, to tell another of paths to the right and to the left, and that he is not to choose this, but is to take that; and as you listen you at last get inoculated with a notion of its easiness, and allow yourself to commit the folly of starting off alone. But once in the wood the pathway is hardly discernible, and across the mountain-top there is no trace of footsteps to be seen; so at last you come to a stand, fully convinced of having done

a very foolish thing.   For years I flattered myself with
the belief of possessing in a superlative degree the organ
of locality; and it is only after having more than once
missed my way in the forest and on the mountain, and
discovered my reckoning to be almost always wrong,
that this crotchet of mine has been given up, and the
acknowledgment forced from me that there is as much
chance of my going astray in this physical world, as in
the one where we are apt to take our passions for guide-
posts.   Once, when lagging behind my companions, I
lost my way on the mountains; and after having traversed a space which no one would have credited but for
my description of some peculiar features of a remote spot
reached while thus wandering, I was at length fortunate
enough to see afar off an old human being, who, on my
forcing him to go with me, put me on the right track.
Had I not found that poor weather-beaten creature just
then, my bones would now be lying up amongst those
heights.

In the mountains all is on so large a scale, the stranger
is constantly deceiving himself as to distance. A trifling
change of position, too, makes everything look quite
different.   In descending from an eminence the forms
selected as landmarks are at once lost sight of; on getting nearer to the foot of the mountains the seemingly
narrow valley opens into breadth : hill, mound, dell, all
unperceived till now, start into sight; you become confused by a multitude of objects not calculated on before,
and, having already perhaps deviated from the straight
line to evade a precipice or to cross a torrent, are wholly
at a loss what direction to take. You look back to
reconnoitre the ground and find your starting-point.
But it is not to be found; all is changed; other forms
are seen up against the sky ; no single feature that was

there before is now to be recognized. You turn round, and ask yourself if in coming downwards yonder peak with snow was not on your right, and you are not sure of the answer, for there is another very like it where snow is also lying :—how then distinguish between them? And if you determine to go straight on toward the distant ridge, on getting there at last after two hours' desperate climbing, all again is like an unknown land, and not a single mountain-top that forms part of the new horizon have you ever beheld before. Landmark you have none—the few you had are now irrecoverably lost. There you stand in vast space, utterly helpless. Far, far around you rise those sharp lines against the sky which bounds your present world. How gladly would you look into the space beyond, and strive to catch at hope! But this "beyond" is shut out from you as impenetrably as that vague unknown which is beyond the grave. And you still keep your look fixed on those impassable barriers: a strange irresistible power seems to rivet your staring eyes upon them, and you gaze on with awe, and dread, and longing!

Ay, with awe! for they stand before you, those huge forms, in overpowering, unparticipating stillness. All is motionless. Nothing stirs that forms a part of them. A shadow may flit across their face, but that is an extraneous thing, and when it has swept by, there they are, still in the same cold, rigid imperturbability. If only a tree were there, with its softer outline, and its boughs, though not moving, at least conveying the feeling that they *might* move as being a thing with life! But no, the hard lines of those fixed features are unrelieved by one milder form ; stillness, unwaning stillness, sits on them everlastingly, like Death! And yet you gaze on them with longing,—the longing that with your vision you could penetrate what is beyond. It is a yearning such as the soul feels to know of that " other side" which will be seen only after death.

On the finest day too the mists will suddenly rise, wrapping all in their flowing cloud-like folds. When thus overtaken in the mountains by dense fog, if it last you may look upon it as your shroud.

In crossing the barren heights of the Valtelline, I remember to have met, on the summit, a little altar raised by friendly hands from the stones which lay strewn around, in a niche of which shone a human skull and a heap of bones. They had belonged to a contrabandista, who, while smuggling his wares across this scene of desolation, had been overtaken by the mists sweeping upward from the valley, and, unable to proceed, had sat down and been frozen to death. " On such occasions," said my guide, " nothing is to be done but to lie down and die." Long after having passed the monument I could see, on looking back, the white bones gleaming in the sunlight, for the elements had bleached them to a snowy whiteness.

In going to Fischbachau, however, there was no fear of my becoming the hero of a " lamentable occurrence" in the columns of a newspaper, or of having an *ex voto* erected to my memory. I lost my way however, as might very well have been expected; but I regained it after a while, and came upon the road that leads from Schlier See. The rain had now ceased, and the sun looked out cheerily and with his very brightest smile, as if determined to make amends for not having shown himself earlier. Schlier See was before me, a little island in the middle of its clear waters, and which, from its glittering brightness, might, for aught I know, have risen out of the lake just before I came. I looked at it a long time, for its beauty and freshness reminded me of England.

The forester's house at Fischbachau had once been a cloister; and the clergyman of the parish still inhabited one half the building. The corridor was filled with rows of antlers, and the sitting-room of the family was decorated in the same appropriate manner. All round the top were ranged the bent horns of the chamois; below these the more majestic antlers of the stag; and lower down, interspersed also at intervals among the others, were those of the roebuck. The windows were filled with ivy and creeping plants, and these trailed along from antler to antler, and hung down in careless festoons, or they were twined round the frames hanging on the wall with engraved portraits in them, among which I recognized some well-known faces. At the further end of the room was a row of rifles and fowling-pieces, with here a strangely-fashioned powder-flask or cramping-irons for the feet in winter; on a nail hung the rücksack, the green hat above it with a gay flower on its brim; while a guitar in a corner, and a cithern on a table, gave evidence of gentler pastime than the chase affords. But the neatness and the creeping evergreens had already told of feminine care that presided here. All was as simple as possible, but the place looked comfortable, and everything was deliciously clean. Having changed my wet clothes, I returned and talked with the forester. "It is no pleasure now," he said, "to have to do with the chase. I do not like even to think about it. The mountains opposite—those you see from the windows—were full of chamois, the Miesing especially. From this room you might often with a telescope see thirty or forty together; and now on the whole mountain there are perhaps not twenty."

" And there were stags, too?" I asked.

"Stags and roes in abundance. But now all are shot. The peasants shoot everything. There," said he, pointing to the antlers between the windows, "is the last stag that Berger, my assistant-forester, shot. It was a good one, as you see, and I have put up the antlers in remembrance, for I dare say he will never shoot another —it will be his last."

" It is hardly credible," I observed, " that in so short a time almost every head of game should have been exterminated. It is very sad, for it would take a long time to have all again as it once was."

" No, it is not surprising when you think that the game had never any rest. Day after day it was disturbed, shot at, scared and driven from place to place. The peasants did not get much, for if they wounded a stag or chamois they had no good dog to follow it with, and so it was generally lost. And all game must have quiet—that is as indispensable as food. A great part therefore went across to the Tyrol; and the gamekeepers too shot all they could, rather than let the peasants get it."

And then he told me how he used to go into the mountains, and sit for hours and watch the chamois and the young kids as they disported themselves on the green slopes, or stood upon the rocks and leaped from crag to crag; but now, he said, he would go up there no more, for all his pleasure in doing so was gone, and his occupation rejoiced him no longer.* I already

* In a letter received from the worthy forester since this was written, he says :—" Although late in the autumn, after you were gone many chamois collected here again. I much doubt if we shall see any next summer, for the poor creatures that are now looking for their winter haunts are so scared and hunted about, that their utter extermination must be the consequence. No one can possibly tell the pain all this causes me; and I therefore never express what I feel to

knew what excellent hunting-grounds all this neighbourhood afforded; for though it belonged to the Crown the
whole mountain-range had been rented by a gentleman,
who, by carefully preserving the game for a year or two,
and by the excellent order he maintained, had greatly
enhanced the value of the chase. He had his own foresters stationed in all parts; young active fellows, and
moreover excellent chamois-hunters, who understood
their duty well, and did it. Just as all was in high
perfection and the game abundant, those political changes
took place which gave the right of shooting to every
individual of the community. In order somewhat to
diminish his pecuniary losses, the Count, to whom the
chase belonged, ordered that the game should be shot
by his own people rather than by the poachers; and
venison became so plentiful that it fetched but threepence, twopence, and even a penny a pound.* But
in the plain it was exactly the same. In the extensive forests of the Prince of Tour and Taxis, with whom
I have enjoyed the privilege of shooting for the last ten

any one but a hunter, and one who loves the chase, and of whom I
am persuaded beforehand that he will understand and sympathize with
what I suffer."

* The circumference of the chase was about sixty English miles.
The Count calculated that in a few years he would be able to shoot
there *every year* three hundred roebucks, eighty (warrantable) stags, and
one hundred chamois. It must however be said, that there is not a better sportsman to be found than Count A., and that such a state of things
could only be brought about in so short a time by his excellent manage-
ment. He had twenty-four gamekeepers, all picked men, fellows as fear-
less and daring as they were excellent hunters. In the short time that
the chase was in the Count's hands, they had shot seven poachers in
conflicts with them. One of the keepers, he who had killed four, was
himself shot soon afterwards at Berchtesgaden. The neighbourhood
of the Tyrol was the cause of this influx of poachers. They would
come across the frontier at the Kaiser Klause and Fallep, and were
at once on Bavarian territory.

years, all the red-deer have been destroyed. From forty-
five to fifty-two or fifty-three good stags were shot every
season, and now there are not half-a-dozen in the whole
forest range. Although the peasantry may occasionally
have had to complain of the superabundance of game in
the lowlands, there could be no excuse for this total
destruction of the chamois, which from its habits could
do no possible injury to the crops of the husbandman.
The higher mountains were their dwelling-place, and the
herbs they found on their green sides, with the young
sprouts of the latschen,* afforded them nourishment.
But the intoxication caused by the possession of a new
right blinded the peasantry even to their own profit and
advantage ; and rather than let a chase for a good
price, as is done with the moors in Scotland, they harried the game, and, having depopulated the mountains,
find at last that what might have proved a constant
source of profit and pleasure is now thoroughly exhausted.
But excess characterizes every social revolution. It is, too,
the very spirit of all proscriptions that they be carried on
unrelentingly, and with a view to extermination ; and the
red-deer and chamois became suddenly a proscribed race ;
a ban was upon them, and none escaped but those that
fled into the deepest recesses of the forest, or sought
an asylum among the inaccessible fastnesses of the
mountains. Their names stood first on the dread list
of the victims who were to fall ; and so the people rose

---

* *Latschen—Pinus Pumilio*—is a sort of pine found on the mountains, growing on their barren sides or out of the crevices of the
rocks. It does not at once grow upwards, but creeps along the
ground for some distance before its branches rise perpendicularly. Its
foliage is dense and bushy, and forms a good covert for the game. This
shrub might be called "The Hunter's Friend," for on its boughs he
may always rely, as they never break with the strongest pull. He must
only be careful not to bend them, for then they snap at once.

E

with a shout to take their life indiscriminately wherever they might find them.*

One great charm of the woods is now therefore gone. They are empty; they have no inhabitants. You now meet no stag's face peeping through the leaves; nor are you stopped on your path by the sight of well-known pointed footmarks on the soft ground.

The assistant-forester was not at home; nothing therefore was to be learnt about the probability of getting a shot. He had been out on the mountains for several days, but was expected home that evening. While at supper we learned that he was returned, and a little later, after having changed his dress, he made his appearance.

" Well, Berger, good evening !" said the kind old head-forester, as he entered; " you have had bad weather—eh ? Now, sit down. What have you seen ?"

" On the Wendelstein yesterday I saw a good chamois buck at about two hundred yards distant. I could only just see the haunch, but still I would have fired, only I had not set the hair-trigger."

" And you met nobody ?"

" No, all is quiet. It was terribly cold up on the Wendelstein, and the weather has been as bad as it could be."

" Well, Berger, do you think there is any likelihood of getting a shot at a chamois when the weather clears up ?"

" Yes; chamois are there, that's certain; and on the Miesing is the best place," he said, turning to me. " We'll go up the Steinberg, and then stalk up the steep part near the latschen. I think we are pretty sure of a shot,—if only all has been quiet, and no poachers have been there to disturb them."

* See note at the end of the Volume.

"Well, if the rain ceases and the weather clears, we will start tomorrow early. When you are ready, call me."

At least twenty times that day I had been to the window, peering, or rather trying to peer, through the clouds of mist, to see if no blue sky were visible. Sometimes the heads of the opposite mountains—the Klein Miesing, the Jäger Kamm, and others—would show themselves just above the gloomy mantle whose undulating folds floated around them; but then the spirit of the storm would come sweeping on to recover his supremacy, bringing up an array of dim clouds from the chasms that divided the mountains, and soon all was again enveloped in impenetrable gloom. It had rained the whole of that day and the preceding night in sullen perseverance, and there seemed no hope of change; when in the afternoon the wind gave sign of his approach, for fragments of mist like flying banners came hurrying past, and bearing down on the cohorts of clouds that had, till now, in sturdy masses defied the sun, tore great rents through them, and sent them flying in all directions. How glad we were of his victory, and how we rejoiced to see the scattered remnants of that vast army of clouds trying in vain to re-assemble! The strong wind put them utterly to the rout. We now saw that snow had fallen on the tops of the mountains. Over the flat land the sun was again visible, and there was every prospect of fine weather on the morrow. We looked out again at night, and the firmament was strewn with stars. What more could we desire?

E 2

❧

CHAPTER VI.

UP THE MIESING.

The morning was clear and bright, and not a breath of wind was stirring, an essential thing for the chamois hunter; for if the air be not calm, all his skill, perseverance, and daring will avail him nothing. At best even it is difficult to calculate on the gusts that will sometimes come suddenly rushing up a chasm, or sweeping downwards just as he gets round the shoulder of a mountain. Thus, when he thinks all is won, and he rejoices in his panting heart at the success which is about to crown his labour, the taint of his presence will be borne along on the rippling air, and the herd on whom for the last hour his longing eye has been so intently fixed looks round affrighted, conscious of the neighbourhood of an enemy, utters a shrill whistle, and, mounting over the sharp ridge of an opposite mountain, is seen for one moment in bold relief against the sky, and then disappears on the other side. But we had no cause to fear that our hopes would be marred by such a circumstance.

Whilst I breakfasted Berger got ready the rifles; for not having calculated on being able to go out here, I had not brought mine with me. We went past the little chapel of Birkenstein, whither many a pilgrim resorts, and on through pleasant meadows shut in by gentle slopes

covered with wood. And now we emerge into a broad
valley, and before us is the Miesing, and to the left the
Wendelstein, with its high conical summit, whence, according to the song, may be seen the two tall church
towers* "of the great city where the King dwells." It
is a striking feature in the mountain-chain, for, though
not the highest of the peaks, it seems to be so, rising
as it does abruptly and alone. A few cottages were clus-
tered together beside a stream at no great distance from
our path, and cattle were grazing in the several fields,
while a little peasant-boy poured forth his orisons, for
such I took his gladsome song to be, in that fair temple
not built by human hands.

As we went along, the neighbouring mountains sug-
gested many a tale of interest to the hunter. "There,"
said Berger, pointing to a wood on our right halfway
down the hill-side,—"there, two years ago, was a stag of
sixteen. Such a stag! his antlers were splendid; and
what a size he was!"

"And who shot him?" I asked.

"That I don't know. The foresters saw him often,
and could have shot him many a morning had they liked;
but Count A. had given strict orders to forbid them, and
at last he was seen no more. He disappeared suddenly,
—most likely the poachers got him. It was such a hart
as will not often be seen again."

And some distance further on:—"Up yonder to the
left, quite at the top of the mountain, I one day shot
three chamois."

"How did you manage that?"

"Why, first I shot two, right and left; and then, knowing where the others would cross the mountain, I ran

---

* Of the church of Our Lady in Munich.

forward to meet them, and sure enough they came as I expected, and just as I was re-loading too. I was ready with one barrel, and shot a third. Had I thought of my pistol I might have brought down a fourth, for one stood not twenty paces from me."

"What!" I asked, "do you carry a pistol with you?"

"Yes, always," he replied, drawing a double-barrelled revolver (with four barrels) out of his pocket: "one must always be prepared for whatever may happen; and with that, if I only have a place to lean against, I should not mind one or two."

"But do the poachers attack you if you do not begin with them?"

"Their hearts are set on the Jägers' guns: their own are not good for much, and they know that ours are, and they would rather get one of them than almost anything. And they'd give us a good thrashing too, if they could," he added, laughing; "and you know to be half-beaten to death is not so very agreeable. Besides, if you meet with such fellows in a hut, where everything is so close together, and there is little room to move, you cannot do much with a rifle, it's too long—in close quarters like that a pistol may do good service."

"But how did you bring down your three chamois?"

"One I put in my rücksack, and the other two, as there was snow on the ground, I dragged down. On the Wendelstein once I shot a chamois, and afterwards a roebuck. The chamois I put in the sack, and the buck across it over my shoulders. One can carry almost anything so, and capitally too."

We now came to the broad path or mountain way that leads up the Miesing, made to enable the woodcutters to bring down the wood in winter, as well as for the cattle which in the summer months are driven up to the high pasturages. Beside us, on our left, a clear stream was falling over the blocks of stone that had tumbled into its channel, and beyond it rose a wall of rock, well-nigh perpendicular, eight hundred feet or more. This was the Gems Wand, a famous place in other days ere the new laws had been put in force, and where, on ledges so narrow that it seemed a bird only might cling there for some moments, the chamois were always to be seen, standing at gaze or stepping carelessly along. But now the rock was indeed desolate. Over the face of this high wall of stone were scattered the friendly latschen, with here and there a pine that had been able to twist its root into some gaping crevice. It was as nearly perpendicular as might be, and, except that the strata of rock formed projecting ridges, there was hardly a footing to be obtained. However, if there are latschen one may climb almost anywhere. We stopped occasionally to look across with our glasses and scan its rocky face, in order to see if perchance a solitary buck were loitering there alone. But not a thing, animate or inanimate, was stirring. As I looked up at the precipice I observed to Berger, " To get along there would be no easy matter— eh? What think you, could you manage it?"

" I went along there some time ago, when out with Mr. * * *. He wounded a chamois, and it climbed upwards along the wall. It was difficult work, for there was nothing to hold on by; and what grass I found was not firm, and gave way in my grasp. Once I was rather uncomfortable, for while hanging to the rock with both arms raised my rifle swung forward over my arm."

" Ay, that is a horrid situation; let go your hold

you dare not; and how to get the rifle back again one
does not know either. When it swings down and knocks
against the rock, it almost makes one lose all balance.
The rifle is sadly in the way in such difficult places.
Without it—"

"Oh, without it," said Berger, interrupting me, "one
could go any and everywhere. Without it I could climb
through the world. The rifle makes an immense difference. But, as I was saying, at last I got up and reached
the chamois. The coming down was the worst part.
However, I took another way than in going up. I pulled
off my shoes, for you can then feel your ground better,
and take hold of every little projection with your toes."

"But that must have hurt you terribly?"

"No; I was then accustomed to go barefoot, and
would formerly much rather have climbed so than with
thick nailed shoes on. Once before I came down yonder
wall from over the ridge: it was ugly work, I can tell
you. We drove the game that day, and I had to go
over the top and roll down stones to make the chamois
cross to the other side."

We had now wound upwards for about an hour, when
we left the path and turned off to our right among some
latschen and huge blocks of stone. We had not gone
many yards when Berger dropped to the earth, as
though a shot had passed through his heart. He raised
his finger to indicate silence, his eyes were opened wide
with expectation, and his lips drawn apart as if uttering a "Hush!" though not a breath passed over them.
We cowered behind the stones, and he whispered,
"There are chamois!" We crept on a little further;
the end of my pole shod with iron touched a stone
and made the metal slightly ring. Berger turned round
with a reproving look, and made me a sign to exchange

mine for his, which was not shod. We advanced and
lay behind a bush, and drew out our glasses. Five
chamois were there, grazing on the slope, skirted by a
wood. Berger's whole frame was alive with expectation;
his face wore quite a different expression to what it
had before; his eyes seemed larger, his body more
supple, his powers of motion other than in everyday life
—the whole creature was changed. "Now then," he
said, "come along, quick *und schön stad!*" (quickly
and *nicely quiet.*) We moved on, but a breath of air
stirred, and they must have got wind of us, for they
began to move towards the wood, and soon disappeared
within it. There was now nothing to be done but to go
round and get above them, for it was late, and the current of air had already set in from below. Just as we
had reached the top I heard a slight rustle, and stopped
to listen; when in an instant there was a rushing down
the steep and over the broken ground as of an animal
in full flight. By the step I was sure it was deer
(hinds), and said so to Berger. "They were not chamois—they made too much noise; nor was it the rush
of a stag. It must have been a hind."

"You are right," he cried; "there they go! I see
them down below—two hinds—they heard us moving
along above them."

"Do you think they will take the chamois along with
them?"

"No, I think not. We shall most likely meet them
further on; if not, we will sit and watch for them."

This is one of the great difficulties of stalking in the
mountains,—to do so almost unheard. Fragments of
stone are lying about, latschen with their long trailing
branches and dense foliage, or steep beds of *Geröll*, cross
your path, which the lightest step will set in motion, and

yet you must advance quickly, and pick your way quite noiselessly.* I always found the exertion and attention this required fatigued me more than climbing for a longer time when such caution was unnecessary.

As nothing more was to be seen of the five chamois we had met with on the Steinberg, we sat down and peered into the vast hollow that lay before us. Rising upwards to our left was barren rock, sharp and broken, grey, bare, and weather-beaten: it looked hoary with age.

Where the rocks ceased to be perpendicular the geröll began, and continued far downwards, till here and there latschen began to show themselves. We sat in silence, examining with strained eyes every inch of ground, and looking down among the stunted bushes, and upwards among the crags, in hopes of seeing a chamois that might be lured forth by the cheering sun. From time to time, as one of us fancied that some spot at a distance looked like the object of his search, suddenly out flew the glass, and the other, full of hope and expectation, with eyes turned from the mountain-side to his comrade's face, would watch his countenance as he looked through the telescope, to learn, before he spoke, if a chamois were there or not. He needed not to say, "'Tis nothing!"—the other saw this at once, by his expression. But when the glass remained up to the eye some seconds longer than usual, and the Jäger, as he still looked, said, "'Tis chamois! there are three together!" how exciting was the expectation. The glass of each would then in-

---

* *Geröll.* Loose rolling stones on the side of a mountain, like the lava on the sides of a volcano. At every step the whole mass gives way beneath your tread, and slides downwards, carrying you with it. The difficulty therefore in crossing such Geröll without noise may be conceived.

stantly be turned in the same direction, to find the spot
on which the hopes of both were now centred. " I have
them ! One is at rest; the one to the right is a yearling, I think. Now it's among the latschen;—now—
now he has come forward again. What high horns that
other one has !"

Such are the remarks to be heard on these occasions,
made in a subdued voice, uttered quickly, and broken
into short sentences—mere ejaculations called forth by
the stir of the emotion, by the feelings of the moment,
and leaving no time for them to be fashioned into a connected form. But neither of us heard from the other
such pleasant tidings; and after having eaten a slice of
brown bread and a morsel of goat's-milk cheese, we slung
our rifles over our shoulders, and each taking his staff
went down the mountain.

We looked around on all sides, but not a chamois was
to be seen. Before us rose the Roth Wand, now (October 10th) covered with snow; on a verdant patch of
pasture-land where we stood was a solitary hut, long deserted ; and on the mountain-side, to our right, it seemed
as if some fiend had dug his nails into the ground, and
torn away from top to bottom all the earth that he could
clutch. Right through the green latschen came a long,
broad strip of loose stones, some hundred feet in width.

On going along at the foot of this geröll, Berger
suddenly stopped; and dropping behind a large block of
stone, whispered, "There's a chamois !" High up amongst
the *débris* a black spot was visible, and this was the chamois. We saw by our glasses that it was a yearling buck,
and for a time watched him at our ease, as we lay on
the ground protected by the fragment of fallen rock. It
stood at gaze for a moment.

" Does it see us ?" I asked ; " does it look this way ?"

" No," said Berger; " but the thing is, how to get near it. Up the stones we can't go—it will make too much noise; and if we cross over the crest of the mountain, and so walk down towards him, it will be too far to fire. If we could only get up through the latschen! but I fear it is impossible, he would be sure to see us. However, let us try: be still, very still."

We were just on the point of making the attempt, when, on looking round to scan the sides of the Roth Wand, I saw a chamois about five hundred feet below the summit, on a green spot quite free from snow, and at the foot of a wall of rock. " Hist, Berger! there are chamois!"

" Where?"

" Look up yonder; don't you see them?"

" No."

" Look, don't you see a black spot, right across to the right of the geröll, and the snow. Now it moves! There is another!—one, two, three!"

" I see them now! Confound it, they see us! Let us move on—don't stop to look; keep away from them, up to the right." And up we went, keeping in a contrary direction, and then stopped among some large loose stones.

" Look, Berger! now you can see them well; they are crossing the snow, but not quickly. What! don't you see them? Why now they are moving round the wall of a rock that goes down quite perpendicularly; yet now I see but two,—where can the third be?"

" Now I see them. Give me your glass: make haste and reach those latschen yonder; when once among them, all's right. I'll lie here and watch them, and come after you directly. But for heaven's sake get up the geröll quietly, for if a stone move they'll surely hear it, though so far off; and be quick, and get among the latschen." Giving him my telescope, which was much the better one, I moved on over the slanting mass of loose stones.

With body bent as low as possible I tried to creep noiselessly upwards. I dared not use my pole to steady myself, for the weight would have forced it among the loose rubble, and made as much or more noise than my footsteps occasioned. Taking it in my left hand, on which side also my rifle was slung, I steadied myself with the right, and so at last reached some larger fragments of stone, which were firmer to the tread, and over which I could consequently get along more rapidly. The sheltering latschen were at length gained, and I flung myself down behind them, quite out of breath with excitement and from moving thus doubled up together.

In this safe haven Berger soon joined me. "They are at rest," he said. "Now all's right! we have them now! But how shall we get across?" he asked, as he looked round to reconnoitre our position. "Yonder they'll see us; we must pass over the ridge above, and go round and see if there is a way."

This we did, and once on the other side, kept just sufficiently low down to prevent our heads being seen above the sky-line. But after advancing some hundred yards, we came to a spot where the ridge swept suddenly downwards, forming a gap between us and the chamois. To proceed without being seen was impossible. On our right it was rather steep, but we were obliged to descend a good way, and then the same distance up again further on, in order to reach the Roth Wand unobserved.

"Here we are at last! Are they still at rest, Berger? just look across through the branches of yonder latschen above you."

"Yes, they are still there! Now then, we must get to the pinnacle right over our heads, and then along the ridge, and so have a shot at them from above."

The shoulder of the mountain where we stood was steep enough certainly, but it still presented sufficient inequalities to enable us to clamber up it. Elsewhere, except on this projecting buttress-like shoulder, the declivity was so steep as to be not many degrees from the perpendicular. I proposed therefore that we should choose this less steep ridge to reach the broken rocks above us, on whose jagged forms we might obtain a firm hold, and so creep upwards to the very crest of the mountain. "Oh no," answered Berger; "we dare not venture that : they would be sure to see us, for we should be quite unsheltered, and our bodies being thrown against the sky would be distinctly visible. No, we must try yonder —up that *lahne*,"* pointing to the steep declivity before us, to see the summit of which it was necessary to fling the head quite backwards. I confess it was not with the pleasantest feelings that I saw what we had undertaken ; for the slope was covered with snow, making the ascent doubly difficult, and upwards of two thousand feet below was a huge rocky chasm, into which I could look and calculate where I might at last stop, if my foot slipped and I happened to go sliding down. Where the lahne ended beds of loose stones began ; and, as if to remind

---

* *Lahnen* are smooth, steep declivities covered with long grass. In the summer, when this rank herbage has been dried by the sun and air, it is so slippery that a firm footing is almost impossible; and in winter such an ascent is not made more practicable by its covering of snow. When slipping on such a lahne you shoot downwards as on one of those artificial mountains or slides which form a favourite amusement in Russia. They not unfrequently rise above a precipice ; a false step here, therefore, and a miracle only can save you from going over into the abyss.

one of their instability, and how hopeless it would be to think of holding fast even for a moment on their moving surface, there rose from minute to minute a low, dull sound, made by some rolling stone, which, set in motion by its own weight, went pattering downwards into the melancholy hollow.

However, to stand looking upwards at the steep snowy surface of the mountain, or gazing at the depth below, was not the way to get a shot at the chamois; so giving my rifle a jerk to send it well up behind my back, and leave the left arm free, I began to mount, keeping in an oblique direction in order to lessen the steepness of the ascent. Berger was before me, sometimes on his hands and knees, sometimes on his feet, and looking every now and then anxiously behind to see what progress I made. Neither of us got on very fast, for a firm footing was impossible. If you slipped, down you came on your face, with both feet nowhere, and the rifle swinging over the left arm into the snow, most inconveniently. Once, when I was quite unable to plant either foot firmly, Berger, who was just above me, and had, as it seemed, a safe spot on which to stand, was obliged to let down his long pole that I might hold on by it, and, with his heels well dug into the ground, gave me a helping pull. We had mounted halfway when suddenly both my feet lost their hold on the snow, and somehow or other down I went over the steep declivity on my back, like an arrow sent from a strongly-drawn bow. It was disagreeable, for I knew how difficult it is to stop when once gliding at full speed down a lahne; and all my endeavours to do so, with help of my heels or my hands, were ineffectual. But I remembered the advice my friend Kobell had once given me: "Should you ever be unlucky enough to slip when upon a lahne, turn round so as to get on your stomach as quickly as possible, or else you are lost." While shooting downwards therefore I turned, and grasping my stick, which was well shod with an iron point, I dashed it with all my force into the ground. It stuck fast; I held on by it, and was stopped in my career. While gliding down, my eyes were turned upwards to Berger. I saw fright expressed on his countenance: our eyes met, but neither uttered a word. Only when I had arrested my further progress, and was cautiously preparing to find a sure footing, he called out, " It was lucky you were able to stop; for heaven's sake be careful, it is dreadfully slippery." At last, by making a zigzag line, we reached the top of the lahne. Here were rocks by which we could hold, and getting amongst them came to a perpendicular wall about seven feet high. Its face was as straight as a plummet-line, but it was rough, so that some crevices were to be found which might serve as steps in passing over it. At its base was a small ledge, on which one person could stand, holding on with his own face and the face of the rock close against each other, and behind, below, was— what was not quite pleasant to think of. Berger got over first, having previously with one hand laid his rifle and pole on a ledge of rock above him to have both hands free. Handing up my rifle to him, I followed; and though the place seemed rather formidable, in reality it was easy enough to climb. As I stood on the ledge face to face with the perpendicular rock, I debated within myself whether I should look behind me or not. I knew that below and behind was nothing but air, and I decided on proceeding without turning round; so I searched for the most favourable crack or roughness in the rock to make a first step, which moment of delay

Berger attributed to indecision and to fear; and stretching out his hand to me, he cried roughly, " Come, what
are you thinking of? give me your hand,—that's right.
Now then!" He was wrong in his supposition, for I
was neither undecided nor afraid, but he feared that if
I grew alarmed I might let go my hold; and as the
moment was critical he thought to rouse and re-assure
me by his manner, and by holding my hand firmly in
his grasp. " Patience, Berger! patience! I shall be up
in a second; I only want to find a place for my foot;
don't think I am giddy. There, now I am up." And
then one of us, lying down at full length, reached with
one arm over the ledge of rock, to the spot below where
the rifles and poles were lying.

With bended bodies we now stole along the crest of
the mountain as noiselessly as possible, for the chamois
were below us on our left, just over the ridge. We
presently looked over. I could not see them, on account
of a projecting rock, but Berger whispered, " There they
are! Quick! they are moving." Still as we were,
they must have heard us coming upon them, and, suspecting danger, were already in motion. But they had
not yet whistled. By " craning" over, as a fox-hunter
would say, I just obtained a glimpse of one far below
me on a small green spot, and standing at gaze. To
fire in this position however was impossible. Berger,
all impatience and fearing they would escape, was in a
fever of anxiety. " Look here! can you see them
now?" as with the left foot planted on an advancing
crag not larger than the palm of my hand, I stood as it
were in the air, immediately above the spot where the
chamois were.* A crack from my rifle was the answer.

* While firing at a chamois under exactly the same circumstances, a
terrible accident happened to a Swiss chamois hunter, Ulrich Zurfluh,

F

To aim nearly straight downwards is always more difficult than in any other direction, and standing as I did
made it much more so; but still I thought I had hit
him.

"He remains behind," cried Berger; "you have hit
him! Well done! 'Faith, that *was* a good shot—a
hundred and thirty yards at least. Quick, quick! we
may get a shot at the others as they go over yonder
rocks;" and darting up the ridge before him, he ran
on along the edge of the precipice as if it had been a
broad highway. At another time, without a rifle in my
hand, I should have followed him with caution; but the
excitement of the hunter was upon me, impelling me
to undertake anything, and I sprang after him, and on
along the edge, driven forwards by a longing and a
thirst and craving which made everything seem possible.

"There they are! they're crossing that patch of snow.

in August, 1855. He was out with his son, following a buck along the
north side of the Engelhörner, when at last, by craning over the brink
of the precipice, he was just able to get sight of the game. To obtain
a fuller view he, like myself, rested one foot on a small projection of
rock, when, at the very moment he was about to fire, the stone crumbled
away beneath his tread, and over he went into the abyss. What is most
remarkable is that his son, as yet a boy, seems from that moment to have
been unconscious of what he did. All he knows is, that he soon after
found himself beside his dead father's body, holding his shattered head
and kissing his face. Afterwards he went to his uncle in Rosenlaui to
bring him the sad intelligence. It was too late that day to go for the
body, but on the morrow four of the most experienced and agile mountaineers proceeded to the spot with ropes, etc., to help them in getting
down to the chasm. The difficulties were so great, however, that one of
the men would go no further, but gave up the task. At last, and after
incredible risks, they reached the corpse, and brought it to Rosenlaui.

And yet the boy, in the excitement of anguish, and blind to the surrounding obstacles, without help surmounted them all; and in the total
unconsciousness of danger, passed safely through the most fearful perils.
It is a psychological mystery.

Getting a shot

Now they 're stopping again—but too far off; let us go back and look after the wounded one."

The wounded chamois was standing some distance further down than when I had fired. It was evident by his look that he was very ill—*sehr krank*, to translate literally the German expression made use of in like cir-cumstances. Stretched out at full length upon the rocks, we looked over the edge, and examined him with our glasses. We saw distinctly where the ball had struck him,—rather high up behind the shoulder. He presently moved off, crossed the snow, and getting among the latschen, after turning round four or five times, lay down. "All 's right now; we must let him rest for an hour. Let me see; it is half-past two exactly. We 'll try then to come nearer to him. But where can we get down ?" said Berger; " here it is impossible."

"A little further on, I think, we may manage it; some latschen are there, and they will help us. But let us stop a little ; there is no hurry, and if we wait some time, it will be all the better."

I now looked around me. The scene was magnificent. The spot on which I stood was near six thousand feet high; and to the south the view was bounded by ranges of mountains covered with snow, whose peaks rose up one behind the other in every variety of abruptness. Over the vast fields of snow fell here and there a broad shadow, and the brilliant whiteness of the peaks facing us formed a strong contrast with the darker sides that looked towards the east. With my glass every snow-drift was distinctly visible, and terrific places amongst those awful solitudes where no living creature had ever moved. Stretching far out to our left they formed an amphitheatre before us; and behind, all distant view being shut out by the Miesing, was the valley between

the mountains, where, just visible among the rocks, the
deep blue of the Soen Lake showed how clear the air
was, and how bright the sky.   Opposite this lake the
sides of the Miesing were covered with the dark green of
the latschen ; but nearer to where we stood all was desolation :—against the sky the barren and blasted rock,
and thence to its foot a bed of loose rolling stones, cold
and monotonous in hue.   But it was towards the distant mountains that I turned and gazed, and yet never
could see enough.   And then again I looked at them
through my glass, and peered into their dark places, and
at their bold projections, and at their very highest pin-
nacles, as though I might at last be enabled to unravel
the mystery—to discover something that might clear the
doubts, and so remove the strange awe that hung over
and around them.   And still I looked, and watched, and
pondered, and the spell that bound my gaze grew stronger,
and I could not turn away.   For me mountains have a
fascination ; and in their presence I sit down, and with
fixed look scan their unexplored summits, not in wonder, but with an overwhelming sense of awe at the frozen
stillness of their deserts, so far beyond the sphere of all
human sympathy,—where all life has ceased, and where
nothing ever moves, save the storm and the avalanche.
It is not a region of death, for death speaks to us of
change; but it is one of numbness and rigidity,—of life
that, once warm, has become still and stark.   It produces an effect as different from ordinary death as the
sight of the motionless soldier on the plains of Russia,
still standing upright and looking as though yet alive,
differs from that feeling awakened by death in any other
form.   He with the scythe and the hour-glass *kills*,—
he *destroys* life and turns it into death ; but that power
which sits on the frozen mountain-tops seizes on warm

life and enlocks it in a glaze which chills vitality, while
the semblance of life remains. It is not of *death* these
icy solitudes remind you, but of *benumbed life.*

Berger came and roused me from my musing. He
took my telescope, and looked at the plains of snow on
the distant mountains. He too felt all the magnificence
of the scene, and gazed around him with delight. Then
awoke in him the longing to climb some vast mountain,
where difficulties were to be overcome such as men who
had once encountered them like not to think of, and
who, while they relate, feel a shuddering and a fear. " I
never was on such a one," he said, " but I should like
to venture. If only *once* I could see such places !" And
I told him of the Ortler Spitz, deemed inaccessible until
a few years ago, when an old chamois hunter found a
way to its icy summit; and how a short time afterwards
he went up again with his son, that he too might find the
path when the father was gone, and that thus the knowledge might not die with the old hunter; and how the
son, a youth of eighteen, had said there were places to be
passed that made his flesh creep as he hung over them;
and how he vowed at the time, as he stood amid the
frightful chasms and walls of ice, while his heart almost
ceased to beat for very horror, that if God should let
him reach the green valleys alive, no power on earth
should ever make him attempt the dreadful way again.
And as I related, Berger stood before me with lips apart,
and his very eyes were listening, as he heard of those
unvisited regions which had for him such a mighty
charm, and inspired so inscrutable a longing.

But it was time to look after our chamois. We went
forward to the place I had indicated as being the one
where we might best descend from the summit of the
mountain. The spot was steep enough, but there were

latschen growing about, and wherever they are found anything may be undertaken.

"Let us mark the place well where he is lying," said Berger, "otherwise we shall not find him when once down below; as we have no dog we must be careful what we are about. Let me see! he is just below yonder high piece of rock with the tall latschen."

"Look, Berger," I said; "from the top of the Roth Wand a line of rough-pointed rocks stretches downwards to the valley."

"Well, I see them."

"They form two ridges beneath each other. Now, over the second ridge the chamois is at rest. If we mark those high ridges well, we cannot be at fault."

And observing attentively the form of the rock where we now stood, in order that it might afterwards serve as a landmark, we prepared to descend. Berger went first over the bed of geröll. He stopped a moment, and said, "Now give me your rifle; you'll get on then much more easily." He slung it over his shoulder with his own, when suddenly his foot slipped, and down he went, sliding on his back over the loose stones; and, though he turned himself round immediately, was quite unable to arrest his progress. At the foot of the bed of stones there was fortunately no precipice, or over it he would most certainly have gone.

"Are you hurt, Berger?" I added, when at last he stopped.

"No," he answered laughing. "But what a noise it made! how the stones came rattling down! Now then, carefully! Stop! Rest one foot against my pole; it is planted firmly, and will bear your weight!"

"Quick, Berger! quick! take care;" and at the same moment down came a great stone that had been loosened, and dashed by close to his shin. But he moved his foot, and it passed without striking him. We had proceeded some distance, and the question now was, " Where is the chamois?" The rocky ridge was close to our right hand, but every feature looked different when seen from below to what it had done before.

" He must be on the other side, just over that rock."

" No, he is certainly lower down," I answered. " Look! we are still comparatively near the summit of the mountain ; and if you remember, from thence it seemed some distance to where he was at rest ; from yonder ridge however we should certainly catch sight of him." Having clambered thither, Berger suddenly exclaimed, " Hist! there he is! It is far, but still within range : take your time!" The report of my rifle thundered among the rocks, and again and again it reverberated, till at last, like thunder heard afar still faintly rolling, it gradually died away.

" You have missed him !"

" I don't think so. I had him capitally, and the rifle went off just as I could wish ; I was as steady too as possible."

" It may be ; but you see, he is moving away," said Berger gloomily.

" I see he is going : but he moves quite differently now. Look, he staggers ; his step is uncertain, is it not?"

" He is off nevertheless."

" Well, I'll go to the spot where he was standing, and then we shall soon see whether I have missed or not."

There we found hair strewn about, and a pool of fresh blood. At the sight of it Berger's face cleared up, and with light hearts we followed the slot of the wounded animal. The snow was dyed red where he had passed, and the herbage was wet and crimsoned on both sides of his path.

"He cannot be far of, Berger," I said; "look at the
blood. That's the right colour—deep red! Here he
stopped for a moment; but how strange that with two
such shots he should still climb that rock!"

Mounting over a block of stone, Berger looked down
among the rocks, and presently cried out, "There he
lies!" I soon joined him, and looked at the spot where
he had made his last effort and had given his dying leap.
We slid down and stood before our chamois. My first
ball had gone right through the body in an oblique direction downwards; the second too was well lodged. We
laid our rifles aside, and Berger, taking out his hunting-
knife, prepared to *gralloch* the chamois. It was a doe,
that had no kid. I looked around while Berger was
busied with his work, to see the wild spot whither the
chamois had led us. It was a narrow chasm among the
rocks; behind us the high, grey, weather-beaten walls
rising perpendicularly, and below a slope of barren stones
of all forms and sizes flung together indiscriminately.

The chamois cleaned, I opened my rücksack, and laying it on the ground, put our chamois into it—all four
feet together, and the head hanging out of the opening
in the middle. Then, staff in hand, we went down over
that wild sea of stones. Though such a chamois as I had
shot that day might not weigh more than 40lb., it is still
an impediment to one's free movements where the road
to be traversed is uneven or difficult: such a dead weight
settles down and hangs against your back more heavily
than would be imagined. But when once the road was
gained that led to the valley, we tripped along with footsteps as light even as our hearts were, and beguiled the
downward path with recounting the thousand episodes of
our epic of that day. It began to be dark as we reached
the meadows in the vale; but that mattered little, for

we had intended not to return to Fischbachau the same evening, but to stop at the village of Baierisch Zell, at the foot of the mountains, and ask a night's shelter and hospitality of the Solachers—a family well known to all who in those parts had ever watched for the stag in the forest, or climbed up the mountain-sides after the chamois.

A light was shining from out the cottage window ; we crossed the trout-stream that flowed before the garden, and, passing the little wicket, were at once at the door of the old hunter's dwelling. We laid the chamois upon the stones, and lifting the latch went in, and were met with hearty and friendly welcomings.

CHAPTER VII.

AFTER THE CHASE. THE SOLACHERS.

To every one who has followed the chamois or the red-deer in the Highlands of Bavaria, the name of Solacher is a familiar word. And though he may not have carried a rifle in those parts, yet if he be a lover of the chase, that name will still have reached his ears, and be known to him in connection with many a story of adventurous climbing, of desperate encounter with poachers, and of trophies borne off from the shooting-matches at Munich or the village festivals. If, when sitting round the table of the little inn of an evening, you hear some old fellow telling when the last bear was seen in the mountains, and whence he came, and how great the excitement when the news ran of his arrival, you may be sure it was a Solacher who was first in the pursuit, and that, whether they killed the monster or not, to one of that name the honour of the day was due.

Each and all of them have been " hunters of the hills," shunning the plain, and any other occupation save that hard one which they have always followed—father, son, grandchildren, and uncles. The name of Solacher to the hunter of the chamois in Bavaria is like that of Napier with us in England,—*it carries with it reputation:* we at once expect to hear of pre-eminence in him who bears

it; and we look as certainly for boldness of deed in a
Solacher as we do for boldness of thought, of action, or
of word, from one who is a Napier. A Solacher is an
authority in all matters of the chase in the mountains.
They have all been hunters from their youth upwards;
from their first childhood they have heard exciting stories
of the chase, and have been fed with traditions of the
times before them. To follow the chamois is, with them,
rather an instinct than a passion; the air of the mountain-tops seems their proper element, and they have preferred that, and freedom of breathing and of limb, to all
beside where these were not to be obtained.

Max, with whom I became acquainted later, told me
how once a nobleman had proposed to take him into his
service, and made him very advantageous offers. And
on my asking if he had not been inclined to accept them,
he laughed at the thought, and said, " What! quit the
mountains! why I don't think I should be able to endure it for a day. Had he offered me ten times as much
I should have refused. For my part, I can't imagine a
happier life than that of a forester; I know very well
that *I* would not change with anybody in the world!"
And thus they are all; the very maidens look upon a·
hunter's life as the most enviable lot that could fall to
the share of man; and the daring climber, the skilful
stalker, and the unfailing shot, are sure of due apprecia-
tion at their hands. All such do they hold in high
honour. They speak of their brothers with genuine sis-
terly pride, and right pleasant it is to hear them.

At the same moment with ourselves these daughters
entered the room of the cottage. They had, it seems,
been to a neighbouring village wake, and had only just
returned. It was dark when we came in, but now a
light was brought; and as I turned suddenly to look at

her whose voice and friendly manner had already prepossessed me, I was struck by the beauty that was close
beside me, and bursting at once upon me through the
dispersing gloom. It took me by surprise, and she must
have been other than a woman not to have rightly inter-
preted my long astonished gaze. There was not even a
shade of coquetry about her; if there had been, she
would have kept on her becoming green hat a minute or
two longer; but she smiled on seeing the mischief she
had done, and with friendly words inquired where we
had been.

She was of commanding height, this fine-featured second sister, and the long dark-coloured cloth cloak made
her look still taller. It was simply drawn together at
the throat; and, falling in natural folds closely over her
shoulders, gave dignity to the figure without preventing
you from discovering the outline of the womanly form.
On her head she wore the picturesque high-crowned green
hat peculiar to these valleys; over the brim hung the
tassel of green and gold, and at the side were a bright
red rose and other artificial flowers. Her braided brown
hair showed itself beneath the broad brim of the hat;
and as I afterwards looked at her finely-marked features, and at the beautiful outline running from the tip
of the ear to the chin—which by the way is more seldom seen in perfection than any other part of the face—
I could not help thinking that such a bonnie green hat
was, after all, the most becoming head-gear a girl could
wear.

But beside the full-blown flower was another; a full
bud just about to unfold and burst into opening loveliness. It was the youngest sister—Marie. She hardly
ventured to raise her large dark eyes to the stranger,
and quickly left the room to lay aside her hat and cloak.

She returned however soon after; and never did I so
earnestly endeavour to inspire confidence as now, when
doing my best to win trust in my good faith from this
sweet-mannered village maiden. It was difficult at first
to entice her into conversation; but later, when she saw
that the rough-looking creature before her was gentle in
his demeanour, and treated her with comely deference,
she would gradually lift her eyes as she smiled a reply;
and eventually, though timidly at first, would let them
rest full and fearlessly on the stranger's countenance.
Yet later, when our supper came, and I begged them all
to sit at table and sup with us, I could not prevail on
this coy girl to eat with me, or drink out of my cup.
It was not fitting that she should do so, she answered;
yet when my companion made her the same offer, she
at once accepted it, and laughed and chatted with him
right merrily. If I could only have made her believe
that I too was an assistant forester; or, by my faith,
have really become one for that modest lassie's sake!
Here is her picture:—

The Verderer's Daughter of Baierisch Zell.

WE since dawn had been out stalking,
And returning now were talking
Of the chamois; all in walking
   Very slowly:—we did dally
   On our way down to the valley,
     The Vale of Baierisch Zell.

For 't is pleasant, homeward walking,
To beguile the way with talking
Over what you've seen in stalking;
   And though we did sorely dally,
   Still at last we reached the valley
     Of peaceful Baierisch Zell.

There may be palm-treed oases,
Well-deserving all their praises ;
But such pastures strewn with daisies,
 Uplands musical with wellings,
 You will find but round the dwellings
  Of verdant Baierisch Zell.

Looking up, my comrade started,
Gazed and gazed, with lips still parted,
At a maiden who, light-hearted,
 Singing, village-wards came wending,
 Where the trout-stream makes a bending,
  Not far from Baierisch Zell.

'Twas a piece of spotless nature,
Fresh of soul and fair of feature,—
A young, guileless, healthy creature,
 Tripping on beside the water.
 " Who is she ?" " The Verderer's daughter,
  That lives in Baierisch Zell.

" We will at his cottage tarry,
And our chamois thither carry ;
You may then converse with Marie."
 " What, you know her ?" " Since two summers ;
 She is shy though of new-comers,
  This maid of Baierisch Zell."

So we entered.—Within, neatly
All was ordered ; plain and meetly ;
She was there too, she who sweetly
 Through the valley had been singing,
 Till with echoes it was ringing ;
  This vale of Baierisch Zell.

Brown her cheek, but fresh and glowing,
Health, and strength, and vigour showing,—
A wild flower of Nature's growing.
 She was modest as a daisy,
 Springing up beside the mazy
  Brooklet of Baierisch Zell.

Some power with a spell did arm her
Stronger than of wisest charmer,
For nought evil dared to harm her.
        And when near, you felt her winning
        Presence kept you too from sinning ;
            This flower of Baierisch Zell.

As round Bethlehem's humble manger,
Where the Mother, fled from danger,
Bent above her little stranger,
        Beams of softened light did cluster ;
        So round her was shed a lustre—
            This maid of Baierisch Zell.   .

Purity, which was her dower,
Did this radiance o'er her shower,
Giving too a queenly power.
        So like Una in the story,
        On she stepped in maiden glory,
            The pride of Baierisch Zell.

Sisters, brothers,—each would measure
By her his own pride and pleasure :—
She was their chief household treasure.
        Done by her, each common duty
        Seemed to win an air of beauty,
            Like her own Baierisch Zell.

Hers a sense, an instinct nearly,
Guiding rightly, surely, clearly :
Was it then a fancy merely,
        If to them their sister Mary
        Were the good and guardian fairy
            Of happy Baierisch Zell ?

It is no poetic sally,
But she and her native valley
Did accord most musically.
        Hers the voice belonging to it,
        Trilling, as she wandered through it,
            Some song of Baierisch Zell.

Even as the merry thrush's
Note belongs to hawthorn-bushes,
Breezy whispers to green rushes,
     Noisy bees to bloomy heather ;
     So too did belong together
     This maid and Baierisch Zell.

The eldest of the sisters was no beauty, but there was
an open honesty about her—indeed this they all had—
and she possessed a store of such genuine, healthy, sound
common sense, that I always liked to talk with her.
She was a famous knitter; and many of the peculiar
sort of stockings, richly ornamented, worn by the young
foresters both far and near, have been produced by her
skilful fingers.

The three sisters lived here together with an old aunt
—a Solacher, in whose withered features lines were still
to be seen which proved that, in bygone days, she might
have been counted among the fairest of the dale. She
was tall, and still walked erect ; she spoke little, and all
her household duties were done in stern silence. The
elder brother, the chief of the family, was not at.home :
he had gone to Munich to be present at the great
annual shooting-match, and was expected back on the
morrow. In former days, when game was abundant on
the hills, the gentlemen who came here to shoot would
take up their quarters in the dwelling of this worthy
family. Prince L—— was constantly here, and the
Princess too would accompany him : they enjoyed the
beautiful scenery around, and loved the simplicity and
kindly-proffered service of their peasant hostesses. Nor
do I wonder they so liked them, for gentle-mannered
they are all.

The cottage is their own, and the pasturage around it,
as well as the trout-stream that runs beside the garden.

The building is low, having only one story and the
ground-floor; but it is roomy, and, like all houses built
of wood, extremely warm. It had been bought and
given to them by a few of the gentlemen who used to
stay here, in proof of their regard for the worthy old
forester, and as a means of rendering a lasting service to
his family. They spoke of the circumstance with evident
satisfaction, and perfect freedom from all false shame;
on the contrary, they rightly looked on the gift as an
honourable token how much their father had been respected. The beams and wainscot of the room where
we sat were dark with age; the usual bench ran round
the sides, as well as round the stove, which occupied a
large space; and in one corner was a small square table
where we sat and supped.

When I went out into the kitchen, I found Berger
busily occupied with Nanny, the second sister, in preparing our meal. As usual he was full of fun; and
while making the dumplings, or boiling the potatoes, he
was joking with his pretty helpmate, and laughing so
heartily that it was quite a pleasure to hear him. We
cooked the liver of our chamois, roasted a piece of venison that was luckily in the house, and with our dumplings and potatoes served up a right famous supper.
And how we enjoyed it! If anything were wanted
besides my wolfish appetite to give it a zest, this was
furnished by Berger's fun and merriment. How he
contrived to satisfy his hunger as he did, and yet to talk
so much, was to me a mystery. Now he would play
Marie some trick, who would give him a gentle pat as
a punishment, while her laughing mouth—laughing in
spite of herself—would threaten a severer penalty; then
Lisl, the elder one, would be tried with some satirical
question, but she was clever enough to turn the intended

joke against the questioner, and cause a hearty laugh at
his discomfiture.   Now would come a sly innuendo
about a lover, or a tale told me with the utmost gravity
of how Nanny had promised she would marry him, and
how he had refused—for which unparalleled effrontery
he was of course duly made to suffer.   But nothing
could stop his good humour and his flow of spirits; on
he went in the fullest joyousness, and seldom, I think,
have heartier peals of merriment resounded in the cottage than on that pleasant evening.

Hardly was supper over when Berger took down a
guitar which was hanging up in a corner, and playing
upon it challenged the girls to accompany him in a song.
At first they would not; but it was not likely he was to
be disconcerted by a refusal, so he began alone, now
some song about the chamois-hunter, now a merry
Schnadahüpfl; and even in singing he contrived to have
his joke, by the choice of a verse with some sly allusion,
and by the look of intelligence he would then give this
one or that as he rattled out his noisy rhymes.   But all
was taken in good part; he was an old friend of the
house, and evidently a favourite.

One of the girls played the cithern, and the others
accompanied her with their voices.   Marie was also at
length induced to sing, and with cast-down eyes, and as
embarrassed at my presence as though a large audience
were listening, warbled forth a charming little song, in
which a Sennerinn reproaches her hunter-lover for his
long absence from her hut.   Everything this sweet young
mountaineer did had a charm about it.   I thought at the
time, and think so still, that I had never seen such
modest grace in any girl—she was so truly maidenly.
In her presence you felt that there was a power which
guarded her, protecting her even against evil thought,

and which, following her steps, would shield her from
any harm. And such a power *did* protect her,—it was
her own pure womanhood.

To understand and feel all the beauty of these simple
ditties, they must be heard under like circumstances :
beneath a cottage roof, and sung by such a group as were
assembled round our little table. They belong to and
form part of the mountains and mountain life, and
nowhere else do they sound so beautiful ; just as a common wild-flower shows most bright in its native lane or
hedgerow.

Berger now jumped up, and pushing aside the table
to make more room, was in an instant dancing first with
one then with another of the sisters. It would have
made the prettiest picture in the world that dark wains-
coted room, with its low ceiling also of dark wood, the
girl playing the cithern and the other group dancing to
its music, with the impenetrable, imperturbable, silent
old aunt sitting quite in shade in the background, and
calmly looking on. There is nothing more infectious
than the dance ; as soon as Berger stopped I took the
other sister and danced with her ; a matter requiring
some little skill, so small was the space we had to perform in. When one pair stopped the other began ; the
walking and climbing of the day was forgotten, and we
changed partners many a time that evening before we
thought of going to our beds. However, as we were to
be up early on the morrow, some hours' rest was not to
be disregarded. My little bedroom was as comfortable
as possible ; everything was homely, but neat and deliciously clean.

IN a preceding chapter I spoke of the high estimation in which the Solachers hold their calling; how they love it above every other, and look upon all other joys as tame and insignificant, when compared to those which their free mountain-life affords. Some such feeling Kobell* has embodied in a little poem, of which the following verses are a translation; and I give them here, because they seem to be not misplaced in a picture of mountain life.

The Chamois Hunter.

Where Edelweist blooms on the bare rock's face,
Up there right well do I know each place;
Up there how gladsome is life, how free!
Methinks it could nowhere more joyous be.

No praters are there to watch and pry,
It's too far for them, 'tis up too high;
Up there you are with your God alone,
And mild and better your heart has grown.

And let them say whatever they will,
By night 't is there so solemn and still;
And when the peaks in the starlight gleam
To pray more readily then I seem.

---

* Franz von Kobell is well known as the author of some volumes of poems in the Bavarian dialects.

† *Edelweis—Gnaphalium Leontopodium*—a flower met with only on some of the highest mountains in certain parts of Tyrol and Bavaria. It is to be found in Berchtesgaden, and on the Scharfreuter in the Hinter Riss. It is much valued for the snowy purity of its colour, as well as on account of the difficulty of getting it. The very name, "Noble Purity," (*edel*, noble, *weiss*, white,) has a charm about it. Strangely enough it always grows in a spot to be reached only with the utmost peril. You will see a tuft of its beautifully white flowers overhanging a precipice, or waving on a perpendicular wall of rock, to be approached

A chamois-hunter you think is poor
And more forlorn than the veriest boor ;
Yet it is not so ; for, look you, if 't were
How sad his fate should his foot but err?

The nearer Heaven, more sure you are
Your guardian angel cannot be far ;
But down below in the crowd he might
Not always find you or see aright.

And mark ! the Devil, who is no fool,
Prowls ever there when he wants a tool ;
Where men together so thickly herd,
He has a handful without a word.

---

but by a ledge, where perhaps a chamois could hardly stand. But it is this very difficulty of acquisition which gives the flower so peculiar a value, and impels many a youth to brave the danger, that he may get a posy of Edelweis for the hat or the bosom of the girl he loves ; and often has such a one fallen over the rocks just as he had reached it, and been found dead ; in his hand the flower of such fatal beauty, which he still held firmly grasped.

It has been made the theme of many a verse, and by no poet has its praise been oftener sung than Kobell, of one of whose poems on this flower the following is a translation :—

EDELWEIS.

The mountains deck their rocky crowns
  With flowers which are the rarest ;
For only on the highest spots
  Grow those which are the fairest.

Hence in my songs, the Edelweis
  I praise where'er I wander,
An image of pure love, within
  The stony realm up yonder.

Like that flower should it germ, beyond
  The reach of every rover,
And bloom above the common world,
  And last when life is over.

But here 't were not worth his while, and all
He'd get by coming would be a fall:
His God protects him, the hunter knows;
The Devil has none, so down he goes.

Ay, up on high do I love to be,
Where bounds the chamois so wild and free;
Where the marmot whistles from 'neath the stone,
There love I to be with my God alone!

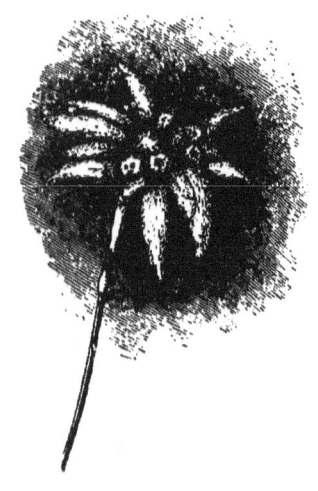

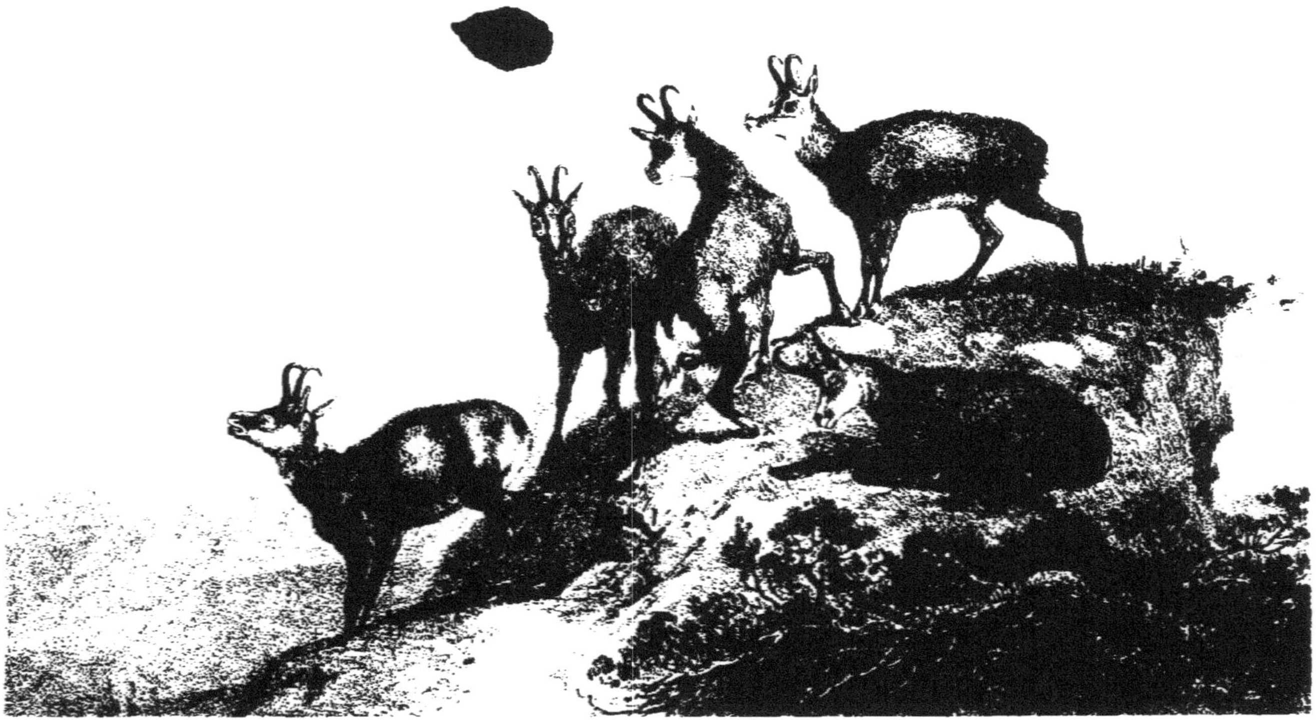

CHAPTER VIII.

THE CHAMOIS.

HAVING come thus far, it is time, I think, to give some account of the chamois itself. First of all be it known that the chamois is no goat,* but belongs to the antelope genus,† of which it is the only specimen inhabiting Europe. It is larger and more strongly built than a roebuck, and is much heavier. A good buck will weigh 55lbs., and one above 60lbs. is a particularly fine fellow. Some however have been shot that weighed 74lbs. and 82lbs.‡ But such are rare and difficult to get at; for these old bucks remain alone in their inaccessible fastnesses and the most secluded places; and it is only when the winter has set in, and the rutting season begun, that there is any chance of seeing them. In order to do so the hunter must brave the intense cold as well as all the dangers of a region of snow and ice, for he will be led

---

* " Well, Peter, I do not think that the sport was so bad after all; for I believe that the chamois, in chase of which the Swiss risk their lives, and are out for days together on mountains of eternal ice and snow, is little better than a great goat after all."

" I didna hear of sic a beast mysel; but I ken, by yer honour's account, he is no worth the speering at."—*The Art of Deer Stalking, by W. Scrope, Esq.,* chap. vii.

† *Antilope rupicapra.*

‡ In 1856 I shot one in the Tyrol that weighed, when cleaned, 75lbs.

to spots where good nerves are required not to feel over-come with horror at the scene around.

The hair of the chamois changes in colour at various seasons of the year, as is the case with the roe, and red and fallow deer. In summer their coat is of a red yel-lowish-brown ; in autumn it grows much darker, and in winter is quite black. But though the changes here in-dicated may be looked upon as a general rule, there will often be found in the same herd one or more differing strikingly from the rest, of a buff-colour perhaps, while all the others are of a reddish-brown. The hair of the forehead, around the nose, the lower jaw, and the in-side of the ears, is of a yellowish tinge, and remains throughout the year the same. The belly, the inside of the legs, and the shaggy hair that overhangs the hoofs, are also of this colour, and never change; the black stripe too, on both sides of the head, extending from the eye to the corners of the mouth, remains a striking fea-ture under every circumstance.

The outer hair is long and coarse; that on the ridge of the back is of greater length than on any other part of the body, especially in winter, and of this the orna-ment called " Gems-bart" is made   Each hair is tipped with white ; so that when a number of exactly the same length are bound together and spread out like a fan, a white line is seen to border the black surface, and pre-sents a pretty appearance. The longer the hair the more it is esteemed for this purpose.

The eye of the animal is large, dark, and intelligent ; it is full of animation,—but this, in its expression of keen watchfulness, is the animation of fear. It carries its head erect, and its graceful ears pointed, as if pre-pared against surprise.

The horns, which are black, rise from the head just

above and between the eyes ; they are round and rougher
at the base, but incline somewhat to flatness towards the
top, which is smooth and polished. They do not stand
up perpendicularly, but slant forwards at a right angle
with the forehead ; their points, which are very sharp,
being bent back and downwards. This feature is not
peculiar to the buck alone; there is however considerable difference between the horns of the male and female,
which often assists the sportsman in distinguishing the
two. The horns of the male chamois are thicker and
altogether stronger-looking than those of the female ;
and instead of diverging from each other in so straight a
line as hers generally do, their outline describes a slight
curve as they rise upwards and apart from each other.
But a still more striking characteristic of the buck is,
that the points of his horns are bent much more inwards
than those of the doe; hers form a semicircular curvature towards the back, while his, turning over abruptly,
form rather a hook. This gives the head quite another
expression ; it has something more resolute about it, as
well as a dashing air and a look of bravado. The horns
of a very good buck will be seven inches high, but I
have seen some that much exceeded this measurement.*
Although, when near, all these peculiar differences in
the horns of the buck and doe are easily discernible, at

* The finest I ever saw are in the collection of Count Arco of Munich,
and are 9½ inches high. The buck to which they belonged was shot by
poachers at Berchtesgaden a few years ago. This collection of the Count
consists of antlers of the red-deer and the roe-buck, with a fair number
of the horns of the chamois, and is perhaps the finest in the world.
Never before were antlers of such magnificent size and such strange
formation collected together ; and the room in which they are placed,
built expressly for the purpose, and the tasteful arrangement of the whole,
contribute greatly to the beauty of this superb collection. £30,000 has
been offered for it, and refused.

a distance the distinction of course is not so striking,
and the male is then recognized by his stronger build,
by his general appearance and more gallant bearing. It
is the same thing as with the stag, which, as he passes
through a wood, though you should not see his antlers,
you recognize instantly. How different his carriage from
that of the hind, and particularly the way in which he
bears his head! But it requires a very practised eye to
distinguish thus with chamois, and it has often astonished me to witness how quickly and with what certainty the foresters have decided, almost at a glance,
whether a buck were among a herd.

The head of the chamois is admirably constructed for
uniting strength with the greatest possible lightness.
The frontal bones are extremely thin,—so much so indeed that they would of themselves be liable to fracture
on the slightest casualty. But to make them strong,
and at the same time retain their lightness, a second
set is thrown over the first, and the space between is
divided into cells, formed by the arched girders of solid
bone which uphold the roof and bind the whole together. The system which Nature has here adopted is ex-
emplified in the cells in the upper and lower part of the
tube that forms the Britannia Bridge. Just as these
thin iron plates would separately be unable to bear much,
but placed above and united to each other present an
amount of strength and firmness capable of resisting
almost any opposing force, so these fine thin bones of the
chamois' head, thus beautifully united by an arched cel-
lular construction, become as firm as the rock on which
the creature stands, and are at the same time so light as
not to hinder any of its agile movements. The arched
girders which occupy the space between the upper and
lower surface rise, bridge-like, with a spiral twist, and

here and there a flying buttress will give additional strength to the walls, or a lateral arch help to support the vault above.

The horn of the chamois is hollow up to a certain height; thence to the point it is a solid mass. This hollow part of the horn however is fixed on, and filled out with, a bony substance which grows with and forms part of the skull itself. By a forcible twist the two may be separated. Among the many stories related of the chamois, it was said that they made use of their crooked horns to let themselves down by, in places where descent by other means was impossible. Ridiculous as the tale is, many believed it; but of such hereafter.

The food of these animals consists of the herbs found on the mountains, and the buds and young sprouts of the alpine rose and the latschen. This is their sole sustenance; no creature therefore is more innoxious than the chamois, and the wholesale destruction of them which has taken place since 1848 cannot even be excused on the plea that, like the red-deer, they occasionally tread down and injure the crops of the husbandman. They keep to their rocks, delighting in the highest and most inaccessible places; and it is only when winter sets in with all its rigour, that they descend to seek shelter and food in the woods somewhat lower down the mountain. At this season they feed on such grass and leaves as they can find, and probably also on the Iceland moss, which is met with on the mountains. In their stomach a hard dark-coloured ball is often found, bitter to the taste, but of an agreeable smell: this is called Bezoar, and owes its formation to the fibrous, resinous nature of the substances the chamois feeds on; and which, conglomerating by degrees, at last grows into a stone-like mass.

Chamois cannot endure the neighbourhood of sheep.

When these appear they leave the spot at once, so great is their antipathy. They have no such dislike to cattle, and I have often seen the two in close proximity. But if, when on the mountain, you hear the dreary bleating of a sheep, you may turn back at once, for there is no chance of seeing a chamois among those rocks.*

The rutting season begins in November. At this period a sort of bladder forms beneath the skin at the root of the buck's horn, the lymph within which has so strong a musk-like smell, that if the animal be shot at this time the odour will remain for years. Now too the stronger bucks make their appearance, and desperate battles take place. In fighting they give each other such gashes, that they bleed as though they had been shot. One combatant will lower his horns under the throat of his opponent, or turn his head sideways, so that the sharp points may catch the other's shoulder, and then drawing them back, he endeavours to inflict a wound. You may be startled also by an occasional bleat, uttered with angry impatience in the fervour of desire. If able to imitate the call, you will soon see a black form leaping along through the latschen or over the rocks, and coming

---

* It is strange that the sheep on the mountain pastures often grow quite wild: the lambs however are, in this respect, still worse. When they have got into this state there is little chance of recovering them; and after a certain day (Nov. 10) the Jäger have a right to shoot all the wild sheep they find on the mountain. Before leaving the hut, therefore, to winter in the plain, the herdsmen go out to search for any of the flock that may be missing. This "Schaf-suchen" lasts sometimes a day or two, for it takes a long time to scour such vast tracts of country, to climb into the dangerous places where a sheep may have got without being able to escape, and to examine every spot, on those dreary heights where a truant animal may have strayed. Such "Schaf-suchen" is hard work. *But the goats never grow wild*, although they rove as freely as the other animals, and, from their agility, climb to much wilder spots. (*See Note at the end of the Chapter.*)

towards the spot whence the sound proceeded. In this way they may be attracted from a considerable distance. If too they see some object that they cannot well make out, their curiosity will drive them to the spot to see what it can be.* The period of gestation in the doe is twenty weeks. In May her young kid may be seen beside her, playing in the prettiest manner, leaping into the sunny air and rolling on its back upon the soft herbage. With a bound it will turn heels over head; not however forwards or backwards, but sideways; a proof of the wonderful strength and elasticity of its limbs even at this young stage of its existence.

There is something very amusing in the wiseacre look of such a little kid. Its bright eye twinkles like a star; its silly little face is full of drollery; and, pricking up

---

* Two striking instances of this were told me by the late Prince Leiningen, as good and thorough a sportsman as might anywhere be found; one too who knew the habits of game, and had watched and studied them for years.

He was out stalking in the Vorder Riss late in the season; there he saw, at a good distance, a capital chamois buck. He pointed him out to the forester that accompanied him, who said, "We'll soon have him nearer!" and taking off his cap, stooped down just behind the ridge, so as to have nothing visible on the sky-line but his bald crown. This he kept on bobbing up and down, then turning his head on this side and on that, till at last the chamois could not help remarking it. After looking at the unusual object for a time, he set off to see what it was, and came within range of the Prince's rifle, but by chance stopped to gaze just behind a projecting stone, so that it was not possible to fire. After standing there for some time quite near, he scampered off.

On another similar occasion the Prince merely turned back the cuff of his coat so as to display the white wristband of the shirt; and putting it up just above a bank behind which he lay concealed, moved it up and down and sideways, as though it were a thing with life. The buck at last perceived the white something that was in motion, and came leaping along to examine into the matter. While he looked, a bullet striking him, solved the mystery.

its pretty velvet ears, it will turn its head most knowingly on one side, and seem to cogitate on the meaning
of a flitting shadow; and then, not from any fear, but
out of mere fun, will start away as though the shadow
were its playfellow and were running after it in sport.

But I have seen others, of riper years even, diverting
themselves in the most fantastic manner. In the Hinter
Riss, at a spot called the Wechsel, I for a long time
watched the antics of a buck, who seemed to me to be
"sheer deleerit." He was in a hollow, on a large field
of snow, which he had all to himself. There he was
quite alone, and round and round he kept racing, like a
horse in an equestrian circus. Then he would turn and
go round in the opposite direction. Now he stopped,
pretending to attack some invisible enemy; then looking round astonished, bounded into the air, and off again
at his equestrian performances as before. How long he
continued at this game I do not know. I stayed looking
on for a good while, and he was still going on with it
when I went away.

When chamois play such pranks as these, and jump
about "ganz wild und när'sch," the mountaineers say it
is a prognostic of bad weather.

A doe has generally but one kid at a time; that she
should have two is however by no means of unfrequent
occurrence. The little creature at its birth is of a dark
brownish-yellow colour; and when a day old is no longer
to be caught.

There is perhaps no animal so peaceful and at the same
time so timid as the chamois. Nature therefore, besides
endowing it with a facility of climbing into the most inaccessible places, and thus avoiding pursuit, has enabled
it to guard against the approach of danger by the great
acuteness of its senses of sight, smell, and hearing. It is

this which makes it so very difficult to get near them. A rolling stone or a spoken word at once attracts their attention; and they will look and listen to discover whence the sound has come that breaks the silence of their mountain solitude. For an incredibly long time they will then stand gazing fixedly in one direction, quite immoveable; and if it happen to be towards something in your neighbourhood that their attention has been attracted, you must lie still and close indeed to escape their observation. The eyes of the whole herd will be fixed on the spot in a long steady stare; and as you anxiously watch them from afar they almost look like fragments of rock, so motionless are they while they gaze. You begin to hope they have found no cause for alarm, when "Phew!" the sharp whistle tells they have fathomed the mystery, and away they move to the precipitous rocks overhead: unless panic-stricken, they stop from time to time to look behind; and then suddenly uttering the peculiar shrill sound, again move on.

It is true that on the mountains, where an awful silence ever broods, the slightest noise breaking the stillness is heard with wonderful distinctness a great way off; but even making allowance for this, there is sufficient evidence that the senses of these animals are particularly acute. If but the gentlest wave be moving in the air, flowing from you to them, they at once become aware of your presence, long before you may perceive them or they see you.

In the human being this particular sense is, comparatively speaking, less developed than the others.* It is

---

* This sense of smell is developed in a very high degree in the wild boar. I have often been surprised, when stealing upon one in the woods, to observe how soon he has become aware of my neighbourhood. Lifting his head, he would sniff the air inquiringly, then, uttering a short grunt, make off as fast as he could.

the one which man least needs, not wanting it for his safety, but possessing it solely to minister to his pleasures. When therefore we find it extremely acute in another animal, it strikes us more than any example of an unusually sharp sight or an extraordinary power of hearing; just as we are always more astonished at that in another which we are least able to achieve ourselves. A chamois, when dashing down the mountains, will suddenly stop as if struck by a thunderbolt, some yards from the spot where recent human footprints are to be found in the snow, and, turning scared away, rush off immediately in an opposite direction. The taint which the presence of the hunter has left behind is perceived by it long after he has passed.

Chamois are instinctively very cautious in passing a spot exposed to avalanches. They do not cross altogether, but one advances slowly towards the middle of the passage, and then darts on with all speed. So the others. Should snow come sliding down while one is passing, he does not run *onwards,* as a man in his fright would no, but *side*wards to the shelter of the overhanging rock.

The agility of the chamois has become almost proverbial; but to have any idea of what it is, one must be an eye-witness of the bounds they make, and see the places they will race down at full speed when pursued. A smooth surface of rock, so smooth that a footing there seems impossible, and of nearly perpendicular steepness, is no obstacle to their flight. Down they go, now bounding, now gliding, with a velocity which seems to ensure their being inevitably dashed to pieces.

The chief strength of the animal is in its hind legs, which, if extended, would be longer than the others. On this account it springs upwards with more ease than it

descends the mountain, and on level ground its walk is
clumsy and ungraceful. It is not made to run, but
bounds along over the ground. The hoof is cloven, long
and pointed, and the slot of the chamois resembles that
of a sheep. The edges are sharp, which causes it to slip
easily on the ice, and on this account it rather avoids
passing the glaciers. When standing, the hind legs are
always bent, as if the animal were preparing to lie down,
which no doubt helps considerably to break the fall when
leaping from a great height. Notwithstanding this, the
croup is still somewhat higher than the fore part of the
body. The elastic force which the hind legs possess is
immense. With a sudden bound the chamois will leap
up against the face of a perpendicular rock, and merely
touching it with its hoofs, rebound again in an opposite
direction to some higher crag, and thus escape from a
spot where, without wings, egress seemed impossible.
When reaching upwards on its hind legs, the fore hoofs
resting on some higher spot, it is able to stretch to a
considerable distance, and with a quick spring will bring
up its hind quarters to a level with the rest of the body,
and, with all four hoofs close together, stand poised on a
point of rock not broader than your hand. On narrow
overhanging ledges some thousand feet high they walk
and gaze about, enjoying the security from pursuit which
such spots afford.

But astonishing as their dexterity really is, much has
been related of them that has no foundation in fact, any
more than the tale of their placing sentinels to announce
when danger is near. Indeed there is something very
strange in the imperfect information obtained about the
chamois, and the marvellous stories related of it, and of
those who went in its pursuit. That this should have
been the case for a time is very natural, especially in

places remote from where the chamois was to be found.
I conceive too that even later, and where men dwelt who
followed the chase, there still hung about the chamois-
hunter's life somewhat of mystery. We can well imagine
that he was looked upon as one familiar with places
where ordinary men would fear to venture,—accustomed
to have Death stalking beside him as a companion, and
to meet him face to face. His departure for the mountain—an unknown region hidden in cloud, and mist, and
mystery,—his absence for whole days together, his start-
ling accounts of the wildness, the silence and the solitude, and then occasionally the going forth of one alone
who never returned,—all this gave a dim and dread uncertainty to the pursuit; and where uncertainty is, imagination will be busy at her work. His very countenance
—his widely-opened eye, always on the watch—even this
must have awakened strange surmises of sights more
fearful than he had yet hinted of.

But that much ignorance on the subject should have
continued to the present day is still more remarkable,
since the home of the chamois—Bavaria, the Tyrol,
Switzerland, Styria—are not remote lands, but lie in
the very heart of Europe. Had it been otherwise, this
haze and indistinctness might have been accounted for
by distance, which effaces outlines, and invests objects
with tints, and shapes, and proportions that are not their
own.

One author of recent date acknowledges that little is
known of the habits of these animals, and accounts for
it by the circumstance of the "chamois-hunter being
generally a rude, uncultivated being; and that, as to
naturalists, they have seldom had an opportunity of observing this animal in its solitary and dangerous haunts."
The writer of this ' New and Perfect Art of Venery ' re-

peats also an account to be found in many earlier works, which as a curiosity is worth extracting :—" One really great peculiarity is the way in which the chamois cross the fields of snow without sinking in. On account of their narrow and sharply-pointed hoofs they would naturally fall through, and the snow would be unable to carry them. They therefore hasten their flight in the following cunning manner. The last chamois jumps on the back of the one before him, passes in this way over the backs of all the others, and then places himself at their head; the last but one does the same, and the others follow in order; and in this manner they have soon passed over such a field of snow." The same writer tells us also that " it is their inner heat which impels them to seek those places where snow is to be found."

A most curious opinion seems to have been prevalent —for I find the same thing related in old books of natural history, as well as in the recent publication from which the above extracts are taken—with regard to the chamois, when hard pressed and unable to escape its pursuers. I give the whole passage :—" The most dangerous chase of all is that of the chamois. The hunter must manage all alone, as neither man nor dog can be of any service to him. His accoutrements consist of an old coat, a bag with dry bread, cheese, and meat, a gun, his hunting-knife, and a pair of irons for the feet. He then drives the chamois from one crag to the other, making them always mount higher, climbs after them, and shoots them if he can, or if he finds it necessary ; but if that should not be the case, and he has driven one so far that it is no longer able to elude him, he approaches quite close, puts his hunting-knife to its side, *which the chamois of its own accord pushes into its body,* and then falls down headlong from the rock."

H 2

In another work published at Frankfort-on-the-Maine in the year 1661, it is also said:—" At last, when the chamois can go no further, and the hunter is about to throw or thrust it down from the precipice, if he draweth his knife and will thrust the same into it, *the chamois pusheth its own body with force upon the knife;* whereupon it is caught, and falleth downwards from a great height. The skin remaineth generally quite unbroken."* The same old writer tells us :—" Some hunters do drink the blood and the fat, that they may thereby obtain a steady head and freedom from giddiness when they come to steep places, and when they must hold on very firmly."

It is not at all unlikely that these properties were attributed to the animal's blood; for the hunter, like all men who live much with Nature, and make companionship with her various aspects, is by no means free from superstition. At the present day even the peasantry of Bavaria consider a certain part of the stag, when dried and powdered, a potent remedy in diseases of the bladder ; and the resinous-looking drops which are found in the corners of the hart's eyes, called by some the " tears" of the stag, are looked upon by many as a sure specific in various disorders.

Strange are the shifts to which it is said the chamois-hunter is sometimes put, when, like the animal he is in pursuit of, " he can go no further." The author of the ' New and Perfect Art of Venery,' who has given so

---

* This is true. Though the body be never so bruised, the skin always remains whole. It is also a peculiarity of the skin of a chamois that it is of the same thickness throughout. By this you may always distinguish it from other skins, which are much thinner in some places than in others. Dealers who wish to palm off doe for chamois leather assist the deception by cutting a slit in some part and sewing the hole up again, such being always found in real chamois-skins where the ball has passed. If however you *feel* the skins carefully, you can hardly be deceived.

amusing an account of how the chamois play at leap-frog over the snow, says that in such cases, " when the hunter can get neither forwards nor backwards, and is unable to save himself by a leap, nought is left him but to fling off everything, and wounding the soles of his feet cause the blood to flow, so that by its stickiness he may be enabled to hold himself better on the slippery rocks."

In the ardour of pursuit, indeed, one might easily get into a place whence, unassisted, it would be quite impossible ever to get out. A spot may often be seen below which can be reached by a jump or by sliding downwards; but the question is, whether, when once there, it will be possible to get further or back again; for though you may let yourself *down* the smooth rock, there is no climbing *up* its steep surface. It is therefore necessary to be assured of this before taking such a leap, or you may find yourself, like the Emperor Maximilian, on a narrow ledge of rock, at your back the smooth stone, and before and below you nothing but the yielding air.

The danger of such a proceeding is illustrated by the following adventure of another chamois-hunter, Rudolf Bläsi of Schwanden, (born in Ennenda in Glarnerischa). One day he went out with his friend Walcher up through the Sernft valley, out of which lead two of the wildest and most difficult passes across the mountain-tops to the valley of the sources of the Rhine. One of these towers over the ice-covered point of the Tschinfel. On their way they found the fresh traces of a chamois, and from the direction the animal had taken they knew that if they were to advance from different sides, the game would not be able to escape them. They parted, therefore, agreeing to meet at the Falz Alp. Bläsi soon perceived the chamois, and in the ardour of pursuit jumped across a chasm to a narrow ledge, when to his horror he remarked that the spot where he then stood was lower than that whence he had sprung, so that return was impossible. The ledge where he had landed was, too, so narrow that he could not sit down there, but only stand ; and thus, leaning on his rifle, his back against the smooth perpendicular rock, and before him an abyss, he stood awaiting his fate. A step would have precipitated him below. Night came on, and to add to the horror of his situation a thunderstorm roared and poured down torrents of rain over the rocks.

His comrade meanwhile had arrived at the meeting-place, and missing his companion, began to fear an accident had befallen him. The following morning, as soon as it was light, he set out to search, and towards eleven A.M., Bläsi to his great joy sees his friend looking down upon him from a rock. A rope is let down, and he who may be said to have already tasted of death, is drawn up and saved. That one night, however, was enough to bleach entirely the hair of the mountaineer.

Note.

I SUBJOIN a few points of difference between the Goat and the Chamois. Their skeletons, it seems, are not the same; for not having myself examined the arrangement of the bones in the two animals, I quote, regarding their formation, from 'Histoire Naturelle, générale et parti-culière, avec la Description du Cabinet du Roi. Tome douzième. Paris, MDCCLXIV.' " L'apophyse épineuse de la seconde vertèbre cervicale dif-fère de celle du bouc, en ce qu'elle est moins haute et presqu'aussi saillante en arrière qu'en avant, ce qui ne se trouve ni dans la gazelle, ni dans le cerf, le chevreuil, etc. ; la branche inférieure de l'apophyse oblique de la sixième vertèbre n'est pas échancrée comme dans le bouc : elle ressemble à celle de la gazelle, du chevreuil, etc." The frontal bone of the chamois, just before the horns, is concave ; that of the goat, convex. The horns of the latter recede ; those of the former animal always advance. The goat's horns too are flat near their base, and wrinkled ; the chamois' are round, and not indented. The goat has frequently a beard, a chamois never; nor does it emit any disagreeable odour except during the rutting season, whilst the effluvium of the goat is always insupportable. The nose of the chamois is not drawn back like the goat; consequently the upper lip projects less beyond the nostrils. Its upper teeth advance slightly over the lower: in the goat they rest exactly on each other. In the chamois there is less depth from the top of the head to the lower jaw than in the goat, which gives the head more lightness and greater elegance of form. But the most decisive proof of the non-affinity of the two animals is that they *never* generate together. Although in the mountains herds of goats are constantly wandering about near the haunts of the chamois, no one instance is known of a she-goat having brought forth young which were a cross between the two breeds. The chamois indeed always avoid the places where goats have strayed. They dislike all intrusion on their solitude. The Steinbock (*Capra Ibex*) on the contrary, classed by naturalists among the goat genus, cohabits occasionally with the tame animal; and offspring presenting the peculiar features of such mixed race have been seen not unfrequently in Switzerland. The author cited above says that chamois, when taken young and brought up with the domestic goat, " *vraisemblablement* s'accouplent et produisent ensemble." In this he is mistaken. He adds, however, that he never heard of any example of the kind. " J'avoue cependant que ce fait, le plus important de tous, *et qui seul déciderait la question* (of homogeneousness of race), *ne nous est pas connu;* nous n'avons pu savoir, ni par nous, ni par les autres, si les chamois produisent avec nos chèvres; seulement nous le soupçonnons."

It is quite evident then that chamois are not merely *feræ capræ*. It was an *originally* wild animal, and not one become so by having wandered away into the wilderness. Animals wild by nature always retain somewhat of that original state, if taken even at their birth and attempted to be tamed. Goats, though quite at liberty, still like the society of man, and will come skipping to the spot where he is; indeed from the earliest times the goat is always mentioned as a *household* animal. The chamois, on the contrary, will flee at the very approach of a human being; and its terror and natural timidity can never be overcome, even though you may have reared it as a kid, and it has lived among men for years.

CHAPTER IX.

KREUTH.

On coming down next morning I found coffee awaiting me, which Nanny had made in order that I might have a warm breakfast before starting. We took the same road as the preceding day, till near the summit of the mountain; we then directed our steps at once to the ridge, whence a view could be obtained far down its sides and into the deep bottom. Here we waited a long time, in hopes that some chamois would be on the move, but in vain. One of the delights attending the pursuit of game in the highlands is, that, even should the pleasure of a successful day's sport be wanting, the grandeur of the scenery amidst which you move is in some sort a recompense for the labour endured. It is ever varying; and should the cloud-drift or the sun-rays not produce their endless changes, you are sure that in going a hundred steps further some new feature will present itself, or that you will see the same under a totally different aspect. Our view here extended over fields of snow, stretching along the horizon into endless distance—one vast range of desert and of frost.

As nothing was to be seen we descended, intending to go toward the Kaiser Klause, where we confidently expected to find game. Passing at the foot of the rocks where the day before my chamois had dropped, Berger went to fetch his knife, which he had forgotten, while I kept on to the left. Here the whole declivity, which was long and steep, was covered with large blocks of stone, lying in all positions, some firmly wedged, and others so loose that without the greatest care your foot slipped down between them;—nothing more easy than to break an ankle in such a place! After crossing this sea of stone for nearly three-quarters of an hour, fog and mist came drifting towards me, followed by a thick rain, while the wind increased at every moment; and by the time I was nearly at the end of my stony passage, it came blowing furiously over the ridge in front. The rain too now poured down in torrents, the wind was bitingly cold, and in a few minutes I was wet to the skin. With such weather all stalking was at an end : so I began to look about for Berger, whom I at last saw far off combating with the blast and with the difficulties of his position. I made a sign to return ; and when we got lower down, the wind, coming up from the other side, rushed by over our heads without much inconveniencing us.

" I looked well at the place you fired from yesterday," said Berger; " I am quite sure it was more than a hundred and thirty yards. When looking upwards from below, one sees how far it is."

By the time we got to the green hill-side where we first saw the chamois, the rain had ceased, the gloom had disappeared, and air and sky were bright again. Berger proposed that I should take my stand at a certain tree, while he would go down to the path, and entering the wood some distance off, pass through it in an oblique direction.

" Most likely it is not empty," said he; "and if chamois are there, they will come out near yonder trees, pass within shot of you, and then bear away in a curve for the higher ground.*   Here you have chance enough, and if anything comes, you will have a fair shot, though perchance a long one.   However, any you may get here will be easy after that of yesterday."

I took up my position beside the withered trunk of a tree, anxiously listening for any sound.   At last there was a rustling, and Berger emerged from the wood: he had seen nothing.   It was too late in the day to think of trying elsewhere; we therefore at once set off homewards.   When we had proceeded some way down the mountain, a bounding was heard among the underwood, as of an animal in flight.   We listened: there were two. Berger ran forward, and saw a couple of chamois making for the rocky pastures on the other side of the Miesing, just below its summit, and where no one could follow.

" There the wall of rock is perpendicular," Berger observed: " that is their usual retreat when pursued.   It would be useless to follow them, for they pass along the narrow ledges, and wait in places where there is no approaching them."

---

* It may often seem unaccountable to one not a sportsman, how the movements of the game can be predicted with such certainty.   It depends of course very much on the nature of the ground, as well as on the habits of the animal in question.   Sometimes however, as in certain steep gullies, there is but one single path by which man or beast can get out of them : and if the hunter can reach that spot unobserved, he is sure of a shot eventually ; for as soon as the chamois are disturbed, by the rolling of a stone or any other means taken to make them move, on they come to the well-known path.   Perhaps they may observe their danger : if they do, they will stand still and gaze before attempting the pass ; and then, well aware that it is the sole place of egress, they will rush headlong forwards, braving in their extremity every danger.   Chamois perceive in an instant the perils of their position when retreat is thus cut off, and their consternation is great and evident.

" But how low down they were! Who would have thought of meeting them here?"

" Ay, who indeed?" answered Berger. " I came nearly as far as this when I went through the bushes; I thought it was far enough. Had I but gone a little further, they would both have gone upwards, and have come out, as I said, where you were standing. You might then have brought down both."

" If we had gone toward the Klause today, do you think we should have seen anything?" I asked.

" Yes," he replied, " for some capital places are there. If we had seen no chamois, we might still have met with deer. The number of stags there formerly was astonishing. Even now, after so many have been killed, fifty were shot quite lately. The order was given to destroy them, so the under-gamekeepers shot all they could find."

" But what a pity to exterminate them in that way!"

" Pity, indeed, for they do no harm to anybody,—there is nothing for them to destroy. But you see it is close to the frontier, and poaching now is carried on so audaciously that we have no alternative but to shoot everything."

" Had you ever an adventure with any of the poachers there?" I asked.

" Oh, yes," said he; " and once in particular I acted foolishly enough; I went to a hut, and finding the door fastened on the inside, suspected there were some fellows inside. Foolhardy as I was, I went to the back window and tried to get in there. I had got my shoulders through, when what should I see through the door that divided the hut but a band of poachers who had taken shelter there? Back I squeezed myself quick enough, you may be sure. The fellows saw me too, but I was off and behind a tree just in time."

" Did they not follow you ?"

" Not they; some came as far as the door, but when they found I was not to be seen they did not trust themselves any further; for had I liked, the first that came out might have had a ball sent through him; and that they knew."

" And how did you get off?"

" Oh, easily enough; I went from one tree to another, and when I was out of shot walked away at my leisure."

We now went to the cottage of the Solachers to fetch the chamois, and without delay set off for Fischbachau, which we reached before dusk.

On the morrow I bade my friends farewell, and set off betimes for Egern. In the afternoon I left for Kreuth, and went at once to the forester.

If ever a man had an honest open countenance it was this one. His bared throat was, like his face, ruddy from exposure to wind and weather. I felt sure of a good reception as soon as I looked at him, and presented my letter with confidence. He promised to do what he could; but then came the old tale of the scarcity of game, and the many difficulties attendant on granting the permission required. He told me that the following day nothing could be done, for none of the assistant foresters were at home : they were out on the mountains, and it was uncertain what day they would return.

The next morning on rising I heard it was raining, and this continued the whole day. In the evening the young foresters returned, and as Max Solacher sat over his tankard of beer in the parlour of the inn, I made his acquaintance. He has a name for being an excellent sportsman, and is considered one of the best climbers in the mountains. I found him below the middle height,

—a great advantage in certain difficult places; but his limbs were firmly knit, and it was always a pleasure to look at his sinewy legs as he stepped lightly along up the mountain before me. A chamois-hunter has never any superabundant flesh; he is spare of habit, and I have remarked, or perhaps only fancied I did so, that in his eye is something peculiar, common to all of his class. It has seemed to me that, animated as it is when on the mountain, or under the influence of surprise or excitement, at other times when meeting him by chance in common daily intercourse its expression is wanting, as though the feelings that gave it life were slumbering. If there be anything in this beyond mere fancy, I can well account for the circumstance. A chamois-hunter on the plain is like a sailor on shore,—he is surrounded by uncongenial objects, and these and the incidents that exist and take place about him are to him matters of little interest: they in no wise awaken his sympathy. As the seaman is ill at ease on land and wants to be afloat again, so the hunter is impatient to get back to his mountains. There he is at home,—in all that surrounds him he feels an interest. But the flat land and its occupations are to him tame and tedious; and so he saunters along, and the sparkle of his eye is dimmed by listlessness. Let however but a sound be heard which calls his attention, and at once the eye is dilated; it is wide open and prominent, the lids drawn far back, and the pupil is seen in a large surrounding space of white. The habit of attentive watching, of ever-constant vigilance, the frequent presence of danger and the narrow escapes from risk—all these cause the eye to acquire a certain fixedness of look, as if it were guarding against surprise. That this is not mere fancy on my part is proved by a circumstance which occurred to me while writing this.

After having spent some weeks in the mountains I returned direct to Munich, and the very first observation
a friend made on meeting me again was, that my eyes
had a different expression : "You have got," he said, " a
chamois-hunter's eyes." He had not, probably, remarked
the peculiarity in this class of men as I had done ; but
he saw something strange in my looks, and knowing
where I had been, at once attributed the appearance
which so struck him to my recent pursuits.*

I remember too, when once at the Königs See, and
while at the house of the forester, waiting till the rain
ceased, an under-gamekeeper came into the room. He
had been out three days on the mountains and had just
returned. The man's look would have struck any one.
At that time all relating to mountain life was strange to
me, and the whole appearance of the new comer excited
my curiosity. He was tall, gaunt, and bony ; his brown
and sinewy knees were bare, and scratched and scarred ;
his beard was black and long, his hair shaggy, and
hunger was in his face ; the whole man looked as if he
had just escaped from the den of a wolf, where he had
been starved and in daily expectation of being eaten.
But it was his eyes—it was the wild staring fixedness of
his eyes—that kept mine gazing on him. The bent eagle-
nose, the high, fleshless cheek-bones, added to their
power. There was no fierceness in them, nor were they
greedy eyes ; but they were those of a man who had

---

* Not a week after penning these lines, I happened to be looking
through a volume of Hazlitt, and found the following remarks, which
at once reminded me of my own observations on the look of the chamois-hunter. I was very pleased to find them, as they confirmed what
I had said. He is speaking of Raphael : "His figures have always an
in-door look . . . and want *that wild uncertainty of expression which
is connected with the accidents of nature and the changes of the elements.*"—*The Round Table: On Gusto.*

been snatched from a horrible death, in whom the re-
collection was not yet effaced nor was ever likely to be.
They were always wide open : the whole creature seemed
vigilant, and awaiting at every moment to have to
wrestle with fate. But this was observable in the eyes
alone, not in the other features ; for the nostril was not
distended nor the lips clenched, as they must have been
to harmonize with the meaning that was in his eyes. I
thought I had seen the man before : when it suddenly
occurred to me that it was the head of the " Ugolino "*
I was staring at.

I entered into conversation with him, and he told me
that not long ago he had slipped on the ice and slidden
down a long way without being able to stop himself. He
was in expectation every moment of going to the bottom
of the abyss, where, even had he not been dashed to
pieces, he could never have got out again, when his foot
was caught and he went no further. His pole and
rifle flew down into the gulf. To go after them was
impossible ; for fields of ice were there, with large clefts
in them, and into one of these frightful crevices both had
doubtless fallen.

Had he told me that, Prometheus-like, he had been
chained to a glacier for a whole winter amid the icy world
of the mountain-top, exposed to the rains and tempests
and the dreary darkness, I could almost have believed
his words, so in unison were his features and his whole
appearance with such a tale.

I was glad to find that I should be able to go out in
company with Max Solacher, or Maxl as he was familiarly called ; for many friends had told me that with
him, being one of the best stalkers, there would be more
chance of success than with any one else.

* The Ugolino of Sir Joshua Reynolds.

The next morning at five o'clock he came to the inn to fetch me, and we sallied forth at once into the grey dawn. After following the road for some distance we turned aside and entered the forest; and when the light of the morning had come over the hill-tops and penetrated into the hollows, and through the gloomy boughs, it showed that even already the characteristics of mountain scenery had begun. Beside the rugged path a wild torrent was tumbling over blocks of stone, that in some preceding spring had been loosened and washed down from the higher ground by the rush of a thousand streams. Some huge tree had been felled, and in the deep part thrown across it as a bridge, the branches hanging down in the water, and its trunk mercilessly split and hacked. It was a region of wood, where a whole tree would perhaps be taken to mend the pathway, or mighty stems cut down and left to rot during succeeding winters. On the hill-side great pines were standing out against the sky, half-uprooted by the blast that had descended upon them suddenly from above; and others, scathed and shivered, were crushing with their weight a young forest that had sprung up beneath their shade. On looking upwards, on both sides and before you was dark solemn foliage, and afar off perhaps and high up a sharp line, beyond which was the welcome sky. We were indeed in the mountains.

Continually ascending, we went on till we came to a steep slope. Above us the trees were not so dense, and we were able to see far from the spot where we stood. We looked, and in silence. Presently, with his eyes still fixed on some object above him, Max pulled out his telescope and made a survey.

"There are chamois," he said. "I see *one*, but there are others, I know."

The chamois he now pointed out to me I had seen some minutes before; but as it was a great way off, and quite motionless, I had not recognized it. Indeed one is constantly deceived; for at a distance a chamois is but a small black spot, and stones and bushes often assume the appearance of the game; it is only when you examine them through your glass, that you see what they really are.

" But how are we to get at them ?" observed my companion, looking round and examining the relative position of the chamois and ourselves. It really was no easy matter. They were some two or three thousand yards from where we stood, and between us and them was a very deep and precipitous ravine; not rugged however, but covered with a few trees and a scanty herbage.

" We must go back again," said he, " get down the gully, and up the other side over the lahne. It is troublesome work, but there is no other way of getting at them. We must then stalk through the trees, and get as near them as possible." So looking well at the place where they stood and at the surrounding objects, we went down the gully, along some projecting rocks, and up the other side. Solacher constantly kept one point in his eye, in order not to lose the direction of the spot we were making for. At last he stopped to look about him, and to determine with exactitude where the game might be. Our plan was, to get round and above it; we had therefore to be cautious not to describe too small a circle in our approach. Max now advanced stealthily, while I remained behind; and " craning " over a bit of rock he espied them to the left.

" There they are !" he whispered ; " they have winded us and are moving. Quick ! A little more forward,— don't you see them ? There, by the stump of a tree !"

I

I only saw one, and that was more than half hidden by the stems; but as there was no time to lose I fired.

"He's down!" cried Solacher; and we ran forward to get a second shot as the others should come into sight. But they were too quick. We went to the one I had shot, and found to my chagrin it was a kid. This was vexatious, but it was the only one I saw, and being partly hidden, I had not, in the shade of the wood, been able to distinguish it. While we were cleaning it there was a croaking and a rustling of wings in the air.

"Ha! there are the ravens," said Solacher; "hardly has the rifle cracked, before those birds are on the spot. Where they come from I can't tell; for though not one was to be seen before, as soon as anything is shot they appear directly."

As my companion would have to carry the chamois the whole day, I believe he was not sorry it was only a kid; for to him this was nothing, and he felt the difference no more than if an additional bullet or two had been put into his rücksack.

We went up higher, and then kept along the side of the mountain; we presently crept forward, and looked over into an immense chasm. Solacher drew back with a start. "Chamois are there," he whispered; "but they have heard us. What a pity! They are off—they are moving," he said, again peeping over. "Ah, the devil take you and your whistling!" he continued angrily, as one of the herd uttered the shrill long-drawn-out sound that betokens fear. "There they go,—but slowly," and the whole herd passed along the bottom of the stony hollow.

It was a wild place, that hollow! We stood on the

brink of it; and before us, reaching up to the very sky-
line, was the rent in the mountain that frost or water,
or some other of the powerful agents by which Nature
works her changes, had made in its steep side. It was
like a stone-quarry, but of gigantic size,—wild, forlorn,
and desolate.

"There they go, but slowly," said Solacher, watching
the retreating herd. "Now they stop and graze. There's
one lying down,—the maledite brood!"

"Could we not get down to the right, and stalk up
round the mountain, and so meet them?" I asked, not
knowing the ground.

"Yes, we might, but the wind is now coming upwards,
and they would be off: it is no good. If I had only
seen them directly I looked over, we might have crept
round and had a capital shot."

We sat down and watched them—the usual consola-
tion on such occasions; and we pulled out and ate our
crust. From here we saw the massy Plau Berg, slightly
covered with snow. It is the first considerable mountain
between Tegernsee and the Tyrol, and rises like a strong
rampart above the narrow valley of Kreuth.

We now went downwards, and across a lawn-like
meadow, on which stood a hut. In a glade lower down
we soon after tracked a good stag; "And he has been
here lately too," said my companion, distending his
nostrils and sniffing the tainted air.

As we were going homewards we discovered among
the trees a man with a rifle at his back. On approaching
nearer we found it was old Solacher, the uncle of Max
and brother of the old aunt at Baierisch Zell.

"He is seventy-two years old," my companion told
me; "and he will still go up any mountain. *He has no
breath at all!*" by which he meant to say that he never

was out of breath, let the ascent he had to mount be long as it might.* It was he who once had an affair with a bear. When it was known that the animal was in the mountains, a general turn-out took place and the pursuit began. Old Solacher—young then however —contrived to wound him, but the bear did not drop, and though he followed the red track for hours, he was unable to come up with him again. He got away then, but was shot four years after in the Tyrol.

The next morning I was up betimes; but on looking out of the window and finding the mountains covered with mist, I turned in again. It afterwards cleared up, and Max proposed we should set off in the afternoon for a hut, where we could sleep, and go out the first thing in the morning. "We shall then be close at hand," he observed, "and can have a splendid stalk. Where I intend to go is the best place we have, and after the two drives reserved for the King, it is the one I like most. We must take something with us, to cook our *schmarren*—some meal and butter, and some bread. We shall be warm enough in the hay."

" Well, when shall we start?"

" Why, it is dark now by five o'clock, so it will be better to leave at one." And having got our things together, off we set, in good spirits and buoyant with expectation.

* See Note on Poison-eating, at the end of the Volume.

CHAPTER X.

THE ALM HÜTTE.

At one o'clock we set off. The snow was gradually disappearing from the summit and sides of the Plau Berg, and in place of the smooth, unbroken, equal surface, the rugged dark rock showed itself in patches through the glittering covering.

"It must be warmer up yonder than it is here," observed Solacher. "The snow is creeping slowly away, and will soon all be gone."

"Is there any stalking to be had there now?" I asked.

"No, it is a hundred chances to one that we should find anything. You see, being just on the frontier, the Tyrolians come over the mountains; and formerly even they were constantly trying what they could get. However, on such a mountain as that the chamois will hardly be exterminated. They have so many places where they can maintain themselves against pursuit; and be sure, long after every chamois is destroyed in the neighbourhood, on the Plau Berg they will still be found."

"Are any ugly places there?" I asked.

"Yes, some are ugly enough. But it is not absolutely necessary to go where they are, with the exception of one, and that cannot well be avoided. You have to step along a very steep and narrow ledge; and then a place is to be crossed,—you have to spring across it,—which, if not sure-footed and free from giddiness, one could hardly manage, for below it goes down a tremendous depth. That is the only place you are absolutely obliged to pass, and there you *must* go, for by no other way is it possible to get out."

"There is a ridge, too, is there not, which is very narrow, with a precipice on each side?"

"Yes, but that is not much: it is narrow, but if you are only steady, you may walk across it easily."

"Not so easily though," I said; "a friend of mine walked along it, but after a few steps he was obliged to sit down, and with his legs dangling on each side to cross it astride. Did you ever meet any poachers on the Plau Berg, Maxl?" I asked.

"Yes," said he; "I and two assistant-foresters were on the mountains, and we saw seven men, Tyrolians, all armed and looking for chamois. We called to them, and off they ran. One of them however I overtook; I kept his gun, hat, and powder-horn, and then let him go."

"But as there were seven of them, I wonder they made off."

"Oh," said he, laughing, "the Tyrolians are afraid of the Bavarian bullets: they never hold out, but directly they espy one of us they take to their heels. Some years since a Tyrolian was missed: he had come over, it seems, and had been on the Plau Berg, but he never returned. His friends came and searched for him, and made every possible inquiry, but all in vain; he was never heard of again. Well, since then the Tyrolians have grown shy: they think perhaps that if they come, they too may not find their way home again."

The manner in which my friend Maxl told this story, made me strongly suspect he knew very well why the Tyrolian never went home again. Of course he vowed that he knew nothing of the matter, and it certainly is possible he did not; but there was an archness and a gusto in the way he spoke of it, that made me feel sure of the contrary. As the man's friends never found him, there was certainly a possibility that he had fallen over a precipice, and that the body had rolled down into some deep impenetrable chasm. Such a mountain is of immense extent; the rents, and clefts, and hollows are innumerable, and if the body had by chance slipped under one of the thousand fragments of rock that are lying about, this circumstance alone might be enough to hide it from the eye of the most careful seeker. Long after, perhaps some chance passer-by might stumble over a few bleached bones, but no one would know whose they were or aught of the dead man's story.

The case of the Tyrolian on the Plau Berg is by no means a solitary one of the kind. Occasionally, too, the forester's wife will wait and watch in vain for her husband's return. It is not long since that the body of one of the assistant-foresters of Berchtesgaden was found upon the mountain: it had been drawn aside from the path and flung among the latschen, which accounted for its not being found until several months after he had been shot. The poacher was evidently hidden from view, and had allowed him to come along the path within a yard or two of the muzzle of his rifle; for the dead man's clothes were still black and singed where the ball had entered. It had passed through the middle of his chest.

In about two hours we arrived at the hut. It stood
on a pleasant pasturage, and facing it rose the mountains partly covered with forest, while on one side a
high rock jutted abruptly up into the sky. Behind was
a gentle wooded slope; thither we now went, and looked
toward the mountain opposite us. We examined every
part with the naked eye and with our glasses, but not a
creature was to be seen. We watched for more than an
hour; and then turning toward the rock that rose above
the valley, presently saw a chamois grazing, now visible
and now disappearing among the herbage. Shortly after
we discovered another nearer the summit; when, as it
was getting cold and dusk, we turned toward our hut.

"We won't disturb them," said Maxl, "for today we
could do nothing, and they will be there tomorrow for
certain : we shall then be able to get at them better, and
may make sure of a shot."

The hut where we intended to take up our lodging
for the night was, thus late in the season (October 15),
of course deserted. The cows had gone down into the
valley, and with them the blithe dairymaids. But
when they leave their summer abode the door is not
locked; a latch only keeps it from being blown open
by the wind; so that the hunter, should he be overtaken by night or by a storm, can enter there and find
a comfortable shelter. We went up the steps, lifted the
latch, and entered. Nothing could be neater than the
room : it was as clean and nicely arranged as if prepared
for a visitor. On one side was a raised hearth of stone,
about two feet and a half from the ground : it was large,
and necessarily so, for there in summer-time, in a huge
copper vessel suspended over the fire by a sort of crane
fixed in the wall, the preparations for cheese-making
are carried on. The wall above the hearth was neatly

whitewashed, as well as the stones round the hearth itself. Above it was a pile of dry thin laths for lighting a fire, and in one corner a goodly stack of logs for fuel. On a shelf near were some lucifer-matches and a horn spoon; and there was a simple broom, fan-shaped and made of heather, left as a hint for the sojourner there, before he left, to make all as tidy as he had found it. Max went down a few steps in one corner of the room into the cellar, having first lighted one of the long pieces of resinous wood to serve as a flambeau. Below were the utensils used by the little household during their residence on the mountain,—all bright and clean, and arranged in perfect order: large brown pans for the milk, and smaller ones too, ranged beside each other like the plates over a kitchen dresser; wooden bowls and pails; all of which had been well scoured before being stored away for the winter. We brought up such things as we wanted,—some pans to make our *schmarren*, and a pail to fetch fresh water in. Three other huts stood on the meadow beside the one in which we were, and a rivulet ran gurgling through the herbage, and might be heard tumbling into a rude basin of stones on the other side of a green hillock. Thither Maxl now went to fill the water-pail. Had he been alone he would hardly have gone even thus far without taking his rifle. It is well to be prepared for every risk, and in such situations one can never be safe against a surprise. Should a poacher also come to the hut to pass the night, and the forester be at that moment gone to the spring for water to cook his supper, and his rifle left in the hut, not only would he lose it, but being unarmed he would be entirely at the other's mercy. As long as you have a rifle in your hand, and a tree or a stone to stand behind, the odds are as much in your favour as in that of your adversaries.

While my companion was gone to the spring, I stood
at the door of the hut and looked out upon the scene
before me. It was getting dark, and the outlines of
the mountains opposite were already indistinct. A cold
gust came up from the valley, and in a moment after
huge ghost-like forms swept by, followed by others in
long succession; grey trailing clouds passed solemnly on
over the meadow, and in a few seconds the whole space
between the mountains was filled with thick mist. It
is astonishing how quickly the landscape is sometimes
enveloped and shut out from view. The meadow was
hidden from sight, as well as all else except the nearer
hut, which loomed through the vapoury gloom.

We were both glad to be so comfortably housed, and
bolting the door set about making a fire. It was pleasant and cheering within, as soon as the blaze lighted
up the walls and roof, and the dry wood crackled and
flung round its sparks upon the hearth. Stowed away
in a secret place known only to himself, Solacher had a
frying-pan of his own in this hut; for it seemed he often
made it his temporary home, as well when the dairy-
maids were gone into the vale as during their summer
sojourn here. The frying-pan was fetched, and he at
once set about the supper, each of us however having
first taken a long draught at the freshly-filled water-pail.

The rücksacks were opened, and their contents brought
forth. In Solacher's was the usual small bag of flour
and the wooden box with butter, which the chamois-
hunter always carries with him; and out of the midst
of the flour two eggs came to light, which he had put
in that safe place for me, in order that the *schmarren*
might be light and delicate. Being an epicure in his
way, he had also taken care to have a few apples with
him, to make his own mess the more savoury. I had some

white bread, the remains of a dried sausage, and a small
bottle of rum. We inspected our store, and I then blew
the fire into a blaze, while Maxl prepared the usual dish
of the hunter and mountaineer. It is made in this wise :
some of the flour was turned out into an earthen pan ;
a certain quantity of water with the yolk of one egg was
then added (the other being kept for tomorrow's breakfast); and the whole having been well stirred, water
was poured in till it grew sufficiently thin. The frying-
pan, containing great lumps of butter, was now put on
the fire, and, when this boiled, the contents of the pan
were emptied into it. The cake was allowed to get brown
on one side, care being taken however that it did not
burn; it was then turned, and with an iron instrument
the whole was chopped up into pieces varying in size
from a filbert to a small walnut. An apple was sliced in,
some more butter added, all well stirred up together,
and when every little piece was nicely brown, it was
turned out smoking into the pan ready to be eaten.

Sitting on the raised ledge, with our feet inside and
towards the hearth, we ate our supper, and well pleased
was Maxl at the praise I bestowed upon his cookery. The
schmarren was really excellent: to make it well is said
not to be so easy as it appears, and without due attention the cake becomes heavy and dough-like. A slice
of bread and a good draught of water completed the
repast. We had lighted one of the long dry resinous
strips of wood, and stuck it into the wall to serve as a
lamp while supping; but now, while sitting over the
embers, we from time to time flung a dry chip or two
upon them, and the flickering flame they made threw
around a sufficient light. The shutters of the windows
were well closed and fastened on the inside,—a very necessary precaution, for should a poacher chance to ap-

proach a hut whence he saw a light gleaming through
the crevices, it would be an easy matter for him, as the
forester was sitting over his fire, to gratify revenge, and,
stealing quietly to the window, send a bullet through
his heart.   It is one of the first things therefore on
such occasions to see that all is safe.*

As I sat there enjoying to the full all the comfort of
my situation, I could not but feel thankful to the dairy-
maids who had left the hut in so neat a state, and enabled us so easily to satisfy our wants.   I said as much
to Maxl, but he did not seem to think it called for any
praise.   " A fine thing indeed," exclaimed he, " if the
wenches were to go away and not leave all in order !   I
should like to catch them doing such a thing !   A good
rating they'd get for their laziness.   No, all must be
cleaned up and put aside, that one may know where to
find what is wanted ; and wood brought in and stacked,
so that a fire may be made directly.   Suppose we had
come here and found nothing—no dry wood, no pans or
hay—we should not have spent a very comfortable evening, I think !"

I was amused at Maxl's looking on all this as a right,
which the chamois-hunter, as lord of the creation, might
duly claim.   The fact is, the young foresters when
out on the mountains in summer constantly repair to
some particular hut for a warm meal or a night's shelter.   They are welcome guests, for they bring with them
mirth and news of the great world and of what is going

---

* Not long before I was at Fischbachau one of the keepers was sitting
at table with his wife and her little baby in her arms, when a blunder-
buss loaded with slugs was fired through the window into the room.
The wall opposite still had the shot-marks scattered over it.   Luckily
no one was hurt.   And this summer (1851) one of the foresters near
Ratisbon had a gun fired into his room at night when his family were
around him : this time too all escaped.

on in the dale. And although perchance none of the lasses is the sweetheart of the youth who is the most frequent visitor at the hut, still the friendly intercourse of many a summer and an interchange of little acts of kindness will cause them to provide, with all a woman's thoughtfulness, for the poor fellow's comfort when he comes to spend a solitary night there in autumn, and the hut is quite deserted; so before leaving the mountain pasturage they will set in order everything for the friend and favourite, who is sure to visit it often when they are gone.

There was a door in the room in which we were sitting that led immediately into the cow-house, and above it was the hay-loft. Over this door was written, "Catharina Hess." I asked Solacher if that was the name of the dairymaid.

" Yes," he said, " that is her name. She is the prettiest girl on all the mountains round. Her sister Lisl is a nice girl too; such a pair you will not easily match."

" 'T is a pity they are not here now," I observed.

" Ay, if they were, what fun we would have! They should sing and *jodeln*, and we would make the old hut ring with our merriment."

But as they were not there, to cheer us with the music of their laughter and their voices, we flung some more wood on the fire, and tried to make the place look bright with the ruddy blaze.

" If I had but something to boil water in, Solacher, we might have a glass of grog," said I; " and that would warm us well before going to bed."

" Grog—what is that? As to boiling some water, that is easy enough; we shall be sure to find something in the cellar." Taking a firebrand he went below and brought up a couple of pipkins, in one of which we set the water on the embers to boil; into the other I poured some rum, and having sugar with me we soon had a hot and fragrant beverage.

"What is it?" asked Maxl, as he sipped at the edge of the pipkin; "what capital stuff! Why, it's like wine, but it is too strong." And though it was far from being anything like a nor'wester, I was obliged to add much water before it suited his palate—so unvitiated by strong drink was the taste of the hardy and frugal mountaineer.

We talked about Baierisch Zell, Max Solacher's home; and he related to me how his father during the war had received a shot through the lungs, "close to the hill," said he, "which you passed in going there."

"But how did it happen?" I asked.

"Why, you see, he and seventy-five more went out against five hundred Tyrolians, who had come with carts to plunder the village. The men of Baierisch Zell of course took care to get behind the trees and rocks; and being good shots, each one brought down his man. My father had already killed three, when he himself was hit—perhaps he had shot even more, but of those three he was certain."

"It was a pity he was wounded so soon, for being so cool and a good shot, he would have knocked over a few more."

"I remember," he continued, "my father used in particular to tell us of one man, an immense fellow, who kept on loading and firing away like the devil. He was a good shot, and almost all his balls told. He was standing behind a pile of wood, quite protected. Well, my father marked him, and thought to himself, 'I'll soon stop you, my boy!' So he kept his eye on him and waited; and just as he leaned a little forward to fire again, my father was too quick for him; in the same second his rifle cracked, and the Tyrolian doubled up together, bent forward, and fell. They were obliged to retreat, and had to use the carts which they had brought to fetch plunder, to carry off their own dead."

" And your father recovered ?"

" Oh yes, he lived a long time after that, quite well and hearty."

" And how was it, Maxl, that your brother Henry got wounded in the foot so badly ?"

" That the poachers did : those of Miesbach and Schlier See are the worst; they fire directly they see a forester, no matter whether he attacks them or not. It was near Schlier See that it happened. Henry came suddenly upon five or six poachers, and immediately called to them that he would stand aside and let them pass, without attempting to stop them or to fire. And so he did; but one of them, when he got near, fired and hit him in the ankle. He fell directly, and the poachers went on and left him there. With great difficulty he dragged himself to the nearest Senn Hütte, and the Sennerinnen bandaged his foot and he was carried home."

" And what about Kreuth, is there much poaching going on now ?"

" It was not long ago that Ignace, the son of my old uncle, he whom we met yesterday as we were coming home, had an adventure with some of them. It was just on the hill where you shot the kid. He was going up the mountain, and saw the footprints of several men in the snow. He wondered who could have been there, so he followed the track for some time, and presently observed a fellow with a rifle in his hand, waiting and watching for game. He drew nearer and looked well at him, but still without knowing him. At last he asked him what he was doing there, when up jumped the man, crying out, 'You rascal of a forester, lay down your rifle, or I'll send a ball through your body.'"

"And did he?"

"Of course he did not," replied Max; "Ignace is a young fellow, only seventeen years old, but he sprang behind a tree and levelled his rifle. The man ran off, and Ignace vows that, if he had not, he would have shot him on the spot."

And now we talked of old times, when game was plentiful on the mountains, of the chamois that had been shot, and by whom and where, and of those matters which to some appear trifling, but which to the hunter are full of interest. We chatted on so long and earnestly that we let the fire get low, and our faces looked almost spectral as the glowing embers threw a faint light upon them. But we flung on more wood, and soon fanned the heap into a cheerful blaze.

"Let us boil another pipkin-full of water, Maxl," said I; "a little more of what you find so capital, and then to bed."

He had still many a question to ask, for I had told him about the herds of game in America, and it had set his imagination on fire. How much he would like to go there! but then the water! Water he did not like, and he asked how long, in crossing, he would have to be upon it.

"But what makes you dislike it?" I inquired.

"Once, you know, I was stationed at the Königs See, and in going over the lake in winter when it was frozen I slipped through a hole. I came up under the ice; but by a wonderful chance, after going down a second time I rose at the hole again, and my comrade pulled me out. Since then I have quite a horror of the water. I should never have left the Königs See but for that: however as

I had often to go on the lake I asked to be stationed elsewhere, for that dread of the water I never could overcome."

" You would of course rather be there than at Kreuth ?" I asked.

"Certainly, much rather. There is no place like Berchtesgaden—what mountains and difficult places! And there too we used to have a right merry life, so many gentlemen came to shoot. Once," he continued laughing, " something curious happened to me, but though I was sadly disappointed at the time, it amuses me now when I think of it."

" What was it, Maxl? let us hear the story."

" Well," said he, " a certain Baron von C——— came from Munich for some shooting. I don't know who he was, but he was sent with a recommendation from some one at court to the head-forester. I was to go with him. The day before we went out, he told me that if he missed the first chamois, he would give me a hundred florins !"

" If he hit it, you mean," said I, interrupting him.

" No, no, if he missed, he said I was to have a hundred florins, and if he hit, he would give me ten : I was astonished, and asked if he was in earnest. 'Oh yes,' he answered, ' quite so: if I miss the first shot, a hundred florins are yours.' Well, I thought, it is strange enough,—but a hundred florins! that's a sum worth having ; and I began considering how I could manage to make him miss the first time he fired. All night I lay awake thinking the matter over, but I could not hit upon any plan whatever. Next day I was going up the mountain to show him his stand before the drive began, when down below us in a gully I saw some chamois. That's just right, thought I ; now then

K

for the hundred florins. So I told him to wait there, while I went on to drive the chamois, to enable him to have a shot at them. When I got to the head of the ravine there lay a great piece of rock that I could hardly move; but by leaning my back against the block I at last succeeded, and over I sent it into the gully below. You may think what a noise it made! Down it dashed, tearing and crashing, and leaping from rock to rock, into the very midst of the chamois. They were frightened out of their senses, and off they went as fast as they could bound. This was just what I wanted, for I knew that my gentleman was so hot he would fire directly he saw them, whether far or near. And I was right; bang! went his rifle not a second after. Now, thought I, the hundred florins are safe; he has missed for certain. When I got back to him I asked if he had hit or missed. He had not missed, he thought. This however we would ascertain on coming back, for to stop then was not possible, as we should have reached the stand only after the drive had begun. I was very pleased all the time, being sure he had not hit him. On our way down I went to look after the chamois; and sure enough, there he lay, quite dead. The Baron gave me the ten florins as he had promised, but the hundred which I had calculated on having I did not get."

Our cheerful fire, the warm beverage, and the merry stories we had to tell each other, made the long evening pass away quickly enough.

"It is a pity the maids have left no cheese here," said Max, who, like myself, was getting hungry again; "they would if I had told them. They would leave anything if they thought it would be of service—cheese, salt, in short whatever I chose to ask for."

There was something very pleasing in these little acts

of kindness,—this thoughtfulness of another's wants,
when there should be no one to minister to them but
himself. But indeed there is much good-heartedness in
these people; and I never left the mountains and my
trusty friends the foresters, to move again among the
conventional forms of town society, without a regret for
their many gracious services, rendered always with the
best of all politeness—that of a willing heart.

"Now, Maxl, it is time for bed; empty the pipkin
and then let us turn into the hay. But we will first
see how the weather looks." And I opened the door
of the hut. Without was darkness as profound as that
which must have weighed upon the world when all was
yet chaos: not a star was in the sky. I never yet
looked upon such darkness: before and around me was
one mass of gloom. The gurgling of the rivulet was
heard as it crossed the meadow; a low moaning wind
moved among the rocks. I shut the door quickly, and
Maxl, as my chamberlain, kindling a piece of pine, prepared to light me to bed. Having bolted the door, my
companion gave me my rifle. "It is better to take
it with you," said he; "one can't tell what may happen;
and at all events it is safer than to leave it down here."
I scrambled into the loft, whilst Max held up the fla-
ming brand at arm's length that I might see to arrange
my bed. The bright red flame flung a wild glare over
my strange chamber; the beams of the roof that were
nearest caught the light, and the bed of hay where I
stood was illumined by the blaze. But further back
were shadows huddled together in deep impenetrable
corners, as if they had all fled there on the approach
of the lurid light. Max now joined me, and with our
rifles beside us, and buried in the fragrant hay, we
soon fell asleep.

CHAPTER XI.

AN UNLUCKY DAY.

If not accustomed to such things, you find it rather strange, on awaking in the night, to hear—almost to feel, so near it is to you—the continued patter of the rain-drops on the shingle roof not many inches above your cheek. As I turned in my warm bed, and wound myself still deeper into the dense fragrant mass that composed it, I heard the gentle falling of the rain just above my face, and grumbling inwardly at the unfavourable morrow it foretokened, again fell fast asleep.

I should have been much better pleased had it come down in a good shower, rattling on the shingles as though about to shake them all to pieces, instead of that dull, monotonous, sluggish drizzle, which might continue any number of hours. The moment of half-waking consciousness was just long enough for the discontented thought.

When I next woke it was at the sound of the quarters which Solacher's repeater was chiming beside me. Five and three-quarters—it's time to be off! So kicking away the heap of hay with which each of us was so comfortably covered, we crept down into the hut. Unbolting the door, to let in the light, we put all in order, replaced everything as we had found it, and sweeping the floor made the place as neat as it was on our arrival the night before. It had ceased raining, but the sky and mountain-tops wore signs of no good promise.

We went to the rock where the two chamois had been the preceding evening. At the moment of reaching the summit the chamois sprang away in front of us, stopped at a distance, whistled, and then were off again. They had winded us as we were coming up, and had retreated before the apprehended danger long before we could approach them. It was an unfortunate beginning, for we had looked on those two chamois as our own. "It's all my fault," said Max, vexed and angry; "I never was here yet but I stalked up the other side; and last night, as I lay thinking it over, I made up my mind to go the same way as before, and yet I took the opposite one. I don't know why I did so; I never went on that side before. If we had gone more to the right we should have got above them, and had a shot for certain. *Himmi! Donnerwetter! Der Teufi!*" he exclaimed, as he stopped a moment and reflected on the matter, and on the chance which had been thrown away.

Below us thick mists were rolling, so that it was impossible to see anything. Presently however a sunbeam fell here and there on the peaks of the distant mountains; and, as a sweet smiling face has the power of dissipating tears or sulkiness, anon the whole snowy range was glowing in the morning light. The fog dispersed, the sky became blue, and all looked bright and cheerful. We walked on, and came to the brow of a hill from which we could overlook a large space, partly bare and partly covered with low stunted shrubs. It was a long while before we saw anything, but at last Max perceived five chamois at a distance browsing among the latschen. He

pointed out to me the spot, and exactly described where
I was to look for them ; but in spite of all his explana-
tions and my endeavours to find them, I was unable to
make out one of the dark specks which he said were
chamois.   We now went after them, keeping just below
and on the opposite side of the ridge, and advancing far
beyond the place where they stood, came round upon
them in front.   On our way we fell in with a solitary
chamois.

"Is it one of them, think you ?" I whispered to Solacher.

"I think not," he answered ; and luckily we succeeded
in passing without his disturbing the others.   There is
nothing more vexatious, when stalking, than to come
thus suddenly upon some single animal, causing it to
start off and alarm the very buck or red-deer that you
might have got. within reach of in a moment or two
more.   But this time no harm was done.   Solacher went
first, creeping along on tiptoe over the grass, with his
hat off and his neck stretched out to catch a glimpse of
the game we were approaching.   Quickly lowering his
head, and bending together as if to make himself invisible, while his whole body was alive with excitement, he
motioned me to advance.   I crept forward : the chamois
were already on the watch, and gazing, somewhat alarmed,
towards the place where we were hidden.   Another step,
and I was before them : they bounded off, but I selected
one, and as it moved away I fired.   Maxl looked at me,
first in astonishment, and then with an expression of dis-
satisfaction.

"Why, what's the matter with your rifle ?" he asked :
"the powder must be damp, or you have not the full
charge : it hardly made any report at all."

I was as surprised as he.   It had indeed made hardly

more noise than a pop-gun, instead of the usual roar
that caused the hills to reverberate.

"I don't know the reason," said I, greatly vexed at
the mishap, and not a little angry at his displeasure:
"such a thing never happened to me before."

"If you go on so, you won't shoot much," said Maxl,
growing more and more angry at the misadventure, and
evidently longing, had he dared, to give me a good scold-
ing for what he conceived was owing to my carelessness.
"Why, the bullet did not go a quarter of the distance
to the chamois: I would lay a wager it fell not a dozen
yards from where we are. You cannot have had half
enough powder, or your rifle would never have gone off
in such a manner." And with his usually merry face
overcast he walked on in silence.

After having missed a shot a change comes over everything. You are no longer light-hearted as you were
before, when expectation made you buoyant; you feel
discontented with yourself, and, enacting in your mind
the whole occurrence over again, wonder how it could
possibly have turned out so unfortunately. You are not
only dissatisfied with yourself, but dissatisfied with all
about you. Nothing gives you pleasure; you care for
nothing: one single thought alone occupies you, and
that is, "If I could only have *one more* shot at him! he
should not escape a second time." And all those things
that at other times are looked at with delight now afford
you none: you hardly cast a glance at the barrier of snow
yonder, high up in the sky; the sunshine does not glad-
den you; and in a sort of desperation you seek comfort
by looking at and following the track of the game you
have just missed. I do not see much sense in this,
though I have often done it, and have hung over the
footsteps in the soft earth or in the snow, and examined

the size and depth of the impression, as though by so
doing I could conjure up the animal and bring it back
again.

It was now too late in the morning for any chance of
a successful stalk; we therefore returned to the hut and
cooked some schmarren for breakfast. As we sat over
the fire with the dish between us, eating our meal in
silence, I could not but think how great the contrast between the present moment and the cheerful evening of
yesterday. Then how merry we were! now both were
dissatisfied and spoke little. We swept up the hearth
and went on our way.

In the afternoon, on our way homewards, we came to
a ridge that overlooked the broad side of the mountain.
It was a most desolate scene: the wood had been cleared
away, and felled trees were lying scattered in all directions, just as they had fallen where the axe of the woodcutter had laid them low, and the stumps that remained in
the ground were sticking out on every side. The surface
was broken, and torn up by rain, and by the great stems
which had been dragged downwards. A log-hut some
few feet high might be seen a long way off: it rather
added to the dreariness and melancholy, for there was
no sign of life in or near that human habitation. Not a
sound was heard; nothing stirred above the whole surface of that sad place. The grey of evening spread over
the sky; the very atmosphere wore the same monotonous
dull hue. It was oppressively still and very dreary; and
I was glad, after long looking round in vain to catch
sight of some living thing, when Maxl proposed to descend into the valley.

"Schlier See must lie yonder," said I, pointing north-
ward; "it must be somewhere in that direction."

"Yes," said Max, "it is not very far off. A pretty set

they are there! the poachers of Schlier See and of Hundham, near Fischbachau, are the most daring of any:
they would as soon shoot a forester as look at him. And
how the rascals served Probst once! You know Probst,
don't you? he is a capital sportsman, and as courageous
as a lion. Did I never tell you what happened to him
near Schlier See?"

" No, what was it?"

" Why, one day he was on the mountain,—it was on
the Wilder Fell Alp,—and as he was looking about for
chamois he saw two men with rifles, also on the look-
out for game: they were not far off, and presently they
went into a hut. He waited for a long time, till he knew
they had made a fire, and would be busy cooking: it was
perhaps three or four hours before he saw smoke rising
from the roof, but as soon as he did down he went. He
knocked open the door, and called to the men to come
out and lay down their rifles; but no one stirred.—all
was still. Probst then rushed into the hut, and, seizing
the first fellow he saw, caught him by the throat; at
the same moment the other poachers came upon him
from behind and pulled him down backwards; they then
beat him unmercifully, took away his rifle, watch, and
hat, and, binding his hands and feet together, left him
there on the ground. The Sennerinnen were all gone
down into the valley, so he might have lain there long
enough before any one came near the hut, and have died
of hunger and cold. Well, after lying there all that night
and the next day, and after trying all he could to get
loose, at last on the second day towards evening he was
able to free his hands, and with his teeth to undo the
cords that bound them, and weak, stiff, and exhausted, he
set off homewards. It was late at night when he reached
his cottage; but, ill as he was for a long time afterwards,

he thought himself very lucky to have escaped with his life."

It is hardly possible to conceive a more terrible situation: the prospect of death, the solitude of the mountain, the pains of hunger and cold during the long dreary night, as he lay bound hand and foot, the thoughts of home, and many other thoughts,—it must indeed have been a state of mental agony. It seems to me that the possibility of being saved, poor as the chance was,—for who was likely to pass over the mountain?—must have added to his torment. The constant expectation, the hope from hour to hour, still unrealized and yet clung to with desperate tenacity,—all this, I think, was calculated to make his sufferings greater than if there had been no hope. With what intense longing, with what an acute sense, must he have listened for a sound! And through the night, as he lay looking up to the stars, how must he have yearned for the morning, and have been solaced when at last he saw it stealing upwards over the sky!*

But although the poachers always took signal vengeance on the gamekeepers whenever they got them into their power, on one occasion they refrained from ill-treatment; it is true, however, in this case the person whom they met was not a forester: it was the young Count D——, then quite a youth, and who, being passionately fond of the chase, was always out on the mountains, sometimes with the foresters, sometimes alone. He had one day given a rendezvous to Max Solacher, and was already on the mountain near the place of meeting, when he heard a shot. He fancied it was Max, who on his way had fired at a vulture or some bird, and took no notice of the circumstance. Soon after he went toward a spot

* Probst has since married Maxl's eldest sister.

where he thought he might find Max, and coming to a
kind of "saddle" in the mountain, looked over. His dog
had been for some minutes very restless, and thinking
it was game he had scented, he reproved him silently by
a sign with his hand. But in peering below, instead of
chamois he saw a hat, and then another and another;
several poachers were there, close beneath him, making
their arrangements for the day's operations. He was so
near that it is a wonder they did not see his face. Behind him all was bare, with only a single latschen where
he might conceal himself. He slid back as noiselessly
as possible; and when some yards away from the ridge
he cocked his rifle, and passing through a ravine went
up the side of a mountain opposite. Here he was quite
exposed to their view, and they might easily have seen
him, which indeed was the very thing he wished; for he
knew that if they perceived him they would be sure to
watch his movements, and wait to see in what direction
he went before setting off themselves, and he hoped in .
the meantime Solacher might come. He went slowly up
the path, sitting down occasionally, as if wholly unconscious of their neighbourhood. It seems, however, they
did not observe him. The young Count then made a circuit, and reached a spot among some rocks, whence he
could see the men as they came up out of the hollow.
The path they would then have to take crossed an open
piece of ground, with hardly a bush upon it, so that they
would be quite exposed, whilst he was sheltered by the
blocks of stone. Presently he saw their heads appearing,
and soon after they came on, one behind the other. He
had meanwhile double-shotted his gun, and was now in
the act of raising his rifle and calling to the foremost to
lay down his weapon, when a voice from the latschen
cried out, "Drop your rifle, you fellow of a Count, or it

will be the worse for you!" Quick as lightning the
other men turned round on hearing these words, and
every muzzle was pointed to the spot where the youth
was hidden. He of course did as he was bidden; and
the men, not without plenty of abuse, went cautiously
on their way, one of them always keeping ready to fire
in case he should move or attempt to send a bullet after
them.

It was evident that the man behind the latschen must
have been there already when the Count took his station
among the rocks, having been stationed as sentinel in
case of alarm. The poachers knew the youth, which accounts for their letting him escape so easily : had Max
Solacher been in his place, he would hardly have lived
to tell the tale.

The men had not been long out of sight when the
Count heard a shot; he imagined it was from Maxl's
rifle, and that, on coming up, he had met the poachers
and killed one.

But he was mistaken : Solacher, as he went along, had
merely fired at some animal below him. Hardly had he
done so when six men, the same mentioned above, rushed
out of a hut on an Alm lower down, and looked about
scared and astonished. But they could not discover
whence the shot proceeded, and this bewildered them all
the more. In order to be safe from a surprise they went
to the middle of a large bare spot, without shelter of any
kind, where grew a solitary tree, and beneath this they
seated themselves. Here they knew they were secure,
as no one would approach thus unprotected within shot,
and the surrounding rocks were too far off for a gamekeeper, if lurking there, to do them any harm. So they
waited till it grew dark, and Maxl all the time lay above
watching them. At dusk he stole away, and hastened

off to a path where he thought they would pass on their
way down to the valley. From the spot where he had
been watching them were two paths only which it was
possible for them to take; there was no other way of
getting down the mountain. He chose the one which
he thought the most probable, and waited in silence beside the path, well concealed, intending when they came
to fire both barrels into the midst of them. He staid
until eleven, when he heard at a distance the sound of
their voices, by which he knew they had taken the other
path.

Evening was closing in, and we hastened our steps.
The light bounding motion of Solacher as he sprang down
the mountain was really admirable. Over all the inequalities, stones, holes, or stumps of trees, he leaped like
a roe: leaning on his long pole he jumped over everything that came in his way, or swung himself down where
the broken ground caused a sudden fall in the descent;
no chamois could leap more lightly. He would stop every
now and then, and look round to see if I was near, and
then bound forwards, and again stand and wait; for I
was tired and lagged behind, which I was not wont to
do. But after such a day as this had been, and when
you have missed one or two shots, the limbs seem to
have lost their usual elasticity, and you plod along more
wearily than at another time, when the fatigue has been
twice as great, but the sport and shooting good. The
path was however so bad that it was not possible to go
very quickly; it was dark too, which made it still less
easy. Sometimes the road was formed by the stems of
trees laid side by side, now rendered slippery by water
and long use. In one place, while going down-hill, my
foot slipped between the stems, one of which crossed my
shin about half-way between the ankle and the knee. It

was with no small difficulty I prevented myself from falling forwards; had I done so, the shinbone must inevitably have snapped. There is no end to the mishaps one is exposed to in the mountains, even under favourable circumstances; hence the care the hunter always takes to reach the valley while it is light; for where the path is narrow, or the descent precipitous, it would sometimes be an awkward thing to be overtaken by the night.

Long before we reached the village it was quite dark. The several foresters were at the inn that evening, and there was laughter, music, and merriment; gay as it was, yet to me, somehow or other, the evening before in the Senn Hütte seemed much more pleasant and cheerful, —the thing was, *yesterday I had not missed a chamois.*

Kobell, in one of his poems, has well represented this state of mind. He has taken a little incident of everyday life, and made of it a complete picture. It is a Teniers scene, if you will; but it is a genuine touch of Nature nevertheless.

Vexation.

Father's so cross and grumpy,
  He keeps on scold, scold, scold;
Just now he beat poor Trouncer,
  That is so good and old:
There's nothing right, no nothing;
  All in the house is wrong.
That Dobbin's lame since Monday,
  Sure that won't vex him long;
The after-math's all in now,
  So he may well be spared.
What *can* then be the matter?
  To ask, if I but dared!

" He comes !   Be still, ye children ! "
   The children all keep close,
And still as mice, and wonder
   What makes him so morose.
The old man cleaned his rifle,
   Then shoved it as it lay ;
Lolled in the chimney corner,
   And drove his dog away.

'T is very late already ;
   At last he falls asleep,
When on tiptoe the youngest
   Into the room does creep,
And whispers to the others,
   " I 've found it out, good luck !
'T is not about old Dobbin,
   He has missed a chamois buck !"

CHAPTER XII.

THE RISS.

On arriving at Kreuth we heard that the King had announced his intention of going out shooting there in a few days. It was therefore useless to remain any longer; for, until the royal hunt had taken place, all the assistant-foresters would be busy in making preparations, and there would be none to accompany me to the mountains. It may be asked, how can such an event occupy so many persons for days beforehand? In order to ensure a good day's sport, the outlying game is collected as much as possible, and made to move forwards into the neighbourhood where the royal party are to hunt. For this purpose the young gamekeepers pass along the places where the chamois have their haunts, and, by occasionally rolling a stone down the crags into the *graben** below, disturb the game and cause them to bear away for ground more within reach of the approaching operations. This is not a task soon done, or easy of accomplishment: from one mountain to another—though when viewed from

---

* *Graben.* Literally translated, "a ditch, or trench," but in the highlands it means the rifts in the rocks on the sides of a mountain, and is used indiscriminately whether speaking of one that is five or five hundred feet deep. Sometimes the deep ones are also called "Clam," as "Schwarzbach Clam," etc.

below they do not seem far apart—is an intervening
space, which it may take a good half day to get over.

On such occasions the foresters do not go down into
the valley at nightfall, but pass several days and nights
on the mountains. They must be on the watch too for
poachers, and see that none are about, scaring the chamois
and sending them scampering away from their accustomed
places; for when disturbed the game is off at once, and
does not return again for several days.

At Tegernsee an anticipated day's sport was frustrated
in this manner. I was to have gone out on the Peissenberg, where there was every chance of being able to get
a shot, when the foresters came in with the intelligence
that poachers had been there: reports of their rifles had
been heard in that direction, and it was vain therefore
for me to think of stalking with any prospect of success.
Once before, when the King had intended to shoot there,
the same thing occurred. The head-forester had sent
some of the under-gamekeepers to watch on the mountain, with orders to remain out till the appointed day:
on account of the lawless state of the country at that
time (1849), he sent a gendarme to accompany them,
thinking that the presence of a police-officer would over-
awe the marauders, should any be met with. As might
have been foretold, he was wrong in his calculation;
for the power which such an individual exercises is a
moral one, quite independent of his constable's staff, or,
as in the present instance, of his bayonet and side-arms.
Obedience to him is ceded out of respect to the law,
which happened just at that time to be as devoid of dignity as power. Even in the plain the laws had ceased
to be respected; it was something to excite a smile
therefore thus to see stationed, high up on the mountain-top, out of the world as it were, and in presence of

L

wild nature only, where courage and physical strength alone availed anything, one " dressed in a little brief authority," expecting to curb rough and reckless natures. While on the look-out the gamekeepers and gendarme were surprised by thirty poachers, each armed with a rifle, who at once ordered them to descend and leave them to drive the game according to their pleasure. Where the numbers presented such odds, opposition would have been ridiculous; the foresters and their companion therefore had no alternative but to return home, and announce that the intended hunt must be postponed.

These grand hunts in the mountains are very interesting, on account of the immense quantity and variety of game that is often seen, besides the opportunities afforded of observing the habits and movements of the various animals when influenced by fear, surprise, or bewilderment. At early morning the keepers and their scouts are at the appointed places on the mountains, and at a certain time—at the hour when it is calculated the several sportsmen have reached their stations—they are all on the move. Here and there a stone is let drop; further on a young mountaineer will pass along the perpendicular descent, holding on by the trusty latschen, in order to drive out the chamois, and also to reach a spot inaccessible in any other way.

On such a day perilous places are passed. Each óne takes an interest in the work, anxious that the day's sport should be satisfactory; and as the chamois love to lurk in the wildest retreats, and nooks guarded by precipices, if the men do their work well they are sure to be led along some dangerous passes. None of course is willing to lag behind or avoid the peril, but, trusting to his steady foot and unreeling brain, each dares whatever may come in his way. Thus led on by an adventurous

feeling, a hunt of this kind hardly ever passes without
an accident of some sort happening to the men employed.
Occasionally too the mists will rise suddenly, and spread
their impenetrable covering over the whole mountain-
range. They lie upon the air like a solid thing, and then
to move even is indeed perilous : a single step, and the
beater may tread, not on the firm ground, but on yielding cloud, and toppling over go sinking through an ocean
of vapour to the craggy bottom.

About such matters I heard much from my guide as
we walked on towards the Riss; for as soon as I found
there was nothing more to be done at Kreuth, I packed
a few things in my rücksack, and driving to Glass Hütten, took thence a bye-path leading into the valley of the
Isar. The peasant who accompanied me was an intelligent fellow, and knew many a story about those merry
times when the mountains were fuller of game than now.
And Prince Löwenstein! how often had he been out with
him when he hunted there, and what sport they had!
He talked about the gentlemen who used to join the
shooting parties, and was pleased to find that I knew
most of them. He had, it seems, been employed as
beater, and knew the mountains well, and every *Wand*
and difficult place. And still he kept on recounting
about the past, as one does who has a yearning after remembered joys; at moments cheerily and with bursts
of pleasure, and then with somewhat of sadness in thinking that such days would never come again.

I was all the while admiring his nimbleness, as he
sped on before me over the broken ground. There was
an elasticity of step and an evenness in his pace that
never varied up hill or down, across the stony bed of a
torrent or over the smooth sward. He wore the usual
short leathern breeches, and as I looked at his red-brown

legs I well understood how, in former times, the English gave the name they did to their northern neighbours as a distinctive appellation ; and this led me to think how in Scotland the whole country used to be roused by just such messengers as he who was now dashing along before me,—a fellow with the least possible clothing, with little flesh, but tendons like whipcord, who knew the passes and short-cuts over the mountains, and could breast the steepest without stopping to take breath.   I now comprehended how in an incredibly short space of time all the fighting-men might be called together,— how

> " Each valley, each sequestered glen,
> Mustered its little horde of men," —

when messengers swift of foot were thus sent out to spread the alarm in every direction, causing district after district to burst into a blaze ; as though the burning brand that was borne along and passed from one fleet runner to the other had the power to fire men's hearts and to kindle enthusiasm.   Indeed it was Malise himself who was before me, hastening on with the words of Roderick still ringing in his ears :

> " The muster-place be Lanric Mead—
> Instant the time—speed, Malise, speed."*

We presently came upon the high-road, and were at once at the Fall.   A large house, singularly neat and clean-looking, with cow-house and barn adjoining, all indicative of substantial prosperity, is the dwelling of an under-forester.   He was out when we arrived, which I regretted, for I had heard much of a deed of his that gave proof of his resolute intrepidity : it was as follows.

One evening, rather late, Rietsch happened to look

---

* The Lady of the Lake : The Gathering.

out-of-doors to see what weather it was; and as he cast
his eyes round toward the mountains, what should he
espy but a light high up in the direction of some Alm
Hütten! It was dark, and he could not see the huts,
but he knew exactly where they stood. The Sennerinnen had come down to the valley some weeks before,
and, as none of the under-gamekeepers were out that
evening, he was sure the light could only be caused by
poachers who were making their fire. Rietsch was not
long determining what to do. Taking with him one of
his assistants who happened to be at home, they started
off for the mountain : there was a path all the way up,
so that, although it was night, they reached it easily;
besides they knew the road well, and had a lantern with
them. On arriving at the hut, they waited till all was
quiet ; no more smoke rose from the roof, by which they
knew that the fire was out and the men had lain down to
sleep. They still waited, when presently Rietsch with a
large stone dashed open the door, and both rushed in
together. Startled and confused, and waking up suddenly out of their first sleep, for a moment the poachers
did not know what to do, but directly after they instinctively reached out their hands for their rifles hanging
near. In their flurry they could not get their weapons
off the pegs ; nor did Rietsch and his companion give
them much time to do so, but charging down upon the
band with the muzzles of their guns, they soon overpowered them. They seized their rifles directly, and the
men surrendered, for unarmed they could do nothing.
There were three of them, and they begged hard to be
released, making the most solemn promises for their fu-
ture good-behaviour; but it was in vain : the next morning at daybreak Rietsch marched his prisoners down to
the head-forester's house.

Such events as these give a zest to the Jäger's life : they afford him the highest excitement, and he prefers, I am sure, a moderate number of poachers to having none at all. Would a sailor so love a sea-life were there no danger of tempest and wreck ? It is the *perils* of the deep that work the charm. It was the saying of a young gamekeeper—one whom the poachers had not spared, for he had been so beaten by them that he was nearly killed—" Without poachers a Jäger's life were nothing !"

In going along we met one of the keepers, who wished us good-day as he passed ; my companions told me that a few years ago this man had shot a poacher whom he met on the mountain, adding, " The ball struck him in the very middle of his forehead." He spoke of the circumstance as though it were a target at which his comrade had aimed.

From the Fall to the Vorder Riss the character of the scenery is profound sadness. At last the road leads through a pine-wood—almost black, so dark its colour ; when suddenly in the distance are signs of human habitation, of care and culture, and in another moment the house of the head-forester appears.

Opposite rise the Karwendel mountains, where the Isar has its source, and on the right the summit of the Zug Spitz is seen. It is a lonely spot, but the snowy peaks impart grandeur to all within sight of them, and in their sharp outline there is no monotony. Nor does the desolateness of the high mountains impart melancholy, as it is in keeping with the wildness ; the vastness of the forms around fills the mind ; their grandeur however does not overwhelm, but elevates it, and leaves no room for anything like fear or sadness. One feeling only you are unable to escape—it creeps upon and holds you like an inevitable fate, and you cannot shake it off,—a sense of the awful stillness amidst which you are.

As the forester was not at home, nothing could be decided on. I looked about me and chatted with the under-gamekeepers, one of whom had just brought home the good chamois I saw hanging from the paling on my arrival; among them too was a Solacher, brother to my friend Max and of the girls at Baierisch Zell, so with him I made special acquaintance.

"You must have a good depth of snow here in winter," I observed: "there is not much chance of getting out except with snow-shoes, I suppose."

"No, indeed," was the answer: "I have myself seen the snow thus high," pointing to a finger-post which was much taller than himself. "And you know in the Hinter Riss, if any one dies in winter, the peasants cannot even get out to bury the body."

"What do they do then?"

"They lay the corpse up in the loft under the roof, and it freezes as hard as a rock and remains quite unchanged. When the thaw comes it is carried to the churchyard and buried."

And there were antlers to be looked at, of stags shot that season,—the last indeed but the day before,—and questions enough to ask about the game, and the places where the stags were most plentiful. Here, as everywhere, the game had been greatly thinned; but chamois were still in the mountains, and on the cold mornings during the rutting season the low hoarse bellowing of the stags might be heard reverberating across the valley.

The right of chase here had belonged until lately to His Serene Highness Prince Leiningen, and nothing could be in finer order than this whole forest while in

his hands : all was done not only with princely magnificence, but with skill and even taste, and the arrangements were admirably adapted for a thorough enjoyment of the chase.   Up the steep wooded sides of the
mountains narrow zigzag paths were cut in various
directions, to enable the stalkers to move along more
stealthily when looking out for the stag.   On the different mountains snug hunting-lodges were built, where the
Prince and his friends would stay for weeks together in
the shooting season, thus avoiding the fatigue of descending to the valley when each day's sport was ended :
from these lodges to the valley a mule-path was made,
by which each morning fresh provisions were brought
up.   With his usual liberality he would allow a party to
take up their abode and stalk on one mountain, while
he remained on another opposite, and of an evening the
result of the day's sport was telegraphed across.

The road hence leads on to the Hinter Riss, lying in
the Tyrolese territory.   The Scharfreuter, upwards of
7000 feet high, forms here the barrier which divides the
Tyrol from Bavaria ; and beyond this again the Graben-
kahr lifts its massy shoulders 9000 feet from where you
stand.   In the Hinter Riss all is wilder; the mountains are less wooded and more craggy ; the dark green
of the pines gives way to the grey of the rocks, and
sharper lines and more abrupt forms are seen against
the sky.

On the morrow the forester returned, and he was kind
enough to propose that I should go out the same afternoon, and try if I could see a chamois towards sunset,
when they emerge into the more open places.   At three
o'clock therefore I and Xavier Solacher started.   We
crossed the Isar, and were at once on the Grass Berg,
which rises immediately over the river.   Though steep,

the narrow pathway cut in the side made the ascent easy
enough ; and as we looked upwards, or cast a glance almost straight down on the boisterous torrent, the value
of that little path was felt at once : similar ones were to
be found crossing and diverging from each other on all
sides, leading to the ledge of rocks or to some sheltered
nook, which could not otherwise have been approached
noiselessly.

Above us occasionally rose masses of bare rock, and
at their base was often such a green plot of herbage as
the chamois love to resort to at evening. Once we came
to a gully in the mountain-side, whence rose a confused
hum of waters, and a better place for a chamois could
hardly be found. Xavier told me he usually met one
there, yet now we scanned every part in vain.

We were nearing a turn in the path; Xavier was a step
or two in front. I heard something move on one side of
me, and a little in advance of where we stood. In order
that the slightest sound might not be heard, I stretched
out my pole to touch Xavier on the shoulder, that he
might stop, or at least move carefully ; but he rounded
the corner without being aware that I had heard something. Hardly had he done so when he started back,
and bending down, pointed to the spot whence I had
heard the gentle rustling, while I quickly moved forwards
to get a shot. A two-year-old buck was standing on the
edge of the steep, but before I could level my rifle he
was dashing downward among the bushes, to pass over
to the opposite side. At once I saw three together ; for
a moment one stood at gaze, and at the same instant I
fired.

"You have hit him !" cried Xavier: "he dropped at
once : now then, let us go and fetch him." So climbing
down the ravine across which I fired (called Speien Käs

im Korst Graben), and up the other side, we found the chamois hanging by his bent horns to a branch trailing near the ground. We cleaned him, the carrion crows croaking above us, and then turned homewards.

"I wonder you did not hear the chamois, Xavier," I said, as we went down the hill. "It is a pity you did not, for then we might have had the two-year-old instead; not that it much matters though."

"I don't hear as well as I did," he answered. "I was at the great festival at Munich this year, and shot in the shooting-match: the thousands of shots that were fired have almost deafened me; and though I now hear better, I have still a buzzing in my ears."

"Did you get a prize?"

"I believe I shall, but it is not settled yet. Most likely the second. Out of two hundred shots eight only missed the bull's eye, and of these five were fired at the running stag."*

"But, Xavier, if you don't get a prize with such practice as that, who could possibly hope for one?"

"Oh, there were many who shot better than I did. The first prize my brother Joseph will perhaps get."

I inquired about the game he had shot, and he told me that last year thirty-six stags had fallen to his rifle. This will give an idea of the abundance of game that formerly was on the mountains. He added, that one morning, when out early, he had counted seventy-five red-deer and a hundred and fifty chamois as he went

* This is a figure of a stag made of wood, and put on wheels running in a groove; on the shoulder is a target, with a red heart painted on it. At 125 yards from the spot where you stand are green bushes. The stag is drawn back out of sight, and at a given signal he runs by, and in crossing the open space between the bushes the target is fired at. As the animal moves along it has quite the effect of a real stag passing through the forest.

along; once at Tegernsee he had seen a hundred and seventy-five chamois together; and the average number of warrantable stags shot in each district every season was twenty-four.

The quantity in other parts must have been immense. A friend of mine, who was lately on a visit to Prince Lamberg in Styria, told me what the Prince himself related to him : that since the revolution not less than ten thousand head of game have, according to his computation, been stolen from his domain, consisting of red-deer, chamois, and roe-deer. To the English reader this seems hardly credible, but from the number known to have been there formerly, and what are now left, it is certainly not an over-estimate.*

These are exciting stories for the sportsman; they stir up all his latent longings, and something very like envy creeps into his heart as he listens to them. I have always thought how natural it is that the Indian should furnish *his* heaven with the rarest hunting-grounds.

The forester came out to meet us as we approached the house : he had heard my shot, and was curious to know the result. That evening we had a consultation about the proceedings of the morrow, and it was agreed I should try my luck on the Krammets Berg, as the surest place of meeting chamois.

"Yonder," said he, pointing toward the mountains in front of the house,—"yonder, below the ridge, are broad bare places, where in a morning you are almost sure of seeing something. Should nothing be there," he con-

---

* To give a proof that it is not so, I may state that the keepers found every year eight hundred pair of antlers, which the stags had shed. As the number not found is always considerable, some notion may be formed, from this circumstance alone, of the quantity of red-deer which must have been there.

tinued, speaking to Solacher, "then stalk up to the ridge, and so on to the Clam. In this way you will have chances enough, for chamois are always about."

The Krammets Berg was the best mountain of all, and I was very grateful to the forester for his kindness in allowing me a day's sport there.

CHAPTER XIII.

A DAY'S SPORT ON THE KRAMMETS BERG.

By half-past three the next morning I was downstairs, and while breakfasting, Solacher was busy with his frying-pan cooking the usual meal of schmarren. We were soon off. The stars were shining brightly, yet as we passed along the pine-wood I rather followed my companion by the sound of his voice and his footsteps than by the aid of sight. By the time we got to the foot of the Krammets Berg however the darkness was waning, and one by one the stars disappeared. The strange faint dimness, similar to that which hovers over the earth during an eclipse, began to spread; the gloom rolled back, and presently red tongues of brightness announced that day was at hand. The Zug Spitz first saw its coming, and flushed in growing refulgence over the still night-bound world. As the day streamed down its sides, the mists and vapours receded, and the mountain-tops came forth, rising from out the cloudy ocean below us as from the midst of the waters on the third day of creation. Soon the whole chain of the Tyrolian Alps was uncovered, and lay beaming before us in the first glad flush of the morning.

Above us, in the more immediate neighbourhood, the forms of things now grew more distinct. It was no wild spot nor much broken : here and there the latschen trailed along, sometimes in dense clumps and sometimes singly. In looking to the left amongst fragments of rock we saw a splendid buck : he was leisurely nibbling the buds of the green branches he found there, quite unconscious of our presence. Between us and him was a broad deep fissure, and all the intervening space was bare, so that to get near him unobserved was almost impossible, While looking at his fair proportions, and wishing that it were practicable to get even a long shot at him, he put an end to our hopes and speculations, by moving slowly away. Before doing so he turned his head in the direction where we stood, and lifting it high in the air gazed for a moment, and directly after was among the latschen. We saw him again at intervals, as he bore away to the opposite side of the mountain. It was very tantalizing, for it was a chance if we should see so good a buck that day. The older bucks are generally alone : they keep too in solitary nooks and inaccessible places ; and if at early morning they are with the herd, they leave it betimes to stray and feed alone.

"Look ! there are chamois !" said Xavier, pointing to the crest of the mountain a considerable distance to the right of where we were ascending. "Don't you see them ?—yonder, right up against the sky."

On the right were several black forms moving about, —now vanishing, then re-appearing. As we got higher we saw them quite distinctly even without the glass ; and it was a pretty sight to watch them as they disported themselves, leaping and bounding over the ground. When a stag is thus seen in bold relief against the blue background no sight can be grander : his majestic form appears of a portentous size, and as he tosses his antlers in the air they seem to shake the sky.

" We must keep away to the left, or they will see us," said Xavier. "There are many together, and no doubt more are lower down, although we don't see them from here: those above will soon be moving downwards. It is lucky we were off in such good time this morning; this is just the right moment for them."

"There will hardly be a buck among them, I fear: you can't make one out, can you?"

"No, as yet those I see are all does; but there may be one perhaps lower down among the latschen."

We now kept to the left, and passed over the shoulder of the hill, so that our heads might not be seen by them as we ascended in a line parallel with the spot where they stood. The latschen through which we crept were thick, and it was difficult to get along. Once on the ridge, we still remained on the other side, and so advanced, just keeping our heads below the sky-line. To do this is often not easy; for the face of a mountain on the northern and southern side is not only quite different, but the change begins from the very crest; on one side the surface being smooth and grassy, and on the other an abrupt and precipitous descent, with a ledge perhaps so narrow as scarcely to afford a footing. This ledge too is not flat, but steeply sloping; and if snow be lying on it, the difficulty and danger are pretty nearly on a par.

On we went, hardly daring to raise our heads, lest the chamois, which we knew must now be near, should see and be startled by our forms. Suddenly Xavier, who was a step or two in advance, dropped to the earth; I knew what that meant, quite as well as when, a second afterwards, he said, "There they are!" pointing to a deep rent or gash in the mountain's side. This yawning chasm, or *clam*, as such are called,* began just below

* The name of this one was the Röthl Clam, on the Stahl Joch.

the summit of the mountain, leaving the ridge unscathed. In this clam three chamois were feeding: they had not yet perceived us. I cocked my rifle and stole forwards, while Xavier watched behind. They were moving along one of those narrow ledges, on the face of the rock formed by the projecting strata, and as I advanced some acute sense told them danger was near, for they lifted their heads and listened. One began to retreat; I fired, and saw the ball had told. The others sprang forward, but a second shot brought another to a stand. Neither fell at once, but both were disabled: each one went some distance along a ledge of rocks, choosing, as they always do when wounded, the most inaccessible places.

I wanted to go down along the edge of the clam and, firing across it, finish at once the two wounded animals; but this Xavier opposed.

" No," said he, " leave them for awhile: it is much better. They are both in a bad condition, and by leaving them undisturbed they will get much worse. They won't go away from the spot, and perhaps presently we shall find them dead. If you go after them now, they will make every effort to get off, and as we have no dog with us it might not be an easy matter to track them through the latschen."

" By getting down yonder," I replied, " I might certainly be able to have a shot and finish them at once; true it is far, but I would sit down to take a steady aim. As to hitting them, I am quite sure about that."

" 'Tis further than you think," he replied; " besides if we leave them at once we can go after the others. These three are not the chamois we saw first."

" But they will have heard the shots, and are no doubt off by this time."

" No, they won't have heard them, for they are over

the shoulder of the mountain, and lower down.   Now
then, let us go."

I confess I did not like Xavier's plan, for it was most
painful to me to leave the chamois there, both badly
wounded, to suffer until we came back.   I honestly avow
I am not one of those excessively humane persons who
find cruelty in the chase.   To send a ball through a stag
or roebuck, and so take his life at once, does not give me
a pang, for I do not deem it cruel; although whenever
I stand beside an animal whose life I have just taken,
a sudden emotion within always keeps me silent.   The
taking life, the destroying that which only God can give,
seems a so daring deed; and, contradictory as it may
appear for a hunter to say so, my first feeling, as I look
at the heap before me, which but now was such a thing
for wonder, is to be astounded at what my hand has done.

For be it remembered that it is not in *killing* his
quarry that the hunter's delight consists, but in the excitement of the pursuit, in the varying chances, in the
" hope deferred," and above all in that crowning moment
when whispering to himself, " Now he is mine!"* *Then*

---

* In these verses from ' The Ballad of the Royal Hunt in the New
Forest,' some of these pleasurable moments have been referred to.

" Oh, that's delight to be in the greenwood,
    When all is solemnly still,
And there's hardly a breeze to move the leaves
    Atop of the wooded hill;

" And watch with expectant and longing ear
    For the merest coming sound;
And, breathless, at last hear a rustling step
    Move stealthily o'er the ground;

" And then to behold, with exulting eye,
    The creature with antlered crest
Emerge from a thicket, whose leafy boughs
    Give way 'fore his broad, brown chest;

M

is the real climax : in that short exquisite second *before*
the death,—before *quite all* has been obtained,—when
the prize, the reward of all your toil and risk, is surely
won, but not yet possessed,—*that* is the moment of the
highest joy. You fire,—he falls, and you are well pleased ;
but the sensation is tame compared to the subtle, qui-
vering intensity of what you felt before.

No true lover of the chase can he be, who estimates
his pleasure only by the number he has killed : 'The
Noble Arte' teaches another lesson.

Few things are more painful to the sportsman than
when, by some mischance or want of skill, he causes an
animal unnecessary suffering. Unfortunately the very
circumstance I am always so anxious to avoid was afterwards to happen with one of these chamois ; the saddest
to witness that ever occurred to me in my hunting ex-
periences.

Giving way to my companion I left the clam, and
going along the ridge above it, we crept softly down the
mountain-side, so as to get on a line level with the spot
where the chamois was standing. The latschen were
scattered about everywhere pretty thickly ; and it was
as difficult to get through the stubborn branches without their rustling or rebounding, as it was to see the
chamois, even when within shot of them. At last we
reached a spot where we could look upon a glade, as it

> " And watch how with caution he cometh forth,
>   And how in his pride of height
> He walketh erect o'er the sunlit sward,
>   Encircled in golden light.
>
> " And behold him then stand before you there,
>   In that still forest glade alone,
> Not a bow-shot's length from your own right hand,
>   *And to feel he is all your own.*"
>
>   *Verse*, by Charles Boner.

were, among the bushes ; and here they passed or paused a moment or two as they chased each other : it was a merry company. We lay flat on the ground, with our chins in a bush, and watched them.

"I dont see a buck; do you, Xavier?" said I.

"No, I hardly think there is one. It is almost too late now. But a doe is there," he continued, with his eye still to his glass, "with curious horns : one is upright, and the other grows forwards straight out of her fore-head.* Look," pointing with his glass, "don't you see that one to the right, half standing on a fragment of rock?—that is the one. It is a long shot, but you would hit it."

I looked and saw the curious growth, and wished to possess the trophy. But then too I longed for a buck—to get a fair shot at a buck—and still I hoped there might be one among the herd, and that I might see him before he made for the latschen. Thus was I divided in my intentions; and hesitation, whether in stalking or in the affairs of life, is sure to lead to no desirable result. While half resolving to make sure of the fine doe before me, the whole herd began to move. They must have got wind of us, for, gazing round, they were all out of sight in a moment. We went upwards again, and along the side of the mountain.

"Hush!" cried Xavier, "there's a chamois quite alone."

"Where? Is it a buck?"

"Yes, but make haste—it has heard us."

"Here, your rifle!" said I, holding out my hand to take his, the sights of which were very much finer than

---

* Strangely enough I saw these very horns again eight years later hanging up in the collection of his Serene Highness the Duke of Saxe Coburg-Gotha, when on a visit to Reinhardtsbrünn in 1857. Their peculiar growth struck me instantly, and on inquiring I learnt that the doe had really been shot on the mountain where I once had seen her.

mine; and as the chamois was far off,—a hundred and eighty yards for certain, I in this case preferred his to my own.

"Does it shoot high?" I asked, sitting down and resting my left elbow on my knee to take a steadier aim.

"No, where you aim there the bullet strikes; but hold it a little forward, for the wind is now coming up from below."

"As I have it now, the ball would graze his breast," I said, about to fire.

"That's right: you will hit him in the middle of the shoulder."

Bang! went the rifle. "He has got the ball for certain, no shot could go off better."

"You have not touched him," said Xavier, who had been watching the result through his glass: "the ball passed just before his shoulder: I saw it strike the bank behind him."

"Confound it, that's the effect of allowing for the wind! But for that I must have hit in the best place. Nothing on earth can fire truer than your rifle."

"Yes, I know it; but being so far, and as the wind is coming up from the valley, I thought it safer to make an allowance for the draught."

There was no use in being irritated; besides Xavier was so good-tempered and willing a fellow, that it would have been difficult for me to have continued angry long, had I been inclined. We kept along the ridge until we came to a descent: here we sat down to reconnoitre, and with our glasses examined the ground below. We soon espied a buck, as usual alone: he kept on the move for some time, always holding a downward course, and at last, to our great joy, lay down among some scattered latschen.

" Now, then, Xavier, will you try for him ?"

" Of course I will: he is certainly a good way off, and the ground is bad enough for stalking, but it is worth a trial at all events."

We noted well where the chamois lay, for though we could see the spot plainly from our eminence, we should soon lose sight of it on getting lower. It was to the left of a stony channel that the water had torn in the side of the mountain ; this therefore, and a pine about two hundred yards further off, were taken as landmarks. One more look, to be quite sure of the point to be gained, and we went down the steep. Broken as the surface was, I could not but think how admirably we both crept along. Not a stone rolled ; at each step the heavy-nailed sole came upon the ground like a paw of velvet ; neither of us made use of his pole, lest it might clink against the rock and cause a sound. Not once did we slip ; and when the ground was so uneven that we had to step lower than usual, each steadied himself with his hand, and then the descending foot was dropped gently to the ground. A woman's step in a sick chamber is not more lovingly gentle than was that of us two iron-shod male creatures.

We halted. Xavier made signs that he thought the buck must be yonder. Here were the stones the water had washed down, and there stood the tree. True, the place appeared quite different now to what it did from above, but still on looking round we felt sure this was the spot. We moved towards the latschen, and peered downwards into the space below, but no buck was there ; he must have gone away as we were coming down. As a proof that *we* had not disturbed him, but had done our work most cautiously, two does were lying not far off, just below us on a patch of green : had the buck been disturbed by us, he would, in dashing off, surely have caused them to move away also.

"Well, Xavier, now for the clam! How far may it be from here?"

"It will take us two good hours to get there: we have come a great way down, you see, and the clam is on the ridge."

"Is there no water near here?"

"Not a drop: do you want to drink?"

"Yes, my mouth is as dry as these stones. Shall we find no spring as we go along?"

"No, the only water is down yonder. It is not very near, but if you like I will run and fetch you some."

"No, no," said I, "let us go upwards; we have no time to lose."

The day was fine and the sun shining, but the heat, though oppressive in getting up the steep, would have been nothing if I could only have assuaged my thirst, which became almost intolerable. There was however no help for it but to go on; some hours more and we might perhaps be able to obtain drink.

"How far is it now?" I asked, breaking silence, for I had been chary of my breath and was choking.

"We have an hour's walk still," answered Xavier; and we went on again in silence.

Just before we reached the clam I stumbled on a puddle. The water, which was dirty enough, had collected in a hole in the mud about as large as both my hands.

"Ah, there's water!" I exclaimed, about to stoop and take a draught.

"You surely will not drink *that*," said Xavier, in a tone and with a look that seemed to say I was going to commit an abomination. His manner was such that I confess to the weakness of not doing as I wished and drinking of the pool.

Thirst is one of the severest trials to which the hunter in the mountains is exposed. To hunger he may get accustomed—as indeed he generally is obliged—but thirst *will* be assuaged, that *must* be satisfied. Meat is the worst thing he can take with him, for it increases his drought to an unbearable degree. Schmarren is found so admirable, not only for the facility with which the ingredients can be carried and the meal prepared, but also on account of its being very nourishing and not exciting thirst. The fatter the food the better; a roll with the crumb scooped out and a lump of butter put in its place, is as good a thing as any to take in your rücksack.

At last we reached the clam. We saw one of the chamois only on a projecting rock, beyond which it could not go. I determined now to do what I had before wished—to get on a line with the animal and give it one last shot. With this intention I therefore crept down along the edge of the clam, keeping myself as much hidden by the latschen as possible, in order not to cause the chamois to move. On coming nearer I saw that Xavier was right; it was really further across than I had thought. However the chamois must be had, and the only way to get the animal was to despatch it first. To climb further being impossible, I sat down where I was; and having been pleased with the precision of Xavier's rifle, I told him to give it me again, promising that this time the chamois should drop dead on the spot.

" Mind, 'tis downhill," he said, " therefore aim low. Besides there is a strong current of wind coming up the clam, and it is well to allow for that."

In the last remark there was, I thought, some truth;

for the rent in the mountain-side was as a funnel for the
wind, which at this hour of the day would of course be
from the valley upwards. So I took a deliberate aim
just below the shoulder, at the top of the right fore-leg;
according to my calculation the bullet should have lodged
in the very best spot on the shoulder.

"You have broken his fore-leg,—high up close to the
body!" said Xavier, who was watching for the shot
through his glass.

I was so vexed that I could have hurled the rifle into
the depth below me; not that it had failed in its duty,
for nothing could have surpassed it in precision, having
struck the animal on the exact spot at which I aimed,
but that I should be prolonging the creature's sufferings
—this was what incensed me; and venting my anger on
Xavier, who was in no way to blame, I said, "This is
the second time I have missed by following your advice."

The chamois had moved so as to be out of shot;
I therefore told Xavier I would go into the clam, manage to reach the chamois, and fetch it down.

"Stay here," he answered: "I will go across and
fetch it."

"No, I shall go; but you can go too if you like," I
replied.

"Indeed you had better stay," said Xavier; "you
don't know what it is: if you get into the clam, you
will hardly come out again."

"Nonsense, Xavier! why, look you—first down yonder
ledge, and then to the rock. It is not very easy, but it
may be managed. And once in the clam, we can climb
up the other side somehow or other. Now then, come!
I want to put an end to that poor beast's suffering."

"You had better not go," said Xavier, gravely, and
without moving a step: "you don't know what it is, I

assure you.   None of the gentlemen who have been out
stalking here ever went in.   Indeed you had better not,
—you cannot tell what it is till you are in it."

" Have you been there?" I asked.

" Yes, but it is an ugly place."

" Well then, come ;" and I cautiously moved toward
the spot I had before indicated, as the only place where
it was possible to get down into the chasm.   I saw that
Xavier did not at all like the expedition, and felt uncomfortable—on my account,—but he said nothing.   At last
we were in the bed of the clam, and a wild spot it was,
—much deeper too than I had believed, and wider ; and
jagged rocks, now that I stood beside them, were grown
to twice the size they had seemed before.   There was no
verdure anywhere,—all was sharp, bleak, grey stone.   It
was an uncomfortable feeling to look up at the blue sky,
and to *feel* yourself in an abyss of rock, with no visible
outlet by which to regain the living world ; for here was
no vestige even of life.   And what a stillness !

To get up the rocks where the chamois lay was indeed
not so easy as I thought.   Though none of them were
high, some were almost perpendicular, and every little
projection sharp as a needle ; but, what was worse than
all, each piece of stone that might have served to hold
by, or as a support to rest the foot on, crumbled away
beneath a moderate pressure ; so that if you placed your
toe or the side of your foot on such a little projection—
hardly broader perhaps than the face of your watch, but
still sufficient, if firm, to help you upwards—just when
you thought it might be trusted, and your whole weight
leaned upon the ledge, it would suddenly break like a
dry stick ; and if you happened to be some way up, you
came slipping down again, tearing your knees, while
your hands clutched at the sharp points to save yourself

from rolling to the bottom. To the bottom however you were sure to go, and the less the distance it was off the better. Presently we got up again, Xavier in advance, and soon after he was above me on a narrow ledge, and sprang thence to another small crag opposite.

The space to be cleared was nothing; but it required great nicety in landing properly on the crag, and in stopping the instant your feet rested on it, in order not to go over the other side. This pinnacle of rock was very narrow, and all below sharp and pointed. Xavier, with his rifle well up behind his back, and the pole in his right hand, was over in a second, and stood as firm and upright on his lofty narrow footing as though he had but stepped across. I doubted whether I could manage the jump: the opposite side was where the danger lay, for if I made the leap with only a little too much impetus, I should not be able to stop myself, and over I must go.

"Is there no other way, Xavier, of reaching where you now are, but by jumping over?"

"No," said he, examining the place, "you cannot cross except by jumping; it is not wide."

"No, but the other side—that's the thing: it is deep down, is it not?"

"Why yes, rather deep; but come, you can do it."

"I feel I cannot, so will not try," I replied, and began to look for some other way. The cleft itself, across which Xavier sprang, was only about twelve or fourteen feet deep; I was at the bottom of it, and while standing between the two rocks I thought I might manage to climb upwards, with my back against one wall and my feet or knees against the other, as a sweep passes up a perpendicular flue, to which this place had a great resemblance. My heavy rifle inconvenienced me, but still I contrived

to ascend.   I was nearing the top of my chimney, when
the chamois, seeing Xavier approach, leaped down into
the chasm below, so that we both had our trouble for nothing.   Coming down the chimney, it not being narrow
enough, I found to be more difficult work than getting up.

The chamois was now some distance lower than ourselves ; before going after it therefore we looked for the
slot of the one that had made off.   The traces of blood
on the rocks showed it had taken a direction that led
out of the clam.   Higher up was a much worse place
than where we had just been.

" It is very difficult to get out yonder," said Xavier.
" The chamois has gone there, and has probably stolen
away among the latschen."

" Have you ever been out that way ?"

" Yes, once," he answered : " I was up here one day,
so I thought I would see if there was a way out or not ;
'tis a terrible place, I assure you."

There was a broad, slanting surface of crumbling rock
where we now stood, like an immense table, one end of
which was lifted very high.   It seemed as if this must
lead out of the clam, or at least to a good height up its
side ; on this therefore I advanced cautiously.   The slope
did not end on the ground, but about twenty-five or thirty
feet from it, and then fell abruptly to the jagged rocks
below.   The plane was so inclined that to walk there was
hardly possible.   Every now and then the brittle surface
would crack off : however, difficult as it was, and in spite
of a slip or two, I managed to proceed.   At last I was
obliged to go on all fours.   Some minutes after I began
to slip backward.   The stone crumbled away as it came
in contact with my thickly-nailed shoes, which I tried
to dig into the rock, and thus stop my descent.   I strove

to seize on every little inequality, regardless of the sharp edges : but as my fingers, bent convulsively like talons, scraped the stone, it crumbled off as though it had been baked clay, tearing the skin like ribbons from my fingers, and cutting into the flesh. Having let go my pole, I heard it slipping down behind me, its iron point clanging as it went; and then it flew over the ledge, bounding into the depth below: in a moment I must follow it, for with all my endeavours I was unable to stop myself. I knew the brink must be near, and expected each second to feel my feet in the air. Xavier, who by some means or other had got higher, looked round when he heard my stick rebounding from the rocks, and saw my position. To help was impossible,—indeed he might himself slip, and in another moment come down upon me. He looked and said nothing, awaiting the result of the next second in silence.

I had made up my mind to go over the brink, and thought all was lost, when suddenly one foot, as it still kept trying to hold by something, was stopped by a little inequality, arresting me in my descent. I was very thankful, but still feared the piece of rock against which my foot leaned might crumble like the rest, and let me slip further. Hardly venturing to move, lest the motion might break it off, I gently turned my head to see how near I was to the brink : my foot had stopped not a couple of inches from the edge of the rock,—but thus much further, and I should have gone backwards over it. The depth of the fall was not enough to have killed me, but quite sufficient to break a leg or arm and a rib or two. Slowly and with the utmost caution I lifted my rifle higher behind my back, and, hardly venturing even to do so, drew one knee up and then the other, and again crawled forwards.

"Be careful," said Xavier, now for the first time breaking silence, seeing the danger was past; and he went on.

He presently called to me not to come further, to stand aside and look out for stones; and directly after one came leaping down and whizzing through the air. I went toward a wall of rock that rose upright beside the inclined plane above referred to, and hardly had I reached it when larger fragments of rock came leaping by me into the chasm below : they passed close before my face, and then for the first time I comprehended the terrific force of such missiles, and the havoc they are capable of causing in mountain warfare. They were pieces of rock that Xavier had detached in climbing upwards, and the impetus with which they came whizzing by made them bound back with renewed force from every object in their way, and shoot out far beyond the brink before they fell. They then swept on, out of sight, while the clam re-echoed with their rolling; but deep and oppressive as was the stillness of that yawning place, the silence thus broken had something discordant, something unearthly in it, and I was almost glad when the sounds died away in some distant hollow.*

At length I saw Xavier making his way back again. The chamois was not to be seen. We followed its traces some distance, first however binding up my torn fingers, in order not to confound the drops of blood falling from them with that of the chamois : we saw that it had got out of the clam, and was doubtless among the latschen. Without a dog we could then do nothing, for by this time the chamois had probably ceased to bleed; and to follow it by the slot alone on the hard ground, crossed

* The drawing facing this page is not a sketch of the clam in question, but there is much resemblance between the two.—C. B.

and recrossed by that of others which had passed there lately, would be impossible.

I forgot to say that, when slipping downwards, I had, in order to stop my descent, convulsively clutched at a piece of rock with my right hand, hoping to save myself. It came away like the rest; yet it caused a momentary strain on my shoulder, and seemed to jerk it out of the socket. For a second or two the arm fell helpless. I had now time to examine the limb, and finding I could lift my arm concluded all was right, and trusted that the pain would cease by the time we got home.

We now clambered down to the chamois : all was so jagged and broken that there was not a place broad enough to stand upon which was not sharp and cutting. At last however we reached him, and glad enough I was to know the poor animal was out of suffering.

On looking round for a convenient spot whither we might drag the chamois, in order to clean it before putting it in the rücksack, I espied drops of water dripping from a crevice. "Water! water! Xavier," I cried with as much delight as when Cortes first beheld the sea from a peak on Darien. A cup which we had with us was quickly fixed so as to receive the precious oozing fluid, and then, with the addition of a little rum from my flask, what a delicious draught did it afford !

"Here, Xavier, drink ! Was there ever such water ! How icy cold, and clear !" We sat down and ate a crust of bread, while fresh drops were welling into the cup, which we had propped up with stones. How exquisite was our repast ! and how strange all the features, deep down in that stony place, telling of a power which made you feel a crushing sense of helplessness !

The water came out of the solid rock drop by drop in a marvellous manner, as though Moses' rod had touched

the stone and made it yield us nourishment. It was very
like that ancient miracle; indeed I have many a time
thought that miracles still often happen to us, only our
thankless hearts fail to recognize them.

How strong and quickened we felt by our meal! and
Xavier relished the smack of rum in the cup of water as
much as his brother had done in the hut near Kreuth
over our evening fire.

"I will look after the chamois tomorrow, with the
dog," said Xavier: "there is no fear of our losing him,
he is badly wounded, and is, I dare say, not far off. But
now we must think of going homeward, for we have a
long distance to walk and it soon gets dark. Let me
see, where is the best way out?" he continued, examining
the steep rock: "up yonder I think we can manage it:"
and lifting the chamois on his back he at once set off.
But to get up a smooth rock with a dead weight of fifty
pounds at your back is not so easy; holding my pole
therefore for him to step on, and disencumbering him
of his rifle, which I handed up to him afterwards, he
mounted the rocks, and we were soon out of the clam
and on the green mountain-side. Now then homewards!

In a few hours' time we saw the forester's house
among the trees, and as we came nearer—yes, surely it
was no delusion—green arches erected over the road
that led thither; the doorway too was festively adorned
with green wreaths, and all looked gay enough. We
soon learned that the King had arrived; and the whole
house was in a bustle of preparation, getting the rooms
in order, preparing dinner, etc. etc. All were busied
sufficiently without having an extra visitor; so I determined to go on to the Fall that same night, and the next
morning walk to Hohenburg, a castle formerly the resi-

dence of his Highness Prince Leiningen, but now belonging to an acquaintance of mine. I therefore bade Xavier promise he would not fail to look after the chamois on the morrow, and, taking a glass of ale and a mouthful of bread, once more slung rücksack and rifle over my back and set off.

There was no time to lose; the evening was drawing in apace, and I had several miles before me. It was quite dark before I entered the warm room of Rietsch's house. Although I had that day been on foot for near seventeen hours, I cannot say I was desperately tired,— such is the invigorating effect of the mountain air.

CHAPTER XIV.

THE FALL. TO HOHENBURG AND KREUTH.

COMFORTABLY smoking his pipe, I found Rietsch sitting over a tankard of ale with a companion. Without asking his name I knew at once it must be Hohenadel. Before starting for the mountains a friend had said to me, "If you go to Glass Hütten, mind you see Hohenadel; he is an *Ur-mensch*"—a primeval man. And in truth many such are not to be found. He is very tall, broad-chested, sinewy-armed, and his muscular legs seem as though they could support a world; he certainly would stand more upright beneath the load than Atlas is always represented as doing. And yet, despite his height and evident strength, there is nothing clumsy or even heavy in the appearance of the man. His face wears a good-humoured expression, and gives the assurance that he is as peaceably inclined as though he had no advantage over his fellows. Woe betide him however whom he finds, rifle in hand, encroaching on his domain! Hohenadel is under-forester to his Royal Highness Prince Charles of Bavaria, and has before now carried down from the mountains a warrantable stag on his shoulders. Those who know anything about such matters, the weight of the animal, and the difficulty of stepping thus laden down a rugged steep, will understand

N

the arduousness of the task.   His knees trembled, it is
true, beneath the weight; he bore heavily on his staff,
and was obliged to rest from time to time; but—he
brought it down, and alone.

As I sat over my supper, chatting with him about the
chase, I asked how many stags he had shot in his life,
and how many chamois.

"Oh," said he, "of stags I kept no account, but chamois I know exactly;" and he named a number which,
no longer remembering it with exactness, I would rather
not indicate at all.   I could not but smile at the little
estimation in which he held the noble red-deer, when
put in comparison with his favourite chamois.

"A chamois!" he continued,—"ah, that is a different
thing altogether; there is nothing equal to a chamois.
I have heard a great talk of hunting wild animals in
America, and I don't know where besides, but after all
it can't be as fine sport as in our mountains.   For what
creature is there like a chamois?   As many as I have
shot in my time, there's no trouble, no risk that I should
think too great to get a shot at one. And what a pleasure
it is to watch them!"

I intended to start early the next morning for
Hohenburg, and to spend a day or two there; and
Rietsch wanted me to return in about a fortnight,
kindly promising that if I did so I should shoot a good
buck.

"By that time the rutting season will have begun,
and the old bucks be on the move; they will come
out of their lurking-places, and we shall be sure to
get a shot.   Only come," he said, "and if you were to
shoot a good buck in my circuit I should be right well
pleased,—only come."

Tempting as the proposal was, I was obliged to resist-

having arranged to return to Kreuth, if anything was to
be done there, to go out again on the mountains, and
then to visit the worthy old forester at Fischbachau.
By daybreak the next morning I set off, and in an hour
or two reached Hohenburg, rising a little over the picturesque village of Länggries. Never before, I think,
·did I so appreciate the "creature comforts" of this
life as now. After the detestably bad inn at Kreuth,
the broad, lofty corridors, the large cheerful bedroom
looking out upon the lawn, the neat arrangements, the
nicely served breakfast, and the observant attendance,
—mindful of everything, forgetting nothing,—all was so
delicious a change, that it seemed to me as if until that
morning I had never understood what such things were
worth. How did all that I had hitherto looked on as
mere common comforts now appear luxuries fit only for
a Sardanapalus !

My Sybarite reflections were suddenly put a stop to
by observing, in the mirror opposite, a projection on my
right shoulder which was not on the left one, and a
nearer examination really showed that one of the bones
which met at the shoulder-joint was out of its socket. It
was this which had pained me so when slipping down the
rock in the Röthel Clam, and the sudden helplessness of
the arm was now accounted for. Little could be done
however, and I left it as it was.

After some pleasant days passed at Hohenburg, I
took a guide to show me the path through the woods
to Kreuth. It poured with rain during the whole day.

"Just there," said my guide, a tall fellow who had
been a cuirassier, "a year or two ago I killed a good
stag. It was winter, and the snow lay very deep everywhere. We were coming up early, as usual, to bring
the wood down into the valley, and saw him stuck

fast in a snowdrift which was over his haunches.   I
got near him, and knocked him on the head with my
hatchet."

" But you might have helped him out, which would
have been much better."

" He was half-frozen," he answered, " and quite exhausted with struggling : he would not have got over it
if I had."

" And what did you do with him? Did you take him
to the forester ?"

" No, we kept him ; we divided him between us and
took him home."

" What ! you kept him !"

" Oh, at that time a stag was not so much thought of
as now. However it was the first and last time I ever
took one, though I might often have done so.   Yonder,
you see," he continued, pointing to a little declivity,
" was the place where they regularly crossed from one
wood to the other—one might have had a shot there any
morning ; and in passing the hollow way as usual, that
stag fell into the deepest part and could not go further.
In winter-time, up here in the woods, 'tis hard work to
get along, I assure you."*

---

* When the winters are severe, a great amount of game is sure to
perish.   It is not hunger only that they have to contend against : the
deep snow is also quite as frequently fatal to them.   In attempting to
cross it their slender limbs sink through the slightly-encrusted surface,
and, utterly unable to extricate themselves, they are at last frozen to
death or overwhelmed by a fresh fall of snow.   In the winter of 1854-
55 the following red-deer and chamois died from the above causes.   This
neighbourhood, be it observed, abounded in deer, it being one of the preserves of the present King of Bavaria.   In district Oberammergau, 30
good stags, 100 old hinds.   In district Buching, 13 good stags, 20 old
hinds, 64 calves, 9 chamois, 20 roes.   In another chase the remains of
30 head of game were found in the spring.   Chamois being so much
less heavy than a stag are less liable to immersion in the snowdrifts ;

" Have you much to do in the forest in winter?" I asked.

" Yes," he said, " when there's snow, and it is hard enough to bear, we bring down the wood that we cut in the preceding months, which it would be impossible to do at any other time; for there are no roads up here, and the paths are so stony that no cart could move over them. But as soon as we can make a *Bahn* (a smooth hard surface on the snow) we load the wood on sledges, and so bring it down the mountain."

" ' Tis hard work, is it not?" I asked.

" Ay, and dangerous too," he said : " such a load of wood is heavy, and on the smooth snow comes down with a rush : if you slip or fall, or cannot stop yourself, and the sledge goes over your leg, it is broken in a moment : some accidents are always happening."

" But in summer it must be a right pleasant life, out in the forest all day long, and living on the mountain. You stay up there the whole week, do you not?"

" Pleasant enough it is," he said, " but 'tis hard work ; and in felling the trees, seldom a summer passes without one or other of us being hurt,—a foot or an arm crushed by the stems as they fall, or something of the sort."

" And how are you paid?" I asked.

" That depends : sometimes thirty-six, sometimes forty-two kreutzers a-day.* But 'tis a long day from four

they moreover manage matters very skilfully when crossing such beds not yet hardened by frost. They spread their hoofs as far apart as possible, thus providing themselves for the nonce with a pair of natural snow-shoes ; they often too will bend back their haunches so much that the whole of the hind legs up to the knee rests *flat* on the snow.

* 1s. or 1s. 2d. a day. But at present (1851) the six-pound loaf of excellent bread costs 24 kreutzers, or 8d. English. In the spring it was so low as 4d., and for a short time even it cost 12 kreutzers, or 3¼d.

o'clock till dark. We begin at three, for it is light then in summer; and by the time we reach our hut in the evening, what with the air and the work, we are glad enough to cook our supper and lie down to sleep."

"And you have nothing but your schmarren," I said, —" schmarren and water?"

"Nothing but schmarren; always schmarren and good fresh water. If we had beer or anything else but water we should not get on at all for thirst. On a Saturday night, when we come down to the valley, and then on the Sunday, we drink a can of beer or so, but the whole week through not a drop. But the water we get is capital."

"And on Sunday I suppose you have meat for dinner."

"Meat!" he exclaimed, quite astonished; "why none of us ever touches meat from one year's end to another, except may-be at the village wake and at Christmas."

"And how much fresh butter does a man want in a week—five pounds?"

"Why yes, about five pounds I think; that is as much as would go into my wooden box, which I take with me every Monday morning, and by Saturday evening it is nearly or quite empty. For you see by about six or seven o'clock in a morning we are glad of our breakfast, so we make a fire and cook some schmarren; at eleven we have our dinner; and then about four we eat something again, and before we go to bed the frying-pan is on the coals once more. All that, you know, takes a good piece of butter every day."

The huts which these woodcutters inhabit during their summer stay on the mountain are log-huts of the roughest construction. Such buildings are just high enough to stand upright in,—indeed sometimes it is not

possible for a tall man to do so; but this is not necessary,
for when in the hut they are either sitting round the
stone hearth in the centre of the dwelling, cooking and
eating their meal, or else lying down on their bed of dry
leaves and straw. As there is no chimney in the roof,
nor any opening beside the door or window, all within
becomes in time quite black, as though the great logs
were charred by the flame. Yet in a storm, or at dusk,
the sight of such a poor place of shelter is greeted with
a heartier welcome than we ever bestowed on the most
luxurious hotel: its low door, as we push it open and see
the cheering blaze, seems then the portal of a palace.

The dwellings in the mountainous parts of Bavaria are
also very different from those of the flat country : they
somewhat resemble the cottages of Switzerland, and, in
the same manner, harmonize remarkably with the scenery amid which they are placed. So much indeed is
this the case, that for their particular style of architecture the mountains seem a necessary background; the
two belong together: indeed the mountains are here as
necessary to complete their character, as the landscape
background is indispensable to the figures in the Peter
Martyr of Titian.

Put any other building of brick or stone in these valleys, and the discord, so to speak, will be immediately
felt. As it is, the eye finds the gently-sloping lines of
the low roof—so low indeed that all its surface is discernible—again repeated in the bolder outlines rising up into
the sky : there seems an affinity between them, and there
is just enough connection to make them component parts
of a well-ordered whole.

The same feeling which guides a painter in the composition of his picture, which urges the removal of uncongenial forms, which strives after unity by the harmonious

blending of the parts,—an intuitive sense of the beautiful, in short, which when put in action becomes Art—this
feeling it is, which, unconsciously to himself, has guided
the mountaineer in the construction of his picturesque
dwelling.

Unpretending, simple as they are, even with all their
rustic adornings, they never fail to be admired by the
stranger. The pleasing effect they produce on every be-
holder arises, in no small degree, from their displaying
no disparity between end and means: on the contrary, a
sense of perfect purpose is experienced as you look at
them; both the forms and the construction seem to have
sprung naturally from the material employed. And they
did so: their arrangement was dictated by the various
wants and habits of the peasant, and by the climate of
the country; their construction was in accordance with
the material used, and adapted to the simple tools, mechanical contrivances, and particular architectural knowledge, which the self-taught peasant had at his disposal
in building his dwelling. Growing up in this way,—
taking a form according to the man's necessities,—not
hiding, but rather displaying, the homely material which
nature had provided for it,—such a building could not
fail of being impressed with a decided character. There
is no endeavour to conceal the simple woodwork, or to
make it appear of some more valuable stuff than it
really is; nor, above all, are forms or a construction attempted, characteristic of, and legitimately belonging to,
some other material. The house always looks what it
is, *the house of a peasant built of wood*, fetched perhaps
from the neighbouring forest; nor does it pretend to be
anything more.

With the ornamental part of these buildings it is the
same. Here "ornament" is no extraneous thing, but be-

longs exclusively to, and springs naturally from, this style
of architecture. Hence the circumstance that these buildings have a peculiar and decided expression, as much and
exclusively their own as that which marks the Greek,
Moresque, or Pointed style of architecture. The protru-
ding beams naturally suggest a rounding off into a more
pleasing form ; in the far-projecting water-spout is an opportunity for carving some animal's head and throat; and
where the converging lines of the gable meet, they are
allowed to run on, and crossing each other to present an
additional occasion for the introduction of some characteristic decoration.

Colouring too is often used ; the shutters of the lower
windows will be pranked with a bright centrepiece, while
the balcony and the carved design that gives such a finish
to the projecting gable, will wear perhaps a more sober
brown.

There is a great variety in these houses, yet every orna-
ment, however rude in execution, is always appropriate
to, and in harmony with, the dwelling it is intended to
adorn. The style of ornament too is always dictated by
the material in which it is to be executed.

It is not a little remarkable that these houses are constructed according to the most scientific rules. Necessity has here proved an excellent teacher : the parts are
put together with a mechanical knowledge which, as I
have learned from an experienced architect, is not to be
improved on. Within they are dry and warm ; they have
an air of comfort too, and in passing one of them you
think it must be pleasant to dwell there, and snug and
freundlich within ; and even should you not see a bright
winsome face at the window, the forehead and brown
braided hair shaded by the brim of the green hat, with a
golden tassel pendent from it dancing in the sun,—still,

without such inducement, you feel that you would much like to enter there*.

My guide now pointed to a high peak on our right : "A year or two ago," said he, "a peasant was lost up there : he went out on the mountain, and never came back."

"Out poaching, I suppose—eh ? "

"Yes, he was out with his rifle, and alone. For three whole days his friends—a band of them—scoured the mountain in search of him, but could find nothing. They knew he had gone there, because he said he intended doing so; besides, the last time he had been seen alive was by a boy who met him on the way; but with all their trouble they discovered nothing.

"And what did they think had become of him? " I asked.

"Oh, no doubt he was shot, and the body hidden somewhere. A mountain, to be sure, is a large thing; yet if he had slipped down anywhere, some trace of him would surely have been found, for every part was searched day after day, and I know not how many there were out looking for him. They were in a great rage, suspecting he had been shot; and if they could have had the slightest proof of this against any of the gamekeepers, they would have taken a terrible revenge."

At last we saw Kreuth below us, while crossing the

---

* Should the reader of these remarks be curious to know the cost of such buildings, it is to be computed thus: one florin per square foot contained in each story, and half as much for the construction of the roof. Thus a cottage forty feet long by thirty broad, and one story high, would cost as follows:—40 × 30 = 1200 florins for the ground-floor; the same for the first story, 2400 florins; which, with 600 for the roof, makes 3000 florins, or £250 for the whole building. For this sum it could be built with a certain finish and with all the decoration usually found in such cottages. The foundations are always of stone.

oozy meadows on the hill-side; and, soaking as we both were, the smoke that crept lazily upwards through the misty rain from the chimney of the inn was a welcome and cheerful sight. I had a warm meal set before my guide; and as the days were now short, and it was important he should reach home before it grew dark, he soon set off on his way back. My first visit was to the forester's house, where I learned that Max Solacher had shot a good stag the day before, and was now out on the mountain looking after poachers. Shots had been heard, it seems, in the direction where we had been lately, and Maxl was off at once after the invaders. Woe betide him who comes within reach of his rifle, and alone!

The stag was one of twelve, and had he been shot earlier would have been a splendid prize. But now, his lank shrunken sides made me doubly regret the necessity of thus killing everything, whether in or out of season.

On Monday it rained; on Tuesday I went out again with Max, but could not get a shot. It was afternoon, and we were going slowly upwards, when close above us we saw five men, each with a rifle at his back. Down we dropped behind a block of stone, to watch them. They were going along one behind the other on a narrow path, and talking loudly.

"Do you know them?" I asked Max, who was examining them attentively.

"Three of them I know, but I cannot make out who the two others are. Let us go on, and see what they intend to do."

We proceeded accordingly,—at first, on account of the unbroken surface of the ground, keeping below and parallel with them, but afterwards following in their very footsteps. Sometimes we waited to let them pass on, and

only when they were a considerable distance in advance
did we rise up from behind a low bush where we had been
lying, and go after them again. Once, on coming to a
ridge, we lost sight of them. Before us was a vast hollow,
broken here and there, and partly filled with high latschen. We sat down, and peered around for them in
vain. Yet they had passed there, for we distinctly made
out their trail upon the ground. Presently an unusual
sound rose on the air, and came floating up from the dark
hollow—it was their voices; and we now saw them going
up the other side, where they all sat down, while one
took out a glass and examined the slopes above which we
were sitting.

"He is looking at us," said I to Solacher.

"No, he could not distinguish us where we are; besides the others are talking and laughing," he continued,
still looking through his glass, "and if he had perceived
us they would *all* be looking this way."

When they moved we rose and followed, till at last
they stopped at a hut built on a clearing of the mountain: just below them lay a tree, blown down by the
wind; behind this we took up our position, so near that
we could almost hear what they said.

"I see!" said Maxl, "they intend stopping there to-
night, to be ready betimes tomorrow morning. Ha, ha!"
he exclaimed, "the door is locked and they can't find
the key." The men were evidently hunting for something in all directions. Some climbed up and searched
beneath the eaves, while another felt in holes and corners
where the missing object was likely to be. At last it was
found, and they all disappeared within the hut.

The right of chase in that neighbourhood, Max told
me, belonged to the parish within which the men dwelt;
there was however little doubt they would not be very

scrupulous about overstepping their boundary, if a chance of getting something presented itself.

From our covert we had a full view of the hut: the men had cooked their supper, and came out and sat under a tree to enjoy themselves: one went and fetched a pitcher of water, and set it down in the midst of them. Maxl all this while was abusing them between his teeth to his heart's content, and muttering all sorts of maledictions upon their heads. This however was not so much for what he then saw, as on account of what in imagination he saw them doing on the morrow; he knew very well that they would not stand on much ceremony about boundary-lines and limits; and even should they not shoot any of his game, their very presence disturbed the chamois, and perhaps drove them over to the adjacent territory, and once there they became lawful booty.

A constant warfare is unceasingly carried on between these two classes of men; their reciprocal hate never slumbers, any more than their ingenuity in devising plans of vengeance against each other. Seven years ago a keeper whose game had suffered considerably from repeated depredations, and who had been unable, in spite of all his endeavours, to overtake the marauders, hit upon the following contrivance to work them injury. He knew that when they were out on the mountain they generally took shelter in a certain hut, where they made a fire and cooked their meal. He therefore procured a bomb, filled it with powder, and buried it in the hearth a little way below the surface. He hoped that by the time their schmarren was cooked, and the men were sitting round the fire enjoying its warmth, the glowing embers would have ignited the combustible mass and caused it to explode: cowering as he knew they would be round the blaze, he rightly judged the effects would be tremendous. The forester was disappointed however; the men came and kindled their fire as usual above the spot where the bomb was hidden, but from some cause or other, from being too deep perhaps, no explosion took place.

"I'll take good care they shall not get much here, at least," said Max; and cocking his rifle, both barrels thundered one after the other, and broke for some minutes the quiet of the still evening scene. "If any game is on my side of the mountain, it will be off now," said he; "and if they want a chamois they must go on their own ground. But look how astonished they all are at hearing a shot so near them!" And then, after waiting a few minutes to see what they would do, we went leisurely downwards to the valley.

CHAPTER XV.

BAIERISCH ZELL.

On leaving Kreuth I started once more for Fischbachau, and it was with sincere pleasure I looked forward to finding myself again the guest of the worthy forester. I should also be glad to pay the Solachers a visit, and tell them I had met their brother; to pass again a pleasant evening in their comfortable dwelling, and see once more that sweetest picture of maidenhood, the gentle and blushing Marie.

From Berger I heard that the chamois had re-appeared; he had seen several during my absence, and had besides tracked a good stag near the spot where we had met the deer on the first day of our going out. He felt sure we should be able to get a shot or two, and this assurance made me all the more anxiously long for the rain to cease and the weather to clear up. But still it kept pouring down, and the whole of Saturday and Sunday not even a glimpse of blue sky was to be obtained. On Monday afternoon all changed; the thin vapoury mist which had filled the atmosphere was swept away; in the direction of the plain glimpses of brightness were discernible, and soon the crests of the mountains showed themselves with sharp outline in the now clear air. All wore a cheerful aspect, and buoyant with hope I set off

for Baierisch Zell, intending to pass the night at the Solachers' cottage, in order to be out betimes the following
morning.

When thus setting out for the chase after a long im-
prisonment, a delicious feeling of gladness, an elasticity
of heart and limb, possesses the whole being: it is an
exquisite sensation. *Your* nature feels the sweet influences as much as the external nature around you. The
refreshing, softening rain, that has filled every valley
with a humming sound, makes your heart leap like
those rivulets; the blue sky above you seems to have
pervaded your mind with its serene colouring, just as it
reflects itself in the glittering landscape, still trembling
with rain-drops, and sheds over it a peculiar azure brightness. Expectation is rife, and as you chat with your companion while stepping lightly along, pleasantest thoughts
rise with the hopeful excitement; for as to the chances
which you feel sure are before you, why you would not
cede them for a kingdom. Every trifle contributes to
your delight: it is a pleasure even to be so well shod,
and to defy the water and the pointed stones; you exult
in your strength, and in the feeling of independence
which that, and a firm heart, and your good rifle give
you. The very obstacles you meet on your path produce a pleasurable sense of power to overcome them.
The smell of the moistened earth, and the gum-like ex-
halations of the pine-forest, are more grateful to you
than all the odours of Araby the Blest.

As we went along, I asked Berger about the elder of
the brothers Solacher, and how he was so badly wounded
by the poachers. I knew he had been disabled by them,
but all the attendant circumstances I had never heard,
or had forgotten them.

"That happened," said Berger, "about an hour's walk

from Schlier See. A great number of the foresters had
had a rendezvous, to watch for poachers. I don't know
how many there were, but from all the neighbouring
forests some came—from Tegernsee and Baierisch Zell,
Schlier See, Kreuth, and Fallep. There were altogether
fifteen Jäger. They had already been out three days,
and it came on very bad weather, with pouring rain. It
was useless staying out any longer, so they separated to
go home. The others had gone some distance, when
Joseph Solacher and an assistant-forester who was with
him heard a shot. They both ran forwards as fast as they
could to where the report came from, and said, 'There
are those rascally Kranzberger boys* shooting again ! but
we have caught them now, and they shall repent it.'
The Kranzberger boys were two youths who lived in a
hut not far off, and who, it was known, used whenever
an opportunity offered to carry on poaching in a small
way. Well, as I said, Joseph, and Bauer, who was with
him—you know Bauer, don't you? a fine handsome
young fellow as you would wish to see—he and Joseph
ran forward, and when they came to the brow of the hill
they heard some one loading a rifle, ramming the ball
into the barrel, and a moment after saw before them,
about eighty or ninety yards off, the two fellows standing
over a roe they had shot. It was a little green spot,
with a tree or two on it, and not too far,—just a good
shot from where Joseph stood. But he did not want to
fire at them ; he thought he would take away their guns,
and give the young fellows a sound thrashing, and then
send them about their business. So, as I said, he did

* In the mountains the word "boy" ("Bube," or in the dialect "Bua,")
does not always imply one in the age of boyhood, but is used when
speaking of young men generally, as Burns does the word " lads," which
is equivalent to it.

not fire, but went round, to be able to get nearer before
he sprang forward to lay hold of them; for by going
round the little mound where they stood he could steal
close up to them unperceived.   They must have heard
something however: for at the moment that Joseph
showed himself and was going towards them, one of the
poachers—for Joseph now saw it was not the boys,
as he thought, but two men—snatched up his rifle to
fire."

" They must have been quite close to each other, were
they not?"

" To be sure they were, quite close; perhaps eight or
at most ten yards apart.   If Joseph had not felt sure
that it was the Kranzberger boys he would have been
more cautious, you know, and not have exposed himself;
but he thought for certain it was they.   He had gone
round, on purpose to get quite close up to them before
seizing them.   Well, directly he saw the man level his
rifle at him, there was nothing left him, unprepared as
he was, but to spring behind a tree which was close by.
Just as he did so the poacher fired.   Joseph gave a turn,
but he thought the ball had hit the stock of his gun,
which he still had at his back, and it was that which
caused the shock he felt; and he was going to lay hold
of his rifle, in readiness lest one of the fellows should approach, when he found he could not move his arm.   It
hung down quite helpless like a dead thing, and then only
he discovered that he had been shot.   At the moment
he had not felt it at all. Turning to Bauer he said, ' My
God, Bauer, they have hit me !' Both stood behind the
tree for a while, but Joseph naturally could do nothing
with his shattered arm.   At last he said to Bauer that
the pain was so great he could not bear it any longer, and
that come what might he must go.   The others heard all

he said, for you know they were quite close, behind another tree at most seven yards off. Bauer told him to go,
and he would watch the others ; and if one of them moved
forward to fire, he would let fly at him the same moment.
Joseph went off, and they did not attempt to shoot at
him. As he went along he ate a mouthful of gunpowder,
and got safe home at last."

" And what did Bauer do afterwards ?"

" He kept where he was behind the tree, with his rifle
raised the whole time, ready to take advantage of the
least movement of the poachers which should present
never so small a mark to aim at. Once he thought,
if he took great care and was very steady, he might
hit one. He only saw a part of his head : he fired, and
shot the poacher's cap off. The bullet just grazed the
tree in passing, so little did the man's head project beyond it ; but Bauer thought he might manage to hit him,
and, you see, he very nearly did so."

" Well, but how did the affair end ?"

" Oh, there they remained opposite each other till it
grew dark, and then they went off : for in the dark,
you know, neither could see to fire at the other in
going away. The next day they found the roebuck and
the cap lying on the ground, and saw where the bullet
had grazed the tree. Joseph's arm was shattered above
the elbow, and it is the greatest wonder that he did not
lose it entirely. He cannot use it much, but it is better
than having none. It is stiff and very weak ; but being
the right arm, he can still shoot with a rifle, which he is
very glad of."

At the Solachers' all were at home, and Joseph the
elder brother too, who had returned from Munich, where
he had been when I was last at his cottage. He had got
a prize—the first if I remember rightly—consisting of a

o 2

most splendid flag, besides a sum of about £6. The
flag was of blue silk, with the royal arms embroidered
in relief in the centre, and bordered with silver fringe
and tassels.   It was a trophy that any one might have
been proud to carry off.

Though the severe fracture of Joseph's arm had been
cured, so as to enable him still to fire at a target, it
had caused a lameness in that side of the body, and
the right leg was weak and palsied.   He had received
a pension for his services, and now lived with his
sisters and aunt on the little estate, which, though
small, was his own.   The girls all welcomed me with the
kindest greeting, and right pleased was I to be again
among them.

Note.

IT may be well to give some account of the way in which the shots are reckoned at these shooting-matches. The target is eighteen inches in diameter; the bull's-eye six. This latter however is marked with three circles, equidistant from each other. A shot in the innermost circle counts four, in the next three, and so on; while any out of the bull's-eye is not counted at all. The very centre of the target is marked by a small copper pin, and only those whose balls have touched this can have a chance of a prize. When the shots of two or more persons are of such equal pretensions as to make it difficult to decide on the priority of their claims, a fresh target is set up, and a single shot fired by each is the ordeal they have to undergo.* The usual distance at such matches is 125 yards; and the length of the barrel of the rifle is not to exceed 30½ inches in length, nor are the bullets to be fewer in number than twenty-four to the pound. It was good shooting therefore of Xavier Solacher to hit the bull's-eye 192 times out of 200 shots, and of these eight which he missed more than the half were fired at a moving target.

As each shot is fired, the hole in the target is stopped with a wooden plug, having a number on it. This number is then entered in a book, and opposite it a 1, 2, 3, or 4, according as the ball was in one of these rings. On a second paper, which each person who takes part in the match has in his pocket, is also inscribed the number of the ring. When all is over, and after the prizes are awarded, the stakes are divided, as well as the money paid for the shots; for I should have remarked that the stakes enable you only to a limited number of shots, and all above that number must be paid for extra, generally six kreutzers, or twopence each. The

---

* At a shooting-match at Partenkirchen I saw a young forester strike the point, drilling a hole through the very centre of the target. But as there was another who had as good a shot to show, he determined to decide *at once* who was to be conqueror, and had a fresh target put up for that purpose. He fired, and his bullet again cut a hole in the centre of the inner ring, and this time so exactly in the middle as if it had been marked out with a pair of compasses. The other was less fortunate. There was of course some chance in thus firing two such shots in succession.

whole sum thus obtained is added together, and also the number of circles entered in the book; one is divided by the other, and the result
shows how much can be given for each ring on the target.   Thus, if I
fire a hundred shots, and hit the bull's-eye seventy times, sometimes in
the third or fourth circle, so that I count altogether one hundred and
seventy rings, and if on inspecting the money in hand it is found there
is enough to pay 10 krs. for each ring, I should get for my seventy shots
30 fls. 40 krs., or something more than £2. 10s.

To add to the gaiety of the festival, the targets are so constructed that
when the head of the pin in the centre is struck a cannon goes off, and
the figure of a Tyrolese, or perhaps a pair of flags, suddenly rise up
from behind.   The marker at the target has generally some fantastic
costume, and when you have hit the very centre he plays all sorts of
antics, as if for joy; and while bringing the target to the umpires, dances
and shouts exultingly, knowing that he will receive a small present from
the lucky marksman.   Altogether it is a merry scene.

CHAPTER XVI.

ON THE MOUNTAIN.

WE were up and ready long before dawn, and Nanny
with her accustomed kindness had prepared my breakfast, and stood by and chatted with me while I drank
the excellent coffee which was her making, well pleased
that I found all so good. It always caused me pleasure
to see her bright intelligent face, and the *patois* in which
she spoke gave, to me at least, an additional charm to
her lively, sensible talk.*

"Joseph is going with you today," she said, "he will
like to accompany you if you have no objection."

"Of course not; I shall be very glad to have him.
Who would not like to have a Solacher with him on the
mountain?" And so she thought too in her heart, I
know; for though the last part of her sentence was added
for politeness, she no doubt deemed—and was quite right
in doing so—that the gain and the honour were entirely
on my side. It always pleased me to see the love and
pride with which these girls invariably spoke of their
brothers. There was all the sister's affection, all the
genuine woman's pride, in being able to talk of them
as *their* brothers. It was a theme they never tired of

---

* "A sort of Doric dialect," as Humphrey Clinker says of the Scotch,
"which gives an idea of amiable simplicity."

listening to, although they never began it; but if *you*
spoke of them, their countenances betokened satisfaction, and they would say perhaps, " Yes, all the gentlemen like to go out with Maxl;" or, " Xavier is a good
boy, and a good hunter too : he's a sure shot, and has
won a prize this year at the great shooting-match." And
when Joseph brought home his richly-embroidered flag,
they were more pleased and prouder of it than if he
had bought each of them a bright kerchief or a boddice
worked with silver.

" Nanny," said I, " you promised me a flower for my
hat, and you have not given me one yet."

" Ah, ah ! because you cannot get one of the younger
sister you come to me; is not that it?" she said archly.

" No indeed, my good girl, it is not so. It would, I
know, be useless for me to ask Marie to give me a flower,
though there is some one else, I think, who would not
ask in vain."

" Well, I'll see if I have one," she said ; and giving
her my green hat, she went to her own room, and soon
returned with a bright flower stuck jauntily beside the
tuft of hair from the throat of a stag and the downy
feathers that were already there—decorations in which
the mountaineer takes no little pride.

Joseph, Berger, and myself now started, taking our
way through the meadows and long wooded slopes, all
dark, and solemn, and indistinct, despite the innumerable stars. We went towards the Miesing, and soon
after daybreak were already a good distance up the
mountain. Nothing was to be seen save a doe with her
kid. We crossed a field of snow, and Berger, creeping
forward to the ridge that overlooked a profound depth,
started back suddenly, exclaiming in a whisper, " There
are chamois !" They had seen him however, and were

already on the move. I ran forward to meet them, and
as they came on but slowly, to get ahead of them was
not difficult; then lying down at full length, with my
left arm resting on the ground, and the rifle pointing
almost perpendicularly downwards over the rocks, I took
a steady aim. I was in no hurry, in no fever of excitement, but quite calm; and, though the shot was a long
one, feeling quite confident in my rifle, and certain I
should hit the mark. I knew perfectly well that, firing
downwards, I ought to aim *low*; and yet, instead of
doing so, by some strange unaccountable perversity I
aimed *high*; and purposely so, conscious all the while of
what I was about. I fired, and the ball went just over
the animal's back. There was no excuse for having
missed; it was all owing to my own stupidity, and this
only made the matter more vexatious and provoking.
After the shot they turned back, and we counted eight
as they passed along far below us. With our glasses we
discerned a buck and a doe a great distance off: we determined to try our chance of approaching them, and
looked for a place where we might get down the rocky
steep. Good practice it was too, coming down that
Handsheimer Eipel Spitz! Joseph, on account of the
weakness of his right arm, was carefully searching for a
spot where, under such circumstances, he could manage
best. Berger and myself tried elsewhere, and began to
move carefully over the ridge. At first sight this seemed
hardly possible, so abrupt was the descent. Snow too
was lying here and there, making the little projections
on which it rested a very slippery, unsure footing, and
there was nothing to hold by, no support save the iron-
shod pole which we carried with us.

To come down the rocks is always more difficult than
to climb up them. As you invariably descend with your

back to the steep, and consequently looking forwards and below you, the terrible depth is all the time before your eyes: in mounting this is not the case; and though, if you are so unwise as to think about it, you know there is a precipice at your back, it is however unseen. Carefully and steadily then down you go, your feet forwards, your body sloping back, and your trusty pole grasped with both hands, and firmly planted behind you.* Every coming step must be decided on beforehand. "There," you say, " the right foot can be placed, and on that point the left: yonder grows a solitary latschen; if I reach it I may then hold on and let myself down to the bit of rock below, and once there the rest will be somewhat easier." Now, your companion, who is below you—and two can always get on better in the mountains than one —drives the point of his pole into a crevice, and holds it horizontally for you to step upon; or you plant yours upright, and keeping it so, he holds by it while letting himself down over a slope of rock, whose surface is so smooth and steep that not even a cat could pass there; and when he is down he returns you the same good office, as, lying on your back with your feet in his hands, you slide slowly downward till you have found a footing.

Joseph was at a distance, among the thick branches of some latschen, and by their help he got on famously. We crept silently to a sharp rocky ridge, and looked over.

"They are still there!" whispered Joseph; "now which is the best way of getting near them? That buck is worth having."

After reconnoitring the ground, it was arranged that

---

* In going *up* hill you always have it *before* you. If the ascent is so steep as to oblige you to take a zigzag course, you plant it beside you about on a level with your hips, the upper part pointing outwards;

Berger should remain where he was, while Joseph and myself passed along the ridge, keeping our heads just below the sky-line, and go on thus till we reached some latschen ; then creeping quietly through these, advance as near as possible to where the buck lay at rest, and fire. We reached the first latschen, and still the chamois remained where they were, as Berger signalled to us. Joseph went first, winding himself through the stubborn branches with all haste ; for when we had gone half-way a huge volume of mist rose suddenly from the valley, and we saw it, in thick folds, advancing with threatening speed. Once over that stony spot where the chamois were, and he knew they would be snatched from our sight ; therefore it was that he made such precipitate haste, causing him to be less cautious than he would otherwise have been. The elastic branches, instead of being put gently, almost lovingly, aside, rustled as he pressed through them, and the chamois heard it.

" Be quick !" he said, " or we shall be too late ; the mist is sweeping on fast."

And just as we reached the edge of the latschen, the vast form, indistinct in outline, but of gigantic stature, trailed past. The chamois were already gone, and we afterwards saw the buck some hundred yards before us, making for the fastnesses where he knew none could follow him. He walked slowly, stopping every few paces to look back, and then uttering a shrill whistle went on again.

Right trusty friends as the latschen always prove to the chamois-hunter in his need, equally troublesome are they on other occasions. To pass a thick growth of them is an arduous business. You have no ground to tread

while your body, resting with all its weight upon it, inclines inwards toward the mountain.

on, so thickly are their creeping stems interwoven ; and
if you place your foot on their branches, it slides down,
and they spring up with a jerk, knocking you probably
off your balance. But it is not your body only you must
contrive to wind through them ; the long pole in your
hand and the rifle at your back must also accompany
you, and every twig then seems a hand and fingers
grasping and pulling them back. But when your work
is to be done *quietly*, you groan inwardly at every step
you take. Indeed the caution which, in this respect, it
is necessary to observe, adds immeasurably to your difficulty. If you dared trample across the loose *débris* at
will, you would find the passage much easier; and if you
were not obliged to bend yourself into deformity, to
achieve some yards of open space over which you dare,
on no account whatever, look like the biped that you
are, you would cover the ground in half the time, and
every muscle would ache much less.

In going home that evening a beautiful appearance
presented itself. The valley in front of us, where Baierisch Zell lay, was filled with a mystic radiance, and no
one saw whence it came.   For it did not hover over one
part only, as shed by a foreign influence, *but it was in
the air*, and emanated from it; it was the very air itself,
which by some wonderful transfusion had become softened
light. But as everywhere else it was dark, whence came
the halo-like brightness that filled all the vale ?   It was
as though angels had descended there, leaving behind
them those faint traces of their glory long after they
were gone.

It was only the moon. Though she had not yet risen
on us, from the other side of the mountain she was shining on the valley through a dip in the hills.   Presently
however, high, high up to our right, a white brilliancy was

seen coming on over the ridge. But no round orb swam into sight: great spokes of silver came instead, and frostwork, and fringe, and bars of light,—strange shapes we had never seen before. The moon had got behind the dark green branches of a latschen, and was shining through it. Berger stopped to admire and wonder: I thought of Moses and the burning bush.

The next day we were out again, and opposite the Roth Wand espied thirteen chamois. The herd was on the side of the mountain, where, by some ancient phenomenon, all had been laid waste, and covered from top to bottom with loose rolling stones. There was no bush, no prominence, behind shelter of which it was possible to advance on them; the whole broad expanse was nothing but dreary barren rubble. Ay, there they were, and here were we; but how get at them? It was arranged that Berger and I should go back, and passing up the shoulder of the mountain reach the summit; and then, keeping just beneath the ridge, make the best of our way to a certain gap, towards which, when disturbed, it was thought they would bear. So Joseph thought. Berger said they would go further on, and cross the ridge at another spot; but being the younger he gave way, and we both started off for our appointed station. Joseph staid behind, and it was agreed that in two hours he might show himself, so as to make the game move; for in about this time, it was thought, we might get to the top. We walked fast and did our best.

As seen from below, a mountain-ridge presents gaps seemingly not of great size; but when you stand close to them they wear a different aspect. Torn, broken, crumbling, the sides overhang a gulf. Up one of these we climbed. The blocks of stone were loose, and as I clung to some of them standing but a little out of the perpendicular—so steep was the place in parts—I could feel that a vigorous pull would bring them down upon me,—an unpleasant sensation where there is a fair depth below, into which you would inevitably roll! Once, when halfway up, a stone on which my hand was laid gave way. I was already falling back,—I knew I was lost, and in that second of time thoughts came crowding on my mind as though each would have a hearing in the one moment which was left, and after which it would be too late. I remember quite well my sensations; that I clenched my teeth, held my breath, and that *one* word—the last as I thought, escaped me. It was a moment of horror. I felt that the shadow thrown by the wing of the Angel of Death was over me. My hands were still outstretched before me, involuntarily trying to clutch somewhat, and grasping only the air; when my striving fingers felt something touch them, and convulsively seizing it, held on with the locked grip of despair. It was the slender stem of a sapling latschen; it did not snap, nor did its roots give way, and to that young thing I owed my life.

After a like escape it seems a blessed privilege to breathe the sweet air in safety; yet having, as it may be said, already tasted of death, you hardly know for the first instant or two if it is quite in character to breathe or not. You look round you on the earth and sky, as as a man looks on a cherished thing that he thought utterly lost, but now has found again; and you seem to love all better than before, and much more tenderly. You feel very thankful, and you carry that feeling in your heart, till you see the chamois; and then another thought possesses you,—" Shall I be able to get a shot?" I do not mean to say that the feeling of gratitude does not return—it would indeed be very sad if it did not—

when you go over the whole occurrence once more, as you will be sure often to do; but the truth is that the physical exertion, the excitement, and the necessary caution, prevent your dwelling long on anything save the present moment: that is all-engrossing.

Once on the ridge, it was necessary to be very careful lest the chamois should see our forms against the sky; but with snow on the ledge, and that ledge sloping outwards, I found it rather unpleasant walking, for close beside it the crags went down precipitously full a thousand feet or more.

But the chamois must have seen us, and are moving; they are making for the gap to which Berger predicted they would go. We rush forwards, to try to head them, but it is too far. They pass, and are among the precipices of the other side before we can get there.

Thus we had spent the better part of our day in trying to approach them, and were unable to fire a shot. Going downwards now was a quick affair. The loose stones give way beneath your weight, and slide forwards, carrying you with them twenty feet or more perhaps at a time; and in this manner, leaning back on your pole, with your heels dug into the rubble, you are soon at the bottom. We were only thirty minutes thus sliding down.

We went home by the Gems Wand. We saw two fine bucks below us in a green valley, but far as they were they scented our approach.

When in the evening we gave the forester an account of our doings, on telling him about this latter herd which we had tried to get near, he said we might perhaps have been more successful if we had stuck a stick up among the stones, and placed on it a hat or handkerchief.* "Many a time," said he, "have I done so when

* In Catlin's work on America there is a print of an Indian who has

out alone, and wishing to attract their attention in one
particular direction, while I got round near them in another. There is no animal more curious than a chamois;
if he sees something he has not observed before, he looks
and looks to make out what it is. They will stare at
and examine a thing for hours in this way; and they
are then so busy with the novelty they see, that they do
not look about with their usual watchfulness. I think
if you had done so they would not have observed you."

The mention of the Gems Wand reminds me of a circumstance that once occurred near there; and, being
very characteristic, I relate the story as it was told to
me a short time ago, by a friend who knew the particulars well. These were his words :—

"It was to the young forester's assistant, K—, that
the adventure happened. He was going along the ridge
of the mountain—the Geidauer Eibel Spitz it is called
—and looking down, what should he see but twenty-
three men standing by the hut. There is a single hut
there, you know, on a green alm at the foot of steep
wild rocks. Well, he looked at them a long time, and
watched what they did, and thought and thought, 'If I
could only get a shot at one of them—only at one !'
And so he kept on thinking how it would be possible to
manage, and did not go away from the place, but observed them through his glass, until at last they began
to move. There is a little path that leads from the hut
right over the Eibel Spitz, and he saw that they were
coming up, one behind the other; so he lay still among
the latschen, and waited till they approached. By-and-

adopted the same plan. He is lying in the grass near a stick, on
which a cloth is fluttering; while approaching within shot is a herd of
antelopes, following one behind the other, and looking at the novelty
with countenances expressive of wonder and curiosity.

by—perhaps it was three-quarters of an hour, or may be
an hour after—he heard their voices. Presently he saw
them winding up the path that led towards him. He
allowed them to advance till they were about eighty
yards distant, and then let fly at the foremost: he hit
him right in the middle of the breast, and the man
dropped down on the spot, stone dead. When they
heard the shot, they all stopped, and ran back some distance, and grasped their rifles. They were exceedingly
astonished, for they saw no one, and could not tell where
the shot came from. K—, as he lay among the latschen,
could hear them talking together, and deliberating what
they should do. Some were for going back, when one
of them said, it was a shame to think of going away
without knowing more about the matter. If even there
were six or seven foresters there, why should they mind?
there were twenty-three of them, and it would be a cow-
ardly thing to turn back for a mere handful of men.
Come what might, he said, he would go on, and as to
the others they might follow if they liked. So with rifle
in hand all ready to fire, on he went alone, straight toward the place where K— was lying concealed. He let
him come on to about sixty paces, and fired : the shot
turned the fellow quite round on one side; he stopped
short and then fell, and when the others saw this they
all turned, and were off as fast as they could go. K—
now crept down the mountain among the latschen on the
opposite side, keeping in the bushes, and passing through
the woods so that nobody might see him. I don't know
how it was, but when he came down by the Gems Wand,
instead of going the way he always did, he took the path
that led to Baierisch Zell. It leads, you know, over the
mountain stream, and there is a very narrow path along
it, and across it is a bridge—you passed it when you

P

came down from the Roth Wand on your road to the Solachers'. Well, when he came here he stopped to load his gun; while he was doing so—it was dusk already—he thought, as there was no knowing what might happen, he would load one barrel with shot: so in one barrel he put a ball, and a handful of shot in the other. He then sat down among the bushes to watch if any one came, for he fancied it was not un- likely that the fellows he had met on the mountain might take that path downward, and if so, they would then have to cross the narrow plank, and as they came on he might give them another welcoming. He had sat about an hour when he heard voices; they came nearer, and presently he saw men across the water, and could just make out that they all were armed. That's right, he thought, they are the same; and when near, just as they were all crowded together, about to cross the bridge, he fired his shot-barrel into the midst of them. You may suppose their consternation, after hav- ing had two of their comrades shot on the mountain without seeing who it was that fired, now in the dark- ness to have the same thing happen once more. K— went leisurely through the bushes, and walked quietly home; but they were terrified almost out of their senses, and did not know what to do, for they never thought themselves safe, and could not tell if another shot might not come peppering in among them a moment after."

"Did he kill one with the last shot?" I asked.

"No; he said he heard quite well the shot falling among them after he fired. He hit one only in the breast; of course he wounded him badly, but the man recovered."

"And the two he shot on the mountain?"

"One only was dead—the first he fired at; he fell directly, and never moved after. The other he hit in the shoulder, and broke his arm, so that it was obliged to be taken off. At first he thought he had killed two, for the ball knocked both over at once; but K—, you know, after the second shot, made off as fast as he could, for he could not tell what the others might do, and having fired both barrels he could not defend himself. But only think what odds—one against three-and-twenty! He must have been a brave fellow, must he not?"

"I suppose they never knew who it was fired at them? Of course K— never said a word."

"Not a syllable: no, they never found it out. The fellow who was shot was the son of a rich peasant near Schlier See,— the only son too. The same night that it happened his parents heard some one knocking at the window, and a man, in a voice quite unknown to them, said that if they would go up to the Geidauer Eibel Spitz they would find their son; and next day they went, and there they found him, sure enough, lying dead."

CHAPTER XVII.

MEETING WITH POACHERS.

ALL-SOULS Day being a great holiday we remained at home, and I strolled out across the meadow to enjoy the morning. I went into the churchyard to look at the graves, each one adorned, as well as might be, according to the means or taste of those who brought their offerings. Some were bordered with rows of red berries, gathered in the hedgerows, with a cross of the same in the centre of the mound; while others had wreaths of evergreens, and a device made out of the cones of the fir. They were indeed very simple; but they were the offerings of affection, and showed that those who had now another home were not forgotten, and in my eyes therefore they looked beautiful. How touching is the gift of a little child, even on account of its poor worth—so incommensurate with the great amount of love it is meant to be a token of!

The forester had marked out a plan for us for the following day, and accordingly we started early, having rather a long way to go. We soon left the road, and took a short cut across the meadows. We had not gone many steps before we came upon the traces of men's footsteps, which were discernible on the dewy grass. We looked, and looked again : there was no mistaking them.

"They are quite fresh," observed Berger; "they cannot have passed here long :" and we distinctly made out
the trail of five men. "When we come to the road," he
continued, "we shall be able to see which way they have
taken; but I have no doubt they are gone up the mountain. Today is a sort of a holiday, and the rascals always
choose such days, as they think we are at home, and that
consequently they are safe. They are from Hundham, I
know it for certain, for they come from that direction,—
the worst set in the whole neighbourhood." This village
was notorious for its poachers, and not one of them but
would as soon send a bullet through a gamekeeper as a
roebuck.

On reaching the road we found by the footsteps that
the men had entered the wood with which the slope was
covered.

"Just as I thought!" exclaimed Berger; "they have
gone up exactly where we are going; there is little chance
now of our seeing anything today. Confound the rascals!
there's a day's sport spoiled!"

We made out that some others had taken a different
direction, and that they had not all kept together. As
we went up the hill Berger said: "It is well to have your
rifle ready: look if all is in order, and it will be better
to put back the stoplock; for there's no knowing what
may happen."

In going up the Heissen Platten we found the track
of a deer in the moss and on the soft ground; and on
nearer examination I saw it was quite fresh, and that the
animal must have passed there but a very short time before. We followed it for some distance, but the men
had no doubt scared it away, and there was not much
likelihood of meeting it again. Berger was behind, and
while waiting for him I leaned on my staff and looked

at the ridge of the mountain before me, high up in the sky; while doing so I thought I saw something move. Although far away, it yet was on the sky-line, where every object is more easily discerned. I looked steadily, and now was sure I had not been mistaken. It could not be a chamois, I said to myself, it was too large for that,—and a stag?—it might be, but I thought not; the movements were not like those of a stag. Keeping my eyes steadily fixed on the object, I put my hand into my rücksack behind me and pulled out my glass. The figure was now clear enough; it was a man who was walking along the ridge, with a rifle at his back. I whistled to Berger: he answered, and a moment or two after joined me. "Look up there," I said, giving him my glass; "there goes one of the fellows we tracked just now. Do you see him? just to the right of that latschen; now he is hidden—there—now he comes again!"

"I see him," said Berger; "that's one of them for certain."

"Now I'll tell you what, Berger," said I; "I would rather get that fellow than the best chamois buck that was ever shot in these mountains. If we could but get him, and bring him down to the forester's house! Come, let us be after him: which is the best way?"

"There is no use in trying, I assure you," said he; "you see yourself what a distance he is off. Why, by the time we reached that ridge he might be far away on the other side, across the valley and up on the other mountain. I should like to catch him well enough, you may be sure, if only it were possible. It would take us some hours to reach the ridge where he is."

"I know that, but we may make the attempt. To take that fellow's rifle from him, and bring him down in triumph—by Jove! it would be the best day's sport I ever had in my life."

But Berger still protested against the experiment, con-
tending that it was perfectly useless to try. So we went
on, keeping away to our right—to the right of the spot
too where I had seen the poacher. The whole time my
thoughts were occupied with the man, and I was still
longing to make him prisoner. We had mounted a long
rough path among the latschen, and could now overlook
the scene. Further on to the right the mountain ridge
made a sweep, and there the rocks were torn, jagged,
and everywhere steep precipices. It was a wild, frightful
place. Far below was a chasm, but nowhere ought else
but loose and rolling stones. Around us was quite a
wood of latschen, and above was the continuation of that
ridge where I had first seen the man. As we moved along
I suddenly stopped, and touched Berger, who was before
me, with my pole, that he might do the same. He looked
round, but my finger on my lips caused him to keep silence. I listened for some time, but the stillness was
unbroken by any sound."

" What was it ?" whispered Berger.

" Did you not hear something ?"

" No."

" Well, but *I* did. Just above us a pebble rolled down ;
it was as if it had been displaced by some one's footsteps." However all was now still, and we proceeded
onwards.

We had reached the ridge of the mountain, and Berger sat down to look over into the space below and try
if chamois were to be seen. I chose a place a little behind him and somewhat higher. By chance I turned
my head to the right, and there to my astonishment I
saw, not thirty yards off, the same figure that I had observed before with my glass. I ducked my head in a
second, and pressing down Berger's shoulders behind a

latschen, pointed in the direction of the poacher. We
lay on the ground and watched him, first with the naked
eye and afterwards with our glass. He was a young
peasant, of about twenty : he carried a bran-new single-
barrelled rifle, and the usual rücksack was at his back.

"We have him now, Berger!" I whispered.

He nodded his head, while his eyes sparkled with expectation. We let him proceed on his path, and when
he was behind a piece of rising ground, rose up and stole
along after him : then we again lay down pretty close to
him. How both laughed, as we saw him looking carelessly about, unconscious of danger; while all the time
we could have struck him with a bullet when and where
we chose!

"Hush! now then, don't laugh," said Berger: "as
soon as we get near enough we'll rush upon him. Have
you all ready?"

"Yes, yes; both barrels are cocked, and my pole—
that I shall leave here in the latschen; give me yours,
I'll put them together."

"But don't fire,—promise me that. You will not
fire?" he asked.

"No, no, don't be alarmed; I won't fire: if however
I see him attempt to raise his rifle, then down he goes."

"Very well then," he said: "now come on."

We moved along with all speed in order to get close
up to him, a block of stone lying right between us; when
we reached it he was only a few steps in advance.
Berger turned his head to see if I was ready: I nodded,
and at the same moment he sprung towards the poacher,
I being close behind him. "Down with your rifle, you
rascal! Lay down your rifle!" In rushing upon him
however his foot slipped, and thus he lost a second, and
the fellow just eluded his grasp. Had a mountain been

hurled down from above, he could not have been more
startled; and no wonder: he thought himself alone, and
suddenly his solitude is disturbed by two armed men, rising seemingly out of the earth and springing upon him.

"Kreutz! Himmel! Donner Wetter! Himmel Sa-
crament!" he screamed with fright and terror, and
dashed at a bound behind a bush not a dozen paces from
where we stood.

"Lay down your rifle, or by Heaven I'll fire!" I
cried, raising my rifle to my shoulder and moving toward the bush, though in reality it was so thick I could
not see any part of him. He knew his advantage, and
cowering close did not speak or move. With the exception of the bush where the poacher lay hidden, all
around was bare as the palm of my hand. My whole
person was exposed had he liked to fire, and I was close
to him. But there was no bravery in this; for the danger
and folly of standing thus unprotected never once occurred to me. When it did, I slowly changed my position. I saw Berger a few paces further back, partly protected by the brow of the mountain, and this reminded
me of what I ought to do. I therefore retreated some
steps, keeping my front towards the bush and my rifle
ready. I had just reached the ridge, when from the amphitheatre of rock—from that horrid abyss of crag and
precipice—loud shouts were heard: they broke strangely
upon the silence, and at the moment I did not comprehend what they were.

"The others are coming!" cried Berger; "there are
seven of them—they have seen us—quick, into the latschen!—follow me!"

I looked at the bush and felt sorry to leave it without driving the game from its hiding-place; but Berger
quickened me, by bidding me come along, for there was

not a moment to be lost. And indeed the wild cries
from the band grew louder with each shout. The
mountain was steep, and we were soon among the latschen, keeping our heads low that they might not betray
our whereabouts, or serve as a mark for their rifles. The
men's cries grew now quite distinct—"Down with the
rascally Jäger!—the villains—down with them!" and
every instant brought the voices nearer.

"Quicker, for Heaven's sake, quicker! they are coming
on fast!" cried Berger, who was far in advance, but who
now stopped to wait for me; "what keeps you so long?"
The thing was, in moving through the latschen, a branch
had caught the leathern strap by which I slung the rifle
at my back, and the metal fastening had snapped. So
now I was obliged to carry it in my hand, which was
very inconvenient.

"Down with the rascals!" was again ringing behind
me—"Fire at the villains!" but though they said this
I do not think they saw us, or they would not have
spared their balls. The latschen were thick and high,
and a branch of one whirled off my hat, and whisked it
away over the tops of the next bushes. To leave that
behind as a trophy for the men of Hundham would
never do; besides I remembered there was the flower
in it that Nancy had stuck there the day before. This
determined me; so I stopped and went after my hat:
I reached it at last. The fellows were near now, and
never ceased their cries. We were at length out of the
latschen, — a reason the more for making all speed.
Berger ran on, and I close behind. He made for a spot,
down which he intended to pass; we reached it. "Good
God!" he cried; "it is a *Wand* (a precipice); we can't
get down!" Further on there was no outlet, no way to
escape; we were therefore obliged to go back again.

We reached some rocks: they were not much less steep than those where we had been before, but Berger dashed down them, now rolling, now sliding, now holding on as he best could. Just above that place was an open spot,—no bush or rock, nothing but bare stones. I looked below, to see how I was to manage it, for the descent was nearly straight. Halfway down a solitary latschen grew out of the rocks on one side, and I calculated that if I could catch that in passing, and hold by it, I should be all right. I was just stooping to descend, when one of the poachers sent a bullet after me, to quicken me in my resolve; it luckily fell short. Berger turned, and looked up to see if I was hit. While standing on that bare spot, I no doubt presented too good a mark to let the opportunity pass unimproved. But this so enraged me, that, had I not been already scrambling downwards, I should have turned and sent a bullet back in reply; for the young fellow being foremost, it was he, I imagined, who had fired,—he whom I had let pass unscathed, though I could have taken his life twenty times had I so willed. It was racking work, racing down that steep over the broken ground: every instant I expected another shot to be sent after us: my mouth was parched, my chest was heaving, and as soon as we reached a wood I declared I would run no further. We sat down therefore behind a tree, where we were safe enough; for if the men approached we should be sure to see them first, and we both agreed, if they did come, this time to fire. Each of us had two shots, and these would be quite enough to stop their advance. But all was still, and having rested we walked slowly homewards.

"I was right you see, Berger," I said, as we went along; "it *was* a stone I heard rolling; the man was just above us at the time, and dislodged it as he passed."

"Yes, he went along the ridge to drive the game for the others, who were among the rocks; they were the same we tracked across the meadows this morning; I was sure they were bound for the mountain."

It was really very extraordinary that the whole affair turned out as it did. The poacher must have passed the spot on the ridge where we sat down, but a minute before our arrival. Had we by chance spoken in coming up he would have heard us, and would very likely have let fly at one or the other. If too we had got there one half minute sooner, we must have met face to face. It is to this moment a matter of surprise to me that the man did not hear our steps; for we were close to each other, and neither Berger nor myself took any pains to step lightly. But not suspecting danger, and walking slowly on in a sort of reverie, his ear must have been less alive than ordinarily to a passing sound. Though the path he had taken along the mountain-top was much shorter than ours, he had proceeded very leisurely, which accounted for our reaching the same point at almost the very same moment of time.

" We won't return the usual way," said Berger; " let us go round by the fields, where we shall be sure to meet no one."

" Why ?" I asked.

" Only look what a state we are in ! how your clothes are torn, and mine too ! If any person were to meet us, they would be sure to suspect something had happened, by our coming from the mountain thus early. We have no pole either,—a stick of some sort we must have ; wait a moment and I'll cut one for each of us. There," he continued, after trimming a couple he had procured from a fence, " there, that's better than nothing in our hands: I would not be seen in this plight for anything ; it is bad

enough to have had to retreat before those rascals, but
for it to be known, and for the people to know who it
was and to talk of it, that's enough to drive one wild."

We came to a stream, and passing through it bare-
footed, sat down on the bank to mend our things.
Needle and thread we had none; so I divided the twist
of a piece of string, and making holes in the torn garment with the point of my knife, in this wise tied up the
rents. I could not help laughing at our droll figures
while thus employed; but Berger looked grave, and I
saw that anger was devouring him.

"Here Berger, drink!" said I, handing him the leather covering which, when it rained, I strapped over my
gun-lock, and in which, for want of anything better, I
had fetched water and mixed with some rum from my
flask; but he refused it, saying, "I can't drink, nor eat
either: something is here that seems to lace my chest together, and there is a gnawing at my stomach, as though
a wolf were inside. Those rascals! For a jäger to be
obliged to run before such fellows! If only they don't
find our sticks,—that would be a triumph for them!"

There was no consoling him. "Had I been alone,"
he continued, "those rascals should not be able to say
they made me run: they have something to brag about
now."

"But Berger," I replied, "why did you do so then?
I followed your directions implicitly, and left you to decide what was to be done. I don't think you can complain of my behaviour in the matter."

"No indeed, that's true enough; but, you see, I could
not know that beforehand; and besides if anything had
happened to you, I should have been responsible: 'twould
be said, I ought not to have led you into the danger, and
all the blame would have fallen on me. But had I been

alone, I should have crept into the latschen and staid there, and I know they would not have ventured after me; and if they had, I should have quietly brought down the nearest fellow, and that would have stopped them. They would have hardly liked to risk having the contents of my second barrel sent into one of them; and even if I had fired that, I could easily have crept away without their finding me."

I am quite sure that all this was true. Once in the latschen, he would have felt perfectly safe; being able through the boughs to watch his enemy's advance, without being seen himself, and thus might bring him down with a bullet, or remain quiet, as he found advisable.

As he knew the ground better than myself, I followed his directions, exactly, without argument; indeed for this there was no time. He, on his part, never having been with me under like circumstances, could not tell how I should get on, and was naturally unwilling to stay on the mountain, since any awkwardness on my side might have proved fatal to me, if not to both of us. Berger's sole anxiety was for my safety, and it was this alone which caused his precipitate retreat.

When we reached home, having taken the most by-ways, in order to meet no one who might tell the men of Hundsham they had seen us returning so unusually early on that day, the forester said it would be useless to go out again at present, for the game having been disturbed would not return to its usual haunts so quickly. I therefore bade my kind host and hostess farewell, and leaving behind a friendly greeting for the Solachers, set off the same afternoon across the Kühzagel Alp for Tegernsee, intending to go on from thence to Munich. Berger, who had a brother at a village on the lake, accompanied me. Night overtook us on the road, and we lost our way in the wood. We waited till the moon rose, and when its broad face looked in among the branches, soon found the path, and in a couple of hours reached the inn.   Berger promised to look after my pole, and a letter which I received some weeks later from the forester, told me he had found it: both his and mine were still lying where we had put them.   He added in his letter :—" All my endeavours to trace this dangerous band of poachers have been fruitless : I have not been able to get the least clue to any of them."

Thus ended my shooting in the mountains for 1849; and I returned to town, carrying with me a rich store of pleasant recollections.

PART SECOND.

CHAPTER XVIII.

THE PREPARATION.

How pleasant an occupation is the arranging all for the coming excursion to the mountains! What an agreeable state of excitement one is in, while mustering the necessary things, and again running over the list in your mind, to be doubly sure that nothing has been forgotten. And then, too, as this or that thing is brought forth from its retreat, where it has lain well taken care of since last October or November, what gladdening associations the sight of it calls forth, and how vividly the mountain and mountain life appear before you! Ha! there is the old rücksack again—stained and discoloured by the rain and the dews, and by the blood of the last chamois that it helped to bring down from the mountain. And there are the dried, prickly leaves of the fir still among its folds; and crumbs of bread, and a hard crust too, reminding of the delicious yet simple meal on the top of the Miesing or the Krammets Berg. What a longing it awakens to have it again at your back, and to be trudging before daybreak over the dewy meadows of the valley! The dear old sack! it is indeed faded and weather-beaten, but its very beauty consists in being so, telling as it does of long and faithful service.

And now for the mountain stick,—here it is, tough

Q 2

and unbending as ever. The good old fellow! he has
been a trusty friend, and helped where none else could,
and when sure and timely support was a question of
life or death. What a pleasure it is to have it once
more in your hand! You are carried away by the impulse of the moment, and, in thought, are again on the
steep declivity with the abyss in front; and so, leaning
the iron point on the floor, with body bent back and your
whole weight resting on the good staff, the four walls
and even floor of your room have disappeared, and you
are on the rocks among the latschen, with the blue
sky overhead. A sudden fit of impatience, that was dor-
mant until now, has seized you : you want to be off, and
begin to think it was foolish not to have started some
days ago, for then you would have been on the mountains by this time. Hitherto you were calm enough,
and proceeded with your task of packing and preparing
with a placid serenity; but as the several objects more
especially connected with the scenes where you are going
again greet you after a ten months' interval, your cool
business-like manner begins to disappear, and, in a word,
you can hardly wait to be off.

Now then a place for these two pair of thick-soled,
well-nailed shoes; and here are grey woollen stockings,
with the clocks worked in green; and the short leathern
breeches, embroidered with green silk,—in with them all
for the present! in a day or two however we shall have
them on. That powder-horn we will put into the very
middle, among the linen, where it will be sure to be quite
dry; and here are two bottles of rum to be stowed away
safely somewhere. Those cramping-irons may be left
out, they are very heavy; besides their sharp points tear
everything they come in contact with. And here are
bullets, in a bag of sawdust to prevent their rubbing.

Now let me see: in the rücksack are the telescope and hammer, and small leathern bag with balls for the day's use; and flask, and drinking-cup, and knife, et cetera, et cetera.

Yes, now I have all. The joppe must not be packed —that is to be worn; and whether on a journey, on the mountains, or in the library, a more comfortable garment is not to be found. It is at once all that may be desired,—is warm or cool, and may be worn over another coat as well as alone. This said joppe, now the national dress of the peasant of the Bavarian highlands, of Styria and the Tyrol, can lay claim to high descent; it is, with slight variation, the ancient short royal mantle that we occasionally see on the stage—such as Harry the Eighth wore—lined with ermine, and made so that it hung loosely on the wearer, or could be wrapped close should he choose, as theatrical kings often do, to cross his arms on his breast and scowl upon mankind. There is nothing like a joppe, grey turned up with green : the ermine has disappeared, but the lineage is to be traced for all that.

And now for the rifle; but before putting it in the leathern case, just one look to see that all is in order; and up it goes to the shoulder, and we are delighted at the fineness of the sights, and should be glad to get a good long shot to test their accuracy. For, be it known, we have had some alterations made since using it last; the sight at the end has been filed away till its pin's-head shape was changed to a thinner form, and the indentation on the bridge in the middle of the barrels has also been made proportionably finer. For in firing at a great distance, if the sight in front is of coarse size, the chamois is quite covered by it; a chamois not being a very large animal. The charge too has been increased for a

longer range; and since all these reforms have taken
place, the rifle has not once been in requisition; so we
have a double interest this time in going out with the old
friend, and in seeing how he comports himself in his
altered condition.   He will do his duty, without doubt;
and if the arm that holds him be but steady, there can
be no fear about the result.

Most persons, I suppose, quite well understand the affection of the rider for his horse, whether that rider
be Arab, fox-hunter, or cavalry soldier.   They find it
natural that the animal, which has contributed to the
pleasures of the one, or shared the dangers of the other,
should be looked upon in the light of a friend, and be
cherished accordingly.   And they are right in thinking
so.   The steed shares the excitement of his master, and
the natural ardour of each is a bond of union between
them.   But will they be able to comprehend the
fondness of the mountaineer for his rifle, between which
and himself there can be no such sympathy? Yet affection he does feel for it : he and it have passed many a
pleasant hour together, and it has been the means of pro-
curing him the most exciting joys.   Why, his very fame
as a good shot, is it not bound up with his rifle? and do
not the two, like loving companions, share with each
other the praises and renown? And a stronger cause for
attachment still—has he not endured manifold disap-
pointments, many a vexation, many a sad failure, with
no earthly thing near him in which he took an interest
or for which he felt companionship, save his rifle?
For should he have missed a stag or a chamois, and
in all the bitterness of disappointment and self-reproach
sits down alone to think over the event and explain
how it happened, the sportsman, if he have a grain
of sense or justice in his composition, will never at-

tribute the failure to his rifle, but to his own over-hastiness or want of skill. On the other hand, when at 160 or 180 paces he has brought down a chamois, he praises his good weapon, and looks at it complacently and with cherishing regard. The reputation of my rifle I maintain as though it were mixed up with my own. Like the monarch in a constitutional state, in my eyes it "can do no wrong;" and when a blunder is committed, I, as responsible minister, am ready to bear the blame.

Moreover I always clean the weapon myself; and, though a rifle is an inanimate thing, the care and attention thus bestowed make you like it all the more, and feel for it a certain regard. Always on my return from the forest or the mountain, let me be never so tired, or wet, or hungry, my first care is my rifle, to see that it is dry, to wipe the locks and look carefully to the inside of the barrels; and then, but not before, do I provide for myself; then comes the refreshing toilette and the pleasant meal.

It is the 14th of September: all the clocks in Munich are striking five, and the stage-coach is rolling noisily through the streets, and going southward. I and my rifle are inside, and when day breaks tomorrow, shall see the sun rising over the snows on the Zug Spitz and the Wetterstein.

CHAPTER XIX.

TO PARTENKIRCHEN.*

It was about eight o'clock when the smart young pea-sant, who drove us from Ammergau to Partenkirchen, set us down at the entrance of the high street of the village, and bidding us farewell, cracked his whip and took the road that, here diverging, leads to Garmisch. From the principal inn issued the cheering sound of merry human voices; and the windows were full of light, and there was a bustle and a hum that, as one approached, rose upon the hush of the night, and had a pleasant influence on the traveller seeking a night's lodging. And there stands mine host—such a host as I always like to see—of fair dimensions, and in whose jolly face good-humour has ensconced itself. He looks as pleased as

---

* Whoever passes through Partenkirchen should take a walk to "The Clam." It is a wonderful place, and the unlearned as well as the learned cannot fail to be impressed by the sight. Even he who knows nothing of geology, will understand that this earth of ours must be very old, when he sees the channel that the water has here for centuries been gnawing through the solid rock. Go and look at it, and stop there awhile; and as you peep over into the deep chasm, try to think of the years that the water has been thus toiling to wear out the hard stone; and how one century dragged on, and another weary century, and the still toiling water had only got a little lower down. After that, and when you see what it has accomplished, the word "Time" may perhaps convey to your mind another meaning than it has hitherto done.

though the light, and gaiety, and hearty laughter emanated from him; as though he were the sun whose rosy
presence thawed all into merriment. And, for aught I
know to the contrary, it may have been so. He was a
right jolly fellow, as I afterwards experienced; and when,
some weeks later, I lay day after day sick and lonely in
bed, I was as glad to see him enter my room as when a
sunbeam looked in through the window-pane.

But the house is full: there is not a bed to be had for
any money, or, what would weigh still more with our
worthy landlord, not even for the sake of obliging another. There is a fair tomorrow, and many are the
comers from the neighbouring villages; so that the lack
of house-room is as great as when independent electors
throng to support independent candidates at a small
country town in England.

After some vain applications elsewhere, we at length
found a lodging, and the following morning I could not
but think how lucky it was the inn had been full; for
on peeping out of the window, there stood before me the
great grey mountains of which the Zug Spitz is the last
and highest peak. The sky was bright and blue, and
cutting against it the sharp, hard outline of the cold
stony ridge; nor could the sunbeams even, as they played
upon that rock's imperturbable face, impart to it life or
warmth. Our little lattice was the frame to the picture,
and I soon roused my fellow-travellers to come and see
what we, in our humble back room, were possessors of.
Long after the others had left the window I was still
looking out; and I gazed and gazed, in order to be quite
assured that I was really among the high mountains.

How often do we hear children, when asking for something, insist on its being a *real* sword, or horse, or whatever it is they wish for, and not a mere make-believe! They

are always fearful they may be put off with something
that is not the reality, and so there be a falling away
from their brilliant imaginings. Somehow or other I
carry this childish anxiety about with me still; and when
a wished-for-thing is just before me, and another step
will enable me to reach it, the doubt and the suspicion
will arise, and I can hardly bring myself to believe that
it is *really* so. And even this difficulty over, all my rea-
soning cannot make my silly self give up the fear that
something may yet happen to snatch away the enjoyment. I must have the toy in my hands, before I can
believe it is my " very own." And so I looked to satisfy
myself that what I saw was all real; and then I looked
again, to be sure that my wishes had not betrayed me
into self-deception. But there was no mistake here;
and it was settled these were indeed thoroughly respectable mountains, and that I with my own eyes was be-
holding them.

Just with such fluttering anxiety did I approach Venice
for the first time. Already at Mestre, I dreaded lest, by
some unforeseen cause or other, I should be transported
across the Lagune otherwise than in a gondola. Could
I by any piece of witchery have been carried thither
through the air, I would still have preferred the gondola;
for that was associated with all my boyish notions of
Venice, and without it therefore the charm of that moment, so long waited for, would have been incomplete.
And only when fairly seated in it, and we had shoved
away from land, did I feel sure that nothing could cheat
me of my hopes. And as we emerged from the Grand
Canal,—ay, there was St. Mark's, and the Masts, and
the Palace of the Doge, all as I had seen them a thousand times in pictures, in drawings, and in my fancy.
All was there—I missed nothing—I recognized every

spot. Yet as the gondola lay moored against the steps, and the waters of the Adriatic gurgled under the prow, I still stared in wonderment, and even then asked myself, Can it really be? And at last when I stood on the pavement, and passed between the columns at the landing-place, I looked up and told myself gladly, I had lived to see the winged Lion of St. Mark.

But now to the Forester, for in his hand lies my fate. His house stood just out of the village, and so crowded was the street that to reach it was a matter of time. The booths and the gaudy throng of peasants formed a merry scene; but the prettiest spot was the cattle-market, where picturesque groups had collected;—here, some young girls with kids; there, two old men bargaining for a calf that a chubby boy was fondling; and, best of all, childhood was everywhere to be seen,—a pleasant sight always, and in any picture.

The kind forester gave me a few words to one of the under-keepers, whose district was a short distance off; and though here, as everywhere else, the game had of late been destroyed by wholesale, he still had hopes that I might get a shot.

"However I cannot promise you," he added; "for all around there are poachers, and from the villages the peasantry go out and shoot everything they see. I think the best place for you to try will be the Oester Berg: it was a capital mountain formerly, and, though it has been well-nigh cleared, it still is the most likely one for a successful stalk. There is a hut about half-way up where you can sleep: that is to say, you will find straw to lie on and milk to drink. Bread you had better take with you."

In the afternoon, putting a few things into my rück-sack, and leaving the rest with the landlord at Parten-

kirchen, I started for Farchant. I soon found the forester, and we talked over the chances of seeing chamois,
and where it was best to go. "You would," he said,
"be more likely to get a shot on this side than on the
Oester Berg. I was there the other day, and saw chamois: two bucks are there for certain, but if we shall
meet them it is of course impossible to say." Then came
the old tale, falling sorrowfully enough on a hunter's
ear, that a year or two ago, had I been there, I might
have had sport in plenty, but now all the best mountains
were quite depopulated. This is a theme which at once
causes a dark look to pass over the face of a forester.
Angry feelings and hatred rise with a sudden gush within him, as he thinks of the times when those mountains'
and forests were his pride, and remembers that the stag
and the chamois which he watched so lovingly have been
since then swept away by bands of lawless marauders. I
may safely assert that, in the breast of no set of men
have the late revolutionary changes caused such dark
and bitter feelings as in those of the foresters and gamekeepers: for not only did they see that which it had been
their pride to guard, at once, partly by law and partly in
defiance of the laws, given over to plunder, but they
found themselves with hardly a shadow of protection,
while defending the little which the new order of things
had left them. At first indeed it seemed as though matters were arranged to protect the thief, rather than him
whose property had been stolen. For the new game-
laws were partial; they were carried out too with a
miserable inertness; moreover the authorities were themselves often possessed by the same spirit, subversive of
order, or were influenced by fear; so that the poacher,
though caught in the fact, had but to bear himself with
effrontery and bravely lie, in order to escape scot free.

He knew besides that the foresters dared not fire at him ; while he, defying the law, cared little for a similar restriction. When hearing of the ill-treatment, and insolence, and danger, to which these men were exposed at the time when this lawless spirit broke loose over the land, one only wonders how human patience could have been found so enduring, and that not more human blood was shed.

For a true sportsman it is a painful thing to see game hunted mercilessly at all times,—the dam shot away from her helpless young, and the kid destroyed when only a few weeks old. And this was going on the whole year round, in every spot where a deer or chamois was to be seen, and the stolen venison sold openly under the very eyes of its lawful possessors. Most of those persons therefore who had a chase, were obliged to exterminate their game themselves, rather than have it shot and carried off by the peasantry, who were ever on the alert.

I proposed that, if we tried the Oester Berg, we should leave overnight, sleep at the hut, and so be on the mountain early.

" You can do so, if you like," said Neuner; "but if you try this side, then we start tomorrow betimes."

" How long shall we be getting up the mountain ?" I asked.

" Four hours."

" Well then," I said, " we will start at four : at five it is day, and we shall be up by eight. You can come for me in the morning." And so it was decided.

CHAPTER XX.

UP THE MOUNTAIN.

THE following day I was up by a quarter-past three. The morning was fine and warm, and the stars were shining with wonderful brightness. Neuner just entered, as I went into the little room below to get my breakfast.

"There is my rifle, Neuner; be so good as to load it, while I drink this cup of coffee. In the rücksack, you will find the powder-horn and balls; here is the measure for the powder. I shall have breakfasted in a minute, and then we'll be off: this half brown loaf we may as well take with us."

We sallied forth into the darkness. As we crossed the fields in the valley, the forms of the nearer mountains could be just made out, inasmuch as the gloom above was not quite so impenetrable as that which shrouded their sides and base. Now came the grey dawn, and then the ever-cheering daybreak, accompanied by that wonderful breath, moving through the air, which is felt at no other time. To the left was the Kramer Berg, with its steep wall of rock and abrupt precipices. From every point on this side the Kramer presents itself in great picturesqueness; the grey stone and overhanging pines, and the deep ravine, are min-

gled together so finely that your eyes turn thitherward
almost unconsciously ; it juts out too, and rises at once
from the plain, and the bold upward line, especially when
seen in profile, gives it a commanding aspect.

"What a thorough chamois mountain that seems to
be," I observed : "what capital places everywhere for
them to maintain themselves in,—just such places as the
chamois love. Are many there now ?"

"Formerly it was one of the very best places : now I
doubt if there are any,—two or three perhaps. You
might go out day after day and not see the trace of a
living creature. And how the poachers used to be about !
You might have heard rifle-shot after rifle-shot on the
mountain continually. Garmisch, you see, lies close at
the foot of it, and the Garmisch people were always
out."

"As it is so conveniently at hand, most of them, I
suppose, were poachers ?"

"Nearly all. They are a bad set there : work they
will not, and so they take their rifles and amuse themselves. I know most of them ; but if I met one on the
mountain, and went afterwards to the authorities to inform against him, the fellow would have a dozen witnesses
ready to swear that at that very hour he was elsewhere,
and I should get no redress. Formerly the Kramer was
in the Ettal district, and then I wished that it had been
in mine. Well, now it is so ; but as things are, I would
rather not have it. Ay, formerly ! that was a place indeed—the best of any here."

"On this side there are some wild-looking spots,
Neuner; yonder, for example, where the rock shows
through the latschen,—a difficult place that, I should
think, eh ?"

"Yes," he said, "ugly places are there. The gullies

(*graben*) are rather frightful to look at—some of them at least. I shot a chamois on the Kramer some time ago, and he afterwards climbed to a spot where he could not get out, nor I after him; so I had to fetch a rope and let myself down by it, and then drag him and myself up again."*

"I suppose as long as the laws remain in their present form poaching will not cease. What think you, Neuner?"

"Oh, the laws are well enough, if they were but executed. We have law, but there is no one to look after it. The fellows know we must not fire, so they don't care: they like to go out, and seeing how little chance there is of punishment, out they go and shoot to their heart's content."

"Do they fire at the foresters here?" I asked. "The Schlier See men do not hesitate a moment, but as soon as they see one up goes the rifle to their shoulder: whether attacked or not, it is all the same to them."

"No, here they don't: they always run away. But once I met a fellow carrying off a chamois, and called to

---

* When a chamois is wounded in the flanks, the ball going through the bowels, it is always best to let it alone for some time, for it is then sure to lie down at the first convenient spot it meets with. If on the contrary you still pursue it, in the hope to get one more shot, the animal will go on and on, climbing upwards till it is at last locked in and can get no further. But the worst part is, you cannot get at it either; or if you should be able to approach near enough to put an end to the business with another ball, the chamois in falling from its narrow ledge will probably roll to such a distance, or come toppling down, dashing from crag to crag, that even if recovered it is of no good to any one, as bones and flesh will most likely be all battered into a pulp. For this reason there are certain occasions when a calm sportsman would not fire at a chamois, because he would know that, if he hit it, the creature would be sure to go tumbling over the precipice.

him to lay down his rifle; he did not, and was just running to a tree, from behind which he would most likely
have let fly at me, when I called to him again, 'This is
the last time, you rascal! now then, or I'll fire;' and as
he did not, I fired.   The trigger worked rather hard, so
the shot went off a little late, or the bullet must have
passed through the very middle of his chest. He reached
the tree however, and afterwards went away."

"And what luck the fellows have," I said: "not many
weeks ago one of the park-keepers of Prince T—— fired
at a poacher he caught in the park.   The ball passed his
ear, just touching it.   And another, since then, shot a
poacher's cap from his head : both got off safe."

"Well," said Neuner, "and it was but the other day
a young forester near here sent twenty-six shot into a
poacher's back. The fellow took four days to get home.
By good luck—or rather by ill luck, I should say—not
one shot touched his neck."*

"Did he take his rifle from him?"

"No, the man crawled into a bush, so of course the
other could not venture near him; but next day he came
up to the spot again, bringing a comrade with him, to
look for the poacher, and see what had become of him.
They thought to find him there still, either alive or dead,
but he was gone."

* As these are actual conversations, and not dialogues invented or
dressed up for the occasion, I beg the reader not to make the Author
answerable for any deficiency of mild forbearance or Christian love, in
these or similar expressions of feeling : that is to say, should he happen
to find there is a lack of either.   It is the Author's intention, to the
best of his ability, to give a plain, faithful picture of what he saw, and
to tell what sort of people these mountaineers, and poachers and foresters
are, *and show how they feel inclined towards each other*. As to a forester
feeling anything like human kindness for a poacher, this is demanding
more than his sinful mortal nature is capable of; but he has plenty of
human hate to give him, inveterate, deep, and unquenchable.

R

"And did you hear nothing more about him?"

"Oh yes, we knew who he was, and went to see him. He never said anything about the matter, nor complained to the authorities; and as he had got punishment enough, we did nothing more either."

I cannot give a better proof of the progress which the lawless spirit of the revolutionary movement had made among the bureaucracy, as well as the peasant class, than by repeating what my companion told me as we walked slowly up the steep mountain path.

"A short time ago, one of my men met some peasants out poaching. Creeping along from bush to rock, he stalked close up to them. He looked at each, but did not recognize any of the party; the rifle however that one carried he remembered; it had been sold by auction not long before in the village, when the fire-arms that had been taken from different persons were disposed of. Well, he laid his information; but the authorities, easy as it would have been to find out the owner, have done little or nothing in the matter."

"I suppose they are afraid to act, and are besides better inclined to the poachers than to the foresters."

"Both one and the other," he answered. "And how savagely the villagers can behave to one of us, when they get us in their power, what I am going to tell you will show. Some time ago a poacher was missing from Partenkirchen. Between one and two hundred peasants went out to search for him, and at last found him shot dead. They instantly fancied he had been killed by one of us foresters; but it was really not the case, for none of us knew anything about the matter. He had, without doubt, been shot accidentally by a comrade. Well, as soon as they found the corpse, the whole band with shouts went to the house of the assistant-keeper, but he was out. At last they found him, and taking him to

the place where the corpse lay, asked, before the body,
'Were you not out in the mountains?' 'Yes,' he answered, 'but not on Thursday.' 'You lie!' they all
shouted: 'you shot him.' They then beat him so unmercifully that he was soon unable to speak, and could
only hold up his hand imploring mercy."

"And what became of the poor fellow?" I asked.

"He was ill for a long time, and will never quite recover; he must have received some very severe internal
injury, for though he still goes about, he is quite a different person to what he was before."

"And were any of the men punished?"

"The doctor, who was a thorough radical, said the
injuries the young forester had received were slight, and
the punishment therefore was also a slight one, as for a
misdemeanour only. Among the mob were two or three
common-councilmen (Gemeinde Räthe), and there they
are still."

We were going onwards up the stony road, when
Neuner said, "Yonder to the left is a salt-lick: it is as
well to look if anything is there."

We left the path accordingly, and passed among the
firs with which all this part of the mountain was covered.
There was little need of choosing our way here, for in
front a mountain torrent rushed along so boisterously,
as completely to drown the sound of our footsteps over
the dry prickly leaves. We came to the edge of the
bed of the stream, a deep and broad gulley torn and
broken up, and desolated by the swollen torrents which
come sweeping down from the mountain-tops in spring-
time. Heaps of rock and large stones were piled in the
middle of the broad bed, besides whole trees, dried and
sapless as the very stones themselves, which had been
flung there like wrecks.

R 2

We did not speak in a whisper, for the waters were filling the solitude with a voice louder than ours.

"There is nothing here," I said, after looking for a minute up and down the ravine; when, just as I had spoken, from beneath a projecting part of the bank forth bounded a chamois, scared at hearing a sound suddenly jarring and breaking in upon the monotonous din that surrounded his loneliness. He leaped upon a high stone, quite unable to make out what sound it was that had intruded on the solitude. His fine ear had caught an unfamiliar tone; the loud equal hum that was in the air, and in the ground, and rolling on with the water, was suddenly interrupted; but what it was the creature did not know. He stared and listened again, terrified as men are when the cause of alarm is unseen. He presently observed us, and springing down from his eminence, turned toward the steep on the opposite side. There he stood and gazed again, not more than fifty yards from me; but as it was only a yearling I let him pass. On he bounded, then looked back, and leisurely passed up among the trees to other haunts on the mountain-top, where his own footsteps pattering on the rock would be the only sound rising through the heavy silence.

On our way upwards we had already passed such a lick, almost hidden among the trees,—a dark and shady spot, but nothing was there. Further on was another. It was in the same gulley we had seen before, and close to a waterfall, caused by the accumulated trunks and branches of trees, stones, and fragments of rock that had here formed an embankment. We crept through the underwood, and as we came nearer I advanced alone. Kneeling among the moss, I could look down into the haunt of the chamois. On one side rose a green hillock,

and about it long grass was growing, and shrubs overhung the nook, making of that patch of ground a bright
verdant spot—a little oasis—amid the barrenness. I
fancied to myself it must be very pleasant behind that
hillock,—a cozy little home such as children, in the
overflowing richness of their imagination, see with their
mind's eye, and in their play will try to build up and
make a reality,—a retreat that nobody was ever to know
anything about, all covered over with nice yielding turf.
While looking at the green bank, and dallying thus with
old recollections (by the way what a simpleton my companion would have thought me, had he known what I
was about), two most delicately-formed little ears rose
from behind it, then suddenly disappeared. They came
again, and with them this time the pretty head of a kid,
nibbling a blade of grass. It was rather toying with the
herbage than browsing upon it; and it pricked its ears,
and bright glances darted from its dark eyes, and it
leaped and disported itself in the very happiest play. I
turned to Neuner, putting one finger on my lips, and
then pointed down toward the watercourse. He was
soon by my side. Hidden by a bush I watched for what
else might come, for I knew it was not likely the kid
would be alone. Its head came forth, now on one side,
now on the other, but the rest of its body always remained concealed. Afterwards another head came in
sight, or rather the ears and horns only, nor could I
once obtain a view of the whole animal. We remained
a long time waiting for it to emerge from this chosen
spot, but in vain.

"That's a doe, Neuner," I whispered: "the horns
are too fine for a buck. When they come in view again,
look and you will see I am right."

"I think so too," he answered; "but we are losing

time here. Let us go up higher; we shall then see behind that knoll, and if a buck is there get a shot."

Stealthily we crept back, and went higher, but on looking over the ravine saw nothing; we could not even discern the hillock which had been between us and the chamois just before.

"Shall we try a little further on?" I asked.

"No, no, it will not do any higher; they would be sure to wind us there."

It was then settled Neuner should stay here, while I returned to my former position; and when he supposed I had reached it, he was to dislodge a stone or two to alarm the chamois; and as they bounded away I should see what they were, and according to circumstances get a shot, or, might be, get none.

Presently down came a stone into the rocky ravine. The two kids pricked their ears, and looked as though they wondered what it could be, but yet not much afraid. A second is heard, hopping along the hard bed of the torrent. There is no doubt now about the danger; and off they go, thoroughly scared,—one, two, three kids! and three does too. They look back once more, and then disappear.

We returned to the path, and soon reached that part of the mountain where the woods ceased. Before us lay the bare steep ascent, with here and there a stunted tree growing out of the rocky earth. Now all wore a different character; we were entering another region. High above us was the sharp line of the ridge's summit; that was our horizon, and thither we had to go. On our left was a deep hollow.

"There, just there." said Neuner, pointing to a wizard-looking dead tree, " I once shot a stag. It was evening, and quite dark. I was waiting for him, sitting here

on this stone. He came along by yonder broken ground,
and through the hollow. I could not see his antlers;
however I fired, but it was too dark to look for him
afterwards. As it was impossible to go home, I sat the
whole night under that tree, and the worst of it was it
rained all the time. In the morning I found him: he
had not gone far, for by chance I had hit him well."

Some distance up the mountain was a rude log-hut.
We went to it, for in such a place traces are often found
indicative of who were the last lodgers, or if any one
has been there beside the herdsman or the woodcutter.
On the door was written—

"IN THE LOWER HUT.

WOLF."

It was fastened with a wooden peg outside, so we knew
there could be no one within. It was a miserable shelter,
just high enough to stand upright in, and round some
stones placed together on the ground were the remains
of a wood fire. A bed of dried leaves and hay was in
one corner, and after stirring and poking it about to see
if nothing was hidden there, we left the place. When a
poacher has rested or passed the night in a hut, he will
often leave behind him some marks of his sojourn; and
an experienced eye will at once discover that the fragments of a meal, the scrap of paper in which something
was wrapped, or the footsteps round the fire or leading
to the hut, were not the traces of its legitimate inhabitants. Among the leaves, too, something or other
will be occasionally concealed, to be fetched away at a
convenient opportunity. Neuner said it was herdsmen
who had been there, and that the fire was of their making. We saw a roebuck grazing among the latschen, but
he saw us too, and soon darted from our sight.

We were now near the sky-line; a few steps more and

we should be on the crest of the mountain. On nearing this boundary of my vision—the line which seems to encircle and form the limits of a world—the same sensations were always quick within me. What was beyond? On what should I look down? On cloud, and vast space, and undefined emptiness; or would wild rocks be there, and dizzy precipices; or should I be surprised by overlooking a new portion of this earth of ours, that my eyes had not yet rested on? Should I see a wide plain, with distant cities and roads and tortuous rivers, and thus, with a single step, be in presence of a new tract of country, and take it in at once with one long wondering gaze? As I had never been on these mountains before, there was always this excitement on nearing the summit—a pleasurable uncertainty about what was to come. And as I crept along towards the ridge, about which, until my foot had touched it, I always felt there hung a mystery, how busily did imagination ply its work! The caution, and the watchful eye, and the breathlessness, arose as much from the awe of the moment as from the heed that is natural to the chamois-hunter. And with straining eye and a tremulous longing, and a sense that a spell was upon me which in a second would be broken, did I creep on my knees to the very ridge, and stare over into what was beyond. But it was not until, with still gradually advancing body, I had cast my eyes over the *whole* expanse before me,—not until with a glance *all* had been passed over,—that the charm was dissolved, and that, drawing a deep breath, I felt the sweetly-oppressive mystery was dispelled.

It is a different thing altogether thus to behold a new country from the mountain-tops, or to see it as he does who advances upon it step by step along the high-road. It does not come upon you gradually, object after object

giving way to others as you approach, but the *whole* land
bursts upon your vision at once, and your senses make
you feel, by the sudden weight that presses on them, how
great the vastness that the mind is labouring to take in.
You have a consciousness of extent, and range, and space,
for some minutes before reason informs you about them,
—a sensation that takes you by surprise, that comes
rushing in upon you, and lording it for the moment over
the faculties of the mind; and though this eventually
gives place to a calm comprehension of extent, reaching
further than the eye can follow, it is after all that *first*
impression which is remembered long afterwards,—that
first sensation of being in presence of a vast thing, but as
yet uncertain, vague, and undefined; for later, when we
look about for forms and mark particular outlines, there
is already a diminution of the glory.

Lying on the earth we wound forwards, and taking
off our hats we looked down into the green valley. Far,
far below chamois were seen: out came the telescopes
quickly, and we counted seventeen of them. On the side
of the mountain we could everywhere see their traces in
the snow.

"They have been here early this morning," said Neuner: "we are rather late; those other chamois kept us
so long. That is the essential thing, to be at the top
early. What a bad wind we have! it comes up from
behind us, without blowing up from the valley in front
too."

"We could not do anything, even if they were not so
far; we should never be able to reach them."

"Besides," said Neuner, who was still watching the
chamois through his glass, "there is not a buck among
them: they are all does."

We lay there awhile, examining the herd, and following their movements with our telescopes, and then I took out our brown bread, and ate, while enjoying the scene.

" Have you an apple?" I asked.

" No."

" What a pity! if you had, we could have a splendid meal. Is there no water near? for I am thirsty."

" None about here; even the nearest place is a great distance off."

Though the mountains opposite us were far away, the bells of the grazing cattle and the shouts of the herdsman came across to us distinctly, floating on the motionless air.

Our dry bread being eaten we went on. To the right was a dip in the mountain, and here we expected to see chamois. It was an inviting spot; and formerly, as Neuner told me, we should have been sure to find some. We looked around, but not a creature was visible. After a time we left our path along the ridge, and advancing among the latschen, sat down and watched. We peered around in vain, examining every dark green patch of herbage, and each spot lying in the sunshine, where at this hour they would most likely be. We were both looking in one direction, and by chance at the same moment turned our heads; when behold, on a pinnacle of rock, rising among the herbage, there stood a chamois! "Look, a chamois!" each exclaimed,—a buck too! and quick as thought my finger drew back the cock of the rifle, and I was cautiously raising it, when the creature was gone. He did not disappear with a bound, but vanished like a falling star. We looked at each other astonished, for neither very well knew how he had got on that point of rock, nor how he had quitted it; but gone he was. It was doubly vexatious, for not once in fifty times might

I get a shot under such circumstances. To bring down
the animal you are after is of course always pleasant, but
the satisfaction is at times greatly increased by the accompanying incidents. The chamois I shot on the Roth
Wand, for example, gave me a hundred times more pleasure than I should have felt in getting one of those first
seen on the Miesing. The spot where the creature
stands, the scene around it and you,—it is this enhances
the charm, and makes the heart leap with delight. Now
here was all I could wish for: from that pinnacle, on
which he was poised, how he would have come toppling
down through the air into the latschen below! And as
I rehearsed the whole scene in my fancy, and grew more
and more vexed that it had not been realized, an angry
"Donner Wetter!" came rumbling through my teeth;
and flinging my rifle over my shoulder I strode away.

"Do you see yonder green knoll?" said Neuner,
pointing to a rock rising out of the valley, and behind
which a path seemed to lead from the lower pasturages.
"Well, just on that spot a poacher was shot."

"Who shot him?" I asked.

"One of the under-foresters. The fellow was a noted
poacher, and had already fired several times at the
keepers. He was the most desperate in the whole country, and being well known as such they had often tried to
get hold of him, and bring him in dead or alive. The
young forester was quite alone, and standing just about
where we are now, when he saw him from afar coming
up the path; so he sat down and waited for him. He
knew the path would lead him to yonder hillock, and
presently sure enough he saw his head appear, and then
his shoulders, and then the whole fellow. He was aim-
ing at him all the while, but it was not until the man
had reached the top of the rock, and stood before him at

his full height, that he fired. The ball hit him in the centre of his chest. It was rather strange, but when struck the poacher pulled open his shirt as if surprised, looked at the shot-wound, and then falling forwards on his face, dropped down dead."

From a sort of table-land below and in front of us, where a group of figures was distinctly visible, rose the sound of women's voices; and all space was filled with their carollings. A very flood of tones came rolling to us in great waves of sound; for the distance, and may-be the soft air, blended them in harmony, and made those loud and sudden gushes of song most musical. We stopped and examined them with our glasses.

"Hang them!" said Neuner, while getting out his telescope, "they are on the mountain shouting and sing-ing all day long!"

"Who are they?" I asked.

"People digging gentian-roots; they are always seek-ing them, and disturbing the game; it never has any peace. There are two women and a man," continued he, examining them with his glass; "they are not from Partenkirchen, but come from a village yonder."

Though far away we could hear them distinctly when they spoke, and their hearty laugh came ringing in our ear, and sounded gladdening among those lonely rocks.

We were ascending the last rise of the mountain, when Bursch (the dog) came running to us in evident fear.

"Himmel, Donner Wetter!" cried Neuner, seizing his rifle with the quickness of thought; instinctively I seized mine, while springing round to meet the danger, and cocked it in a second; for I thought a poacher had stolen upon us and was close at hand. But it was no such enemy that Bursch had run from : a large vulture was wheeling upwards and bearing away from us, and was now so far that it would have been useless to send a bullet after him in his flight.

"Had we seen him sooner, I might have had a shot," said Neuner. "Four florins are given for every one we deliver to the head-forester."

"Are they very large?" I asked.

"Seven feet from wing to wing; and they are strong too; they carry away the young kids. When the chamois see one wheeling in the air, there is a terrible commotion, the poor helpless things are so frightened. I have often watched them: they all run together, and huddle as close as possible with the kids in the middle, and wait tremblingly till their enemy is gone."

After continuing along the crest of the mountain for some time, we again sat down on a commanding spot, to look if anything was to be seen. We saw nothing; so at last I gave up the search, and let my eyes wander dreamily around, just as they listed, without aim or purpose. I saw all, but it was supinely, and with the happy consciousness that not one single object concerned me, or could disturb my delicious inactivity,—a sweet state of utter indolence. The early hour of rising, the fatigue and the excitement, all induce this calm and dozing listlessness. The muscles relax kindly, and the whole body reposes in a state of slothful Eastern ease.

While thus outstretched upon the earth, my elbow buried in the grass, and my head resting on my hand, gradually my eyes wandered to fewer objects, and at last gazed with but little consciousness at a single one. Slowly a thin veil moved before it; I heard the voices of the women floating lullingly on the air, and indistinct remembrances were lazily trying to marshal themselves into some sort of order in my brain, but they could not accomplish it. The carol of the gentian-gatherers was now as a low hum in my ear, and from the valley there rose a mist, and then a rolling cloud. I fell asleep.

Suddenly there came a shock; a hand was upon me, and a voice said, "There is a chamois!" I was wide awake in an instant, and involuntarily cocking the rifle on which my hand rested while I slept, I started to my feet.

"Oh, it is too far to fire," said Neuner. "There he is!"

"I see it!" And there stood, far below us among the thick latschen, a fine chamois. Out came the telescope. His fore-feet were on a fragment of rock, his sloping back was toward us, and his neck stretched out, with the head knowingly on one side, as though he were listening. He stood so for a long time immovable; it was evident he did not know what to make of it.

"Perhaps he hears those women," I observed; "or, as he is looking downwards, may-be a herdsman is passing below. What shall we do?"

"We will wait and see what _he_ does," said Neuner.

But he still remained, and gazed and listened. And well might he tarry, for from the rocks above no danger could reach him; and to approach where he stood without being perceived was next to impossible. Yet he was mistrustful, and soon skipped lightly away. The manner of his leaving the spot, however, showed he was not frightened; prudence, rather than fear, had induced him to change his position. I knew therefore he would not go far: he would not bound headlong on without stop or stay, as when his fine sense of hearing warned him of danger being near, or the taint of the hunter floated toward him on the air, streaming over a sudden dip of the mountain. He was most likely among the latschen, so we hastened back some distance, and down the rocks, in order to meet him should he come that way. But we saw no trace of him, though every bush and spot was examined most carefully.

" He cannot have passed, Neuner," I said : "he *must* be among the latschen. Perhaps he is behind that up-right rock yonder : I will go forward and see." And leaving my long pole behind me, I went carefully through the latschen and looked over the precipice. It went down quite perpendicular two hundred feet, and from my pinnacle I had a good view around, but saw nothing of the chamois.

We regained our ridge by climbing a steep, so long and slippery that I was right glad when it was behind us. We sat down to rest. Opposite was the Kramer, and rising above this was the Zug Spitz range, grand and mighty in its proportions, and the eye wandered over those snowy peaks far away into the Tyrol. On the left the Ettaler Mannl came peeping from amid the verdure-covered rocks. My good friend Franz Kobell has sung his stern virtues ; but I was now hungry, and so tormented with thirst that I cared not one farthing about his virtues or anything else,—*I wanted to drink.* Water was not to be had ; I was obliged therefore to mix some snow with a few drops of rum and eat it. Neuner told me snow would only make me more thirsty, but that I could not help,—drink I must. We ate a crust of bread, and, as the sun was shining warmly, we crept into a shady place, with Bursch beside us, and all three had a sound sleep.

In an hour we awoke, and on we went again. " A buck ! a buck !" flew suddenly from Neuner's lips ; and with widely-opened eyes and his mouth screwed up as though he were saying " Hush !" though he uttered not a breath, down he dropped, so as to prevent his body being seen above the sky-line. We crept forward on our stomachs, with hats off, gently advancing our heads, till at last our eyes could just peep over the ridge. There he was below us, and a splendid fellow too.

" He is quite black," I whispered to Neuner; "that's a good buck indeed! But how can we get near him?"

This was a question of painful interest. To be tortured by the sight of such a capital chamois, within my grasp as it were, and yet not be able to approach him, was most distressing; for in a moment my eye reconnoitred the ground, and I saw all the difficulties of our position. Over the ridge where we lay the descent was nearly perpendicular; latschen were growing there abundantly, it is true, so that to climb down would have been possible enough, but not noiselessly, and that was here a question of the last importance. From out the depth before us, that went stretching away more or less abruptly to the valley, rose here and there a pile of rock like the towers of a cathedral, with latschen growing on its surface, or starting from the gaps and crevices. It was on the top of one of these rocks the buck was feeding. With our glasses we looked down full upon his broad back.

" What a magnificent fellow! If we could but get him, Neuner!" I said, half inquiringly.

" Yes," he answered, " but how? that's the thing."

At first he was partly hidden among the latschen, then his hind-quarters, quite black, emerged from the dark green bushes, as he slowly moved on, perfectly unconscious of our neighbourhood.

" I don't see him now," said Neuner.

" But I do: look there, the black spot to the right of that bare rock,—that's he! Here, take my glass."

" Ah, what a size! Well, we had better go down yonder to the left, and see if there is any possibility of getting nearer: it will however be a long shot in any case. Shall we try?"

"Yes, of course, come along."

And we went to where the ridge dipped somewhat, but yet advanced thitherwards where the chamois stood. Now came the latschen,—those dreadful latschen through whose thick branches it is so difficult to creep without a rustling noise. We stepped with breathless caution. "Hush!" said Neuner with a long drawn-out breath; "Hush—sh—sh!—silently, silently! no noise, for heaven's sake!" And holding back the stubborn branches for each other, we proceeded slowly to the brink. Before us was a wilderness of latschen, growing up from the abrupt steep, and there was a deep hollow between the brink where I stood and the tower-like rock where the chamois was first seen. But now we looked and we saw him not. Between us and the rock on which my every hope was centred there rose another, hiding a part of the first from view. I fancied the buck might be just behind that rock, and whispered it to Neuner. "If so," I said, "he will for certain come in sight again on one side of it or the other;" for the nearer crag, being less broad than the further one, hid just the middle part from our sight.

"How far is it from here to yonder bare rock on the left?" I asked; "it is there I expect he will come."

"A hundred and forty yards; not more I think, but quite as much certainly."

For a long, long time we waited, but in vain. At last Neuner proposed to return to the ridge whence we first saw the buck, and look if he was still there. After awhile I saw him standing motionless on the crest of the mountain, and gazing steadily into the depth below. He made a sign that nothing more was to be seen. This

s

was certainly not cheering, but I did not yet despond, and still believed the chamois was on the rock and would eventually move into sight. But another half hour dragged by, and then another, and at last I reluctantly acknowledged to myself that I gave him up. But as Neuner still stood on high peering from his eyrie, I would not quit my station, incommodious as it was to stand between, and partly upon, the branches of the latschen. And though in my heart I had given up all hope now, my eyes were still fixed on the further rock; when behold! from behind the nearer one the head of a chamois appears—only the head—as he advances grazing. It was on the right. And now he lifts his head, and comes forward. His whole body is exposed; one second only, and the report of my rifle thunders through the mountains. He stops, turns, and goes to the very spot where I first expected he would come. It is terribly steep just there; he stands somewhat bent together, ready to descend the rock's precipitous side. But he is hesitating. He must be hit! The rifle is still at my shoulder, and the ball from the left barrel . . . "By Jove, it has hit him!" Down he comes; he can't stop himself, he rolls headlong over the crag! I watched him till he was out of sight, and then drew a long deep breath. I looked up to Neuner, and taking off my hat waved it in the air, that he might know all was right. He swung his gaily in return, and dashing along through the latschen was soon at my side.

"Did you see him fall, Neuner?"

"Yes, but before you fired I saw nothing. When you levelled your rifle I thought it was only a joke, till the shot came, and afterwards the other."

To be doubly sure, I looked across with my glass, to see if any blood was upon the rock, but I could discover

After the wounded chamois

none. Then came the doubts and anxiety; yet at the same time I felt sure he was hit, and well hit too. With some difficulty we clambered down to the foot of the rock; I looked into the gulf, but could see no trace of the animal.

"He *must be* in there, Neuner,—I am sure he must. No chamois that was not badly wounded ever came down a rock as he did. I'll go down and look after him."

"No, you will not be able to get out again; it is impossible. Let us go lower down yonder, and look up the gully."

We did so, and I stopped to load my rifle. Neuner meanwhile ran forwards to a projecting crag, and by his manner and the expression of his whole body I knew he saw the chamois. At the same moment he fired.

"There he is!" he cried; "he's limping."

"Stop, Neuner, I am sure he can't go far; we shall overtake him, and then we'll let Bursch follow, and he'll bring him to bay." And down we ran, where at any other time we should have gone with slow and careful steps, and presently caught sight of him.

"There he is!"

"Let me fire!" I cried; "do you see him? Ah, now I do, but the latschen half hides him. Now he moves forward!" Fire!—and down he rolls head over heels. Bursch, who till now, though trembling in every limb with excitement, had restrained his desperate longing, was unable to do so any longer. When the chamois fell, he dashed forwards, baying, screaming almost with passionate delight, and the chamois and he were going down the steep together, and we following as fast as we could go; it was a headlong race over loose stones of every size, slipping, stumbling, falling, and then sliding

s 2

forwards several yards with the loose rubble, my feet in front and my body inclined backwards, leaning on my pole behind. Now all was silent; Bursch had ceased his baying, so we knew the chamois was dead. On the grass and rocks were frequent drops of blood: but as we could not see where the hound was, we whistled for him, and at the same moment descried him beside the buck, which had fallen close to the trunk of a half-decayed tree.

Then came the examination of our booty, and of the different shots. On of the horns was gone, broken short off close to the skull in rolling among the rocks after the last shot. I was sorry, for they were high and thick, and had in perfection that short curve peculiar to the buck, which gives him so sturdy an air.

"Look, Neuner, here's the first shot; it has grazed his back-bone badly—a little too high, though. No wonder he stood so bent together after being hit!"

"And this must be the second," said Neuner, examining another just behind the shoulder. "It was that prevented his being able to hold himself up in coming down the rocks."

"Well, I am very satisfied with both: that left barrel of mine shoots capitally. Now then, let us pull him out:—how heavy he is!"

And dragging him to a spot where it was less steep, I gralloched him, and found him in capital condition and as fat as possible.

CHAPTER XXI.

HOMEWARDS.

Not far from where the chamois fell there gurgled a rivulet; and when our buck was put into the rücksack, we sat down beside the pleasant water, and mixing a cupful with a little rum, drank success to the merry sport. Not that I was thirsty now, for the excitement of the last two or three hours had prevented my thinking about it; yet, thirsty or not, it was right cheerful to sit on a mossy stone, rifle in lap, with a good chamois to feast our eyes on, and to taste the delicious water that was playing round the stones. But there was no time for luxuriating thus.

" We must be going," said Neuner, " for it is a good way home; and if we wait much longer night will overtake us before we reach the village."

" Let me carry it," I said, as Neuner was about to sling his rücksack, with the chamois in it, on his shoulders; "I would rather, I assure you,—halfway at least."

" Oh no, it is nothing; I have many a time carried two roebucks, and have still gone on stalking, as though I had nothing. Two I did not feel,—I did not mind them at all. I have even done so with three, and have carried home five. Sixty, eighty pounds, I don't mind now, but more I should not much like.

"Yet that's a pretty fair weight to carry a long time."

"Yes, but I am not what I once was: formerly I cared for nothing;—heat, or cold, or hunger, it made little difference to me. I used to be out day after day, and night after night, and did not return home from one week's end to the other. But once I went out, and in the evening, on reaching the hut where I intended to sleep, found it full of snow; so I could make no fire. I was in a profuse sweat, and of course had nothing to put over me; I got some brushwood and made a bed on the snow, and lay down. The next morning I felt ill, and went home; but I was so cold and stiff that it took me a whole day to get there. I have never been quite well since."

There were no signs of stiffness in his limbs now, for on he went at a smart pace, despite the rough path and the chamois at his back.

In coming down a mountain, there is every now and then some appearance which gives indication of your approach to the valley; and each one, as it shows you are nearing your home, is welcome and makes you glad. We came to a meadow affording capital pasturage, and strewn over it were the rude log-huts for storing the hay.*

"Often enough at evening," observed Neuner, as we stopped a moment or two for him to rest his load, "often enough were stags to be seen here formerly. The meadow, you see, is quite surrounded by the woods, and as the sun was going down they liked to come forth and graze.

"Once, near Ettal, my brother saw twenty stags all

---

* After the haymaking the whole crop is put up in such log-huts, and when winter comes and the snow is hard enough to bear, the hay is piled on sledges and carried down to the village.

together in a pool," said Neuner. "He is forester in that district, you know. It was in summer, when the great horse-fly is very troublesome to them. Another time he met seventeen together. That was a sight—such pushing and rolling and fighting with each other."

"It must have been worth seeing," I observed. "What a splashing, and how they must have been coated with mud!"

"Bauer shot one there the other day,—just there, between yonder woods, where you see a way cut through them," said Neuner, pointing to a grassy avenue leading from the smooth green meadow away into the forest. "Game would quickly be here, if there was only a little peace. The red-deer, that used to quit their haunts at certain seasons, now stay and drop their young here; and in the rutting season the stags have their appointed places too. For some years this has been the case; formerly they never did so. With a little quiet, I should soon have a fair stock again, for all the places about here are favourable for deer and chamois; they can maintain themselves on the mountains, and there are sheltered spots for them in winter, just such places as they like. And you see how beautifully all adjoins and hangs together: I would not wish a finer forest, and it used to be my greatest delight; but now, I don't know how it is, all my pleasure is at an end."

"But things will change," I said; "be sure matters cannot go on as they are now,—they must mend."

"Oh, you can form no idea of the endless disagreeables we have to go through. There are our master's rights to defend; and if we do so, never so mildly, then the peasants, every one of them, abuse us in all possible ways. They think now they have a *right* to everything: they want wood given them, or permission to collect litter* for their stables, and are greatly discontented if they do not immediately get what they require. And yet these are the persons who have been exterminating the game, and would not listen to reason, and who refused every offer made them that was just and fair. No, I've enough of it; my duties give me no pleasure now."

"I well know what the peasants are; formerly I thought something might be done with them, but I now see it is quite out of the question. Besides, of the game here they had no reason to complain, for it did them no harm, as is the case in the flat land."†

"To be sure not," continued my companion; "but even my woods, which I always took such pleasure in, they can't leave alone."

"What is it they do?" I inquired.

"Did you not see, as we were going up the mountain this morning, the bark peeled off several trees? Well, where the bark is off, a worm enters and destroys the tree. I could show you places where there are twenty

* The peasantry in Germany collect the dead leaves in the forests to make litter for their cattle in the stables in winter. Though of course the forester does not mind their carrying them away, he cannot give to each one indiscriminately permission to do so. Formerly, when there were red-deer in the forests, the constant invasion of their solitude disturbed them; for, as everybody knows, there is nothing the deer value so much as quiet. Besides, the young wood might be injured, or timber stolen, if every one were allowed to work for days together in the woods merely for the asking.

† In the flat land the game, it is true, often did harm to the crops of the husbandman. But when the damage was paid for—paid for even beyond its value—the discontent of the peasants did not cease, though many of them calculated on this indemnity as one source of revenue. I have often seen potatoes planted on strips of ground on the skirts of the forest, which no peasant would ever have thought of tilling, had he not hoped to be able to show that deer had been on his field, and so make a claim for loss sustained. The noble proprietor of the forests bordering the Danube, in the neighbourhood of Donau Stauf, paid regularly every

or thirty in that state. The worst is, the disease is infectious; and when one tree has been treated so, it is sure to spread to several others. I think I should shoot a fellow if I caught him at it."

" But what is their motive ?"

" Malice, mischief, ill-will," he answered. " What other motive could they have, as they gain nothing by it? And yet they want us to help them out with wood, etc., and are mightily surprised and insolent if we say a word. My trees used to be my great delight; for as to shooting the game, I don't care about that: it never cost me an effort to see a stag or chamois and not to fire at it."

" And what is the price of venison ?" I asked.

" Eight kreutzers a pound.* We are obliged to sell it cheap, or we should not dispose of it at all. If we asked more than the poachers, no one would take it, so we are obliged to give it at the same price as they."

Rather hard this, for another to be underselling you with your own property !

" Have any been out lately ?" I asked.

year a considerable sum to the peasants as indemnity for the damage done to their crops by the game; and according as the price of corn rose these sums were increased. As the money received was generally more than adequate to the loss sustained, the peasantry were satisfied, and found in the arrangement no cause of complaint; when suddenly, in 1848, although the preceding years the indemnity received by them had been nearly doubled, they discovered that such a state of things could exist no longer; and thus, supreme authority ceding to popular will, a general extermination of game took place throughout the land. Now however, when too late, there is hardly one who does not regret the change, and wish that "the good old times" would come again; for to many a peasant this indemnity was a source of revenue :—it was a part of his income in fact, and, as such, entered into all his calculations.

* One-third of a penny less than threepence. Nine kreutzers are equal to threepence.

" Of course: why they are always out: it was not long ago Bauer met three men on the Enning, where you shot your buck today,—close by where we first saw him."

" As he dared not fire, he could not do much, I suppose."

" He took away the rifle of one,—that was all. The thing was, he stalked close up to the man without his perceiving him, and laid hold of his rifle. The fellow, who was sitting on a rock, was terribly startled, and slipped forward to get away. Bauer caught hold of his rifle, and thought to get the man too, but he just escaped."

" And the others," I said, " what did they do?"

" You see, when Bauer crept up to the one poacher he did not know any others were there. He had not observed them, for they were a little distance off. But when he did, he had his rifle to his shoulder in a moment so they could do nothing but follow their companion, and off they ran."

We now came in sight of the village and its little homesteads, and broad fresh green pastures; with here and there a peasant-girl tripping along on the dewy path, returning from Partenkirchen, or youth whistling gaily, or with a mouth-harmonicon feasting his soul with music, as he lingered abstractedly on his way.

And now we are in the village, and the children stop in their play, and the old people and youths and lasses pause in their work as we pass, and look at the good chamois that Neuner has at his back. And with what feeling of inner satisfaction and delight you meet the passers-by! in truth you are glad they happen to come that way just then, when the rücksack is freshly stained and bulging out with its pleasant load. You feel so cheery and light-hearted, so perfectly satisfied with yourself, and, even if not so generally, I am quite sure that *now* you cannot help being affable. But does not success always make us happy?

We took the buck to Neuner's cottage, and his sister stepped out to welcome us. Now came the sweet words of gratulation,—sweet and gentle-sounding ever, be the language what it may in which they are spoken. Some of the hair was then pulled out to make a *gemsbart;* it was jet black, but unfortunately rather short. Six weeks later it would have waved the whole length of his back in long and splendid tufts. He weighed, when cleaned, 61½℔., and of fat alone we took 5℔. out of him.

"There are calamities in authorship which only authors know," writes Charles Lamb to a friend; and just so with the sportsman—there is many a circumstance which he only can appreciate. All these little incidents therefore I mention purposely; for, though very trifling in themselves, they belong here, and it is such after all that contribute in no small degree to make up the sum of the pleasures of the chase. Just as the place where you follow the game, or the spot where it falls, serves to enhance your delight, so the length and colour of the beard,* the size or beauty of the horns, the casual meeting with some forester or friend as you are going downward with your prize over your shoulders,—all these and a thousand other chance events contribute to your pleasure, and swell the amount of your enjoyment.

We were told that two shots had been heard on the Oester Berg, the mountain that rises immediately behind Farchant. It was probably Bauer, the under-gamekeeper; for he had gone out betimes that morning, and was not yet returned. Nor did he come later. We supposed

---

* The so-called "beard," be it remembered, is the hair growing along the ridge of the back.

therefore that he had wounded a roebuck or a chamois, and would stay that night on the mountain.

As I returned to my little inn, the whole village was crowded with young heifers coming back from the pasturage, each wearing round its neck a differently toned bell; and there was something very cheerful, and far from discordant, in the sound.   Hardly had it ceased, when the evening bell, swinging slow and steadily, again broke the silence, but added to the repose,—reminding all, even the lonely wood-cutter in his poor hut high up on the mountain, that it were well to thank God for another day of life.

THE ETTALER MANNL.

"The Ettaler Mannl," or "The Little Man of Ettal," alluded to in the preceding pages, is a mountain that closes in the vale of Ettal, and whose top consists of an upright bare rock, which rises above the surrounding verdure, forming by contrast a rather conspicuous feature in the landscape.   This "Man" Kobell in a little poem has invested with human attributes, and makes him from his watch-tower look forth over the plain, to see if danger is approaching the land.   When I was last at Ettal it was with Kobell, and the villagers told him that the words had been set to music, and how a few nights before they had sung them amid loud cheers and enthusiastic applause.   The dalesmen love their mountain all the more dearly now; they have identified themselves with "The Old Man of Ettal," since the poet has breathed upon him and made him live.

The Ettaler Mannl.

The Ettaler Mannl is strong and stout,
His bones have a marrow of stone throughout;
Cares not for wind or for tempest wild,
For he's indeed a true mountain child.

The Ettaler Mannl sees far inland,
'Tis a fine look-out where he 's ta'en his stand;
But what 's he watching, what is 't he will,
So earnest always, and always still?

I'll tell you what,—he's thinking, and heeds
What sort of life the Bavarian leads;
If still, as once, he is kind and good,
If still he 's warmed by the same brave blood,

If still to his King he true be found,
That's why the old fellow looks round and round;
And should it not be so, then—God speed!
For days would follow of sorest need.

The Ettaler Mannl in awful size,
His gray cloak round him, doth now arise;
A giant then you will find is he,
The like of whom none did ever see.

And with his feet and his arms of stone,
Makes such wild havoc as ne'er was known,
And on throughout the whole land the same,
Till clean once more from disgrace and shame.

The Ettaler Mannl still stands in peace,
All 's right as yet—there is nought amiss;
So go on bravely, be good and true,
That this Man never have aught to do.

CHAPTER XXII.

THE OESTER BERG.

AT noon I started for Partenkirchen, and walked straight to the forester's house to report myself. He was not a little surprised at my good fortune. Then, before going up the Oester Berg where Neuner had seen two chamois lately, I went to the inn to get some bread, a few lumps of sugar, in case I should wish to make a glass of grog, and a couple of eggs for mixing with my *schmarren*. The landlord's daughter—who, although her wedding was near at hand and she was busied the live-long day with three of her handmaids in marking and hemming, and folding great piles of linen for the household of which she was soon to be mistress, was not always in the best of moods—met me as I entered. "Good day, Christina!" I said; "why, I expected a friendly greeting, —you wanted a chamois, and I sent you one yesterday."

"Ah, good day!" she answered: "one hardly knows you in your green hunter's hat and joppe."

"The chamois was good, was it?"

"A capital one,—who shot it?"

"I."

"No, no! that I don't believe."

"Now for your unbelief, Christina, you must give me

an apple to take with me; for I am going up the Oester
Berg, and dry bread makes a rather insipid meal. So
now for the punishment: come along to the storeroom
and put some of your best into my rücksack, for part
with your rosy apples you must."

What a storeroom that was! well worthy of belonging to the richest man in the village, and a post-master
and landlord withal. It was a large stone-paved room,
light and cheerful and cool; and round the walls were
bright copper moulds, for making jellies and cakes;
and a store of spoons, and plates, and jolly-looking tan-
kards, with huge flagons beside them, that had many a
time descended into the earth, and returned thence foaming and sparkling and bright with the rich treasures laid
up there. And there were mighty stone bottles standing on the dresser, in which it was evident some rebelli-
ous spirit was enthralled, for to make egress quite impossible the corks were bound firmly down; and mountains of butter on fair white boards, and eggs in abundance; and binns broad and deep, filled with coarse meal,
and finer, and the very finest flour. Loaves of freshly-
baked brown bread were piled on the shelves, each a good
five-pounder; and tongues shrivelled and smoked, with
fat sides of bacon, hung from a row of hooks; and sugar-
loaves, and dried fruits, and glass jars filled with luscious syrups and preserves; golden apricots and red cran-
berries, with pots of lucent Tyrolian honey—all was
there in generous overflowing abundance. The fat of
the land, dropping into many channels, had been made
to pour out its unctuous richness here. It was worth
seeing, that storeroom,—a rich granary where the wealth
of the earth was garnered up!

A good road leads a considerable distance up the
mountain: at last, between the hills a green valley is

seen, with a single solitary hut. But it was to the
" Hinteren Hütte "—the hindmost hut—that I had to
go ; so crossing the meadow and following a stony path,
I soon saw smoke rising slowly, and mixing with the
mists which were gathering fast over the landscape.   It
was growing dark, for I had tarried too long at Partenkirchen, and the walk thence had taken me two good
hours.   .

I pushed open the unbolted door, and entered the
room on my right.

" Ha! you are come at last," said Neuner, rising to
meet me ; " it is so late we had given you up."

" And glad I am to be here," I said ; " it is just beginning to rain.   I fear we shall have bad weather ; the
sky is overcast, and the clouds look very gloomy."

" Should it rain in the night so much the better, if it
is but fine in the morning.   After rain the chamois are
on the mountain-tops.   We want rain, for it has long
been too dry, and the chamois have kept low down."

I wiped the moisture from my rifle, and hung it up
against the wall ; and laying aside my rücksack and
thick shoes, was comfortable enough in the warm room.
The hut was rather a large one. It consisted of the room
where all sat, with a smaller one adjoining ; and on the
other side was a kitchen,—that is to say, a smoke-
blackened place three or four yards long by one-and-a-
half or two in breadth, paved with rough stones, and a
rudely-raised hearth in the middle for making fire.   On
the wall hung several large copper saucepans for warming
milk, and an iron frying-pan, and this was all the furniture.   But nothing could be cleaner than these utensils ;
they were as bright inside as if they had been of silver.
On entering the house-door you went along a passage,
leading to a shed or sort of barn, which, though roofed

over, was at one end quite open to the weather. Here
stood a large horse-trough, into which a rivulet splashed
and gurgled unceasingly. At the further part of the shed
was the cow-house, and over this stable, immediately
beneath the roof, was the loft, crammed quite full with
hay. Here I was to sleep that night, and many a following one. You scrambled up to it, by help of a rude ladder; and unless the pattering of the large rain-drops on
the shingle roof just above your forehead were to disturb
your rest, or the jingling of the cows' bells in the stable
beneath, or the noisy rustle of the water falling into the
trough,—sounds which most likely you would not be
accustomed to in your bedroom in town,—if, I say, the
novelty of all this did not keep you from sleeping, you
might pass as comfortable and warm a night up there
in, not *on*, the sweet hay, as in the best chamber of the
Clarendon.

In the room where we sat was the usual large stove,
and round it ran a bench, as well as along the walls.
There was one deal chair besides, and a deal table, a
clock, and a closet where the pans of milk were placed,
that the warmth might the more quickly cause the cream
to form in thick and luscious layers.*

As it was late in the season the greater part of the cows
were gone into the valley, and with them " the Swiss,"
or chief dairyman. The calves only were left behind for
some weeks longer, with cows sufficient to furnish milk
for them, and to make butter for the three herdsmen who
were still here. These had to tend the cattle, cart the

* I here saw a method of skimming milk that was new to me. The
dairyman took out a pan of milk, and passing his finger round the surface, separated, as it were, the edge of the thick layer of cream from the
sides of the vessel ; then tilting up the pan, as if to pour out the contents, and blowing the surface, it floated off, and tumbled, almost in one
piece, into the bowl put to receive it.

T

manure, and keep all in order. The eldest man, under whose orders the others were, cooked for them, skimmed the milk, made the butter, and managed all relating to their frugal housekeeping. They lived on bread and milk and butter. Their complexions, clear and bright as possible, gave evidence of perfect health; and many a lady might have envied their transparent purity. Health shone from the men's eyes: the lids were thin, and moulded themselves to the ball of the eye, causing but the softest outline.

The youngest of the three, a lad of about sixteen, was sitting at the table playing at some nondescript game of cards with two women, who had been on the mountains collecting gentian-roots,* and who had come in to claim shelter for the night. The pale flickering lamp gave a poor light, it is true, but the youth's hearty laugh every now and then, at his own good luck or scientific play, made the place cheerful. It was a singular group; he on one side, his arms and neck bare, and wild as a young colt, watching with an arch expression for his adversary to fling down her card, and one girl looking over the other's shoulder into her hand, and giving her friend sage counsel.

A pan of milk had been put before me on my arrival, part of which I had drunk. The herdsman now asked me what I would have for supper, so giving him the eggs I begged he would make me a schmarren. He soon brought it in a large earthen pan, hot and brown, and just savouring of the apple which had been sliced into it. The young forester who had come with Neuner shared it with me, alternately taking a spoonful of

---

* These are collected in great quantities, and sold for the purpose of distillation. The spirit obtained from them is in high repute: I think it detestable.

schmarren out of my pan, and a spoonful of fresh milk from another beside him. I preferred a draught of water, a pitcher full of which "the boy," as he was called, fetched from the spring and put upon the table before me. It was all very primitive, both the service and the repast,—much, I imagine, like what might be met with in a lonely log-hut in the backwoods of America, where the wilderness stretches away towards the far west. But the service was rendered willingly, and though "the boy" was bare-footed and bare-knee'd, and had on but two articles of clothing, a thick shirt and a pair of short breeches, there was nothing of coarseness or vulgarity about him. Nature—simple, God-fashioned Nature—had been, to him, as a mother, and she had reared him in her own quiet way and very unartificially, giving him no polish, for she had herself none to give; but she had moulded his heart kindly, and his manner was fashioned after the simple human feelings which had taken root there, though of forms he indeed knew nothing. For him the maternal converse had done all.

It was too early to go to my hay; and though the herdsmen looked sleepy, and evidently thought we were keeping recklessly late hours,—it was at most eight o'clock,—I stayed where I was, and chatted with Neuner about the chase, the mountains, and his favourite forests.

"Have you shot many chamois this year, Neuner?" I asked.

"No, I have shot nothing, but Bauer has—twelve chamois and six roebucks."

"And in the Ammergau—do you know how many they got this year? A good number, I suppose: as it is preserved for the King there must be plenty of game there."

" Forty chamois have been shot ; but as to the stags it is quite a riddle where all the good ones have gone. Hardly a single good hart has been seen this year."

As we talked, one or the other of us mentioned the Zug Spitz, and this reminded me I had long wanted to get some information about the ascent, which was difficult, and had been accomplished for the first time only a few years before."*

" It is about five hours' walk from Partenkirchen to the place where you commence the ascent," Neuner told me, in answer to my questions ; " but it is too late in the year to attempt it now. A cowherd there, who is a sort of guide, has been up twice. 'Tis a wild place at the top !"

" What, have you been there ?" I asked.

" Yes, I went up with the head-forester and several others. There are only two places which are ugly and difficult ; one is a narrow ridge, a sort of bridge, which you have to cross, with a precipice straight down on both sides of you three-quarters of an hour deep.† It is very horrible, there's no denying that; all looks so wild, and rent, and torn. If you like you may ride across astride."

" Did you do so ?"

" No, I walked over : that I did not mind at all. But the other place, near the top, is much worse : it is a steep slope of ice ; we were obliged to cut steps with a hatchet all the way, and got on well enough. But the coming down is the worst, for if you slip there's an end of you."

* It is very little less than 11,000 feet high.

† In Germany it is usual to compute thus *by time*, meaning in this instance it would take three-quarters of an hour to arrive at the bottom.

" And no accident happened ?" I asked.

" No, all went on well; however we were obliged to leave some of the party behind, one at the ridge and three at the ice; they would not venture, and waited till we came back. Luckily we had a very fine day; the snow was quite hard in the morning, but later it grew much softer."

" But, Neuner, the other day when I was at the Ammergau, I heard that an idiot who wanders about there had been up and alone; is it true ?"

" Yes, quite true: he has always had a passion for ascending mountains, and sometimes he goes up one, sometimes another. Once he came home and told everybody he had been on the Zug Spitz. They all laughed at him of course, for no one believed it. This, it seems, hurt the poor fellow very much; so off he set, and after being absent several days, came home again and told the people he had been up the Zug Spitz, and that if they looked they would see a pole at the top. No one believed the tale now more than before; yet when they looked with their glasses, there sure enough was the pole stuck on the very highest point."

" Yes," I said, " I have seen the pole: but how get it up there? And then, to find his way quite alone! Why, it's almost incredible."

" But quite true," replied Neuner, " for there was no pole there before; besides he described everything exactly as it is. The most extraordinary part of the story is that he went up barefoot,—the second time at least, and the time before he slept on the mountain. That he was not frozen to death is quite a miracle."

" Did he tell where he got the pole, and how he managed to carry it ?"

" Oh yes," said Neuner, " we know about that. The

pole is a young fir: this he felled as far up the mountain
as possible, and then dragged after him all the rest of
the way.   Once he let it slip, and down it rolled a considerable distance; but he returned, and dragged it up
again.   And only think ! the poor fellow had nothing to
eat all the time, for he merely took a *kreutzer-semmel* (a
penny roll) with him, which dropped on the ice, and
rolled away into some crevice or hollow.   Since then he
has been on the Spitz Berg—the only person, I believe,
who ever was there ; and he says it is so frightful that
he will never go again, but the Zug Spitz he does not
mind attempting.   He has been on the Wetter Stein
too, and on nearly all the peaks you see of that range."

The gentian-gatherers had been gone some time, the
neatherd had been lying asleep on the bench beside the
stove since he had cooked my supper, and I began to
think it would be as well to turn into my resting-place.
The peasants stood up, the elder one said a prayer, which
the others repeated aloud after him, and then all knelt
to say the Lord's Prayer. Wishing me good-night they
went up a ladder behind the stove, and disappeared
through a trap-door, their beds being above the room
where we had been staying. Neuner preferred lying
down on a bench in the warmth. Being unacquainted
with the locality, the young forester went before me with
a lantern, and we thus proceeded to the shed and up the
shaky ladder to our dormitory. The loft was nearly filled
to the roof with hay. We stepped and tumbled along
over the fragrant heaps, and, aided by the dim light, I
soon made myself a right cozy nest. I pulled down
great masses of hay from the pile beside me, and my
companion flung whole armfulls over my body. Except
my head, which rested on a cloth thrown over the hay-
pillow—I owed the luxury of the cloth, by-the-by, to

the thoughtfulness of the neatherd—not an inch of me was to be seen. I was as warm as possible.

" Why, there are the two women!" exclaimed the young forester in surprise, holding up his lantern. They were lying close to us, but like myself so tucked up we had not observed them.

" No matter," I said, " as long as they do not snore: that is all I care about. Good night!"

CHAPTER XXIII.

MIST ON THE MOUNTAIN.

I AWOKE early the next morning, and groping my way clambered down the ladder. It was three o'clock, and as dark as pitch; and the gusts of cold damp air came creeping round my bare knees, which just before had been imbedded so warmly. Outside there was a drizzling rain, and mist, and impenetrable blackness; in short, to tell the honest truth, it looked miserably wretched. With such weather there was little prospect of success, and with—I don't know if it was a sigh, a groan, or a growl of discontent—I drew back my gloomy face, and went into the room to lace on my shoes. This done we took our rifles and started.

Most persons, doubtless, have walked out in a dark night; but if they have only done so on a tolerably smooth road, they will have but an imperfect notion of the unpleasantness attending every single step when the path is strewn with large stones, loose fragments of rock, broken up into holes or intersected by rivulets. You do not see where you are stepping, and thus often plant your foot so as to slip down a bank and let the water fill your shoes brimmingly. This however does not much matter, it is true, for it soon bubbles out again; but in going up a steep and slippery mountain, it is fatiguing, hindersome, and even dangerous to find yourself stumbling over unseen obstructions, or your nailed shoes sliding from under you down a slanting surface of stone. The angle up which you are going being pretty acute, down you come on such occasions on both hands, and, what is far more annoying than having your knees driven into the earth or among the stones, your rifle flies round your shoulder and descends with no little force upon the ground. This always went far to put me in a passion. On such occasions my first thought was my rifle; and if unable to see, I would feel, if all was in order.

We went up in a straight line for some time; at last Neuner said we should soon have better ground. We could now just see black patches, like blots, through the gloom, and soon these grew into distincter outlines, becoming trees and latschen. There was a rude path in the neighbourhood that led to the summit, but how discover the exact spot? Amid stunted bushes, looking one like another, and patches of torn-up rock, and gravel, and stones, it was difficult in the dusk to find the place.

"Yonder is the dead tree," said Neuner, "and the path is to the right, a little higher up."

"I think it is nearer the tree than where we are," answered the other, "and near thick clumps of latschen. Wait a moment," he added to me, "I'll go straight on, and do you, Neuner, keep to the right. We shall soon find it."

Presently a whistle told me the path was found, and going straight toward the sound, we all three proceeded one behind the other. As we neared the summit, the grey rock and snow appeared through the dun clouds, and below us mists were floating, which shut out the living world from view.

The north side of the mountain, as is always the case, wore a totally different aspect. The line of the ridge was the boundary of two distinct regions. From the summit we now looked down upon sharp points; all was broken and wilder in character than on the side where we had mounted. We went downwards, and wound along the slanting face of the rock; here and there stepping along a mere ledge, formed by a projecting layer of stone, our bodies slanting outwards toward the rocks and away from the precipice.* And now we mounted again, and reached the top of Hennenck. The vapours had before partially cleared away, but they now swept by beneath our feet, and we looked down on cloud, on dimness, and uncertainty. Close to us, a yard or so downwards, the traces of chamois were discernible in the snow; but they were old—some days old perhaps. Beyond lay a world of shadows, where no eye could penetrate. Suddenly the forester exclaimed, "There's a chamois!" I saw nothing; but a moment after from out the mist and cloud came the sound of a rolling stone, and as we listened we heard it bounding on till at last it was no longer audible.

We found but one new track of game in the snow, the others were all old. The place seemed forsaken. We still went on, and, creeping up a shoulder of the mountain, looked over into a hollow spread with verdure—for the mists had sailed away just then—in the sure hope of seeing some animal life; but our eyes swept over every inch of ground in vain.

It was now six o'clock, and I was glad to breakfast. A slice of brown bread and one of Christina's apples

---

* The clouds were just below our feet, so that it was impossible to see beyond; but for this circumstance, it might have been less pleasant to walk along that ledge.

furnished the meal. I relished it much, for I was very hungry. Before us rose the Bishop, a mountain of grey rock, on this side almost entirely covered with snow.

" Was that a good place for chamois formerly ?" I asked.

" No, never," replied Neuner; "but further down was one of their favourite haunts. Yonder runs the boundary-line which divides the chase belonging to the Eschenlohe peasants from that of the King. They come across, and leave the game no rest : you may hear shots cracking, all the year round ; in season or out of season, it is quite the same to them. Here we shoot the does too, because if *we* did not, *they* would ; so, you see, we are ourselves obliged to clear these mountains of the game ; indeed all along the boundary we are forced to destroy it."

On such a day as this it is impossible to calculate with any certainty upon a favourable change in the weather. The appearances around vary from one moment to another. Suddenly the mists come trailing by, and bits of floating cloud, smoke-like and vapoury ; and in a second all is shut out from your sight. A damp, cold, dull clogginess, like thickened air, hangs before your face ; you feel it sticking to you ; and to see your comrade beyond two paces' distance is impossible. Even then he looms towering through the fog, an indistinct spectral shape. Every landmark has disappeared ; there is not one single thing for the eye to seize and hold by, and this soon produces a disquieting sensation. All stability seems gone, and your nature is not used to this. Then you discover that the eye, as well as the footstep, needs firm ground to move over ; *it must have something to lay hold of*, and it peers around with a straining intensity into the sluggish, thick vacuity, but finds nothing.

It soon began to rain, and so heavily that we resolved to descend. On our slippery way down we found here and there the genuine Iceland moss. At last we reached a hollow, where the hut of a woodcutter was standing, and, rude as it was, it proved a welcome shelter. We were all wet to the skin. The younger forester took off his joppe, and wrung the water from his shirt-sleeves: he complained of being cold; however I did not feel so, and lying down on the bed of dry leaves, with my face toward the open door, watched the mist and rain so long that at last I fell asleep. After the rain it grew somewhat clearer, and in going along we could see down into a green valley.

" Once upon a time five good stags were there," said Neuner, pointing to the glen.

" It was hereabout that Bauer shot his stag, was it not ?" asked the other.

" Yes, just there, near yonder steep bank."

" And who shot the others?" I asked.

" Oh, poachers no doubt," said Neuner, " for they soon disappeared. Perhaps they were scared away and shot somewhere else; however *we* saw none of them."

" And did you never meet any of the men when you have been out on the mountain ?"

" No ; and had I caught one and brought him to the police, it is a hundred to one that he would have been punished."

" There was a keeper at Schlier See—Bromberger was his name—he once met a whole band of poachers, and among them was a notorious rascal; he therefore thought it better not to lose so good an opportunity, but to make sure of him, and, picking him out from the rest, sent a bullet through his body."

" That was in the old times, perhaps. It was by far

the best way. The poachers expected nothing else : they risked their lives, and we risked ours; they knew before-hand that, should we happen to meet one of them, he was a dead man, and in some places they treated us in the same manner. As I said, both parties expected no-thing else: neither complained; and if such a poacher got a full charge of swan-shot in his body when one of us caught him carrying off a roebuck or a chamois, he never laid a complaint or said a word about the matter, knowing very well he ought not to have been there,—that it was his own fault, and that he deserved the punishment. He was aware of what he risked before he went out; but as he could not gratify his passion without the danger, why he was content to take the venture as he found it."

" But what was the story of Bromberger?" asked the younger forester.

" Why," said I, " the thing happened thus :—A friend of mine, young Count D * * *, who was with Brom-berger at the time, has often told me the story. They were out together, looking for chamois : while sitting on the mountain and peering around, they suddenly per-ceived several men below the ridge, a good distance off, and, like themselves, watching for game. Their glasses were out in a moment, and one of the band was recog-nized as a noted poacher of the name of Hofer. At the sight of him the keeper's blood began to flow quicker, for this fellow was known as the most daring in the whole neighbourhood, and the blood of more than one forester was on his head. Solacher had fired at him once, but missed. Bromberger waited to see what they would do. After a time the men rose and came along a path leading to the ridge where the two were sitting. The whole band presently emerged from the hollow, and

stood exposed on the summit of the mountain, with Hofer
a little in front. Bromberger could not resist the temp-
tation, and determined to have a shot at him; so laying
a handkerchief folded together on the rock to serve as
a rest for his rifle, he prepared to fire. 'It is a long distance,' he said, turning to his companion, who, with the
glass to his eye, was waiting to observe the effect of the
shot; 'so I'll aim rather high, and somewhat to the
right, to allow for the wind coming up from below. If
I take him just between the shoulder and throat, you
will see I shall hit in the very centre of his chest!'
And a second after the rifle cracked, and down rolled
the poacher, with the ball crashing through his shoulder.
As you may imagine, the consternation of the others was
indescribable. Bromberger and young D * * * waited
just long enough to see the men carry off their wounded
comrade, and then creeping into the latschen, stole away
down the mountain, leaving the poachers at a loss to
tell whence the shot had come."

"You said just now he had a narrow escape once
already: what was it?"

"Yes," I continued, "and it was not long before.
The forester at Schlier See caught him in a hut where
he passed the night, and had him tried for poaching;
but he got off, as usual, without being punished."

"How was it he got him? Was Hofer alone?"

"No, there were two of them. The other was as
great a rascal as he—Nicolaus Angel by name, or Anni
Klaus as they called him. But I must begin at the
beginning. Not far from Schlier See is an Alm—the
Stocker Alp—and Andreas, the peasant who was there
during the summer—or Stocker Ander'l as he was named
—was an honest fellow, and one who could be trusted.
The foresters used to keep their meal there sometimes;

and even when he was gone, and the hut was empty,
they would leave their frying-pan or other things stowed
away in some secret place. Well, they knew that Hofer
occasionally passed the night in this hut, when out on
his poaching excursions; so they asked Ander'l if, when
he came again, he would let them know; for they had
often tried to catch him, but never were able. One
night he came as usual, and Anni Klaus with him. The
herdsman had only a boy in the hut beside himself; but
when the two poachers were asleep up among the hay,
the boy crept through the window and ran off as fast as
he could to Neuhaus—it is on the road to Fischbachau
you know—to tell the forester that Hofer and Nicolaus
were in the hut. It happened that none of the keepers
were at home, so he took with him two of the Grenz
Jäger,* who were stationed there, and set off. When
he got to the hut, he left the two men to watch outside;
and then making a great noise, spoke roughly and told
Andreas to get up and make him a fire, that the poachers
might not suspect he was in league with the forester.
On looking round he saw the two guns and the poles
which the men, strangely enough, had left hanging on
the wall near the hearth; and pretending to inquire whose
they were, got some evasive answer from Andreas. This,
he said, did not satisfy him : he suspected all was not
right, and would search the hut. So he went up, and
groping among the hay, seized hold of the two men's
feet, and in this way he pulled them out of their hiding-
place. As they had left their rifles below, instead of
taking them with them when they went to lie down,

---

* Custom-house officers, who patrol along the frontier, to prevent
smuggled goods being carried across. They are, in fact, preventive-
service men, but in arms and accoutrements are quite like our Rifle
corps.

they could do nothing. The thing was, I suppose, they felt so sure of being safe in the hut that they did not mind going to bed without their guns."

" Well, but how did they escape? What happened to them afterwards?"

"The forester, who was somewhat hasty, could not wait till it was broad day, but in his impatience set off with his prisoners at once. It is true they were bound, but not together; and, as they were going down, Anni Klaus made a spring, dashed into the bushes, and was out of sight in a moment."

" And the other, Hofer, what became of him?"

" He was examined, but, as is always the case, he denied everything. The powder in his pocket he said he had found, and invented a story about looking for a goat that had strayed, to account for his being on the mountain. Of course he would not confess, and he got off scot-free."

Chatting thus as we went along, we forgot the wet and the rugged stony path. Everywhere something of interest to the hunter was to be recounted: the story of an adventure with a poacher, a spot pointed out near which a certain good chamois had been shot, or where, in other days, the red-deer might always certainly be seen just as the sun was getting up over the opposite peaks.

From afar we now perceived the meadow on which our hut lay. It was still a good distance off, but the smoke was circling upwards over the brown roof, and the grass looked green, and it was cheerful to see the like after the wildness we had left. Moreover, as we went along, I was thinking all the while of the warm breakfast I would cook myself as soon as we arrived there, and of the snug room where I could hang up my clothes to dry.

Were people to reflect about it, they would often be

surprised at the pleasure which, under certain circumstances, the commonest sights are able to afford them.
When therefore the traveller recounts, and dwells upon,
some trifling incident—a mere sound perhaps—he should
not on that account be set down as trivial.   It was not
a trifle to *him*.   You will perceive this when you have
been a whole day among the rocks, and at last chance
upon a spot whence you happen to see smoke curling in
the air.   Your heart bounds at the sight; and though as
yet you have not even a glimpse of the hut whence it
proceeds, in thought you are already in the human habitation.   From that moment there is an end of your
loneliness,—that handful of blue vapour has filled up
the distance which separated you from your kind.

And when the mists suddenly clear away, and show
you a patch of green, and hard and determined outlines
—it matters not of what—how beautiful you think them!
and your gladdened eye flies to the place to alight upon
it, after having been for hours unable to find one little
spot of earth whereon to rest.

When we reached the hut, the first thing as usual was
to look to the rifles; and then taking off the heavy shoes,
soaked with rain like all the rest of my things, I went
into the kitchen to see after the bread and milk, or " milk
soup,"* as the peasants here call it.   I found the neatherd with a large mass of delicious butter in his hands,
just made.   In a few minutes I had a blazing fire crackling on the hearth, and while a pan full of creamy milk

---

* There ought to be a lump of butter put into the hot milk to make
the genuine " milk soup," and the cow-herd wanted very much to fling
in a piece.   He was surprised I could think of eating it without a pinch
of salt being added, " for," said he, " if you don't put any, the milk will
be quite sweet."   He looked rather astonished when I told him that was
just what I liked, and by his manner I saw he thought my taste a barbarous one, though he did not say so.

U

was boiling, the brown loaf was sliced into the pan in readiness. It was ten o'clock, and I had been out since three; so that, when at last the frothing milk was poured over the bread, and I had carried it into the room, and sat there comfortably drying in the warmth, I enjoyed to the full the luxury of that plentiful repast. The herdsman too brought a large piece of the fresh-made butter on a clean board, and fetching a pinch of salt, put it down with the loaf on the table before me. What could man desire more? There is positive happiness in such a meal, and I cannot think that any one who had himself known the luxury of appeasing his hunger with warm food when cold and famishing, would ever turn away unkindly from the starving wretch asking alms to buy himself bread.

The rain ceased; the blue sky again was visible, and leaving the hut we turned our steps homewards.

CHAPTER XXIV.

THE OLD BUCK.

SHOULD you ever go up the Oester Berg, you will see on
your right hand, quite at the top, and just before you
arrive at the first meadow, a little wooden chapel, with
a rude bank before it, in order that the passer-by may
there kneel and pray. We had just reached this spot,
talking as was our wont of matters that most interested
us, when Neuner, suddenly stopping in his story, exclaimed, "There's a chamois! Come on, don't stop!"
he said, as I lagged behind to examine the mountain-side
and discover where he was. A few steps further, and
we reached the bench beside the chapel, whence with our
glasses we could watch the animal without his observing us.

"Where is he, Neuner?"

"Look," he replied, "you see that long strip of geröll
coming down from the latschen; well, to the right is a
black spot,—that's he."

"Ah! now I see him; he is looking down at us."

"Yes, he heard us talking; but who would ever have
thought of his minding it at such a distance? The thing
is, the chamois have grown unusually shy from being
hunted about wherever they go. They never have any

u 2

peace; the peasants are firing eternally, and even though they may not hit them, the noise scares and makes them as wild as possible."

"'Tis a capital buck," I observed, examining him with my glass. "Now he is going: he is turning round, and will soon be among the latschen. Now he stops again, —just in the middle of the geröll. How capitally I see him now! He is looking down at us again. What *can* he be afraid of!" And at once he disappeared among the rocks and bushes.

What was to be done? To reach the spot where he had been standing would take, at the very least, three-quarters of an hour—besides he was gone; and though, from the way in which he left the open space for a covert, I judged he would not be very distant, still it was an impossibility to reach the rocks above him without being heard, they were so steep and difficult.

"The only thing would be," said Neuner musing, "to wait for him up there. He is often where we just now saw him; a little higher or lower, as may be, but still in the neighbourhood."

"Do you think he will be out again this evening? Far off he is not, of that I am certain; most likely in among the latschen, under the wall of rock to the left, for he went away quite leisurely."

"No, he probably is not far, but whether he will be out again this evening is a question; besides," continued Neuner, looking up to the rocks just over the spot where the chamois had been standing, "the way up there is most difficult. It is no joke, I assure you. There is but one place where you can pass, just above the geröll yonder, past the latschen, and so over the ridge of the mountain: that is the only way out. You have to creep up between and under the crags: 'tis an awkward place, and you see there are no latschen the greater part of the distance."

While I listened to him I was examining the places he was describing with my glass, following him step by step, and looking out to find which would be the best spot to attempt the passage. Once on the commanding crag jutting out over the vale, I should command the whole space where the chamois would be likely to pass, and should have a fair though perhaps a long shot, as he sauntered about on the patches of verdure, or sunned himself on the blocks of stone.

"I see the place where it would be most likely I could get up," said I to Neuner: "the rock is steep, and the ledge in one part very narrow, but still I think I could manage it."

"Bauer was there once, and said it was extremely difficult, but I dare say you could do it; however," he added, after a moment's reflection, "I have been thinking it would be better to try for him in another way. We will go round the mountain, and you," turning to the young forester who was with us, "you wait here an hour, and then go up to the ridge, and keep along it for a good distance. Afterwards you must climb along the steep wall of rock above where we shall be standing, and come out at the further end. Make as much noise as you like, but do not start for a full hour. Let me see: it is twelve now by my watch,—at one you can set off; you will want an hour to reach the top."

"Yes: full that," said the young fellow; "'tis scrambling work there, but in about an hour I can do it."

We went on, and presently were going to quit the path and enter the wood, but Neuner thought it was better to keep even still further down before doing so. "He may see us," he said, "for the forest has been rather thinned here. I know that buck well: he is a most cunning fellow, and so shy that it is the most difficult thing in the world to get near him. Bauer shot at him once, but missed: he has been shot at too by the poachers, so that he is as wary as an old fox."

"Is that his usual haunt where we saw him today?"

"Why he changes his place pretty often. Sometimes he is opposite on the left-hand side, when no cattle are there; sometimes he will wander round to the Fricker. He ought not to have gone away just now, far below him as we were; but that comes from being shot at so often."

We looked at our watch, and found that we had fifty minutes to get to the place where I was to stand; by that time he whom we left behind would be on the move. Twenty minutes—forty—fifty minutes—at last we are there, but it was good climbing to accomplish it in that time. Just above where we stood an isolated crag rose from the steep side of the mountain. "There you will take your stand," said Neuner; "you have a good view below and above you, and if the buck is not gone he will be sure to pass down here when he hears footsteps coming up the other side. Look! you see those loose stones: he will cross those, and you can fire as is most convenient, either then or as he passes lower down. But all that you know without my telling you; so clamber up and choose your place, and keep a sharp look-out, for by this time my comrade will be on the move." And thus saying he left me, to take his stand somewhat higher, nearer the summit.

With my heels well in the earth, so as not to slip forward, I sat down, rifle in hand, where I could command the depth immediately below me on my right, and at the same time see far up the mountain—indeed

nearly to the sky-line. I was gloriously enthroned. To
my left the piled-up mountains, grey or snow-covered,
with the magnificent Zug Spitz forming the last out-
work of the impassable barrier, and the peaks of all just
veiled with a thinly-woven cloud; before me the whole
declivity, with broken rocks and precipices and green
bushes, stretching downwards to the vale; Farchant,
with its red church-spire, its cottages, and road and
river; while further off across the pasturage was Garmisch, at the foot of the Kramer. To the right there
was a sweet sight. Through a dip in the mountain the
high vale of Ettal appeared,—a beautiful expanse of
green-sward, and the stately church too was seen; and
behind this peep in the mountain other distinct peaks
were visible, gradually sloping downwards to the plain,
and losing themselves at last in the flat land beyond. I
looked on all this from my rocky throne, and the sight
and the feeling of self-reliance, and of strength in every
limb, filled my whole frame with a thrill of exhilirating
gladness. And over my broad domain—for mine it was,
but without the care of governing—there lay a murmuring stillness; the hum of life that breathed and moved
below me in the vale,—of distant cataracts reverberating
among the hollow rocks: it hung in the air, or rather
was inwoven with it. It was a very different stillness
from that of the high desolate mountain-peaks; for there
it is a palpable thing, which clings to your heart and op-
presses your chest by its weight; and it comes upon you
surely, like the chill of death, that creeps along the
limbs, and cannot be evaded, despite your inmost striving and endeavour.

It has often occurred to me, when thus looking down
upon a land, how solemnly sad must have been the feelings of Moses when he went up from the plains of Moab

to the top of Pisgah, the highest point of the mountains
of Nebo. Though he was an old man, how must his
heart have swelled at what he saw,—the Jordan and the
groves of palms, and the fat pasturages of Basan stretching away into the distance; the mountains with the
thick oak-woods of their valleys, and on the plain the
herds of the Tribes, while before him he looked over
" The City of Palm-trees," Jericho, and away " unto
the great sea toward the going down of the sun:" and
then the remembrance that he was gazing on that earth
for the last time! But, above all, how in that mountain solitude must he have felt his loneliness! There
is to me something quite overwhelming in the thought
of going up unto a mountain to die. It is an almost
superhuman act, worthy indeed of a Prophet,—of one
" whom the Lord knew face to face,"—but is not for the
men of this generation.

I sat here with my hand on my rifle for an hour and
a half; but the minutes did not pass laggingly: I was
all attention, and eye and ear were watching for the
slightest circumstance that might betoken the approach
of a chamois. Moreover I would every now and then
cast a look at the world at my feet, and let the grandeur
and the loveliness fill my heart. Fancy besides was
busily at work, as is ever the case with the hunter when
awaiting the approach of game. At such times, what
pleasant visions pass before his brain; what delicious
hopes that *may be* realized! The buck I was expecting
was not only a good one, but a well-known one too.
He had been pursued by several, and all had failed
to obtain the prize. Many were the shots that had
been fired after him, but they all had missed. He
had become notorious by his escapes: he was quite
an historical personage. And should he *now* come—

yonder, for example, near those stones—and I be lucky
enough to bring him down, how proudly should I return home and relate that the old buck had at last
fallen! Then too, in after-times, when the keepers
would talk of their exploits, and of the noble stags or
sturdy chamois that had fallen here and there,—each
one remembered as accurately, with place and date,
as a succession of monarchs,—then would this famous
buck be mentioned, and they would tell how he had been
often followed in vain, and how at last "the English-
man"* brought him death.

And these fine imaginings were all I had, for no
chamois came. At length, high up among the latschen
the young forester appeared, making his way downward
as well as he was able: he had seen nothing, it was
therefore evident the wary old buck had betaken himself
to some remoter stronghold.

Such a place as that where I was watching is my delight—is the delight indeed of every hunter; for from
it I could have seen the game, had any come, long before it reached me. And this is always pleasant; not
only because it gives you time for preparation, but on
account of the delicious excitement you feel in every
vein, from the moment you espy the coming creature
till that other moment when you feel it is your own.
Your hopes, your fears, your longings—all that makes
up the sum of the enjoyment—is thus heightened by
being prolonged. You watch its approach with greedy
eyes, and full of anxieties: the excitement would choke
you if it lasted long; yet two such minutes—and they
seem hours—are worth whole ordinary days.

The flutter and nervousness felt by him whose whole
heart is in the chase, when he first is in presence of

* "Der Herr Engländer," as the people always named me.

the stag, is a curious psychological phenomenon. The Germans have a special name for this state, and call it "Hirsch Fieber" (Stag fever). The excitement you are in quite lames you. Of course it varies in degree with different persons, according to temperament, and the phlegmatic will probably never experience it at all. In me it showed itself in the highest degree. When I heard the rush of the stag among the branches, or saw him approaching at a distance, my heart began to beat *audibly*, my breath came quickly, every limb trembled, and I felt half suffocated. To take a deliberate aim was of course impossible, for my rifle rose and fell like a bough swayed by the wind. But I remember one instance in which a sort of magnetic influence seemed to be exercised over me. I was waiting for a stag on the edge of the covert. Presently I heard something rustle, and the fever began; but only a kid leaped by, and I was calm again. Soon after I heard the step of the stag, and in another second his majestic head looked forth from the green branches. On he came towards me, down a gentle slope, slowly and unaware of my presence. The rifle had been raised when first I heard his approach, and it was levelled still; the hair-trigger was set, and a breath almost would have been sufficient to move the trigger; my finger too was upon it, and I wished to pull, yet for some cause or other I was unable to do so. There I stood, the magnificent stag opposite me, and I charm-struck and spell-bound. The slightest movement of the finger would have been enough, *but I could not move it;* and only when he had disappeared, did my fast-clenched teeth relax, and I drew a long breath and felt myself relieved.

Since then I have understood the power of the snake over other animals; how by fixing its eyes on a bird or rabbit the prey will become so fascinated as to be help-less for escape, but awaits the monster's approach, and even walks into his jaws. The influence, it is true, is not quite the same in both cases; for in the hunter this want of power to execute his will does not arise from fear but is probably merely an intense anxiety not to miss the mark,—a violent struggle between suddenly aroused emo-tions. In time the "fever" wears off; yet occasionally, though you flatter yourself you are grown stoically calm, and that an old sportsman like you is not to be disturbed by such freaks and fancies,—occasionally, I say, if you are kept long in suspense, you too will get the "fever;"—you will feel it laying hold of you in spite of all your efforts to shake it off.*

I do not remember any allusion to this *extreme* state by English sportsmen. They acknowledge being "ner-vous;" nothing however transpires of chattering of teeth, of gasping for breath, or of violent tremblings throughout the whole body; yet I do not doubt that the presence of the red-deer of Scotland may have the same potent charm as that of his German compeer; and I am quite sure, if it ever were my good-fortune to get a day's stalk-ing in the Highlands, that such a sight as Sir Edwin Landseer has shown us in his "Drive" would set my heart beating exactly as of old.

It was now three o'clock, and we turned our steps downwards; but still, not to give up a chance, we deter-mined to have a look into a deep ravine that yawned like a terrific gash in the mountain's side. It extended al-most to the very summit,—jagged, deep, and frightful.

---

* I know a forester who has never been able to get over it. I once saw him when we were out together after a stag. "He's coming! he's coming!" he stammered, as he caught sight of antlers between the trees, and his eyes stared, and he trembled as though it had been a ghost.

Hither, Neuner said, the chamois loved to resort; it was a quiet spot, or rather one undisturbed by human neighbourhood; but the roar of the near waterfall resounded in the chasm. We cautiously climbed down towards the brink, and looked over and around. Every crag was minutely examined with scrutinizing eye; our gaze pierced among the stunted shrubs and the withered stems of ghastly-looking skeletons of trees; and then we looked high, high up, where the mountain had been torn, and where the savage rent had left a perpendicular wall of glaring stone. But all was without sign of life,—not a creature was to be seen. Suddenly a sharp whistle came across to us over the broken hollow. We started, and each looked at the other in surprise; and then, with widely-open eye and with head bent forward, gazed and stared toward the rocks whence the sound proceeded. It was a chamois that had observed us; but none of us could see anything. At last I did: "There!" I whispered eagerly, and pointing straightforwards across the chasm.

"Beyond the first or the second ravine?" asked Neuner.

"Beyond the second."

"I see it!" he exclaimed almost immediately.

"A doe!" said the younger forester.

We looked a long while, and the chamois sprang up the rocks, and then stopped to browse: it seemed no longer afraid. Any attempt to reach it was out of the question, so we turned homewards.

Here and there on declivities will be found open spaces, without trees or shrubs, and covered with a long grass, the blades of which do not grow erect, but hang downward with the slope. The sun and air dry the stems, and make their surface as slippery as ice, and these places are perhaps the most difficult of any to descend: if you

slip, down you go, till a tree or shrub or some inequality
of surface stops your descent. There was no danger now;
but when such a grassy slope or *laane* ends on the brink
of a precipice, it is rather perilous if your foot should
glide. Some years ago a dairymaid from one of the huts
on the mountains near Berchtesgaden slipped in coming
down a *laane*. She was unable to stop herself or hold on
by the long grass, and went over the brink at the foot of
the slope into the abyss. When the poor girl was found,
the braid of her hair, which she wore twisted in a knot
behind her head, was lying in the cavity of the brain.
Misfortunes occur almost every year from the treacherous
smoothness of these grassy slopes.

We at last regained the path. It was raining at Garmisch. The effect of the slanting sun-rays on the thin
clouds was of exceeding loveliness. The mountains were
arrayed in pearly hues; vapoury horizontal mists were
lying lightly on the air near their tops, but their grey
and snowy peaks could be seen rising above them. A
magnificent rainbow now blushed into existence, span-
ning the mountain to the very top with its lofty elliptical
curvature: while the part that was earthward rested on
the side of the mountain, showering a halo of rosy and
violet light upon the trees and bushes. The whole scene
was surpassingly beautiful.

A rugged and broken path leads from the road down
to Farchant. We were full an hour descending to the
village, and one hour of such descent fatigues and racks
the joints far more than a whole morning's climbing: it
was a hard day's work, and we had all enough. Tired
and dirty as I was, the sight of the inn cheered and gladdened me. Having first well cleaned my rifle, I attended
to myself; and presently, refreshed and with a good appetite, went down to the little parlour to sup, where I

found my two companions and the other worthies of the village.*

FRANZ VON KOBELL has made the fancies and imaginings of the hunter, while expecting game, the theme of one of his poems. He has, with his accustomed truthfulness of delineation, pictured all the hopes and longings which the chamois-hunter will cherish and dally with on such occasions; and he has given the end of these pleasant castles in the air, with a quiet humour and, as I have often found by unwelcome experience, with comic truth. And comic enough it often is, if we compare our expectations at such times with the eventual reality. Yet we always weave new fancies, and look at the rocks and bushes and the cool ravine, and think and wish so long, till at last we feel sure a chamois *will* spring down yonder slope, or that a good stag *must* soon emerge from the shades of the forest. And at such times all seems so very plausible, and wears so comely an air of truth, that at last good, honest, jog-trot, sober, unimaginative Common Sense yields to the pretty coquetry and winsome ways of Fancy, and believes, and even sees, all that she has been archly whispering in his ear.

---

* I afterwards (Feb. 16, 1851) got a letter from my friend Neuner, containing news of the old chamois buck. He writes :—"The chamois that remain with me the summer through have this winter gone over into the chase of the Eschenlohe peasantry, and have, as I am told, been considerably reduced in number; so that with me, next summer, there will be but poor sport, and the whole season's shooting will consist at most of but a few head of game. The buck on the Fricker Reison has not changed his quarters; he is still alive, and his haunt is in the very same place where it used to be."

The lines I have here attempted to render in English verse, are written in the original in a Bavarian dialect.

The Chamois-Hunter's Soliloquy.

" Ha! what a glorious deep ravine!
    Hence I can see far round :
Here on this spot I 'll sit me down,
    A better can't be found.
A chamois *must* be up among
    Those latschen near yon blocks ;
And if he cross to yonder slope,
    He *must* pass down those rocks.
And down below I tracked a stag
    As big as any cow :
He too will soon be on the move,
    And here I 've chance enow."

So there the Hunter takes his seat,
    The hours roll by apace,
And thinks of all that might appear,
    At such a famous place.
If only he 'd a little luck !
    If but a lynx would come !
" Old Johann once did shoot one so,
    And here I know are some.
A lynx! Ay, that 's not easy though,
    The surface is but small."
Then he takes aim, and thinks that he
    Could hit one with a ball.
" And Michael too,—just such a place
    'Twas where he saw the bear ;
Now if *he* came and trudged along
    Right down the pathway there,
He 'd get knocked over the ravine :—
    What would our Ranger say ?
And how they 'd question me, and stare !
    There 'd be fine work that day !
My lassie would be proud of me,
    She 'd tell it all the folk ;
'Twould bring me seventy gulden too,
    Faith, that were no bad joke !

'Twould be in all the papers too,
　The King of it would hear;
Why, who knows but he'd say, 'I'll have
　Him made Head-Forester'?

" Should a wolf come, 'twould also do:
　Yes,—wolves they prowl far round,
And such a place as this they like,
　Where something's to be found.
A bran-new rifle then I'd have,
　As handsome as could be;
And carved upon the stock a wolf,
　With date, that all might see.
And should one at a shooting-match
　Ask 'From the city, eh?'
'No, no, 'tis his who shot the wolf,'
　Is what they all would say."

And so with rifle ready cocked,
　He sits, and thinks, and thinks,
Till it grows dark; but nothing comes,
　Bear, chamois, wolf, nor lynx.

305

CHAPTER XXV.

THE KROTENKOPF AND THE KRAMER.

BAUER was to come from Farchant, and meet me at the
Oester Berg ; I therefore started alone from Partenkirchen, and went up the well-known path leading to the
hut. As I walked slowly on, with that deliberate pace
which, when you have a long ascent before you, it is
well to choose, I presently reached a bushy spot, where
however a precipitous steep on one side showed the valley, with its winding stream and cottages and pasturage
lying at my feet. On a sudden, from out the green
branches on my right, rose Bauer to his full height,
and gave me a cheerful greeting. It was like one of
Roderick Dhu's men starting up from his ambush of
heather.*

* I must here give some account of the excellent young hunter, whom
I greatly liked for his amiable disposition, his kind and gentle manners,
his daring courage, and his ever-cheerful nature. His open, honest
countenance at once won your favour. He was one of the best climbers
far around ; and he longed to attempt some ascent beset with difficulties.
I expressed a wish to go up the Zug Spitz, and he begged that when I
went he might accompany me. Since then he has been up, and I also ;
but his adventurous descent was so perilous that it may here be noticed.

It was the intention of some of the villagers to plant a large iron cross
on the top of the Zug Spitz (10,094 feet high), to be carried up in parts,
and put together on the summit. Accordingly a party set out one afternoon from Partenkirchen, and it was only when Bauer came home in

x

"I thought you would soon come," he said; "so I sat down here to wait for you, and was looking across to my sister's cottage at Ettal. It is just visible through that dip in the hill yonder. She was in the garden a moment ago, and then somebody came in from the road. I could see all capitally from here."

We went on, and were soon at our old quarters. I fetched a pan of milk from the cupboard, and slicing into it the bread which I had brought with me, had my supper, and then went to bed.

The next morning we were out betimes, and, as we mounted higher, saw, soon after dawn, a couple of stags

the evening, after his day's round in the mountains, that he learned they were gone. He would not lose the opportunity, so without resting and late as it was, off he set from the village of Farchant, to overtake them at the hut on the mountain-side, where he knew they would pass the night. With his rifle at his back and his dog for companion he walked on, and reached the spot at dawn an hour before the party started for the summit. They soon reached it: the cross was erected, and firmly soldered in a socket of rock, and then all turned to descend the way they had come. But Bauer resolved to try if it were not possible to get down on the north side. All wished to dissuade him; and indeed, when you look down that almost perpendicular slope, covered as it then was, and is at all times indeed except in the height of summer, with snow and ice, it is hardly conceivable that any one could ever dream of such an undertaking. As none would accompany him, he went alone; and the others turned homewards. After scrambling and sliding down the frightful slope for some time, Bauer at last came to a place where he could get no further. To climb up again was impossible. There he stood in that dreary desert of snow, high up in middle air, where assuredly till then no human being had ever passed or even thought of passing. He had come to the ridge of a perpendicular wall, down which there was no getting save by leaping below. But something must be done, for he cannot stay there to freeze among the ice. So in order to see if the snow was hard enough to bear him were he to spring down, he took off his rücksack, in which he carried his dog, whose feet had got sore, and flung both below upon the snow-field. The snow bore the weight. He then tried his rifle, for he knew that if this did not sink deep, he

and some chamois on one side of the Bischof. What luck! We crept along over the ground, as though we feared to hurt the blades of grass; and, carefully avoiding the stones, stole softly onwards. And now the spot is reached whence the game will surely be visible, and we shall be able to get a shot; and lifting our heads slowly and carefully, our eyes sweep over the sides of the hollow, expecting every moment to light on the object of our hopes. But there is no need of all this care, for not a creature is to be seen. We then examined the slot, and found that the stag had, at most, eight points on his antlers; he had gone over a shoulder

himself might venture down. At last he too jumps from the brink into the bed of the snow. He flounders out as best he can, and on and on, desperately venturing everything to save himself from a dreadful death of cold and hunger in those regions of torpor and solitude. But it must not be forgotten that he had been walking the whole of the preceding day and night, and again that day, without rest and with but little food; and it is not surprising therefore that at length his strength succumbed to the overpowering exertion of wading through the snow. And he sank at last, unable to move further. He had reached the lower part of the mountain, just above the Eib See, and here he was found lying by some smugglers, who by dangerous circuitous paths evade the look-out men of the Custom-house.

Bauer has never been like his former self since this adventure. I met him a year or two ago at Berchtesgaden, where the King had given him a place as under-forester, and the worthy fellow's face grew quite radiant when he saw me waiting for him on the shore of the lake. Nor was I less pleased to meet him again. His frank countenance wore the same mild expression, but it bore deep traces of what he had undergone. His chest too hurt him.

But since then another sad accident has befallen him. He was always venturesome, and the most daring of climbers still. At seven in the morning of the 21st of July, 1855, while after the chamois, he fell from a wall of rock—the Kehlstein—sixty feet high, turning over three times in his descent, into the Schatzkohl Alpe. He dragged himself to a hut, where he was found still alive, though his head and back were terribly mangled and bruised. His fall was occasioned by the loosening of a stone.

x 2

of the mountain, and across some splashy ground covered with many traces of both deer and chamois.

We were advancing slowly up the Krotenkopf,—a mountain somewhat less than 8,000 feet high; on our left the stony Bischof extended its broad side before us, over which was now spread a thin covering of snow.

"Do you see anything?" I asked of Bauer, who was looking fixedly across at the opposite mountain.

"I *think* it's a chamois!" he replied, with his eyes still fixed on a certain dark spot, and turning his head a little on one side, as if to look at it from another point of view.

"Yes, it *is* a chamois," he continued, as we looked through our glasses; "that's all right! We have plenty of time, for he will not go away. But let us on now: yonder—do you see those rocks—great blocks of stone, just on the shoulder of the mountain?—well, there I think you had better stand; and then I will go over the ridge, and roll down stones, to put the chamois on the move; he will be sure to come round close to where you are, and you can get a famous shot."

We were a considerable time in reaching the place, yet it did not seem far off. But in the mountains distances are very illusory, and you are sure to fancy them shorter than they really are.

"How long will you be crossing over the ridge?" I asked of Bauer, as he was about to set off.

"I can hardly say; it's a good way up and round to the other side. But I will tell you what; as soon as the chamois is on the move, I'll fire off my rifle, so that you may know, and be on the look-out."

"Very well: this is a good place where I now am. I will keep behind these rocks, and shall thus be almost hidden."

"When he comes, he will pass along yonder. Do you see?—just there, where those stones are peeping out of the snow." And off he bounded with a nimble step, and was soon out of sight, as he took a slanting direction over the mountain. There was plenty of snow where I stood ; for the spot being overshadowed, there it lay week after week, safe from the influence of the sun. I brushed some away, and lay down on the rock. I was tired and listless, and then grew angry with myself for being so. I could not tell what was the matter with me ; but, for some cause or other, I strangely enough did not feel the intense interest which always possessed me at such moments of expectation. I took out a crust and ate it, but more for pastime than from appetite. I was annoyed at my own indifference, and at such unwonted apathy. A charm seemed to have been broken, and my eyes now looked at the magnificent forms about me, no longer wonderingly, but as though they were quite common, everyday things. Suddenly a thundering sound reverberates from the Bischof, and rolls up the sides of the Krotenkopf; and then falls back again, like a great wave, that, breaking its massiveness against the rocks, tumbles to pieces with a low, murmuring moan ;—it was from Bauer's rifle. I started up, and something of the old feelings came creeping on, but sluggishly, and not with a sudden rush as heretofore. I was behind a piece of rock, that covered me entirely up to my chin, and looked right in front, where I expected to see the chamois appear, but nothing came. Presently a stone moved slightly ; and turning my eyes to the side whence the sound proceeded, there stood two chamois at gaze on my left hand, one behind the other : both were immovable, and looking steadfastly in my direction. I was as immovable as they ; it was evident they suspected danger, but I did not think they could see me, for they had not whistled as yet; and there was still a possibility they might, in moving on, come a little nearer, for at present they were a long distance off. There they stood for a time, I all the while hardly daring to move even my eyelids, anxious what the next moment would bring with it. The nearest chamois was the smaller of the two,—it was of a reddish colour, while the other larger one was quite black. But he was the further off, so, if I fired at all, I thought it would be better to take the nearer animal. Thus we remained in presence of each other; all was still and silent as the very air,—it was as if everything had been petrified by some sudden spell.

Suddenly the nearer chamois utters the sharp whistle; but he gazes still, and is motionless. I now knew there was no hope of their coming nearer; in a moment they would be off. There was no time to lose; and, bringing my cheek down to my rifle, to take aim, I carefully prepared to fire. The loud report breaks the long silence. "Is he hit?" I ask myself. "No, they're both going away! It cannot have touched him! Yet the one that lags behind—he does not leap up the mountain so lightly as the other! I don't know though—something seems the matter with him—yet—yes, he's off!" Far as he now was, I still fired the other barrel, and knew at once I had missed.

I followed their track some distance, to see if there were any drops of blood on the snow, but to my great vexation found nothing. Bauer now came over the mountain, and at once called to ask if I had got one of them.

"There were two, were there not?" he said. "I only saw the second after I had fired my rifle. You have missed? What, did not they come near? No, you can't have missed! Where were they?" he continued, as he looked for their slot in the snow.

"But I have. For a moment I thought I had hit him, but now I see I did not."

"Where were they standing when you fired?"

"Further on. But it is useless to look: I have followed them already, and found nothing. Further on,—down lower—further still, if you *will* look," I called out, as he inquired about the position of the chamois.

"Here's hair enough however," he cried, holding up some in his fingers, as I ran to the place. The long black hair of the back was lying on the snow, and by its length it was evident that it had been shaved off quite close to the backbone. The supposition that one moved as though hurt, which I had a moment entertained, but afterwards given up as a mere fancy, was, I now saw, well founded I *had* touched him. The ball had just grazed the vertebræ, but so very slightly as to cause only the momentary lameness I had remarked.

"Look how long they are!" said Bauer, examining the speckled hairs. "Well, that was near! an eighth of an inch lower down, and he would have dropped at once. 'Twas a long shot though, that I must say."

The mishap was indeed particularly vexatious; for, had they come but a little nearer, I might easily have shot both,—right and left; and it would have been a pleasant thing to recur to in aftertime.

The rest of the day we saw nothing. At the hut the herdsman foretold change of weather. "The cattle were so wild," he said, "they had broken the pole of the waggon that morning. He was quite sure it would not be fine on the morrow; it's a sure sign when the cattle are so restless. As to the almanack-writers, they may say what they like,—the cattle are never wrong."

We now turned our steps homeward. As we went along, Bauer told me how, close to the spot we were passing, he had once met some poachers. "There were five of them," he said, "and I crept through the bushes, and got quite near them unobserved. At last they saw me, and called out that I should make the best of my way off, or they would fire."

"And did you go?"

"Of course not. I was lying on the ground behind a great piece of stone, and I knew they could not touch me. No; I stopped, and looked at them well. I recognized them all, and gave their names to the Police, but nothing was done to them."

A day or two after I arranged with Bauer to go up the Kramer : though I knew there was little chance of meeting chamois there, I still wished to go ; for it is possible to be prepossessed by the face of a mountain, as well as by the human countenance, and this was now the case with me. There was a hut there,—or rather, as it was of stone, a house containing a single room, which had been constructed some years ago for the present King, should he ever seek shelter or accommodation on the mountain.

"A blanket is there, too !" said Bauer triumphantly ; "and a stove is in the room ; only think, a stove! The place is snug enough, but it is a long time since I was up there."

After crossing the meadows we passed at once into a gulley, where the torrent came tumbling along over its rugged bed. The din of waters drowned every other sound, so that we did not hear the approach of Neuner, who suddenly stood before us, on his way down from the mountain. We stopped a moment, to interchange some questions, and to pat old Bursch's head, and then

we went on up the steep and narrow path.* As we
ascended higher, the wild beauty of the spot became
more and more visible. In some places there were
perpendicular buttresses of rock, of five or six hundred
feet in height, with here and there projecting spots,
covered with grass, or a pine-tree that had managed to
force its roots into some chance fissure. This was a
" Graben," as well as the " Rethel Clam," but very unlike it in appearance and character. Grand as the forms
were, the whole was so shut in by the peculiar shape of
the mountain, and the parts brought so near together,
that verdant nooks were formed, giving the whole a
mild aspect; moreover there was herbage in abundance
among the grey rocks, and the foliage of pines and
latschen to break the rugged and sharp outlines. Here
and there you saw little green spots, that you would
gladly have alighted on, had you had wings to fly there.
On our path was overshadowing wood; and the shade,
and a languor I could not shake off, soon brought me
to a resting-place. It was a delicious afternoon, and,
though the 23rd of September, agreeably warm. I
looked before me, down into the deep gully, and listened
to the waters below, sounding, where we sat, just pleasantly loud enough to tell of their presence, and nothing more. While I was thus contemplating the scene,

* One of those mishaps which occasionally occur in the mountains
happened to this good dog, just before my departure from Partenkirchen. Neuner missed him on the mountain, but as he whistled for him
in vain, thought he had followed the slot of a roe, and would come back
after a time. He however never saw him again, and supposes he fell
over the rocks in the ardour of pursuit. For two days Neuner searched
the whole mountain for his dog, in case he should have got into some
place whence he could not climb out again, and where he might be still
alive. He called him by name, as he knew that, if alive, he could
answer by a bark or howl. In spite of all his endeavours he could find
no traces of him.

I heard the sound of bells. I listened more attentively.
Yes, I was right; but then the thought occurred to me,
how could such a peal as that come from Partenkirchen,
or Garmisch, or indeed any other village? I looked up,
to see if Bauer's countenance betrayed a sign of having
heard them too; but nothing there told me that he had,
and how should he? for it was the well-known sound
of the Bath Abbey bells, that were ringing as merry a
peal as I had ever heard them do in the days of my boyhood. I got up, and stood, and looked round, and convinced myself I was not asleep; but still I heard the dear,
well-remembered bells, that were as familiar as the voices
of old friends. Now they fell, as if borne away on the
wind, and then again came swelling on the ear, as though
the ringers were pulling right lustily. It was so real,
that, had it been some simple church-bell merely, I might
have been cheated into belief; but there was no mistaking those of my own dear native Bath. The author of
that most delightful of books 'Eothen' mentions something of the sort occurring to him on a journey,—if I
remember rightly, when he was crossing the Desert.*

We went on, and still on, and it seemed as if there
was no end to our steep ascent. I could hardly drag
my limbs along, so weary was I; and had I been alone,

---

* I ought perhaps to mention that I had been at Bath but a week or
two before. In both cases the circumstance arose, no doubt, from the
nerves being unstrung by coming illness; for it was afterwards that I
fell sick at Partenkirchen, and the author of 'Eothen,' on arriving at
Cairo, had an attack of fever, if not of the plague. I am inclined to
think that in every instance, whether such sounds are heard at sea or
elsewhere, a state of debility or excitement would be found to be an attendant circumstance, were the matter inquired into. If nothing un-
toward follow, it is thought no more of; but should the person by whom
such music is heard die soon afterwards, it is then looked upon as a
supernatural warning, and a friendly summons is recognized in those
loud sounds of home.

should certainly have lain down to sleep. Bauer was
always far in advance, stopping to wait for me, and
urging me on; for though we were now at last approaching the summit, which was evident from the
changed character of the scenery, and from the patches
of snow that were lying about, we still had a long way
to go, and evening was coming on, and in such a place
daylight was as necessary as air to breathe. The mountain was of vast size; and, as I looked upwards to the
sky-line, and saw the drear expanse, and felt my sinking
strength, it seemed to me impossible that I could ever
reach the hut. I had never before known such an utter
prostration of strength, such a total want of anything
like energy. But still I toiled on as best I could;
though I was obliged—a thing I had never in my life
done before—to give my rifle to Bauer to carry for me.
The evening was drawing in, and we had still far to go,
and the places became more rugged and difficult: every
minute was valuable.

"Pray come on! If we were only down these rocks
I should not care. Once out yonder and all is well; but
here, if it gets dark—you see what a place it is! Exert
yourself—do your best—now then, try once more!"
And Bauer again led the way.

It was quite dark before we got to our destination.
I hoped that, when I had eaten something, I should be
better, and we therefore hastened to make a fire and
cook our supper. Bauer fetched water from a neighbouring spring, and, in the darkness, this was not so soon
accomplished. I meanwhile tried to get the wood into
a blaze,—but oh, the torment of that fire-making! instead of flame, the hearth was involved in smoke, and
the wind, pouring down the chimney, sent whole clouds
into our smarting eyes. In that small space neither of

us could bear it long. Now for the frying-pan, and then
we shall soon have a warm, savoury meal! But what a
state was that vessel in! Covered full an inch thick
with grease, rancid from staleness, and incrusted everywhere with dirt and dust, just as it had been left by
the last lazy comer. This was indeed disheartening—the
last drop in our cup of bitterness. However there was
nothing to be done but to clean the pan, and try to
make it fit for use. It took no little time to accomplish this, but it was fairly done at last. After it had
been well scoured, and water repeatedly boiled in it to
get rid of its impurities, we set it on the fire with a good
lump of butter, while Bauer mixed the batter for the
schmarren. Now all is ready, and the fair white meal
and water is poured into the pan. But what a sight!
it all turns black at once, looking more like the black
broth of Sparta than any Christian food. Grievous as
this was, the whole had in it something so comic that
we could not but laugh. We let it fry however, and
then tasting a bit and finding it not so *very* bad, cooked
and ate a part. Luckily we discovered an old iron ladle,
and having well cleaned it, boiled some water, and mixed
ourselves a ladle-full of grog. This, twice filled, and
some bread that I had in my rücksack, furnished us a
better supper; and I had still a crust left, just enough
for the morrow's breakfast. How different was this place
from the hut near Kreuth, which had been made so
clean and tidy, and left in such perfect order by "Catharina Hess!"   It was a disgrace to a hunter to leave
things in such a state,—nothing washed, the room un-
swept, and whatever had been used, lying about as when
last employed. On some boards, covered with straw,
was our bed; and putting our joppen and blanket over
us, we soon fell asleep.

I was still exhausted the next morning, though I had slept soundly; yet I did not like to give way, and tried my best to keep up, but my step that day was void of elasticity, and altogether it was sorry work. The sight at early dawn from the Kramer was indeed a glorious one. We were almost opposite the Zug Spitz, and seemingly quite near it; and it was as though we looked down upon the mountains and the snow-plains on their tops. And when the sun came, there was a lovely pageantry!

We saw only two chamois the whole day. In going home we met a man, who passed us scowlingly, and without a word,—a most unusual and strange omission, for here every wayfarer greets the other as he goes by.

"That is a poacher of Garmisch," said Bauer, as we went on; "as great a rascal as ever breathed. I have no doubt that his rifle is hidden near, somewhere among the stones or latschen."

This was the last time but one of my going out. I again passed the night at the Oester Berg, and in the morning went out alone, though the overpowering languor still dragged me to the earth. The ground was covered with snow, and mists were on the hills, and a drizzling rain soon began to make everything wet and miserable. At last I found it was useless to try to go on: I was *obliged* to give it up, being fairly brought to standstill, and literally unable to drag one foot after the other. I crawled to the hut as well as I could, and lying down close to the stove fell asleep for an hour. I afterwards managed to reach Partenkirchen, where I found, by every one telling me how yellow I was, that I had the jaundice. My languor of the preceding days was now explained. It was a grievous thing to be confined to my bed for weeks, and the mountains so near; and as day after day I turned and looked at them from

my pillow, their tops clear and distinct against the bright
blue sky, I felt doubly the privations that sickness brings;
and yet I was in some measure compensated for the
loss, for the scenes themselves were brought to my bed-
side,—"transcripts of Nature," as Constable would have
called them, fresh from the open air, and in which tone
and forms and colour were not copied merely, but felt.
I had just before made the acquaintance of Mr. Carl
Haag, who was staying here; and from the moment I
was unable to leave my room, he brought me daily his
portfolio, and left with me the result of each morning's
or afternoon's work. Then there were effects to be
talked of and discussed, picturesque figures to look at,—
new acquaintances perhaps which he had made in the last
walk,—opinions to be interchanged as to which of the
masterly sketches laid out before me on my bed might
best furnish subject for a picture; and in this way the
hours went pleasantly by, and I found that I was not so
greatly to be pitied after all.

From my window I saw one morning a sight which,
touching as it was, had in it much of beauty. It was
the funeral of a little child. I heard the chanting of the
mourning train, and on looking into the street discovered
whence it came. The young child lay in the open coffin,
which was carried in the arms of a man; its placid face
uncovered, and nothing between it and the blue heaven.
All around it were flowers, on its pillow and on both
sides; and its pretty hands too were embedded on roses,
—buds as tender as itself. I had never seen Death arrayed so winningly.

Note.

THE distance a wounded animal will sometimes go before leaving, on the ground over which he has passed, any trace that he has been hit, is most extraordinary, and in some cases appears to me quite inexplicable. But a week or two before penning this note, four or five deer suddenly crossed my path one evening, as I was returning home through the woods. They were a great distance off; but as they stopped to gaze for a moment, I took my chance and fired. I was sure that I had hit the deer, and as they all passed among the trees, I felt still more certain from peculiar motion I observed in one of them. I followed the slot across the snow, but saw nothing. Yet still, not convinced that I had missed, I kept going on and on, and at last saw a single red drop on the white surface of the ground. A little further there were more; presently, on the side of the slot there was a perfect crimson shower; and a moment or two after, the deer was seen stretched dead.

Sometimes a part of the intestines will protrude, and close up the opening which the bullet has made, and then of course it is no wonder the trickling of the blood should cease. But the hemorrhage takes place inwardly, and, after following the slot for many hundred yards, and when perhaps you have given up all hope, you will very likely find the stag in a thicket quite dead, or lying in the middle of a stream, his strength having failed him in making a last effort to leap across.

It requires an experienced eye however to detect a drop or two of blood, amid the dead leaves with which the ground in the forest is covered; and where the earth is hard, or strewn with the dry foliage of the preceding summer, it is difficult even to make out the slot at all; and yet by practice you at last discern the slightest imprint in the ground, and recognize in a moment if it has been made by a deer or not.

When following the slot of an animal that you think you have wounded, without finding on the ground any traces of his being so, it is well, should he pass a thicket, to examine the boughs he has brushed against in forcing his way through. The branches hang close upon his broad sides, and a leaf may have swept over the wound, and a single streak of crimson is sufficient to betray all you want to know.

> " A flower thus stained, to the hunter brings
>   More joy than the reddest rose ;
> It telleth a tale, to his heart as dear
>   As the blush that doth all disclose."

Once I remember shooting at a wild-boar, and, on going to the spot, found only that he had passed on into the wood. A beater who, like myself, was also looking about, called to me that I had missed, and showed me, in proof of his assertion, the hole my bullet had torn in a young pine close by. But even this did not convince me, and I still followed the track of the boar. At some distance I found bristles on the snow, and a little further the boar also, quite dead, but no blood anywhere except on the spot where he lay, although the ball had passed right through the body before entering the tree.

But the strangest sight I remember to have witnessed occurred with a fallow-deer—a buck. I came suddenly upon him while grazing in a glade, and fired. I looked to see the result of my shot, but he neither fell, nor dashed away. In a moment he began rocking to and fro where he stood. I went towards him, but he took no notice of my approach, and continued the rocking motion as before. I pushed him with my hand, and he rolled over and was dead. The shot-hole was quite round, and showed no redness,—not the least sign of blood was visible, and the opening was filled up by the chewed grass on which the animal had been feeding.

CHAPTER XXVI.

PEPI'S COTTAGE.

In looking through Mr. Haag's portfolio, I one day saw
a very fine sketch of a bandit-like figure with a rifle, and
which he had treated as "a poacher."

"Who's that?" I asked.

"That's 'Schützen Pepi,'" he replied, "a most picturesque fellow. I was at his cottage yesterday, and if
you like we'll go there some day together. If we could
manage to find out when there was a 'Heimgarten,'
'twould be all the better, for that's a curious scene,
and well worth seeing."

"What is a Heimgarten?" I inquired.

"Sometimes the young people of the neighbourhood
agree to go on a certain evening to a house they have
fixed on; and then, when the day's work is done, they
all pour in there to dance and sing, and amuse themselves as they best may. It is a sort of evening party
to which the guests come uninvited, just as when a lady
opens her *salons* on certain days, and announces she
will be 'at home.' But you will see what it is, and I
am sure it will amuse you."

From all I heard of Pepi, he seemed to be so original a fellow, that I set off one evening to pay him
a visit. His dwelling was as picturesque as his person,

Y

and the room and the groups there when we entered,
were all that a painter could desire. As usual the ceiling and walls were of panelling, quite dark from smoke
and age.   At a table a young peasant was sitting
playing the cithern, and in a corner, near the large
green stove, their faces gleaming in the flickering blaze
coming from a hearth close by, sat Pepi with his pipe,
while beside him wife and daughter were busy with
their spinning-wheels.   Bare-legged boys were lying
around listening to the music, and one of them every
now and then would throw some pine-chips on the fire to
make a merry flame; and then the light illumined the
whole nearer group from head to foot, spinning-wheels
and all.   A ruddy flash would play too for a moment
round the form of him at the table, and even put the
shadows in the further nooks and corners into confusion. But Pepi himself deserves a particular description.
He had on an old jacket torn and patched, and round
his brown throat a kerchief was loosely knotted.   His
leathern breeches reached only to above the knees, which
were bare, for the thick ribbed stockings came no
higher than the calf.   The old cap could cover but half
of the wild hair that straggled from beneath it, thickly
intermingled with grey, like his beard and bushy mou-
stache.   It looked snug in that dark, low-ceilinged
room; for there is something cheerful in firelight, and
the glare and the skipping shadows, which no other
illumination can give; and then too the low humming
of the wheels and the plaintive tones of the cithern,
each seeming like an accompaniment to the other, so
well did they harmonize, fell gratefully on the ear, and
gave that indescribable something which carries with it
a sweet feeling of "home."

Pepi's wife wanted him sadly to put on another joppe

in honour of our presence; but he seemed thoroughly
to understand the picturesqueness of the old garments,
darns and patches, and would not hear of a change.
"Why the tailor could not make such a one as this!"
he exclaimed, looking down complacently at the thread-
bare surface. The thing was, he had been often painted,
and knew very well what looking figure an artist liked,
and what would do best for a picture. Pleased as he
was to see us, there was a sturdy self-importance and
gravity in his manner which was rather amusing; a
feeling of his own consequence which peeped forth
through the very holes of his jacket. I asked him
about his family. There were four children alive he
said, but he had had twelve.

"No, father, eleven," said the boy.

"Sacra! one more or less," exclaimed Pepi, "who
can be so exact as all that?"

There was an old map of Europe hanging up against
the wall, which Pepi took down and asked me to show
him where I came from. I pointed out Bath, which he
then underlined. It was quite extraordinary how soon
he found the places he wanted. "There's Havre," he
said, "that's where they all go to sail for America.
And there's Schleswig, where they are fighting and
killing one another. 'T will all end in nothing; they
fight and fight, and the others look on, but if it don't
go on as they like, they'll step in and stop 'em. And
here's Partenkirchen,—what a way from Bath!"

My companion now began to make a drawing, and
nothing could be prettier or more amusing than the
group. It had, it seems, been the grand ambition of
Pepi's wife to be painted too; artist after artist had
come there, and she had never once been asked to sit,
while her husband figured in many a portfolio. She

had at first only hinted her desire, but when day after day passed and no sitting was spoken of, she herself proposed boldly, and with somewhat of offended pride, that Mr. Haag should paint her portrait, which he, to please her, good-humouredly promised to do.

And what a momentous affair was that sitting to her! the first and probably the last time. There she sat, stiff and immovable, full of her dignity, and a pleased smile of triumph on her face, "calling up a look" befitting the occasion. She would not have turned her head let happen what might, for a sitting was an important matter; and whenever the flax on the distaff got entangled she dared not change her position or even cast down her eyes, but called to one of the children to do it for her. The full blaze of the fire fell on her face, the expression of which was the very drollest in the world. Opposite sat her daughter, gazing alternately at her mother and Mr. Haag, while over the shoulder of the latter one of the bare-legged boys was peeping, watching the growing picture and comparing it with the original. It was a delightful group. Presently a loud knocking was heard without, the door flies open, and in bursts a whole troop of youths, singing, shouting, dancing; they offer no greeting, they say nothing in fact, but, with cap on head, continue their wild song, and dance round, snapping their fingers as they still pour in. "Hush, no dancing! leave off, I say! Hans, don't stamp so!" cried Pepi, who was now no more master in his own house than he was over the elements. A wild shout and a louder song was the reply. The first ebullition of mirth over, they stood round the cithern-player, and talked and sang: I all the while remained sitting where I was, heartily enjoying the scene. Presently one of the merry troop came up to me and looking at me from head to foot, much as a monkey would at any strange thing thrown into his cage, seemed particularly struck with my stockings. " Where were they made ?" he asked. "At Baierisch Zell." " Die sind schön !"* he said ; and then was off again, leaping and dancing, to join the others.

Presently the whole company stood together in a circle, their arms round each other's neck, and in this way sang to the music of the cithern, whose gentle tones however were overpowered by their louder voices. Standing thus, they continued swaying their bodies backwards and forwards, with a rocking motion, keeping time with the melody, or suiting their actions to the words of the song. Then their gesticulation became gradually more violent : they would turn, and look each other full in the face astonished, or with searching inquiry, as if to be convinced of the truth of what each had said, although both of the parties were singing the same words. Near them were five or six others, linked also together in the same way ; these hummed the tune only, and kept time by lifting up their feet in front of them, swaying their bodies backwards and forwards like the others, and by advancing some steps and again retreating. There was something very strange and primeval in this rude minstrelsy. It was like a fragment of a long gone-by century, cast up at our feet out of the ocean of Time, upon the shore where we are standing.

The resemblance between this manner of singing of the highlanders of Bavaria and that peculiar to the highlanders of Scotland, is, to say the least, somewhat singular. " When a song is to be sung," says Mr. W. Leathart,† " the parties all round the room take hold of each other's plaids, or, if an English dress, they employ

* " How handsome they are !"
† See ' Literary Gazette,' No. 1520, p. 223.

their pocket-handkerchiefs for the same purpose. The song commences, one sings the verse, and all beat time with their plaids or handkerchiefs, rowing, as it were, to and fro; in the chorus all join, still beating time, and thus the song proceeds. This mode of singing, they call *Oran Luathaidh*. Shaw, in his 'Gaelic Analysis,' accounts for it as having originated in the fulling of cloth by the feet, before the improved method was introduced."

And now the circle broke up, and the different groups began to dance. " I won't have it !" cried Pepi, "leave off, I tell ye! it's Friday, for shame!" " Ho, ho ! no matter, we *will* dance !" And round they went in spite of him and his wife. Why, they might as well have tried to stop the streams that came leaping along down the mountains in spring, as to arrest the whirl of those lads' dancing ! The best dancer had now slipped off his shoes, seized a girl round the waist, and all the others had set off and followed their leader in the dance. Pepi, seeing how utterly vain his words were, put a good face on the matter, and looked on not displeased. He seemed to feel he had done what he could to prevent the revelry, and having thus satisfied his conscience, was at ease and quite content. He relished his pipe amazingly; and as he sate immovable, puffing in sturdy silence, the smoke curling around him, and the mad youths leaping and bending before his presence, it was somewhat like a heathen rite being performed before a god half hidden in clouds of incense. But how describe all those wonderful evolutions ! Now in the middle of the dance they would clap their hands, striking one against the other tambourine fashion, while the head was turned knowingly on one side; and then the palm would descend with a smart slap upon the brawny thigh, which at that moment was lifted high in the performance of some won-

derful step, and in the same moment too would fall upon
the broad calf with a hearty thwack, but so quickly
that it caused no interruption in the movements of the
performers. Then they would snap their fingers, and
make a clucking noise with their tongue, and all in
time with their steps, and in a sort of tuneful measure;
mixed with these sounds every now and then a shrill
cry of delight was uttered, something between a shout
and a halloo; and, before you were aware, before you
could conjecture even that such a thing could come
within the range of the possible, a head which you
had been looking at would suddenly disappear, and two
feet were as suddenly in its place; for a second they
would perform *f pas* in the air, and then the missing
head was seen again on a line with the others. As the
dancing went round in a circle, he who had kicked off
his shoes in order to make less noise,—a thick-set sturdy
little fellow, a baker by trade,—had, like the clown in the
pantomime, suddenly stood upon his hands, and, flinging
his heels over so as to describe a wheel, was again on
his feet and going on with the dance before his head
was missed. How he contrived this lateral somersault
without push or hindrance is to me quite a marvel. For
it was not done once only, but every now and then with
a sudden plunge down he would go, and you saw legs
near the ceiling clapping against each other, as if ap-
plauding their own inimitable dexterity.

"Don't stamp so," cried Pepi, as they beat time on
the floor with their heavy shoes; "don't stamp so, I
tell ye, 'twill be heard outside, and they'll know ye're
dancing!" The thing was, as I afterwards learned, the
Bishop had tried to put down dancing on Fridays, and
Pepi was afraid of getting into disgrace with the clergy
for allowing such wild doings in his house. On any

other work-day they might, I verily believe, have done
what they would, and he would surely not have stopped
them.

"How do you like it?" said one of the youths to me.
"It's fine fun, isn't it? and beautiful dancing too, eh?
In the flat land one never sees anything like it. Does it
please you? But I'll tell you what," he continued, in a
confidential whisper, "you should see me and that man
yonder dance together—*that* would surprise you! You
must tell Pepi you want to see us, and then he won't
mind it." I did so, and the two performers began. All
the rest sat round, attentively watching them, and it was
evident by their silent eagerness that great was their admiration. I hardly knew which amused me more, the delight and wonderment of the spectators, or the attempts
at excellence of one of the dancers; it was droll beyond
description to see his mincing steps, his affected attitudes,
and his lackadaisical air, so strikingly in opposition as it
was to the natural romping of my bouncing little baker;
and then their dresses too, and the surrounding groups
must be taken into account, all serving to heighten the
rich comic effect of their superabundant gravity.

"Oh, what a pity it's over!" exclaimed the originator
of the dance when it was ended. "But tell me, how did
you like it? We are merry fellows, eh? Why, when
I was at Munich—I went there to draw for the conscrip-
tion, I drew the last number but one,—you should have
seen how the people stared when *I* danced. They stared,
I tell you, for *such* dancing they had never seen. There
was not one who could keep it up with me : I tired them
all down. But here, you see, it's not high enough. One
might knock his head if he were to jump high. It's
right merry here among us, isn't it? We are the right
sort of lads, eh? Ay, this is Heimgarten!" and away he

sprang to join his comrades and devise some new piece
of merriment.

"A pretty row there was in the village last night!" I
said to one of them. "Ha, ha, ha!" burst forth from
them all; "did you hear it? Was it very loud?"
"Why of course," I said; "such a clatter as that would
awake anybody. Were you of the party?" "Oh no,"
they answered, "not we;" though, as I afterwards discovered, they all were present; and then they described
the whole to me with a gusto they could not repress, and
told me how the party, "*so they heard*," had gone all
through the place, and stopped and knocked at my door.

"We're merry fellows, don't you think so?" they all
asked. "Don't you like being among us? Now then
we'll sing you a song that'll please you," and they began one in which the joys of stalking were described,
every part being accompanied by pantomime. There
were the peering looks as if chamois were discovered, and
then there was the stealthy advance; the rifle was lifted,
and after the shot came the anxious search and the outstretched neck to see if the game had fallen. It was all
dramatic,—a succession of scenes, of simple, natural act-
ing. Every gesture was full of life; and had the crack of
the rifle been really heard, the widely-opened straining
eye could not have indicated more eagerness or longing.

All this to me was most delightful. The dance, the
songs of the uninvited guests, all was rude, it is true, but
it was the healthy wildness of some untamed creature,
gambling and tumbling about in its native strength. It
was a piece of fresh nature, a bit of unreclaimed land,
untouched as yet by "the progress of civilization;" where
no furrow had been upturned, but where you still smelt
the wild thyme in the bracing air.

The noise I had heard in the night was occasioned by

the observance of a custom peculiar to these parts, and which, when a man illtreats his wife, they never fail to put in practice. Mine host of ' The Golden Star' had, it seems, given his helpmate a beating, so it was resolved that night the charivari was to begin. Accordingly at midnight a troop of youths and men assembled before the house of the offender, and having summoned him a set dialogue was gone through. A certain formula is always observed, and the questions put are as follow.* " Today was killing-day, do you want to buy any fresh meat? What meat will you have?" And then a regular bargain is made about the price to be given. This done, the culprit is allowed to retire; the troop gives a good rattle on the wooden bench before the house, and on they go to the next door, to summon the sleepers and propose the same questions.† To evade the meeting is impossible; the inhabitant summoned *must* rise and hold the usual parley; and were he to refuse to open his door, the inquisitorial band would batter it down. The noise lasted from midnight till four o'clock.

In Töltz and the neighbourhood there is also a custom very similar to this; it is however always attended with much greater preparation, and in its observance more caution is necessary. When any person, no matter who it be, has committed some disgraceful act, the young men for many miles round assemble, all armed, and go to the house of the delinquent. He is called out, and he is obliged to appear in the midst. His shameful conduct is then pointed out to him in terms not very complimentary, and when he has been well reprimanded he

---

* The German word " Fleisch " is used indiscriminately for "meat" and "flesh,"—the flesh of a person or animal.

† At other houses they say *where* it was killing-day, in order that every one may be acquainted with the name of the offender.

is allowed to go.   Although on such occasions hundreds
of youths assemble, no injury is ever done to person
or property ; and should, through their instrumentality,
horses or cattle chance to be killed or hurt, *the full price*
of the same is forwarded to the owner.   Should a traveller be passing that way at the time that such visita-
tion is going on, he is stopped till all is over, when he is
allowed to proceed on his road.   To guard against surprise, they have outposts and patrols in all directions
round the scene of their operations, who give the signal
in case of alarm ; for the authorities are, as may be supposed, very averse to such general risings of armed bodies, and have taken every means to punish those who
share in them.   But such is the secrecy observed, that
the Government has always been unsuccessful, not only
being unable to make a single capture, but even to find
out any of the parties concerned.   Indeed to prevent
such a meeting by force would be very difficult, as the
bands assembled are sure to be numerically superior to
any that can oppose them.   Töltz, though a large and
populous village, was unable to hinder such a *Fehm-
gericht* from taking place.   Troops indeed have been
sent to surround and take the parties, but owing to the
videttes extending to a great distance, and the scouts
being on the alert, all had dispersed to their several
homes before the soldiers could arrive.   The secrecy
with which the day and hour and place of meeting are
kept, the extent of their operations, and the perfect success of their tactics in escaping from pursuit, reminds
one of the nocturnal excursions of the Rebeccaites in
Wales some years ago.

Pepi's portrait was now looked at, and all were pleased
with it, but his own children were especially delighted.
Their admiration was boundless.   It was indeed very

like, and rich in colour,—altogether a masterly sketch; but what attracted their attention most, and gave them most pleasure, were *the nails in their father's shoes.*

One of the lads asked Mr. Haag: "It costs a great deal of money, does it not, to have one's portrait taken?" As he no longer had much time for sketching, and was besides pretty well supplied with studies of figures, he answered, "Oh, certainly, a very great deal;" and hoped thus to get rid of him. After a time he returned and said, "Mind, I would not care about paying a fair price. I'd stand a good sum for the picture: now I'll tell you what, I wouldn't mind giving a crown!"*

But it was getting late, so I took my leave of the party, who crowded round me, and begged me to come soon again.

The moon was now up, and lighted the pointed gables and the paintings on the house-fronts. All was still in

* The story that Catlin relates of the Indian who was laughed at by the rest of his tribe because he was painted in profile, and was therefore only "half a man," is not more amusing than many an incident the artist will sometimes meet with in civilized Europe. Mr. Haag once saw a handsome young person sitting before the door of a little inn and playing the cithern. The youth presented so picturesque a figure, that Mr. Haag wished to make a sketch of him. The lad agreed to the proposition. Next day however he refused. *He was afraid, he said, his comrades would ridicule him if he were to be painted.* At last, when all his scruples were overcome, he would fain put on his Sunday clothes instead of sitting in his shirt-sleeves, and with his hair curling about his forehead. Finally these difficulties were successfully combated, and when the picture was finished he was mightily pleased with his appearance, so much so indeed that he wanted to keep the drawing for himself. He argued besides that it *must* be his. *He* had sat for it, how then could the artist claim it? Moreover it was *his* face, it must therefore belong to him, and not to another. To end the dispute Mr. Haag, with his usual good-nature, promised to paint him again, and this time just as he liked, as a present for his sweetheart. He accordingly came, but was no longer the same being as before. He had put on a long coat that reached to his heels, had wetted his hair and plastered it close to his head, and

the village: nothing was heard except the splashing of the fountain in the street, and the occasional chant of the watchman, whose rude verse I always like to hear, calling down, as it does, a benediction on the sleeping hamlet, and acknowledging a higher protection than man can give.

> "Hört, ihr Herrn, und lässt euch sage'
> Die Glocke hat eilfi g'schlage',
> Schütz' uns Gott und Marie!"

Hardly had I reached my room when the noisy laughter of the merry roysterers was heard in the lane that leads from Pepi's dwelling, announcing that their pleasant 'Heimgarten' was at an end.

almost choked himself with a cravat. Caricature as he was, the portrait delighted him and his parents too; and when Mr. Haag paid his bill on departing, the father said, "We are perhaps in your debt too." "Oh no," was the reply, "the portrait was a little present to your son." "But we don't wish to have things for nothing," was the sturdy rejoinder; "we are not the sort of persons for that. We can pay, let me tell you—oh yes, we can pay!" and pushed over three six-kreutzer pieces (sixpence English) to Mr. Haag.

PART THIRD.

CHAPTER XXVII.

THE HINTER RISS.

I CANNOT begin this account of the Hinter Riss without making mention of one who is intimately associated with all my first recollections of the spot, and whose memory I cherish with the warm and sincere regard due to a thorough sportsman and a most kind and trusty friend. Whoever knew the late Prince Leiningen intimately, and had thus an opportunity of learning how many a genial quality made up the sum of his character, how thoughtful he was for those to whom he was attached, and mindful of *little* things which another would forget, —to such a one it will appear a most natural circumstance that I should advert to him here, where every path, and ravine, and mountain-top, and so much of the cheerful past is connected with him and his society. Those sojournings alone with him in the wilderness were pleasant times. Extensive as was the chase, he knew well all the localities even in detail,—no easy matter in such a wild mountain range. The haunts of the game were familiar to him ; and no forester knew better than he, where at dawn or at evening, a chamois or good stag was likely to be found. As I said before, he was a *thorough* sportsman : it was not in the mere slaughter of game that he delighted, but its pursuit by fair means, at

z

proper times and seasons. A rare quality too was his, he never begrudged another *who knew how to appreciate his good fortune* a signal success in the chase, but on the contrary was delighted at his luck, and always shared heartily in his exultation. And the same feeling made him allow me to plan my stalking expeditions, going whither I chose, and staying out on the mountain for days together. His love of mountain scenery was a passion, necessary, absolutely necessary for his happy existence; and his shooting-lodges on the hill-top and mountain-side were sure to be built not only with reference to the game, but on a site where some magnificent view lay open before you, or a romantic glen could be seen in all its wild picturesqueness.

His experience too in woodcraft, his recollections of past times, when noble stags were shot in Coburg, Erbach, and elsewhere,—for in those days there were giants in the land,—made him a companion from whom, on such matters, much was to be learned. Nor on these alone; for he had not only seen much, but had known the most eminent men of his own most eventful time; and his reminiscences of the changes which had taken place in Europe, and of the master-minds who had wrought or had opposed them, made his conversation a singular enjoyment. Would that I still could hear his voice, and receive his friendly welcoming!

End of September, 1854. It was getting late, and the stars already began to twinkle brightly, as we entered the narrow gorge between the high mountains that led to the place of my destination. The road sometimes passed close beside the mountain-stream, now wound through the pine-forest, to avoid the torn-down banks and trunks of trees which the devastating torrent had rooted up in its spring-time violence; or occasionally even took us over those beds of loose stones which give such spots so drear and barren an appearance. Just before the evening began to sink into deeper gloom, a large bird—a cock of the woods or a black-cock—would rise from the dense underwood, and scared flutter away to some neighbouring tree. Soon however nothing was to be discerned except the dark line of the mountain-ridge sharply cutting the pale star-lit sky; and the only sound was that deep reverberation of the rushing water, which may be heard so far off, and, in the quiet of night, seems amalgamated with the very air, tingling and imbued with the sonorous monotonous sound. All space was filled with it: it was on the mountain-sides, and the hollow murmur rose to their lonely summits.

It produces a peculiar sensation to be moving thus at night through such a gorge, locked in on all sides by high dark masses that defy our scrutiny or any attempts to choose a way save that which the gigantic forms themselves prescribe. Being dark the winding of the valley could not be discerned: before, behind, around, all seemed closed; so that it even appeared as though there were no outlet by which to emerge again into our accustomed world. At length a light was seen ahead; and as the carriage rolled over the wooden bridge, others made their appearance, and I soon recognized amid the glare the well-known faces of my friends the Jäger, who had come out to see what belated traveller had arrived at so unusual an hour. Then came the pleasant welcoming, a question or two about the stags and the chamois, and sanguine expectations of what the next few weeks might see achieved.

In the morning a grand consultation was held. Being the rutting season I asked about the stags. They were heard, I was told, only at distant intervals; and if du-

z 2

ring the night and towards morning a low bellowing resounded across the valley, it would cease at daybreak, and there was no saying when it might be heard again. There never had been such a season as this. Stags, and good ones too, were about in plenty : but if they were silent, how was it possible to come up with them and get a shot ?

"The weather has been very mild hitherto," I said to my good friend Hans, who had always been out with me the year before ; "the season is advancing, and we shall surely have a change before long. A clear cold night, and you will hear the stags the whole morning long, for certain. Where do you think were the best place for us to try our fortune?"

"Why, I should say 'twere best to go to Baumgarten," replied Hans. "The ground there is good for stalking, and moreover not a shot has been fired there yet. It has been kept quite quiet. And there are some *good* stags there too," he continued, with a movement of the head that indicated the word "good" meant something really superlative. "Franzl was there lately, and saw two,—both of them stags of twelve, and perhaps more. But such antlers! If you could get a shot at them you would be pleased indeed, that I'll answer for."

That night the weather changed. Thick mists came sailing along between the mountains, shutting out every object from the sight. Then the rain began to pour in torrents, changing soon after to hail, and finally becoming a blinding snowstorm. Through the impenetrable gloom nothing was visible. Day and night this cheerless weather lasted, and there was nothing to be done but fling an additional log on the fire and wait for better days. At moments a rent would show itself in the lazy mist ; and then the head or shoulder of the opposite

mountain would appear, all white in its robe of snow. At
last it cleared up, and a blue sky shone brightly over
the whitened fir-trees and the dazzling craggy peaks.
So we got ready for our departure.

As the place we were going to was some distance off,
it would be necessary to remain absent about four days,
and accordingly a stock of bread and coffee and sugar,
with a couple of bottles of wine, were put into our
rücksacks. We set off in the afternoon, and soon leaving the road, turned aside into the wide bed of a
mountain torrent. This Lechbach is one of the most
destructive of the streams that pour down their waters
to the vale. All around it is desolation. Year after
year it carries away the bridge that here spans its bed:
for though built with all possible forethought, and
though protected by raised dams of large stones, with
whole trees for beams, firmly bound together, as soon
as the snows melts, the Lechbach comes leaping down,
and with one sweep hurls the strong pile away. A narrow path, broad enough for a single person to walk along,
has been cut in the hill-side; and for nearly two hours
we kept on mounting, being all the while within the
gorge formed by the waters during many ages. When
at last you reach the ridge overlooking the scene below,
then it is you see how great the havoc and destruction;
and how the waters, like the scathing fire on the prairie,
lay waste all that comes across their path. Not a patch
of soil is left on which a shrub could vegetate: a bare
waste of stones and sand alone lies bleaching in the sun.

Having reached the ridge, we came upon a vale formed
by a dip in the mountains. In summer this spot must
have been enlivened by the herds sent up here for the
pasturage; but now the huts were empty, and the
ground covered with snow. Here we began to descend,

and following the channel of a stream soon came to a succession of huts, which, late as it was, had not yet been
deserted by the Senner. The huts found in these remote
places are very different from those around Berchtesgaden or Baierisch Zell. Such are neat, clean, and pretty;
and often indeed will fully satisfy those idyllic expectations with which many a tourist sets out to visit them.
In these, too, you always meet dairy-maids :* here only
Senner are to be found,—men who at first sight look
something between a bandit and a savage, with much
of both in their dwelling and mode of life. A person not
accustomed to these huts would start on being told that
it was here he must take up his quarters for the coming
week. But you get accustomed to the semi-civilized life,
and to the discomforts which, at first, seem to meet you
at every turn; and soon invent clever contrivances, and
learn to prize the little conveniences your ingenuity has
supplied.

* It is impossible not to smile on reading the following note, sent
by a Sennerinn from her hut on the mountain to the apothecary in the
little town of ——. In spite of her demand for rouge—to win more
surely, perhaps, some truant-lover—(there is something very unsophisti-
cated in the coaxing epistle; and, being in ignorance of the name and
application of what she asks for, she in it betrays her thorough simplicity : —
  "Ich möchte gern ein solches Ding Wie es so einige Frauen haben
die gar so Schön roth aussehen wir nahmen (nennen) sie halt den an-
strich oter (oder) zinober wie man es nenen soll sie sollten mir aber das
rechte geben sie möchten aber so gut sein und es darin Schreiben wie es
sol angewented werten und ich werte inen (ihnen) dafür zur rererung
(Erinnerung) Etelweis stöckel schiken."
  Of the above, which is an exact copy of the original, the following
is a pretty fair translation :—
  "I should like to have that sort of thing that some women have
who look so lovely red we call it the paint or vermilion as they say
but you must be sure to send me the right but you must be so good and
write inside how it is to be used and I will send you in remembrance a
posy of edelweis."

These dwellings are mere log-huts, in one corner of which, beside the entrance, there is a sort of hole about a foot deep. This is the fireplace. A few stones are piled around it, to protect the wooden walls from the blaze, while it is on the ground itself that the fire is lighted. You sit on the floor of the hut, with your feet on this rude hearth; and the smoke—for there is no such thing as chimney—curls round your face, often causing your eyes to burn and tingle. This is the place of resort for whoever has an idle moment: he steps down in the little pit, warms his bare knees at the cheerful blaze, fills his wooden pipe for the hundredth time, takes in his hand a red-hot cinder which he presses into the bowl, and then puffs away until the hour for milking or some other duty has arrived; unless drawn away beforehand from his ingle nook by the appearance of a goat or a cow looking in at the doorway, when up he jumps, and with screams and threats and denunciations scares the animal back again to the pasture.

The rafters and all the upper part of the interior are, of course, blackened by the smoke. Dust and dirt lie thickly on every spot. A door at the back leads to a cellar, generally a few feet lower than the floor of the outer dwelling, where the cheeses and pans of milk are kept. Here all is clean.

The sole furniture of the hut we stopped at consisted of two large iron frying-pans and six battered iron spoons, for everybody's use, which a strip of tin kept in their places on one of the logs just above the hearth. A large pail of fresh water is always to be found standing against the wall, with a small wooden bowl or copper ladle hanging near, out of which each comer drinks when happening to be athirst. In the cellar, beside the milk and cream, are mountains of butter on clean wooden platters:

a sack or bowl full of flour will also be found there; and this completes the stock of food which the herdsmen have for their subsistence. One of the men attends to the in-door work and household duties, among which cooking and the business of the dairy hold the chief place. With no other ingredients than flour, milk, and butter, it would be difficult to introduce much variety into the *cuisine*; and yet the everlasting schmarren is changed occasionally for dumplings, made in the palm of the hand with curds, and fried in butter; and where bread is to be had, a "Milk Suppe" will be cooked today instead of the old dish of yesterday. A bowl of milk during or after the meal supplies the place of beer or wine. Thus three times a day, for six months or more, they have this simple but nutritious diet.

As we passed a hut we stopped to ask the herdsman if he had heard any stags that morning. "Yes, faith!" was the reply; "heard them and seen them too. Last night they made such a noise, there was no possibility of getting to sleep. Just before daybreak they must have been quite low down and near the hut; and a rare bellowing it was. Up yonder to the left, on that green slope below the trees," he continued, pointing upwards to a spot above a deep ravine, "there pretty nearly every day I've seen a good stag moving about. This morning, 'tis true, he was not there, but tomorrow he's sure to come. As to stags, there are plenty about here."

"What say you to remaining here, instead of going on to the other hut?" asked my companion of me. "As the stags have been heard here, we have as good a chance as if we go further."

I agreed to remain, so we entered, and began to unpack the contents of his rücksack. Seated round and over the fire were four men, bare-legged from the knees downward, their feet resting on the wood-ashes, occasionally using them as pokers to move the embers. Besides the short breeches they each had on a coarse sackcloth shirt, open at the chest, and nearly as black as the charred beams and rafters. When it or the persons of the wearers had last been washed, is a question which would have posed any of the company to answer. Their memories would hardly have reached back to so remote a period. Their long hair and shaggy beards, their begrimed faces and uncouth covering, gave them certainly a somewhat savage look; yet they were friendly and obliging, and were always ready to show me such little courtesies as prove a friendly feeling and kindly disposition. One in particular, who seemed to hold me in especial affection, was always on the alert to do me a service, which he invariably accompanied with a knowing shake of the head, a sly wink, and a smile so friendly, that it would have made the swarthiest face look bright and winsome.

Before making ourselves comfortable for the night, Hans and myself went out to listen for the stags. We mounted the steep for some little distance, in order to get beyond the noise of the water below, which, rushing over its rocky channel, entirely prevented any remote sound from reaching our ears. Presently we heard a low moan, which perhaps might have been unheeded by one not accustomed to the peculiar, almost inaudible, murmur. As we ascended higher it sounded most distinctly,—a hollow, dull, angry tone, which came from the mountain far above us. Again the sound was heard; but this time it proceeded from another direction: there was, too, a difference in the roar; it was in another key from that which had first made us stand still and listen. Thus we knew there were at least two stags about there.

The stars were coming forth, the night-wind began to be cool, and we went down again to the hut; and taking off our heavy shoes, sat round the fire. I soon set about cooking my supper, and by eight o'clock was ready to go to bed.

The cowhouse was on the other side of the pathway, a few steps from the hut-door: so slipping my feet into a large pair of wooden shoes lying near, I told Hans to follow with a burning brand, and light me up the ladder into the hayloft. Such a bed requires little preparation, and covering myself up with a wrapper which I had brought with me, and getting well into the hay, I was soon fast asleep.

CHAPTER XXVIII.

TRACKING THE WOUNDED STAG.

AT a little past three o'clock the next morning I awoke,
and lay for some time listening to the distant roar of the
stags, sounding solemn and lugubrious as it did in the
silence of the night. Hans was soon stirring; and kicking aside the hay, I groped my way down the ladder and
crossed over to the hut. My friend of the knowing wink
was already up, and sat, pipe in mouth, over the crackling fire he had made for us. A breakfast of some bread
and milk, and then taking down our rifles from the
rafters of the hut, we slung the rücksacks over our
shoulders and set out.

We went straight in the direction where we had heard
the stag the evening before, feeling our way up the
mountain-side till we came to the wooded part. Here
we stopped to listen, for it was useless to go on without
some sound or token by which to direct our steps. We
sat down under a fir and waited. After a time we heard
above us a short, impetuous, angry bellow, and we instantly rose and proceeded on our way, silently and very
quietly, yet with all speed. But the stag did not continue
to make himself heard: his roar was intermittent, and
at distant intervals only a low moan announced that he
was still there. We were obliged therefore to halt con-

tinually, in order not to advance upon him unawares.
Now a louder roar told us he was near: and anon we
crept forward with redoubled quickness, but also with
redoubled caution. In mounting higher the ground became steeper and more broken, and though it was broad
daylight, still it was difficult to advance among the roots
of trees and get along over the stones, without displacing
even a single one.

The stag was seemingly now quite close to us; and we
got to a tree and awaited there what would happen next.
Straight before us the hill-side sloped steeply downwards, and there on the rising ground we knew the stag
was. I could not see him, but I once saw the tip of a
bough bend, though not a breeze was stirring, and this
at once told me his whereabouts. Presently I could
hear the stag's footsteps on the stony ground, as he
moved about in his angry impatience, and signified so
much to Hans by moving my fingers over the ground
and pointing thither whence the sound proceeded.
Hans's gaze was fixed across the dell. Suddenly he
looked at me, his eyes wide open, his lips moving but
uttering no sound, and with a slight movement of his
head indicating that he saw the stag yonder.—I looked,
but saw nothing.

"Fire!" he said, in a whisper full of excitement.
"Fire! there he is! It's not too far! Why don't you
fire?"

"Where?—I don't see him."

"Up there, by the tree! What, don't you see him?"

I looked *up* to the stem of a tree standing on the
declivity, but could discover nothing. Hans meanwhile
was burning with impatience. It was indeed vexatious;
for he, it was clear, saw the stag before him all the
while, and I was searching for him in vain. But pre-

sently looking *downward*, I saw the large form of the splendid hart crossing slowly some ground uncovered by trees or underwood. I raised quickly my rifle, but just as it was at my shoulder the last of the stag was seen, as he moodily passed into the bordering thicket. Had I but seen him twenty seconds sooner, he would in all probability have fallen to my shot.

"Of course you could have hit him," said Hans; "why, it was not more than a hundred and twenty yards!—And we had stalked him so capitally! Such a chance too! There he was before you all the while!"

There was no use in being vexed, or in telling my companion that his "*up* over there" was the sole cause of the mischance. We slid quietly downwards, and making a detour, endeavoured to get below the stag, who was moving but slowly, and thus try again for an opportunity of getting a shot. We came upon an open space covered with tall rank weeds and loose fragments of rock, and saw several deer which already had got wind of us, or had heard our movements. We stole back again therefore, and, as there was nothing more to be done, turned homewards. The hut where we were staying was so poorly furnished that not even an earthen pipkin—no vessel, in short, except the two iron frying-pans—was to be had. As we passed by another hut I therefore asked the Senner if he had some such thing, which I could borrow to make myself some coffee. He had none either. "But," he added, "the man who has the still,* about a mile from here, has a pipkin,—that

* In the mountains here, as in Scotland, you will often find in far-off out-of-the-way places a rude dwelling where a spirit is distilled from the roots of the gentian; and not unfrequently the landlord of such little tenement will be provided with luxuries you would hardly expect to find; such as a cup and saucer, sugar, coffee, and a store of Tyrolian wine.

I know;" and so off Hans set to borrow the valuable utensil, that I might cook myself a comfortable break-fast. He returned with a cracked earthen pipkin, bound together by a thick iron wire. The coffee was now soon boiling, and then warming some cream in the iron frying-pan, with bread and large slices of fresh butter, I had a luxurious repast. Sitting by the hearth, the floor of the hut was my table; but that circumstance in no wise dimi-nished the zest with which I ate my meal.

Later I went out again, up to the ridge of the moun-tain, and looked down on the other side for chamois. But not one, not even a trace of one in the snow was to be seen.

Now and then that evening, and during the night, a stag might be heard at intervals, but not continuously, as is the animal's wont at this particular season. This year, indeed, the rutting had a peculiar character, dif-ferent from any preceding years; for even though the nights and mornings were cold and frosty, the occasional bellows of two or three harts might be heard only just before daybreak, and then perhaps for the rest of the day hardly once to be repeated. At other times the stags, when they had hinds with them, were never quiet for a moment: their voices re-echoed from the hills, while now scarcely one was uplifted in the solitude. From afar, indeed, if you listened with most attentive ear, might be caught occasionally a low rumbling as of dis-tant thunder; but even this soon died away, like the faint mutterings of a retreating storm.

The third morning we went out again in another direc-tion. It was early, and very dark, and Hans went be-fore with a bundle of thin strips of resinous wood in his hand, which flickered and flamed brightly, and threw a wild glare around our path. And now we reached the

brook that came dashing and roaring over the stony fragments in its channel: there a light was very necessary.
I could not help stopping for a moment to enjoy the
picture before me. My companion in advance was standing on the stones in the middle of the torrent, waiting
for me to follow. The crackling flambeau threw a red
gleam on his countenance and his bare knees, while all
the opposite side of his tall spare figure was in deep shadow. Stepping from stone to stone, we crossed the brook
and wound up the steep ascent. Beyond our own immediate circle there was utter darkness: now and then
the bright flame illumined the trunk and the gloomy
foliage of a fir-tree as we passed, spreading like a black
pall over our heads. The lurid glare made the night
which was beyond seem unfathomable. A dead branch,
a bleached ghost-like trunk, would start suddenly into
existence, and then as suddenly recede and vanish, swal-
lowed up again by the pursuing shadows that, like a
hungry pack, followed on our steps. Add to this the
stillness which brooded over the earth at that hour,—
for the torrent now reached our ear but as a low hum,
and rather harmonized with, than disturbed the solem-
nity,—and it will be understood that the scene was one
to arrest the attention of even the least impressionable.

But it was time to quench the flame of the burning
wood, for we were getting near the covert, and moreover a dim grey began to be interwoven with the blackness in which we had hitherto been enveloped. To the
right was a wooded slope, between which and us there
lay a deep ravine; and across it now came the hoarse
tones of a stag.

"That's the same one we heard the day before yesterday: there is no mistaking his voice," said I.

"And he must be a good one too, judging by the

deep tone," answered Hans, " a much better stag even than we first saw. If he keep about the same ground a little longer, which he no doubt will do, we may manage to come up with him and get a shot."

We still listened, for it was a pleasure to hear the deep roar. But in our neighbourhood nothing gave sign of life. Hans proposed to go some distance down the mountain-side, and then making a circuit to pass through the thicket, and thus if any game were there, to drive it towards me. I agreed to the plan. We looked for a good place where I might take my stand. The spot chosen was a very steep declivity, covered partly with long tangled grass, and partly with large stones. At a hundred and sixty or seventy yards below me the forest-trees advanced from either side, and left but a small space of open ground, which led down to a distant water-course. Cutting down some branches, I made a sort of breastwork to avoid being seen. But hardly was this precaution taken, when a long cloud of mist came sailing up from the hollow, and as it advanced shutting out even the nearest objects from sight. I did not know whether this vapour might extend further on or not; and I feared that if Hans continued his drive and the mist did not soon disperse, a stag might pass without my being aware of his neighbourhood. I therefore watched this filmy yet opaque mass as it rolled along, now for a moment growing thin as air and letting the blue sky look in, and then taking threatening forms, flinging over every object its damp and clammy shroud. In half an hour it had disappeared.

I had waited an hour and a half, when at a good distance below me a patch of brownish-red colour, as of a stag, became suddenly visible,—and it was one. The antlers grew clearly distinguishable, and he came slowly on. I should have been glad if he had been nearer, but still I was thankful that his movements were not more speedy. I sat down, and putting up the sight for a longer range, took deliberate aim. As he crossed from the wood I fired. He stopped, looked towards me astonished, and I saw by his manner that he was hit. As he slowly moved on I fired the second barrel. He stopped again, lowered his head, and then raising it seemingly with an effort, gazed again and limped into the wood. "The second bullet must have hit the left shoulder; 't was a good shot!" said I, congratulatingly to myself. A deer, bewildered by the noise, now dashed close up to me, then, scared by my presence, flew back, and finally crossed whither the stag had gone.

Hans now appeared, and I hastened to rejoin him. He too had seen the stag, and had watched him after the second shot was fired.

"We shall have him soon, there's no doubt of that: he's ill enough already, but 'twill be better to leave him to himself for awhile, and he'll get worse."

"Yes," I replied, "that was my intention, for we have no dog with us, and must be careful," and I advanced a few paces on the stag's track. I had seen that he limped, that he could hardly walk after the second shot, so that I knew he was hit: moreover his whole bearing, and the peculiar movement of his head, left no possible doubt on the matter. It was not therefore as an additional assurance that I looked on the ground for blood, but from mere habit. Strangely enough not a drop was to be found.

"No matter," said Hans, who had been searching also, "he's hit, that's certain. "Far off he can't be: let us sit down for awhile and then go and look for him."

I now learned from Hans that he too had observed

2 A

the mist floating upwards soon after he had left me; and knowing that as long as it lasted I should see nothing, he had waited quietly till the brightness re-appeared before commencing to drive the forest. He always *thought* about what he had to do; I could safely rely on his executing any manœuvre with skill and without committing a blunder. He was ever ready to carry out any of my wishes, and as to exertion he was indefatigable.

We waited what we considered a sufficient time, and then began to follow the slot of the stag. Over the hard ground this was not so easy; and when it was soft, and on the grass, there were everywhere the traces of the cows and heifers which wandered hither for pasturage. It required the greatest attention to make out and follow the right track: there were moreover the traces, some old and others quite fresh, of other stags in the mire, that had passed backwards and forwards through the thicket. Sometimes I got on a wrong scent, and had to double back again like a hound: the size and peculiarity of the stag's hoof was to be well kept in mind, in order to discover the right footprints among fifty others; and sometimes one which looked very like that I was following would, on being felt, prove to be no fresh impression, but two or three days old. Hans had gone in another direction. I had made out the track as far as a wet meadow, and over a steep bit of clayey ground. Here the stag had evidently slipped—slipped with the forefoot; and this made me feel all the surer that I was on the right track. From here the bank sloped down to the watercourse. Noting the spot I went back to Hans, and told him I would not follow further, but send for a bloodhound, and then we might make sure of the stag. "For," said I, "if he is not at rest, the dog will soon come up with him, and bring him to bay. For us to follow him is out of the question: where the earth is soft, all is trodden down with innumerable footmarks, and in the wood among the dead leaves nothing can be seen. So I will go down to the hut and send off at once to the forester."

On my way I met the Senner, who said congratulatingly, "I have seen your stag." By this I imagined he meant to say he had seen him some time that morning on a glade, as was often the case, when looking upward from the valley toward the steep mountain-sides. "You'll soon have him now!"

"What do you mean?" I asked.

"Why," said he, "as I returned from driving out the cattle, just as I was crossing the brook, there stood before me—quite close—not further off than you now are from me—the stag on the bank; I could have caught him nearly, and with a stick could have knocked him down."

"But how do you know it was my stag?"

"We heard your shots, and soon after down came the stag to the water, and wanted to cross over to the opposite wood. But he could not get along well: one leg he drags, and there was blood, plenty of blood, on his flanks."

"On which side?" I asked, in order to see if he were sure of what he was saying, and to test the narrator.

"The left side," was the answer, which was that on which I had fired.

"And his head," I continued, "how did he hold his head? Was it upright, and did he gaze at you? And when he saw you, how did he go away? Very fast?"

"Oh no, not fast at all. I might have overtaken him; and as to his head, that was drooping, hanging down

2 A 2

low near the ground. He has tremendous thick antlers. they are not high, but strong, sturdy things like
cudgels."

All this verified what I had thought about the stag
being well hit, and I now felt still more sure that with a
dog we should soon be exulting over the possession of our
booty. One of the men was therefore despatched with
an injunction to make all speed.

"It is now half past ten : in six hours you can be back
again. Lose no time, and start."

"I shall be here before four," said the man, and was
soon out of sight.

There was plenty of time to think the matter over,
and for Hope to weave a brightly-tinted web representing the events that are likely to happen in an hour or
two; but while mentally I saw all lit up by a vivid bow
of promise, the real clouds overhead gave signs of bad
omen. Low and scowling they came on over the hill-
tops, and presently bursting poured down a heavy deluge
of rain. Nothing could be more unfortunate : all traces
would be effaced from the ground and the scent utterly
destroyed. However to repine and be discontented is
always the worst that, under any circumstances, we can
do. Things might, after all, not turn out so unfortunately
as this change of weather seemed to indicate.

It is not yet four o'clock, and yonder comes the messenger at a good pace, with Feldmann in a leash trotting
behind him. We were soon in the wood, and the bloodhound was laid on the scent where the stag passed just
after the shot. He took it up readily, but he soon grew
cautious and occasionally was at a loss what to do. He
would stop at times and smell the bushes and low boughs
hanging near the ground bordering the path the stag
had taken. Thus he tested the correctness of the track

he was following, and verified also the assertion of the
herdsman that the animal was wounded on the left side;
for it was on this side always that the dog raised his head,
cautiously and with no overhaste, sniffing a straggling
bramble or trunk of a fir.   Eventually he led us to the
clayey spot whither I had traced the footprints, and near
which the peasant had met the wounded animal.   Here
the dog was also at fault. We took him down to the water-course : he led us some way up the brook ; but after
smelling about for a time he gave up the search.   It
was too much to expect that under such circumstances
he should follow the slot : indeed what could he do there
amid the plash of those eddying waters ? The good dog
had done his part well ; and indeed it was most interesting to watch him, now ardent and impatient, pressing
forward against the leash when the scent for awhile was
good, now carefully doubling and again going over every
inch of ground when at fault, and making sure he was
right before setting off in a new direction.

Indeed to watch a good bloodhound follow a wounded
animal, and observe how, if in difficulty, he seems to
weigh one probability against another,—to mark his
resources when at fault, and see how he will steadily keep
on the trail of the animal he is pursuing even though
crossed quite freshly by others,—this is one of the many
episodes in hunting life which are full of interest and
excitement.

However some resolution must be formed, and a consultation was held.

It was the opinion of Hans that the stag, after being
driven back by the herdsman, had made a circuit, returned to the brook higher up, and crossing it had made
for the forest.   He was strengthened in his opinion by
having found some traces leading thitherward.   Now I

was not of his opinion; urging that a stag, wounded as this one was, would not seek the high ground; and I did not believe, lame as he was, that he could get up the steep bank where Hans believed he had seen fresh traces. That he sought the water was, I contended, quite natural; and, had he not been disturbed by the peasant, would either have remained near the stream, or following its course have got lower down into the wood at the foot of a neighbouring mountain.

It was too late however to continue our search that day, so we turned homewards. At the hut we found two more keepers, who had stopped there for the night on their way to some distant hills to look after the game, and, if possible, drive it from the border. As we sat over the fire that evening the whole affair was again rehearsed, from the moment of firing the first shot till we had lost all traces of the wounded animal; and many a sagacious question was put by one or the other relating to something seemingly unimportant, but from which, in reality, useful information might be educed. It would, I think, have interested even one of the uninitiated to have heard the various opinions as to where the stag should be sought, with the reasons on which they were founded; based as these opinions were not only on an attentive observation of the habits of red-deer generally, but on the habits also of certain well-known individuals among them.

"If it is the stag which, from the description of the antlers, I think it is," said Franz, one of the jäger who had joined us in the hut, "then I have no doubt he is gone back again whence he came, and is in the low wood on the hill-side. All last summer that was the ground he kept to: I have often seen him, and know him well. He has short antlers, but very thick: he is a stag of ten, but

up to the points even the branches are thick and strong.
He would be sure to make for his old summer-haunt : it
is dense there and shady, and moreover he would have
water.   Tomorrow when I see the slot I shall know for
certain if it is his : he has a long and narrow hoof and
very pointed."

"Yes," I replied, " unusually long."

" That's the stag, you may be sure," continued Franz.
" There were two there a year ago, and the slot of each
was peculiar. I should know both again easily. One
of the stags disappeared, but the other remained, and
was always in the same neighbourhood.   Besides, if he
is hit as you say he would never take to the high ground,
but keep in the valley."

Thus we kept on discoursing, as we sat all eight of
us round the blazing logs ; and it was resolved that
the next morning the wood was to be scoured in all directions to find the stag, which it was not unlikely
might already be lying dead.   It was long past seven
o'clock, and we began to think of turning into the hay ;
so leaving the bright fire we crossed over to the loft,
and scrambling up the ladder—Feldmann too managing
to mount—we were in a minute all ensconced in our
warm bed.

When you stand on the mountain-side and see the
dark forest stretching around you, and call to mind the ravines and gullies and declivities which intersect the wide
space ; and when you tell yourself in that tract before
you a stag is somewhere lying which you are to find, the
task seems a hopeless one, and you are almost inclined
to give up the attempt.   My companions however were
confident of success ; and Franz and his comrade set off
to scour the woods in one direction, while Hans, who

still clung to his former opinion, went upwards in a contrary line. I took up my station on a spot where, should the stag be disturbed and come forth, I could not fail to see him, and probably to bring him down. As I sat there quietly waiting in the silence, I dwelt admiringly on the energy and perseverance of my three companions, gone forth as it were on a voyage of discovery. " I shall go up yonder," Hans said on quitting me, "and pass through that wood. I shall then come downwards, looking well through the whole breadth of it as I descend. If the stag is not there, you may be sure we shall have little chance of finding him," thus working out for himself a way of many miles. Such a search is hard work; but it was undertaken with a readiness that showed how great the interest each took in its success.

However it did not prove successful; and some hours after I discovered Hans above me, forcing his way through the branches, and the others soon appeared coming up from the ravine. Thus passed another day. Regret at losing so good a stag was felt by all, by no one so intensely as myself; but it was one of those unfortunate incidents which occur occasionally, baffling alike skill, experience, and perseverance. Franz, who was a good cook, now made some dumplings with curds and flour; and before long we were all sitting round the fire, the frying-pan on the floor in the midst, each one with his iron spoon choosing the smoking brown morsels which pleased him best.

I have been rather minute in this account of our proceedings, although they were followed by no result, in order to show the mischances that attend such mountain expeditions, the little incidents on which success will sometimes depend, and the difficulties which the vast extent and character of the ground bring with them.

The same excellent sportsman whom I have already quoted,—Prince Leiningen, and who for a great part of his life had been accustomed to mountain sport,—once told me he had gained a conviction that mountain stags were much fleeter in their movements than those of the plain. This, he asserted, was especially observable in the rutting season; and he accounted for it from the circumstance that, the distances being so great, there was so much more ground to be got over, requiring an additional degree of speed in order to reach the various spots within a reasonable time. The correctness of the opinion was verified to me the following day. In the morning, as we were on the point of starting, we heard the loud, hoarse bellowing of a stag close to the hut. He was so close indeed, that, but for the impenetrable darkness, I could have shot him from the threshold. He was still there some time after, when we went forth toward the hill-side. Presently we heard him in front of us, and then away to the right: anon he was further ahead; then his voice came rumbling through the pines high, high up on the mountain; and at last, after climbing awhile, we could but just hear it, far away,—a low, almost inaudible murmur. The space he had cleared in that short time was quite extraordinary.

I determined to try for this stag, and continued to ascend. At last the bellowing grew more distinct, and, no longer continuing to recede, was heard proceeding from the same spot. The stag, which before in passionate impatience had been scouring the whole mountain in search of deer, had now, it seemed, found some, and consequently remained where they were. We got nearer and nearer, and the stag's voice now reached our ears with delightful distinctness. His occasional low muttering even could be plainly heard. Now there came a

groan, rising as it seemed from the very inmost depths
of his body, followed by a short, quickly-repeated, loud,
angry snort,—impetuous, defiant, with all the madness
of voluptuous rage. Then all was still. I now felt sure
that we should be able to get near him. For although
as yet no creature was to be seen, I could easily picture
to myself all the dalliance, and behold with mental vision
the now-appeased wooer triumphant in the middle of his
serail.

"Hist! I see him!" whispered Hans, bending down
to the earth, cautiously turning to see that I too com-
pressed myself into the smallest dimensions possible.
"Lie down, lie down! don't lift your head! He has
several deer with him, and they are looking this way."

The spot where we were was a very steep Lahne, in
the middle of which a sort of gutter had been formed by
the rains : letting ourselves slide into this, up we went
on hands and knees till we reached the ridge. A mighty
fir had been torn out of the soil by some tempest, and
lay there, forming an excellent shelter behind which we
could watch the deer grazing quietly on the slope opposite; while between them and us was a dip in the hill of
some hundred yards, and uncovered by bush or tree. The
stag was stalking majestically about in the background.

While thus watching, a chamois came bounding downwards from the uppermost ridge of the mountain, leaping
lightly over the latschen and then disappearing among
them. Hans had not observed him. I pointed to the
spot and told him of the circumstance, which was strange
enough; for in that neighbourhood we had not expected
to find a single chamois. At all events we felt certain
it must be a buck, strolling thus alone quite away from
the herd. For a time we saw nothing more of him, and
continued watching the movements of the stag. Pre-

sently, on turning my eyes, I saw just above me the head
of the chamois projecting beyond the latschen, and looking with an inquisitive stare at the two human beings
he thus unexpectedly had chanced upon. His surprised,
droll face made me smile, and I touched Hans, that he
too might see him. "It's a buck," he said under his
breath; "quick! fire!"

I did so, and the animal turned and disappeared. But
he was hit, and we saw him some minutes afterwards
about a hundred and sixty yards off. Another shot, and
we were soon beside him, as he lay stretched out on the
grass.

"A very fair buck," said Hans, looking at him as he
lay before us; and both were satisfied that it was a buck.
We now turned over the chamois to clean him, when
to the surprise of both we found it was a doe,—a yeld
one and very old, and of a most masculine appearance.
Not only was the head very male-looking, but along the
back was a ridge of long hair, usually to be found only
in bucks. The horns were corrugated and covered with
resin, indicating the very respectable age of their possessor.

We had one day passed before the hut, where it had
been first our intention to take up our quarters. There
was a Sennerinn here, which was rather unusual, and she
with her two brothers attended to the cattle and dairy.
I very much doubt whether a person to whom the un-
becoming dress which the women on the mountains frequently assume was unfamiliar, would, at first sight,
have recognized the sex of the individual in question;
and yet she was womanly in demeanour, despite her
horrid costume, and she had a pretty smile and a mild
blue eye. Happily too—for there is nothing so disgust-
ing as dirt in a woman—her face was clean and bright;

and her hands, I observed, were always washed before meals. Equipped as she was in full male attire, so that at a short distance I could not distinguish her from her younger brother, she needed this palliative of cleanliness to lessen somewhat my unconquerable distaste to her masculine attire.

In such out-of-the-way places you may often perceive a human form stalking along the hill-side, which you very naturally take for the herdsman. On approaching the Esquimaux-looking figure—Esquimaux-like both in filth and dress—you perceive it is not a man, and yet you can hardly bring yourself to believe that the rotund bundle before you has any claim to the name of woman. It seems to you such a sad desecration; and indeed it is so, for every appearance of womanhood is gone.*

On leaving this dwelling I could not help exclaiming to Hans, " What a nice hut! Why it has a table! did you see it? And there is even a sort of bench to sit on; —it looks quite comfortable."

The thing was, our present abode was so rude that even this trifling accommodation of a board on four legs as a seat, seemed to me a luxury. The interior of the hut was also neater than the one where we were staying, owing probably to the presence of the Esquimaux-looking sister.

Thus, after all, comfort, like happiness, is quite a relative idea. Had I seen this out first, with its poor contrivances, it would not have seemed to promise great things; while now I was really anxious to remove to it, in order to profit of its superior accommodation. And

---

* It need hardly be said that this dress is assumed for convenience sake; as the woman's usual attire would be but little adapted for the mire of the cowhouse, or the dews and plashy meadows and tangled underwood of a mountain sojourn.

we did so; taking care to carry the cracked pipkin with us, for my coffee; for here nothing was to be had for cooking but the usual iron frying-pan. In this Franzl made a savoury mess of the chamois liver, and, with some potatoes brought up from the valley, we had a perfect feast. The table was hardly larger than the frying-pan which was placed upon it, but still it was a table; and as we sat round the iron vessel, all eating out of it at the same time, the additional comfort of such a piece of furniture was indeed most enjoyable.

I had almost forgotten, however, to speak of something we had here which was really a great luxury,—a light. There was a small oil-lamp, throwing out as much brightness as a rushlight; and by thrusting a lath into the crevices of the wall, I made a bracket just over our supper-table, on which the lamp was placed. The reader may think this a mere trifle: however it is not so; for it is inconvenient to be obliged to carry always a lighted piece of pine-wood about with you, or to hold it in one hand while with the other you eat, if desirous of not taking your meal in darkness or twilight. To sit there, in the fullest sense of the words, "at table," with a lamp to light us, was in truth as much as the most exigent could require. We were very comfortable; my only fear was that the little tin lamp might suddenly tip over and tumble into our frying-pan.

I went out again, but was unable to get a shot; therefore after five days' absence I returned home.

CHAPTER XXIX.

THE KARWENDEL MOUNTAINS.

THE weather being favourable, I started with my trusty companion for the Eng, a narrow valley between high and abruptly-rising mountains at some distance off. We left soon after noon, and the evening was just setting in when we saw a light twinkling through a crevice in some hut, and knew we had arrived at our destination. The dwellings here are much the same as those where we had lately been. I had been here before, and was therefore prepared for their primitive arrangements.

Day was already coming up over the snowy tops of the mountains opposite when we went forth next morning. On going further we reached a knoll at the outlet of the valley, and here the grandeur of the scenery showed itself in all its vastness. Before us rose the peaks of the Karwendel, broken, sharp, and jagged,—a ridge impracticable save for the eagle or vulture. The mountain was a stupendous barrier: on the right it took a semicircular sweep, hemming you in and shutting out all hope of egress,—no possible outlet, visible at least, anywhere. It seemed like the boundary of a world, and yet just below on the other side lay the Tyrol, the lovely valley of the Inn.

The scene is the more striking, because you come upon

the grandeur and desolation quite suddenly, emerging as you do from between the rocks of the picturesque pass.

The huge shoulders of the mountain receded gradually a considerable distance, forming large plains of snow, dazzling and resplendent with the brilliancy of the rising sun. From out this high frozen field rises suddenly the precipitous wall that forms the torn and blasted crest, which even the boldest climber could never reach. Over the cold wide expanse brooded that awful silence which always reigns in mountain solitudes. The very sharpness of every outline against the blue sky, the distinctness in which the whole is spread before you, added, I thought, to its character of desolation and loneliness. There was no blending anywhere—nowhere a shadow: there was no room left for self-delusion. You were shown clearly and unmistakably that not a single thing had there a being; and while the glaring light discovered every part it gave no warmth, but only showed how frigid, and unsympathizing, and dead was all that lay before you. Within the vast amphitheatre on the right the ground was broken by great chasms; and here all looked very dreary. It was thitherwards we took our way: it looked the more gloomy now from being entirely in shade. Seating ourselves, we gazed downwards and around. We peered long into every part in vain. "It's a strange thing," said Hans; "I would have wagered anything we should have seen chamois here. I was never here yet without meeting them. Two bucks were here regularly for some time past, and now they are missing;" and he peered still more searchingly into every recess, and up among the rocky shelves, but still ineffectually. A long silence followed. "I see him!" he exclaimed suddenly, putting up his telescope; "there he stands on the field of snow, right in the midst. It would be impossible to get near him, but we may drive him. Come along, let us try !" and we descended the slope and into the stony bottom. Here lay whole banks of earth torn down by the floods, and fragments of rock and up-rooted trees and bushes. Through these we went, and up on the other side. Once here, what before had seemed from a distance an even surface of snow, showed itself full of rifts. From time to time we came suddenly on a chasm, that descended straight down eighty feet and more, and so abruptly, that the merest slip of the foot would send you to the bottom. At best it was but bad walking here. The slopes were so steep that in going round them—for we were obliged to choose these places and keep below the ridge, to avoid being seen—we were forced to dig a footing with our poles for each coming step as we proceeded, the snow being deep and not to be trusted. Hans, who went first, would sometimes, if he himself were standing firmly, thrust back his pole with its iron point under my foot, in order to steady it and make doubly sure, for now and then it was perilous work. Once we went along a narrow path—perhaps eighteen inches wide—worn in the side of the rock, just above a chasm. The rock overhung the path a little, and at a turn pro-jected so much that, the better to get by, I rested my right hand on the jutting mass, as I bent my body slightly outwards on the opposite side. Just as I was turning I felt the rock I held by giving way. I had but time to stand firm and quietly, and try to preserve my equilibrium. Instinctively as the crumbling fragment fell, I guided it so as not to let it strike my chest or shoulder, which would have sent me over; but caused it to fall lower down, so that I was able to withstand the shock. Down rolled the loosened stones, dashing over the

rocks below, reminding me where I should have gone if
at the critical moment I had been the least flurried, or
otherwise than collected and calm. The position was
rather an awkward one, and that Hans thought so was
evident by the anxiety with which he watched the result.

At last we reached a spot where I was to wait while
Hans returned the way he had come, and by making a
detour reach the extremity of the Kahr, as such spots are
called, and drive the chamois towards my resting-place.
It was a knoll about two hundred yards from the base of
the wall of rock.

"He will come along below the rocks, and at farthest
'tis always within shot. Keep a sharp look-out, but be
careful not to be seen. Make yourself comfortable, for
'twill be a long while before I get round."

"The wind," I said, "is now blowing down over yonder dip in the ridge,—that's all right; but later, when the
sun gets higher, and the wind comes from below, don't
you think the buck may remark it?"

"No; the sun never shines in here. The wind we
now have will blow in the same direction all day. Come,
lie down," he continued, kicking away the snow, "and
above all don't raise your head too much. Adieu, and
Weidmann's Heil!"*

I took off my rücksack, in order to stretch myself upon
it, and wrapping my joppe closer round me, for I was in
a perspiration from our quick climbing, chose my place,
and lay down with my rifle beside me. It is always well,
when you are waiting at any spot for game, to reconnoitre the ground, and to note the different places where
it is likely to come. By doing so you are not taken
by surprise when it does make its appearance, whether it

* Synonymous with "Good sport!"

2 B

approach over the knoll to your right, as you think it most likely will, or even though it show itself emerging at a greater distance from a hollow on your left. Having acknowledged to yourself the possibility of its moving along yonder, you are not flurried or anxious when you suddenly do see it appear there, as you might be if the distance had not already been measured by your eye. The ground having been well conned too, you know how far you may let the game advance without danger of its escaping you by taking another direction. You have also marked the spot where the stag or chamois will be best seen and most exposed as he steps along; or you tell yourself, "If he come down yonder I will *not* fire, but will wait till he reaches the opposite side, which is so steep that he *must* go slowly in mounting it;" and thus you are not taken unawares, let the game show itself on which side it may. If you are lying down, or in any unusual position, this forethought is the more necessary, in order to be able to bring your rifle to bear on this side or that easily, and without such a total change of posture as to risk frightening the animal. To turn your head even would sometimes not be permissible. You must therefore manage your limbs and body so that, whether standing, seated, or lying down, directly the creature is seen your bullet may fly to meet him. More than one good stag have I lost by my carelessness, by being unprepared for him when coming in a direction other than had been expected. Indeed on this particular subject, "The hunter at his post awaiting game," a long and useful chapter might be written.

It began to get cold in that vast amphitheatre, surrounded as I was by snow and ice, and the wind that blew straight down upon me added to this feeling. When Hans left me I had forgotten to look at my watch: it

seemed however a long time since he started. I could
not see him at a distance, though I carefully scanned the
fields of snow before me. After a time I grew uneasy,
and fancied that he might perhaps have missed his footing in returning by the narrow ledge, or had gone over
the brink of one of those yawning clefts which opened
here and there so suddenly. I waited, but still saw and
heard nothing. It was quite inexplicable; for more than
enough time had elapsed to enable my companion to
make the round, and I ought to see him, at least from
afar. The buck too had disappeared. I resolved to wait
one hour more, and then, following Hans's footsteps in
the snow, set out in search of him.

The time had nearly elapsed, when in the far distance, where the gloomy cauldron closed round, I saw
a black something which moved. Yes, it was a man, and
on closer examination I found it was Hans, carefully
descending into the hollow. It was a great relief to
know he was safe, though his appearance still so far
off puzzled me the more. I got my rifle ready, and kept
a sharp look-out; trembling all the while with cold, and
partly may-be with expectation. Presently at a distance the old chamois came sauntering along over the
snow. He had seen Hans no doubt, but he was not
alarmed. On he came in the expected direction: I lay
close and watched him well. He suddenly bore for the
rocks, and instead of keeping on the broad snow-field,
chose to step along the slightly-projecting ledges, where
no animal but a chamois could find a footing. He
moved on, still very saunteringly, like the veriest
lounger who has nothing in the world to do. He was
further off than I had hoped he would be; but, though
a long shot, he was within range. I put up a second
sight, aimed, stretched out at full length on the snow, and

fired. At the same moment I *felt* that I had missed him : and it was so ;—he gave a bound and disappeared.

Hans soon came, his honest face looking pleased and inquiring. "He's not hit; I know I've not hit him."

"Where did he come?" asked Hans, and we went to the spot where he was standing at the moment I fired. "H—m ! there's the mark of your bullet in the snow : and here he stood. The ball must barely have passed under his shoulder. A little higher only, and you'd have had him. You ought to have hit him too at that distance," he added, looking back to the knoll where I had been lying, " for it's not so very far after all."

"I aimed just at the middle of his shoulder."

" Aye, but you did not make allowance for the wind that bears right down from above here. Such a gust as that presses down a bullet several inches ; and if you did not allow for it, no wonder you missed."

He now told me why he had been so long absent. After going round and descending into the hollow, he looked for the chamois at the place where he had first seen him, but he was gone. He examined attentively every spot, and at last saw far away behind him, at the very further end of the hollow, a chamois at rest on a ridge of rock. It was probably not the one we had first seen. He had therefore to retrace his steps, mount the opposite hill, and thus come down upon the buck so as to ensure his moving off in my direction. After hearing how much trouble he had taken, I was doubly sorry it should have been to no purpose.

We now went higher up towards a point whence a look might be obtained over another wide expanse. In going along we saw a bridge of solid ice thrown across a wide cleft. The arch was of considerable span and height, and had a curious as well as bold appearance.

It was hard work wading upwards through the snow, and by the time we reached our destination I was fairly tired out. Nothing was to be seen to reward us for our pains. Stretching away to the right, the snowy slope rose in a bend to the ridge of the mountain. We determined to return. At this moment I observed a black speck or two in the distance, motionless on the white expanse. Presently one speck moved, and then another. They were chamois. I pointed them out to Hans, who asked if I would go after them. It was a great way up: it would take nearly two hours. However we set off, and after resting several times on the way, we got to a rock behind which we thought the herd must be. Amid that deathlike stillness the slightest sound would betray us; and at each step a stone rising through the snow and meeting our heel risked to make our labour in vain. I now advanced alone, and cautiously looked over the rock. No chamois were to be seen, although the snow in front was marked by their traces. The next moment a doe with her kid bounded from a hollow and away over the expanse. But where were the others? I heard a whistle and looked round just in time to see a buck standing at gaze for a second, and then vanish.

Thus it is with the chamois hunter: he often spends hours in toiling up to a desired spot and at last gets there unperceived: the game is within reach, the wished-for object attained. A moment only and his finger will have pressed the trigger; but in that short interval a something occurs that defies his precaution, the game is already far off, and the labours and watching of half a day have been in vain.

The magnificence of the scenery compensated me in some measure for my disappointment. I had the pleasure too of falling in with a covey of ptarmigan,—a bird of beautiful plumage, being quite white except the feathers of the wings, which are bordered with black. According as the moon is on the wane or is increasing in size, so Hans asserted, do these birds lie quiet on the snow, or rise before you can get within shot of them. When it is nearly full moon, they are so wild as to be quite unapproachable.

"Is it possible to pass the ridge, think you?" I asked, turning to gaze once more at the wilderness we were leaving.

"Yes, it is just possible to get out by yonder rent, extending further downward than the rest. It is a narrow cleft, and steep, but still possible; and the poachers from the Tyrol know the way and occasionally come across. A year or two ago I saw one making for it, when standing where we are now."

"Had you never any adventures with poachers?"

"Yes, once when I was going out before daylight after black-cock. I had a lantern with me to show the way, when suddenly some one gave me a tremendous blow over the head, and jumping forwards caught hold of my gun. Luckily I held fast, but we had a good struggle together, during which some how or other his gun went off. More than once I thought it would go against me, but at last I got him down and wrenched my gun away."

"Did you never fire at one in any of your expeditions on the frontier?"

"No, never. I never shot one in my life; and I am very glad of it, for even in self-defence it is a thing I should not like to think of. I could have done so more than once, but I never did."

We reached the hut at last; and putting our shoes to dry, which, thick as they were, were saturated like a glove, cooked some supper and soon went to bed.

CHAPTER XXX.

ON THE GEMS JOCH.

THE sides of the valley were beginning to grow distinctly visible as we set out on our expedition. We passed opposite a spot where, the year before, I had climbed after a chamois; and now in looking at the place from below, I wondered how it had been possible to get up there. We pressed forwards toward the bed of a stream which had torn for itself a channel out of the side of the mountain. Up this we went, stepping from stone to stone as each rose out of the splashing water. It was pleasantly cool in this watercourse, which we were about an hour in ascending. We then crept along till we reached the edge of a kahr, and taking off our hats peeped cautiously down. Chamois were there. Suddenly Hans sank to the earth, making his body as flat as possible, and signing to me to do the same; while his eyes bade me look opposite, where on the summit of a rock—a pleasant green table-land—a chamois was standing: a fine fellow he was too. With our chins close to the ground, we wound our bodies backwards, till a dip in the hillside prevented our being seen.

Resuming then a more human posture we consulted on what was to be done. "That's a rare buck!" said Hans, "and well worth trying for; but how to do it, that's the thing. Even were we to go down again and round the other side, all is so open there we could not approach him."

"And he'll hardly come down and join the others," I said; "he'll stay where he is, quite alone. But the others,—did you see if a buck was among them?"

"Yes, one was a buck, but nothing like him opposite. However, if you like I will try to drive them, and it is not impossible that he may join the others and come with them. What is your opinion? Don't you think if I get round and appear on the other side, they will pass up here within shot? They surely will never go up the yonder, so come here they must."

I took the same view of the case as himself, for unless the chamois turned back, which was not likely, they could not do otherwise than seek an egress near to where we were lying. "Well, I'll be off," said Hans, "the sun is shining, so be careful not to let your telescope be seen,—it glitters so. I remarked that the other day, and such sparkling is visible afar, and would be sure to be seen by the chamois. It will take me an hour and a half to get to the summit, and about half that time to come down again, so be on the watch then."

As Hans began toiling up the mountain, I could not help thinking, while looking after him, what an indefatigable, good-tempered fellow he was. No fatigue, no difficulty or privation ever for a moment prevented him from starting off to serve me; and he was always cheerful, never out of humour, even though I missed the buck which after an infinity of trouble he had managed to make move towards me.

It was a delicious spot where I lay; I was comfortably ensconced between two large stones, which, while they formed a sort of easy-chair, screened me from the view of the bright eyes which were on my left. The kahr where the chamois were, may be compared to an enormous quarry; but a quarry, be it observed, occupying the whole broad face of a mountain, and deep in proportion to its breadth. On one side rose a vast steep slope of rock, extending in unbroken surface up to the topmost ridge. How great the height was, I first fully comprehended when, some hours later, Hans appeared on the summit, and his whole form showed itself in clear relief against the sky, not bigger than an infant's.

Before us, stretching away in seemingly interminable distance, lay the world of glacier and everlasting snow. Peak upon peak, plain adjoining plain, rising and receding one behind the other, till at last the furthest misty outline was so very far, that it was no longer possible to say what was snowy desert or mere floating cloud. Occasionally I turned to watch the buck on the small table-land, enjoying the green pasturage; but once, when looking for him again, he was no longer to be seen. He had found perhaps some shady nook, and was enjoying the solitude.

At last I saw a small moving figure high up against the sky,—it was Hans. I watched him with my glass, and could remark what caution was necessary in coming down over that steep, smooth slope of stone. But why come down there at all? Why not keep more away, so as to come upon the chamois from the opposite side, instead of approaching them thus? It was inconceivable to me how Hans, who always showed such judgment, could commit such a blunder. He was more than three parts of the way down before the chamois perceived him. As usual they stared, moved forwards undecided what to do, and then—to my astonishment, and that of Hans too, for he stopped and looked after them with great surprise—dashed boldly up the face of the rock, where we both had decided they would certainly *not* go. But it took even the chamois a good time to reach the summit, for to the very top they went, and then disappeared over the other. On my companion reaching me I learned why he had come at once over the rock. He had seen chamois on the other side, and had therefore kept this side the shoulder of the mountain, in order not to be perceived.

We set off after them, and climbing down into the kahr, and crossing it, mounted the green declivity still higher. Advancing cautiously we approached the edge of the chasm, and lying flat on the earth looked over. Many chamois were there scattered in various directions, but all as yet beyond our reach. Two we marked as being bucks. There was nothing to be done but wait, and see if they came nearer. We thought they would, and in some hours' time, pass out of the hollow over the rocks near where we lay. Hans meanwhile took an hour's nap, and I dozed and watched the chamois by turns. They strolled carelessly about, and as I observed them hour after hour, I was convinced more than ever how little foundation there was in the stories generally told about the sentries and outposts that keep strict guard against the approach of an enemy.

The sight and hearing of the chamois are so good that they are in reality in little need of sentinels: they are at all times watchful, and the sound that one of them could hear would be heard by all. Nor would the taint of human neighbourhood borne down to them on the breeze reach one only, to be announced then by a shrill sound to the rest. They *all* would look up and scamper away at the same moment, as though an electric shock communicated *at once with all their bodies*, the moment the current of air came rippling among them. There would be no need, no time indeed, for any such announcement. The sharp whistle moreover is not intended as a signal, for when the animal is quite alone the sound is still uttered: it is rather an expression of wonderment and of fear,—may-be also of displeasure. A deer, if it come upon some strange object suddenly, and quite unable to make out what it is, will gaze, stamp on the ground, and utter a grating noise: and the roe too, when very frightened, has a most discordant cry. But these are all expressions of personal feeling, without reference to others of the herd; though of course such token of alarm uttered by one makes all vigilant; and though the rest see nothing, it will cause them to scamper away more scared than if they knew from what they were running. In the present instance not one was watching.

Quick as are the eye and ear of the chamois, these organs may be termed coarse in comparison with the sense of smell these animals possess. Watchful and alert as they are, I have sometimes passed in places unobserved by them, when they ought to have seen me; but never on any occasion did the slightest breath of air flutter round or move only in a direction from me to them, without their marvellously fine sense perceiving it, and making them alive to the danger. I am convinced too they rely for safety more on the sense of smell than on that of sight or hearing.

At last three came nearer the rocks. "That first one is a buck," said Hans; "don't you think you could hit him? it's not so very far. That other is a buck too, but he is much further." Lying down at full length on the ground, I tried my aim. "I think I can manage it," I replied, and fired. "Well done! he's hit, well hit!"

said Hans, as the chamois made a few uncertain steps. The other was still standing on the same spot as before, looking up quite bewildered at the thundering report, which seemed to shake the very sides of the vast hollow, and was still heard faintly in rumbling echoes. I aimed steadily, and taking him rather high in the shoulder, fired my second barrel. He made one step forward, and then rolled off the ledge where he had been standing on the loose stones below, and continued thus rolling, turning over and over for about two hundred yards. But the other though wounded was still on the move, out of sight immediately below me. I quickly reloaded, and stole some paces lower to look over the brink. There I saw the head of a chamois in listening attitude, and the animal was evidently undecided whether to come on up the rocks or to retreat below. The horns were thick and high, and believing it was a buck I had not yet seen, waited to let him advance, so as to get a better shot. Meanwhile a yearling buck sprang along the rocks not twenty paces from me, and stood and gazed for a moment in great amaze at the immovable human figure it had suddenly alighted on. But I did not fire, waiting for, as I thought, the third prize. By going down the rocks some paces I got sight of the chamois, whose head only I had before seen, and quickly firing sent him rolling over. "That's number three," I exclaimed exultingly to Hans, as the animal fell; and I began to look for the one I had first shot at. But my companion, who from the spot where he was standing could see better into the depth than myself, told me I had but two; my first and third shot having been fired at the same animal. This was rather a disappointment; however it was a pleasant sight to see the two chamois lying stretched out on the slope before me.

We now clambered downwards, and crossed the *geröll*
towards our booty. " A good buck !" shouted Hans, who
was the first to reach the lower chamois, and on he hasted
to the other. After examining it I knew at once by his
silence it was not a buck. " 'Tis a doe !" he exclaimed,
" a very old doe ! There's not much difference between
them in size ; and look at the horns too, how high they
are !"

We cleaned the two chamois, and slinging the rücksacks which contained them over our shoulders, set off
for a hut that lay on our way homewards.

To cross *geröll* is at no time pleasant walking, and
when carrying a load a firm and careful step is necessary
to get along at all. We returned by the way we came,
passing through the kahr where we had first seen chamois.
Here was a place that made you feel the difference between carrying a weight of some forty to fifty pounds
behind you, or having nothing at all to bear. The path
was a narrow ledge, and to get out of the kahr it was necessary to step on a piece of rock about as large as the
palm of your hand, and then swing yourself upwards.
There was no difficulty in the passage ; but the dead
chamois pulled you back, and prevented the elastic bound,
without which you could not reach the spot for your next
footstep.

In about two hours we gained the hut, which was now
quite deserted.

The next morning betimes we set off, and reached
home in about four hours and a half. In crossing a
mountain-stream I nearly got a ducking. The mountaineers often throw a couple of saplings over the water,
from one bank to the other, and on these the passenger
is naturally obliged to move sideways, a step at a time.
Being young trees, they bend and rock at every move-

ment you make. Moreover as you stand sideways, your
heels are on one tree and the forepart of your feet on
the other. Now if one stem happens to be weaker than
its neighbour, or if you press more heavily forwards than
in the contrary direction, or if you raise one foot rather
quickly,—if in short all is not kept in perfect equilibrium,
a jerk is occasioned by one tree or both, and your bending bridge of a few inches in breadth will inevitably play
—you such tricks that over you go into the rapid torrent
beneath. We had to cross such a bridge, and a day or
two before without anything at my back it was easily
accomplished; but this time the additional weight made
the slender stem sink and rise again as if bent on mischief, and now I was in danger of going backwards into
the water, and now forwards on my face. However
neither happened, and we reached home in right merry
humour and well pleased with our sport.

CHAPTER XXXI.

THE TYROL.—SCHARNITZ.

(1856.)

Arrived at the Riss Thursday evening, October 16th. Found the castle pretty full of guests, and for me a letter from Prince Leiningen, who was on Sattel Eck. On Saturday we go to the Wechsel. Many chamois pattering on the rocks above our heads, but none shot.

Some days after to the Hagel Hütte, where we all stay a week. Shot in the Todten Kar one good buck. At dinner one day, the Duke proposed to me and G— to go to Scharnitz and stay there as long as we like. We gladly accepted the proposal; for, in the first place, the territory was new to us, and we knew that the features of the country there were of the wildest character. Moreover, it was much more to my taste to go out stalking, than with beaters to drive the game: for thus, much of the charm is lost; you are not dependent for success on your own skill or venturous daring; and the thousand incidents which attend your steps while approaching the chamois,—all the breathless excitement of expectation and disappointment,—these are in a great degree wanting when you have but to wait quietly at an appointed stand. Stalking too might be preferred for another reason: it causes less disturbance among the game; and, be it never forgotten, quiet is the most essential thing to be preserved in every chase.

The road through the mountains to Scharnitz lies amid the grandest scenery. At the end of the valley called the Eng, a rampart of silvery-grey rock, with zigzag summit, rises to bar all egress in that direction. In turning into the Karwendel Valley the same vast forms are now on either side of you. The line of stone is only interrupted by a rent in the mountain chasm, and you are able to look up and into the awful hollow where Desolation and Death seem to dwell together. There a slope of loose time-bleached stones stretches from receding peaks down and down in almost endless sameness to the foot of the mountain, and leads out of that crater-like place, where the sunlight never enters, into the glad face of day. And over the steep upland huge blocks of glaring stone lie tossed about in disheartening confusion, crushing and obliterating all vegetation, and testifying to the fearful throes of some long-gone century. Perpendicular walls of rock, bare as slabs of marble, are more frequent here than in the Hinter Riss. Here all is wildness, and every rock you look on speaks to you of convulsion, of fiery pangs and suffering. The *geröll* too extends here in much longer lines than in the Riss, and there are few objects which impress so mournfully as such tracts of barren stones. Being late in the season, the herdsmen and milkmaids had all left the pastures with their cattle, so that neither the cheery shout of the peasant-boy nor the sound of the sonorous bells was heard to enliven the valley as we passed.

Arrived at our little inn, after a walk of ten hours and a quarter, the first thing was to consult with the keepers about what was to be undertaken. As we sat at supper our companions were watching with scowling glances a

party at another table; every word on the subject of
game was uttered in a low whisper, and we learned that
yonder in the corner sat a poacher, who would be on
the watch to catch up any word that might give a hint
of our intended movements. It was curious to see how
Bradler, who had himself been a noted poacher, watched
the others from beneath his eyebrows, casting glances
which, could mere hate kill, would have destroyed his
enemy over and over again. This keeper was, indeed,
the terror of all the poachers in Scharnitz, and there
were plenty of them; for they knew his daring, and
were sure, moreover, that were they and he to meet they
need expect no mercy. He once heard a shot in the
mountains, and suspecting a certain cottager to be the
delinquent, waited near the man's hut at nightfall, to see
if he would return. He came as expected; but having
perceived in the dusk the dark figure against the white
walls of his cottage, flung down his rücksack and took
to flight. Bradler pursued him, but fell unawares down
a bank into the brook. He soon, however, gained on
the poacher, who turned and called to the keeper to stop,
or he would fire. For this threat Bradler cared little.
It enraged him the more; so rushing on the man he
knocked him down into the stream with one blow from
his rifle, rendering him for a long time insensible; and
had the poacher not been dragged out of the water he
would inevitably have been drowned. A chamois which
he had shot was afterwards found in his rücksack.

"And if you call to a poacher to lay down his rifle,"
I asked, "and he does not, what then?"

"Why that at once tells me what his intentions are,
and I don't wait long. Should I be near him, and he re-
sists when I take his rifle, and tries to wrestle with me,
then if I am not able to manage him I feel for my knife,

and stab him where I can. It will never do to trust these fellows. While I was at Brannenburg a keeper lost his life by such imprudence. He met a poacher, and called to him : he did as if he intended to give himself up, and when the other approached, attacked him. They struggled together; and each making use of his knife, one was stabbed in seventeen, the other in eighteen places. Both staggered to a village hard by, and there, each in his own house, they died within an hour of one another."

The following morning we three went out together. On reaching halfway up the mountain, we saw on the other side of a broad chasm a chamois grazing.

" He has something the matter with his hind leg," I observed, after watching him attentively. " He tries to spare it each time he moves."

After waiting half an hour to see what he would do, he lay down. The spot where he was, formed a small ledge, with a young birch-tree growing on it, about 130 yards below the ridge that overtopped the chasm. It was a sure spot; so my companion retraced his steps, while we lay down to watch his proceedings. After a while I saw him opposite me, his figure diminutive in the distance, creeping upwards. And now he is peering over the brink into the depth below to look for the chamois. It seems he cannot discover him among the thick herbage, for the stillness is yet unbroken. But now the report of his rifle crashes from rock to rock : he fires again. We start to our feet, and see the chamois rushing down the smooth rock and coming towards us.

" He has missed him !" cries Bradler, and at the same moment springs down the steep immediately before us, to try and intercept the chamois. To see him make this Curtius leap was really frightful. The declivity overgrown with trees and bushes was most precipitous, and

where it abruptly ended there was the deep abyss. But
it must have been more frightful to look at than to do,
for dashing after him with my rifle in one hand and
swinging from branch to branch with the other, I was in
a moment at his side, and craning over into the chasm.
Down there stood the chamois amazed and bewildered.

"You might fire now!" cried Bradler. But to stand
upright on that slope was impossible, and without a firm
footing I could not fire.

"Quick! lean against me!" said B—. "I've got one
knee against this old tree-stump. I'm as firm as a rock ;
there's no fear, only lean!" And doing so, I fired straight
downwards, just as the buck was looking up to discover
what this hubbub could mean. "He's down! Quick!
There he is! Don't you see him? Close to that rock!
Quick, another shot!" and I fired a second time.

My companion from his eyry opposite was now, in his
turn, watching our proceedings; too far away however to
take any part in the affair.

"Now climb back carefully: only take care not to
slip," said Bradler, "and I will go round and get down
to the chamois."

He soon returned. My first shot had entered just above
the shoulder, and the second, further forward, had passed
through near the neck ; that of my friend had merely
grazed the skin. The cause of the animal's lameness was
now discovered, a quite recent shot—fired by a poacher*
—had shattered the hind knee-joint; yet notwithstanding this the buck had been able to pass down the steep
rocks with unabated rapidity.

We returned home, and an hour later my companion
came back, bringing a capital buck he had shot higher up
on the Bronnenstein.

* No keeper having fired a shot there lately.

2 c 2

For the following week it was arranged that one of us should go to Gleirs Thal, and the other take up his quarters at a hut in the Karwendel valley. On Monday morning therefore I was up by half past three, and at four was on my way passing along the banks of the noisy Isar, which alone broke the stillness of the bright starlit night.

It was about half-past seven when, as we were going slowly up Gleirs, I suddenly saw a chamois, feeding right in front. Bradler saw him too at the same instant. Dropping to the ground, and as quickly as possible—for there was no time to lose—I fired. The buck sprang forward a few steps, and rolled on the earth. But what exclamations of wonderment and gratulation arose when my two men looked at him stretched on the greensward! He was indeed a splendid animal, jet black and with hair some inches long waving down along his back in the morning breeze. And how we passed our fingers through it exultingly, and smoothed his glossy coat! We could not sufficiently feast our eyes on the sight. There was no end to the delight.

"You may go out for many a long year," said Wrack, "before you will shoot such another. I have shot five hundred in my time, but have not yet seen one to be compared to him."

He weighed, when cleaned, seventy-five pounds (Austrian weight).

We left him hidden under a bush, and went on up the mountain. Many chamois were to be seen, but it was impossible to get near them. They all moved away, and one after another disappeared in the "Wand." Soon after, when approaching this place, we saw a buck, at rest on a small ledge projecting from the steep side of the mountain. It was but little out of the perpendicular: the only places for the foot to rest on were the narrow prominences here and there where the strata were broken; much the same as if in the wall of a house some bricks, carelessly laid down, were sticking out from the rest. What made the passage more difficult was that fresh snow was lying on the rocks, which not only caused the footing to be less secure, but prevented you from seeing what you had to tread on. But we got on well some distance in the Wand; and with one foot as firmly planted as I could manage, and leaning my whole body against a heap of snow which had accumulated in a nook, I fired, just as the chamois, suspecting danger, had started to his feet. It was a long shot, and my position cramped and incommodious, and I missed him; though by the hair found on the snow where he stood the bullet must have grazed his body. I was afterwards glad I missed, for had the chamois been hit, he would have fallen to a frightful depth, and rebounding from precipice to precipice, would have reached the bottom an indistinguishable mass.

Of all the difficulties a chamois hunter may have to encounter, the most trying is undoubtedly climbing along a "Wand," or wall of rock. Nerve is very necessary, and a steady head and foot. Your position looks, and in reality is, so fearful as you creep along some ledge—seeming a mere speck, full-grown man as you are, on the vast rock's face—that if you dwell on the thought, and allow the peril to stand before your mind in its reality, you must, I think, be inevitably lost. The danger is so palpably evident to your senses: it stands before you bare and in its very nakedness, that there is no means of self-deception; and while clinging to the rock's face, like a bird to a house-wall, you feel and know you are utterly cut off and away from everything like

help. Above your head, high, high up, nothing but bare
stone; before you, on and still on before you, bare stone
again; and beneath, perhaps you cannot see to the bottom
on account of some projecting crag, but occasionally a
stone your foot has dislodged goes whizzing through the
air, and leaping over the promontory is heard, though
faintly, still rolling in the gulf below. How far down
it is! How little every object looks at the foot of the
mountain! Houses and trees are dots; but up here all
is of tremendous size,—all except yourself,—and you in
your own eyes seem the very smallest of dots. Your actual position, moreover, is so peculiar. On one side of
you,—quite close, touching your hip at every step,—is
the rock, so that there is no room for free action there;
while on the other is air, nothing but air, so that here
too, not having wings, you are shut in also.

Your disposition on the particular day or at the moment will often enable you to attempt such passage or
warn you to desist. What you may do today, you
may not be able to essay even tomorrow. You feel you
have not the heart to venture, nor do you. A few days
after going into the Wand where the chamois was, I came
by the place again. There were no chamois there; but
by passing along the Wand and coming out further on,
I should have emerged in the neighbourhood of a herd
in front of me, and which it was impossible to approach
unperceived in any other way. But although the last
time I had gone on without a moment's hesitation, I
had not the least inclination to go there now: for some
reason or other I did not like it; and the more I thought
about it the less it pleased me; so I turned away and
went on. The view from the summit of this mountain
is not only very grand, but is also peculiar. It is so si-
tuated that you see into the whole of the Leutash Vale,

towards Seefeld, and look down as well on the Hinter
Au Vale. All lies before your eyes as distinctly as a
map in relief. You see the mountain-chains diverging
from each other and forming new valleys : the mountains themselves too are beheld from their very base on
the plain clear up to their summits. This point of view
is most interesting.

It was getting late, so Bradler went to fetch the dead
chamois, while we turned downwards in order to reach
the path before night came on. We sat down at a turn
in the road to await our companion, whom we at last
heard in the distance, the irons on his feet clattering
among the stones. He could testify to the weight of our
prize; it pressed heavily on his back as he descended the
broken mountain-side.

The next morning we started again at four, and took
the same path as on the preceding day. We had seen
chamois, and as they were still on the mountain or among
the precipices on the north side of it, it seemed to me
there was every chance of getting a shot. We had moreover arranged that Bradler was to go into the Hinter
Au Vale, which was at the foot of the Gleirsch Joch—
it was on this valley I looked down when in the Wand
the day before—and thence climb upwards through the
chasm to where we should be near the summit of the
mountain. If chamois were there, they would be disturbed by his presence, and would move slowly forwards, and I should be enabled to get a shot as they
came out over the ridge. By one o'clock, when I expected to reach the top of Gleirs, Bradler was to begin
his ascent. When later I looked down into the abyss up
which he was to come, I sincerely repented the arrangement, so truly frightful did the place appear. It seemed
an absolute impossibility for any human being to scale

such towering heights of smooth rock. Yet he did so, and
seemed to think nothing of it. "Only once," he said,
"he did not know how to get further while he held on
to the bare stone, and above and below was nothing but
the liquid air." The chamois came—fifty-nine of them
--slowly one after the other, but not at the place I expected, and so far off that a shot was impossible.

Later we saw a buck below us. Down we went, and
taking off our shoes crept over the stones towards him.
But there was no possibility of getting sufficiently near ;
and after we had watched him for an hour crouched
down on the ground, he moved away.

We now went to a hut lying in a deep glen beside a
torrent, that came tumbling in many a waterfall over the
rocks. It was a wild spot ; and later when Wrack went
out with a handful of blazing pine to light him, and the
red glare flickered over the foam, the whole had a Frei-
schütz air ; and had the Wild Huntsman come yelling
through the air with his spectral crew, it would hardly
have been out of character. There was abundance of
wood, and our first act was to make a roaring fire, which
soon gave a look of cheeriness to our little dwelling.
Potatoes were set to boil, and from some mysterious
hiding-place Wrack produced a piece of chamois liver.
Here was abundance and luxury ! Meat even, which no
one would have expected. And a pitcher of delicious
water was fetched from the spring. We peeled and ate
our potatoes, fried the liver, sliced more potatoes into the
pan, and had a supper good as man could need.

What especially pleased me was the delight which
Wrack's countenance expressed at my satisfaction with
all his arrangements and cookery : nor should the thousand little attentions he showed me be forgotten. He
did the honours of the simple dwelling with zealous and

kindly care; for he considered this a duty that devolved
on him, as for weeks together in the summer-time this
hut was his home.   He had accumulated here all sorts of
useful articles,—pots and pans and pipkins; and at hand
in a cellar was a store of potatoes, some carrots, and
even celery.   It was a Robinson Crusoe sort of household, and Wrack himself was as uncouth in appearance as the poor solitary could have been.   But he took
thought of everything for my comfort, made a bed for
me with scrupulous care, and covered me over to ensure
my being warm enough, as tenderly as if I had been a
child.   Yet he was a wild-looking fellow.   Indeed his
very birth and infancy seemed belonging to a savage
state.   He was born in a cavern below the rocks,
close to the foaming stream we had passed in the morning; and this place, reached by a ladder, was his abode
winter and summer for the first years of his existence.
Here, like the young goats, he had scrambled over the
rocks; and not having broken his neck or rolled over
into the stream, learned in time to pass along a precipice as fearlessly as over a bridge.   He had lived in
the woods and grown up among the wild animals, and I
can well believe they were not afraid of him, but looked
on him as one of themselves.   War was raging at his
birth; foreign soldiery were pillaging and ravaging his
native village, so his parents fled from Scharnitz and
found an asylum in the cave, since called by his name.

Wrack's last service that night was to bring me a
draught of ice-cold water, and I soon fell asleep despite
the incessant tumbling and noise of the torrent close to
our dwelling.

At daylight next morning we started for the valley
leading to the Solstein, a mountain somewhat more than
9000 feet high.   It is rounded in form, and of bare

stone, without the slightest trace of vegetation. At the foot of it we saw fifteen chamois, but after having spent some hours in trying to approach them were obliged to desist. Later we saw eleven, but they too were unapproachable. That night we returned to the hut, and the following day started for our old hunting-ground, Gleirsch Joch. I knew we were certain to see game there, and though the ground was most unfavourable for stalking, I still hoped to get a shot. On our way we saw five and afterwards six chamois.

From a distance we saw the herd disporting themselves on the ridge, then disappearing among the precipices, then emerging again from the " Wand." Most of them, no doubt, were on the ledges on the precipitous north side. The only thing to be done was to send Bradler in where I had been a day or two before, and so disturb the chamois and cause them to come out on the summit. Downwards they were sure not to go. So I set off for the place, and making a sort of screen before me of the stones lying about, I sat and waited. By-and-by I could just see on my right, above me against the sky, a head or two and crooked horns. Then more and more. The herd was moving, but unluckily instead of emerging from the Wand where I expected they would, a little further off *in front* of me, they were all making their appearance so much to my right that I could but glance at them from the corner of my eye, though at last I did gently move my head a little more round. But to turn so as to bring my rifle up to my shoulder was out of the question. They would have been off and down the precipice on the other side in a moment. There they stood on the sky-line, twenty or more together, looking down towards me. I thought they would never have done staring. Some strolled here, others there, but not any where I wanted them to go. How cordially I was abusing them to myself all the while! At last a yearling buck thought he would see what strange animal had come up into their haunts, and walked down to have a better look at me. He turned his head to the right and to the left, but it was evident he grew no whit the wiser. Then he walked further down, and stopping opposite me stared full into my face. But he could not make it out, for I was motionless as a stone; my eyes even did not move. He seemed determined to give it up, and was moving, when, as I saw there was no hope of the others coming in that direction, I fired at him. He bounded away for a few yards, but soon I saw him rolling over and over down the steep mountain, till stopped at last by a stone. I went to fetch him, and then up to the ridge. This was the highest point. From here you looked down into deep craters, jagged, gloomy, horrid. I stepped across to a narrow ledge, and holding by a pinnacle of rock, got round it, so as to see down into the chasm. It was a horrible place; I do not think I have seen any so frightful. From the spot where I stood the rocks went down perpendicularly like a shaft for 150 feet; a narrow, appalling descent. All was calcined and brittle as if from fire, and crumbled away in your hand or beneath your foot. Further out rose from the abyss broken barren rocks, and at their foot were depths your eye could not penetrate. On such a jagged ridge were now about a dozen chamois. They had gone thither after my shot. But even they now could get no further. There was no passage, no egress beyond, and not a chamois could leap down such precipices. They saw and heard us, as we saw them. There they stood gazing, wondering, and scared. It was too far to fire, besides had I shot one, it would have been impossible to fetch the carcass out of the bottomless pit into which it might have rolled. Bradler was watching them too, but lower down. I saw him running forward towards the brink, and knew by his manner he saw a chamois somewhere within shot, and was just calling to him not to fire, or to wait, when I heard the report of his rifle. On reaching him he told me he had hit the chamois; it was lying in yonder chasm, and he could just see its head. I told him how foolish it was to have fired, as he would not be able to get the animal after all.

"Not today," he said; "it's too late, for I want a whole day for that; but tomorrow I shall come and fetch him."

"You intend to go after that chamois!" I exclaimed, not crediting I had heard aright.

"Yes: I shall get down that place where you were looking yonder, and when I have found the chamois, clamber up again the same way."

"Good Heavens! you don't surely mean to try to get down there! Why, it is utterly impossible; it is quite perpendicular, and so crumbling you have nothing to hold by. You *can't* do it!"

"Oh, but I can," said he, laughing; while for my part, the mere thought of the attempt made me shudder and disquieted me.

"I only know," said I, "that were it *my* chamois, nothing should make me let you go for it, and I would take good care too you did not. I should never forgive myself for letting you undertake such a thing for me."

But he went after the chamois quite alone, and got it too, as I learned from the head-forester some weeks later, though *how* is to me still an inexplicable marvel.

In the six days I had been out at Scharnitz I had

seen one hundred and sixty-four chamois, and yet was able to kill but three bucks. In the five days' shooting in Hinter Riss one good buck had fallen to my rifle,--the only shot I had fired during that time. These particulars will show how uncertain the chase of the chamois is, and on how many chance incidents success depends.

On our way homewards Bradler asked me if I knew a certain forester in Baierisch Zell. I said I had seen him, and inquired the reason of the question.

" He had a *malheur*," was the rejoinder.

" Yes," continued Wrack, " he shot my brother."

It was a matter of surprise to me that both my companions spoke of their former lives as poachers without the least reserve.

" In one year I shot forty-seven chamois," said one, as we were slowly going down the hill-side. " For I was ' a shot,' you know," he added, addressing me (a' Schütz bi' i' g'wesen).

" And I," rejoined his companion, " shot forty-six in one year. 'Twas the most I ever did."

" And did you never meet any keepers ?" I asked of Bradler. " Did you never get caught ?"

" No, never," he replied. " I always preferred going out alone : moreover I went into places where few would have dared to venture, so that there was little chance of falling in with the forester there. Once only, on the Plau Berg, I had shot a chamois, and was coming along with it, when I saw a keeper advancing and going up the mountain. With all my might I exerted myself to reach the ridge before him, and by great exertion I did so. I then flung down the chamois, and rifle in hand, went straight towards him. Being above I had the advantage. When he saw me he turned aside in another direction.

"And since you have been a keeper, have you never shot any poachers?"

"No," was the answer; "but I was once present when two were killed. It was near Branneburg, and I and another were going to shoot a roebuck. I was just passing round a small thicket, while my comrade took the other side, when suddenly I heard a shot. I turned back a step or two, and saw a man running away, and at the same moment almost a second shot sent him staggering to the ground. On I went to the other keeper, and on coming in sight of him, saw a poacher making towards him, gun in hand. However, my unexpected appearance made him turn back; and running to the dead man, he took his rifle and escaped. My comrade had shot two: one dropped at once, and the other we found some distance off in the forest."

The poachers round Scharnitz knew that from him they need expect no mercy, if he caught them in their depredations. He had said, and he told me so too, that should he ever meet one out on the mountain who resisted instead of surrendering himself instantly, he would fling him over the precipice if they happened to be near one. And they all knew he would infallibly keep his word. This dread of the man kept the territory, vast as it was, which was under Bradler's care, pretty free from predatory incursions. Though he was here today, that was no reason why tomorrow he should not be on the mountains at the other end of the valley: they were never sure of him except on one point,—that once on their track he would follow them unto death. They dreaded him as though he were some incarnate fiend.

That the animosity is mutual, and that the severity of the gamekeepers toward the poachers is not unfrequently to be accounted for by preceding acts of refined cruelty to themselves or their comrades, the following story will go far to prove. Its hero lived, up to the summer of 1846, in a cottage on the borders of the pleasant Starem-berg Lake, close to the country-seat of one of my friends, who knew the man well,* and who had listened more than once to the terrible recital, and had seen the marks of crucifixion which his feet and hands ever after bore.

Zacharias Wagner, or "Zacherl" as he was familiarly called, was one of those handy fellows who was expert at almost anything he attempted,—at carpentering, gar-dening, fishing, bird-catching; but what he loved best was to be out in the woods or on the mountains watch-ing the game; and, if an opportunity offered, without danger of being caught, to test perhaps the steadiness of his aim and the range of his trusty rifle. At last he got a place as keeper in Reichertsbayern, and it was one evening in June, when returning from his usual rounds in the forest, that his adventure occurred. He had seen nothing, neither stag nor chamois that whole afternoon, but it was too early to turn homewards; and so, in-tending to be out early on the morrow, and with hopes of better luck than he had had hitherto, he determined to pass the night in one of the log-huts which are always to be found on the high-up pasture-grounds.

Here, snugly ensconced in the sweet hay, with his dog beside him, he soon fell asleep.

An hour, or may-be two, had hardly passed, when Waldmann began a low bark, which awoke his master; but he, thinking the dog was dreaming, took no further notice of it, and turned to sleep again; when at the same moment he hears a rush towards and into the hut where he was lying, and he had scarcely time to seize his rifle

---

* It is to this friend I owe the admirable likeness of Zacherl, done to the life, at the end of this chapter.

before three men laid hold of him, exclaiming, "Eh, my lad, so we've got you now!" Out they dragged him, and one beat him soundly with a cudgel while the other two held him fast; but before long he sank down quite insensible. On coming to himself,—roused by the sharpness of a new pang,—he found that the men, poachers all three, whom he once before had caught and taken before a magistrate, were raising him up against the wooden walls of the hut, and, extending his legs and arms, were nailing them to the boards. Having no nails, they had cut pointed wooden pegs, which they drove through each hand and foot; and so they left him on the mountain upreared—crucified.

"My dog, Waldmann," to continue the story in Zacherl's own words, "ran after the men, but soon he came back again to his master. I was too exhausted by agony to call out, and I scarcely took heed of anything; still I can remember how anxious and sympathizing my poor dog seemed. At last I beheld before me, as I hung, the sun slowly coming up behind the mountain-tops; and I was glad to see it again, though for the last time. ' Your morning prayer today,' thought I to myself, ' will be a prayer for the dying !' and I was in despair with my sufferings and the thought of perishing by so miserable a death ; and I began to think of our Lord and Saviour Jesus Christ, who died on the cross, and of his agony. But I soon grew insensible ; and all I know is, that when I came to myself I was lying on the grass. The thing was, Waldmann's barks and howls had brought a boy to the place, who was out with his cows on the pasturage. He ran to get help, and then began the descent from the cross. I was taken down, and with water from a spring close by my wounds were washed; but I could not stand, and some wood-cutters carried me down into the valley.

" In three weeks I was able to go out, but my hands were still bound up, and as to the scars, they of course will remain to my dying day. It was lucky that no nerve or sinew was injured by the wooden nails; but so it was, and right thankful am I to Providence that I escaped so well.

" As to the three men who crucified me, I have often seen them since in the inn-room and out in the fields; but I thought '*I won't be their judge!*' However, should I meet them in the wood or on the mountain in my territory, then I shall do as I have always done yet."*

The mountains here abound in black-cock and ptarmigan. Of a morning we continually heard the call of the former, and the latter beautiful bird we frequently surprised on its bed of snow.

The vulture, even more perhaps than the poacher, is the redoubtable foe of game in the mountains. The flocks too suffer by his presence, and the number of lambs carried away every year from the pastures by these birds is almost incredible. Hence every effort is made by the keepers to catch or shoot them. The latter method is seldom successful; for it is chance merely that brings the sportsman in such proximity to them as to get a shot.

Wrack's cousin, who is noted too for his skill in imitating and catching every sort of bird, told me some curious details about the vulture. He had caught a young one, and hoping to make this a means of catching the old bird, he fastened a strap to its leg and tethered it to the ground on a mountain-top. For three or four days the old birds did not make their appearance, probably not having found out where the young

* There is something quite matchless in the self-complacency expressed in these last lines.

one was. At last one of them comes, bringing a hare for its offspring. The next day a lamb was brought, another time the greater part of a chamois kid, and once only a ptarmigan. Thus the old birds continued, now one and now the other, for several days to feed the prisoner, without it being possible for Wrack to surprise them; for wheeling high in the air, they always scan well every spot before approaching the earth, and the least change from its usual appearance, or any new object, makes them distrustful.

The young bird was always aware of the parents' approach, so Wrack related, long before he was able to discern the vulture in the air; and at such times would grow restless, scream, and flap its wings, as impatient of their coming.

One morning however Wrack was there before them, and from his hiding-place of piled-up stones, shot the old vulture just as it alighted on the mountain. It measured seven feet from wing to wing.

The Hinter Au Thal is, so these men told me, one of the most difficult places in the Tyrol. I looked down upon it and its declivities of rock, from the top of the Gleirsch Joch. Everywhere here, they said, are smooth, steep slopes of bare stone, so that you can hardly get on otherwise than on hands and knees. To walk on them is next to impossible.

Another valley near Achensee, where I had been two years before, is very beautiful. The rocks on its sides, however, are broken and crumbling and pointed; and there in the midst of them you might fancy yourself in an extinct Etna or Vesuvius. Even the hunter who was with me there could not help exclaiming, as we looked over the brink into such a chasm, " Es ist grausig!" But I mention this Fallthurn Thal, because it was here I

witnessed the most magical, most wondrous effect I have
ever yet seen, or perhaps ever may see again.

It was still dawn when we left the house, and a dense
vapoury covering hung low over the meadows. By the
time we reached the Fallthurn Thal it was day; but the
mists still filled the vale, although the brightness of the
rising sun penetrated through them somewhat, and the
morning breeze drove them trailing along over the pasture. Presently the whole world of cloud in which we
were moving began to lose its whitish-grey hue, and to
assume a leaden colouring merging into blue, but as
yet dark and opaque. Suddenly, however, on raising
my head, there stood before me at the end of the valley,
high up above the rolling vapour, an opening into the
blue sky; and thereon rose two high peaks, not of rock
seemingly, but rather of opal, or some wondrous substance that could catch and give back with softened
lustre the sun's effulgence. There on the deep azure
they gleamed, silvery-grey in colour, but radiant as the
spot might be where an angel of God had stood. Just
so, methought, might have shone in lucid splendour
the gates of Paradise. Below and around, the mists still
shrouded every object, yet you could not but perceive
that the whole was becoming of a bluer tint, and the
upper layers more transparent. And now before me
through this thin, floating, half-transparent veil there
shines a vision, as yet however so waveringly indistinct,
that it is not possible to recognize a form. But a glorious burst of blue sky is visible through the vapour,
which is now every moment growing brighter, and the
top of the Sonnen Joch appears. And through the vast
rolling mass, half opaque, half transparent, an outline
of brightness grows into existence, and from the silvery
point, which is already glowing in the light 8000 feet

2 D 2

above you, you are just able to trace it downwards, and to make out that it is the sharp shoulder of a tremendous pile of rock. As yet it is half hidden in sunbeams inwoven with the mist: a divine halo-light is in the air, as though that mountain were a divinity, and only thus veiled might show itself to mortal eyes.

But what before was trembling, and dreamy, and uncertain, grows each minute more defined and real; the clouds fall aside, and the vast form of bare rock is before you in all its size and brightness.

CHAPTER XXXII.

CHAPTER THE LAST.

To be upon the mountains is always an inspiring, an ex-
hilarating event; and the further you penetrate amidst
them, the greater is the feeling of delight. It is a peculiar sensation you experience when climbing among them:
and I know nothing like it, except the thrill of gladness
and exultation which fills the heart when you have given
yourself to the waves, and are forcing your way onward
over the open sea. For mighty as are the forms which
rear themselves around, and sensible as I always am of
their vastness, on me they never exercise an overwhelming power: on the contrary, all my best energies are
called forth by the sight, and by the difficulties to be
grappled with: the mind seems to expand and grow,—
to rise, as with newly-awakened strength, till it is on a
level with the grandeur that it beholds.

On the mountain-top the same silent joy possesses my
whole being as when in presence of the ocean; and as I
have sat on the rocks of the Lizard or Land's End, looking out for hours over the Atlantic, and watching the
long waves that heaved their ponderous weight along,
awe was in my heart, it is true, and a tremendous sense
of God's omnipotence; but there was no feeling of little-
ness: on the contrary, within me rose an elate conscious-

ness of power, an exulting joy that, vast as was that ocean, my human mind could still encompass it,—in thought could traverse it to its very utmost verge:—a great rejoicing, deep and unspeakable, that I, even I, was able to take in such immensity.

And this effect, the grandest appearances of Nature always produce in me. They do not crush the mind into nothingness, but cause it rather to feel

"An equal among mightiest energies."

They incite it to action, and call on it to put forth its strength. For then, when thus face to face with sublimity, one mighty sensation, like an instinct, becomes always suddenly quick within it,—a glad, triumphant consciousness of inalienable divinity.

But there are besides many other minor sources of joy, for the mountains form an exclusive world of their own,—a world with its own delights, phenomena, and wonders; and not only the things themselves, but even their very names have often a strange charm, that awakens the fancy and sets it busily to work. For he who lives constantly with Nature, watching all her moods, nor loving her less, but rather the more, for her changing and waywardness, will not give to familiar things, and to places that are dear to him, a barren name; but remembering each as connected with an event—call it how he will—the word he chooses will have a meaning, a significance. The wider our world, the less sympathy have we for individual objects; but if we make a valley our home, we become as intimate with every part, and with all belonging to the dale, as we are with the children, and the men and women that inhabit it. And, where this is the case, such objects become a part of us; they live in our heart, and we invest them with attributes, and we speak of them almost as though they had feelings like ourselves. Hence the personifications which we find in the talk of the mountaineer,—the vapours, the storm, the torrents, the deep lake, are to him not inanimate things: he has heard or looked on them with dread or with complacent joy; and he knows the ways of each, as though it were a living creature which he himself had reared. And this is the beginning of poetry.

I have often asked the name of a peak, or field of snow, only in the hope I might hear that it was some " Spitz," or " Kopf," or " Firner." The positive pleasure such mere names afford me is greater than I can say. " Wetter Spitz," " Teufels Horn," "Uebergossener Alp," " Gems Wand," " Sonnen Joch," " Steinernes Meer,"—what painting there is in these words; what scenes they call up, and how they invest the dead, senseless rock with a living interest! Yonder peak becomes, for me, more than a mere mass of dumb stone, when I hear that there the wild elements come together and hold their meetings, and descend thence in storm and tempest upon the lower world. Another, perhaps, has a dread story locked up in its name, and as you hear it your fancy conjures up a tale of terrible retribution, overtaking some great sin.

The mists also, as seen on the mountains, are different from anything of the sort ever witnessed in the plain : they sometimes come clothed in loveliness, but they will rise too dread and dimly, and with a fearful and unsparing power. Here they assume great forms, and are a reality, a presence. They rise up, and pass slowly by you, like sad ghosts, or come rushing on along the sides of the mountain, a long array of muffled shapes of superhuman bulk. It is an impressive, a very impressive sight; and not only on account of their vast proportions as they sweep through the air, but because of the change that is wrought by them ; for they separate you at once and entirely from that dear world which you look upon as your home. There you stand, cut off from humanity, and as lone as though you were on the broad sea, a thousand miles from any shore. At such time I think that even one who called himself a misanthrope would acknowledge a returning love of his kind, and feel that he belonged to them, and would long for but one glimpse only of his and their dwelling-place. And when such glimpse at last is caught, through a rent in the dense volume of cloud, how fair the earth appears! it seems fairer and brighter than ever it did before.

One feeling, moreover, was always present to me; and, whether lying down to sleep on the mountain-ridge at noon, or when sitting of an evening with my peasant friends in a cottage or Senn Hütte, that pleasant consciousness, like a merry, laughing face, that peeps in upon you, go where you will, was ever in my thoughts. It was, to use the words of the author of 'Eothen,'—for he had felt it too,—the delight at being beyond the reach of "respectability." I often quite hugged myself at the thought, "Not one 'respectable' person near me, look where I would!" and this thought imparts always a sense of freedom, quite distinct from that which the boundless space and the fresh breeze bring with them: it is the sense of liberty, which he feels who has escaped from heavy thraldom, who has slipped off his handcuffs, and got away over the walls of his prison, and laughs to find himself in the fields and beyond pursuit. There is a feeling of self-satisfaction in the heart, and a very wantonness in your contentment and glee, as you repeat again and again the assurances of your safety,—of being beyond the reach of either the "genteel" or the "respectable."

As I have observed in a preceding chapter, it is not

the mere killing which affords him pleasure who stalks through the forest in pursuit of game. Besides the natural appearances which will meet him at almost every step, and which contribute so largely to his delight, he has another interest,—the observation of the habits of animals. In dense forests this is not so easy; but in the beech-woods, where there is less undergrowth, and where too the sun can penetrate more easily through the spreading boughs, and so illumine the leaf-strewn ground and the beds of green and brown moss, there you often can observe the creatures in their forest-home, and get well acquainted with their family or household life. It is a pretty sight to watch the care of the doe for her fawn, or to see the two playing together, as a happy human mother will do with her baby; or, if very still, you may steal forward near enough to see the majestic stag himself at rest in the shade, and may observe how he enjoys the coolness of the spot, and, with a languid Sybarite air, now lifts, now turns his head, and puts back his vast antlers even upon his broad sides and shoulders. But he hears a sound! or did the breath of air that rustled through the leaves carry to his nostrils the taint of your neighbourhood? He is no longer the slothful Sardana-palus he was before, but with bold front and head erect, is now " every inch a king."

Among a family of wild-boars I have sometimes remarked one—generally a weakling, and more helpless than the rest, for with boars, as with men, the strong like to show their power—who was buffeted and ill-treated by all his brothers and sisters. Do what he would, nothing was right; sometimes the mother, uttering a disapproving grunt, would give him a nudge, to make him move more quickly, and that would be a sign for all the rest of his relations to begin showing their contempt for him too. One would push him, and then another; for, go where he might, he was sure to be in the way. It is true such poor little unfortunate was generally the most awkward of the family; but then constant ill-treatment is enough to make any one embarrassed and awkward.

The caution with which a stag, particularly an old one well versed in the ways of men, will emerge from a thicket into the open space, is very great. With his head almost on the ground, he steals forth as stealthily as a fox. You do not hear a dead leaf rustle, so noiseless are his movements: with his nose low down, and advanced as much as possible, he will stand immovable for some minutes, with no part of him visible except the nostrils and the large bright eyes,—these alone move; and when the ground has been thus carefully reconnoitred, without however at all turning his head, the rest of the creature then steals forth, and with a fleet step he flits across the road, and into the shelter of the opposite thicket. It is a mystery to me how a stag is able to pass through the intricate foliage with his widespreading antlers, without disturbing the boughs,—so cautiously indeed as not even to cause a twig or the trembling of a leaf to betray his approach. He is aware of the danger, and flings them back quite low behind him: when in full flight through the forest he does the same, lest he strike them against the overhanging branches in his headlong haste.*

One thing too will have struck every person who has had opportunities of observing wild animals; the quick-

* " Now on again comes another herd,
    They follow their leader's track ;
  I' the van their chief, his embattled crown
    Flung down on his velvet back."
                        VERSE: *Ballad of the Royal Hunt
                              in the New Forest.*

ness, namely, with which the wounds they have received generally heal. When however we consider their mode of life, and the simple food they eat, there is less difficulty in accounting for it. Fresh grass and herbs and pure spring-water as diet must necessarily act favourably on the state of the blood; add to which, a life passed in the open air, inhaling health at each respiration, and our surprise diminishes at what we here see Nature do when left wholly to herself.

It is not at all uncommon to find old rifle-balls in deer, and the marks of shots that failed to bring them down at the time. But where a bone has been shattered, and the animal has still managed to escape, it is really interesting to see how the splintered parts will loosen and fall away; and the wound then nicely closing, the limb presents the same appearance as if it had been amputated by a skilful surgeon. I once saw a deer that had been injured, no doubt by a ball, in the fore knee-joint; the stump had healed, and was perfectly covered. Last winter (1851) I watched a boar that had also lost the fore-leg; but in this case it was high up, close to the shoulder. It was shot some weeks later, when I was out in the forest, and so perfectly had Nature performed her work, leaving behind no trace of a former fracture, that some were present who insisted the animal must have been thus maimed from its birth. There was no scar, no unevenness of surface, to indicate that the bone had once been broken, which however was the case.

But the hardiest animals I have met with are the fallow-deer: it indeed takes a good deal to kill them. I have myself seen bucks with several balls in their body, feeding some hours afterwards as quietly as if nothing had happened. A roe is a very delicate creature, and can bear little; a shot almost anywhere will bring it down. I have sometimes met one in the wood running away from some real or imaginary danger; and it was quite pitiable to see its condition, agitated and exhausted with exertion, the exquisitely fine limbs trembling beneath its body, and its flanks palpitating as it gasped for breath: every movement showed how little its fragile form was able to endure any unwonted roughness. The chamois is less susceptible than the roe, but a wound soon makes it sicken; when struck, it will immediately climb to some solitary spot, and there remain. If by chance you shoot one that still carries traces of a former wound in the body, you may be sure it was slight and of little importance. But chamois even, as well as red-deer, often get bad falls; and the antlers of the one and the horns of the other frequently bear evidence of a headlong tumble over the rocks.

In old works on Venery strange stories are related about the habits of animals of chase.* In former days the pursuit of the stag and wild-boar was a royal pastime, and those animals which afforded such noble sport were on that account elevated to a rank above the more common brutes. They were—without offence be it said—the aristocracy of the animal creation. For in barbarous times the attributes of the sovereign are always exaggerated; and, as "the fountain of honour," his ennobling influence is extended to the elephant that carries him, the steeds that draw his chariot, and even to the beasts of the forest which he happens to take especial

---

* "Plutarch has put the question, Why the flesh of a sheep bitten by a wolf be more agreeable to the palate? And he says that it happeneth because a wolf's breath is so hot and fiery, that the hardest bone in its body will become soft and tender. Therefore the flesh which his breath hath touched becometh soft and tender. On this account the dainty livers of olden times strove to obtain sheep that had been torn by a wolf."—*Abraham Santa Clara.*

pleasure in pursuing. Hence, therefore, such are protected from being molested by an ignoble hand. Now as soon as a person or thing is hedged about by privilege, as soon as a halo is thrown round either, an unusual interest is at once excited, and with it comes vulgar curiosity. When this is the case, be sure that Fable will henceforth have more to tell than Truth. We may suppose too that the wonderful tales which thus grow current, are rather grateful than otherwise to the pride of him for whom alone such marvellous animals are reserved.

"The stag," so writes Isidorus, "is the foe of serpents; and when he is old and sick, he goeth before the serpent's hole, blows and respires therein, so that the serpent may creep out, which then he presently stampeth on with his feet and devoureth. And he goeth straightway to the water and drinks, so that the poison may spread through his whole body ; and as soon as he feeleth the poison, he commenceth running hither and thither in such wise that he getteth warm and fain would sweat, and hereupon he is so purged and purified by the operation of Nature, that he retaineth nothing more in his body, and so becometh renewed and young again, and changes his old hair. Music he loveth much, and is well-pleased and joyful when he heareth a piping or the sound of a flute, or any gentle song.

"A stone is to be found in the deer after she hath dropped her calf: she did eat it before to assist the birth. The stag liveth to be one hundred years old. Three hundred years after Cæsar's death one was found with a golden collar round its neck, and graven thereon 'Cæsar me fecit.' The stag hath a large heart, and a bone therein. The stag is ashamed when he is without his horn."*

* Abraham Santa Clara, who turned every natural fact as well as

In those ancient books, in which the noble Art of Venerie is bravely upheld, as inferior only to the science of war, and the excitement of the chase deemed scarcely less heart-thrilling than a battle, much weight is always laid on the qualifications of a hunter. "And the hunter"—so it is written in a quaint old volume of some centuries ago—"shall be strong of body, bold, and of gay disposition: in body not too stout, in order that he may bear work, and in time of need follow well afoot. Nor should he be too spare of habit or meagre, in order that he may have strength in him, and so go to meet the wild animals with greater safety. The manly hunter followeth the praiseworthy pastime of the chase, nor doth he let himself be withheld by snow, cold, rain, water, mountain, valley, desert, hunger, thirst, heat, unrest, vigils, work, trouble, nor danger."

Whether on the plain, in the forest, or on the mountain, he who has tarried much with Nature, and made her his companion, will, unless duller than a clod, have at times experienced strange emotions in the solitude; familiar shapes will have assumed unwonted forms, and awe will have seized on him, and great fear; he will have heard "low breathings coming after him," or "steps almost as silent as the turf they trod;" and things, even low sounds, have been to him as a Presence, and he will have felt sorely troubled. And this not merely in the darkness, but in the broad light of noon; when the stillness of midnight seemed hanging in the air, yet the sun-rays were streaming silently down the stems of the beeches, and there was no living crea-

every superstitious belief to account, alludes to this bone as follows :— " A pious and sensible woodman may derive a lesson from the animals of the chase. The stag carries in the middle of his heart a little cross of two small bones ; this may cause the woodman to remember that he should never shut out the cross, nor Him crucified, from his heart."

ture to be seen. At such times I have watched and
listened,—listened long and earnestly, not willing, not
venturing rather, to break by my steps the profound repose. Once, I remember, on an autumn day, when in
a wood in Suabia, I suddenly looked round, and behold!
right before me, on a clear space amid the bushes, stood
a deer at gaze. To me then it seemed no ordinary creature, but of gigantic size, the like of which I had never
seen before. There it rose above a little knoll, encircled
in golden light, and its vast form surrounded with a
glory. We gazed for some time at each other in great
astonishment; and had I beheld a bright cross gleaming
over its head, such as St. Hubert saw, I could not have
been more amazed. Suddenly it bounded away, and the
spell was broken.

Wordsworth, in his ' Prelude,' describes with wondrous truth such visionary appearances, and the mental
organization that called them forth. He tells how in
the dusk some peak, as " with voluntary power instinct,"
upreared its head, and growing still in size, and seemingly " with purpose of its own, strode after him." And
very fine, because so very true, is the picture of him who,
" in majestic indolence," wanders on the hills, and sees
objects, in portentous size, looming through the mist.
Indeed no other poet has passages so full of the *spirit*
of mountain scenery as Wordsworth. It is true they
are the phenomena of such heights only as Westmore-
land and Cumberland present; but though these are not
high mountains, they have a solemn character of their
own, and the mists assemble there, and silence is round
them, except when the sough of the wind is heard. The
generality of persons tarry amid the grandeur but a
short time, and then describe their impressions of its sublimity and their own great wonderment. But it is not

by mere passing visits that intimate acquaintanceship can be formed : he only who lives with Nature long and frequently can obtain an insight into all her hidden ways. Nor does she reveal herself but to him who truly loves her : he must learn to interpret her changeful countenance, not by scientific rules, but by the force of sympathy,—the sympathy of deep affection. And it is such familiar intercourse that forms one of the great charms experienced by him who, with rifle at his back, stalks up the mountain, or sits watching on its summit.

The forest, like the mountain, has a delight of its own,—a peculiar, mysterious influence, which grows around the heart, and holds it with the power of a sweetly-influencing spell. The voices and breathings there are different to those heard among the rocks,— that peculiar rustle, as of passing wings, still heard when not a breath is stirring,—the murmur among the branches, and the whisper which floats above the ground, as though the spirits of the flowers were moving about with a hush in that forest world,—all this keeps the eye, and ear, and mind vigilant, and you tread with caution and expectancy among the creeping sunbeams and quickly-flitting shadows. You hear steps now, and the low footfall sounds strangely in that solitude ; but it is retreating, and soon is lost in the surrounding silence. You saw nothing, and it is this very circumstance which imparts mystery, and makes you listen still when the pattering sound has quite died away. Or in strolling on, you will suddenly look round, and from out a thicket see two large bright eyes and a hairy face meet your gaze, and looking fixedly upon you. It is as though the woods were once more peopled with their ancient inhabitants, and the fawns and satyrs again returned to their old leafy home.

Every people while yet young, while their instincts
are still fresh and their sympathies keen and alive to
natural influences, has made the forest their temple;
choosing, if they built an altar, the dense interlacing
branches of venerable trees for the roof that was to
shelter it.   They felt how solemn was the subdued light,
and the trembling stillness : the low murmur attuned
their simple minds religiously, and a presentiment awoke
within them that there "was a spirit in the woods."

And now even in the songs you hear the young
hunters sing, while sitting round the hearth of an evening after a good day's sport, the forest and its delights
play a prominent part.   Among the northern nations
the forest may be said to have had, and indeed still to
have, a poetry of its own.   There were the "Wald-
Märchen" and "Wald-Lieder," and in its gloom many
a mythe was born.   The Germans have an appropriate
word—Waldlust—to describe the peculiar delight which
the woodland imparts ; and as such solitude is also different from that experienced any other where, for it too
there is a particular designation—Wald-einsamkeit.

But, as many a story in the preceding pages will have
shown, there are other far more stirring causes of excitement, contrasting strangely enough with the calmer
pleasures I have just attempted to describe.   From time
to time a report will come of the depredations committed
by poachers, or that one of the foresters has been badly
wounded, or that a Tyrolese has been shot who had
come across to fetch a chamois in the Bavarian mountains.   Or perhaps, according to a preconcerted arrangement, on a certain day all the gamekeepers will be on
the look-out for miles round, in expectation of meeting
the marauders; and, if you also go out, the report of a
rifle from some neighbouring mountain fills you with

2 E

expectation, well knowing that on such an occasion the foresters would not fire at game. It must therefore have been at a man, unless indeed the shot was from a poacher stalking in his old haunts; if so, he will hardly escape now, for the keepers will close in upon him and cut off his retreat. Meanwhile the rocks opposite, and the well-known passes, are carefully scanned with the telescope, to see if any human being can be discerned among them.

On the frontiers of Bavaria and the Tyrol a sort of border warfare was constantly kept up, much the same as in former days was carried on in our own country in the Northern Marches. And as "the Percè owt of Northomberlande" did make a vow "to hunte in the mountaynes of Chyviat," just so would occasionally a band of armed peasants from the Valley of the Inn set off to drive the chamois on the Plau Berg or the Miesing.

Many a deed of boldest daring occurs at such times, when the foresters, coming up with the freebooters, attack them at once, often without heeding their own inferiority in number. But a dauntless bearing, a knowledge of the ground, a quick eye, and a readiness in seizing every available advantage, will nearly always obtain the mastery, even when the odds are most disproportionate. Tales of such sudden encounters with poachers, or of long and patient watchings for them at some well-known pass, are never-failing subjects of conversation; and told too, as they not seldom are, in the living words of passion, and with the energy and eloquence of strong natural impulse, you become aroused as the narrative proceeds; you share all the excitement of the stealthy approach or the unequal strife, and feel an ardent longing to join in the affray.

The following incident, that occurred a few years ago near Brannenburg, will show what daring and recklessness of human life these feuds inspire.

One of the keepers, while out on the mountain, saw three Tyrolese cross the Inn. He at once suspected what was their intention, and instantly set off for a pass among the rocks, where, if he were right in his conjecture, he knew they would surely come. For an hour or more he waited, without hearing or seeing anything of them. At length however he espied the poachers advancing up the mountain, and, keeping close to avoid being seen, let them approach. The place where he stood was a narrow path, with rocks rising on one side, and on the other a precipice. When the men were at a short distance from him, he stood forth and called to them to lay down their rifles. As they did not obey, he shouted that, cowards as they were, he would lay down his, and challenged them, if they dared, to do the same and come all three of them armed only with their poles. They did so, and the three advanced upon him. Calm and collected, he watched his opportunity, and, as they approached, thrust his iron-shod pole two inches deep into the breast of the foremost man, and sent him toppling down into the abyss. The others, terror-stricken, sprang back to seize their rifles, but the keeper was too quick for them : he had already grasped his own, and levelling it threatened to send a bullet through the first who should dare to raise his weapon. There was nothing left them now but to retreat; and as they did so the keeper fired at one, sending a charge of coarse shot into his back and wounding him badly.

The keepers, on the other hand, well know that, should they fall into the power of their enemies, the retribution will be terrible. An instance of this sort was told me by a friend who well knew all the parties concerned. I give the story in his own words.

"Meier, the forester stationed at Gmund,* was one day out on his usual rounds, when suddenly he heard the crack of a rifle. He went towards the place, and there —it was on the Gschwendter Berg—he saw a poacher standing over a stag which he had just shot. Meier dashed at him; they struggled long together, but at last he overpowered the fellow, and binding his hands together, took him as prisoner to Miesbach, to the house of the head-forester. Here he got a light cart and horse, with a lad for driver; and making the poacher seat himself beside the boy, Meier walked along near the cart, with his rifle over his shoulder. As the man's hands were tied firmly together, he thought there was no danger of his attempting to escape.

"You know the road from Agathenried to Miesbach, and how hilly and rough it is? Well, just as they reached the steep hill, the poacher gave the lad who was seated next to him a shove, and sent him out of the cart; then taking hold of the reins, which he could very well do although he was handcuffed, made the horse set off at full gallop down the hill. Meier, who was a little behind, seeing the impossibility of overtaking him, levelled his rifle and shot him right through the middle of the back. The man rolled out of the cart quite dead.

"This circumstance, as you may suppose, called forth feelings of deadliest hate. All the poacher's friends were mad with rage at their comrade's death. Month after month this state of excitement lasted, and time did not seem to abate their fury in the least. They only waited for an opportunity to take their revenge.

* Gmund lies at the northern extremity of Tegernsee, on the border of the lake.

"It was perhaps a year, or may be a year and a half, after Meier had shot the poacher, that he and Probst and Fuchs caught a couple of peasants out stalking on the Schuss Kogel; and having taken away their rifles, and bound their hands behind them, marched both off to the Justice at Miesbach. On their way (it was a most incautious thing to do, and I cannot conceive how they could act so) they stopped to rest on some moss in the wood. It was a glade-like place, some few yards in extent, with trees all round. They were sitting here with their prisoners, their rifles beside them, when suddenly a band of armed men rushed out of the wood: they had followed the keepers through the forest, and had stalked close up to them unobserved. What could three men do against such a number, attacked too as they were quite unawares? The poachers beat them dreadfully, and only left them when they thought all were killed.

"After a time Probst came to himself, and lifting his head and looking round, saw the others covered with blood, lying motionless on the ground. He got up and tried to rouse them, but he found both were dead— so at least he thought. He then, still bleeding and covered with wounds, tottered homewards. After he was gone, Fuchs recovered a little, and observed that Probst was gone. He spoke to Meier, but found him dead. Stunned and bewildered, and staggering, he still tried to reach the nearest house, and made his way to Gmund, which was about an hour and a half's walk distant. Meier lived here, and Fuchs went straight to the cottage to tell his wife what had befallen her husband, and that he had been killed in the wood. Hardly had he finished his story when he fell forward, and dropped down dead on the floor. The sudden change of temperature on

coming into the warm room out of the fresh air, added
to the exertion and loss of blood, was no doubt the cause
of his instantaneous death.   Probst survived, though the
wounds in his head were terrible.   He had recognized
most of the men, but when thay were called upon for
their defence, each proved an *alibi;* one bringing witnesses to swear that on that day he was at a shooting-
match in a village some miles off, and another that at
such time he was in the Tyrol; and thus they all managed
to escape."

It was my intention, had my indisposition not prevented me, to have gone from Partenkirchen to Berchtesgaden, and endeavoured to obtain a day's stalking
there.   I was particularly desirous to do so, not merely
on account of the abundance of game, but chiefly because
the mountains are different in feature to those where I
had hitherto been.   They are wilder and more rugged,*
and the difficult places far more frequent.   Narrow paths
along a ledge overhanging a precipice are sometimes not
to be avoided : they *must* be passed in order to proceed
further.   In more than one place a wall of rock shuts
out all advance : a path is impossible in such a spot,
and yet if you *could* scale that perpendicular face of the
mountain, you would then be able to pursue your way
according to your pleasure.   You have come so far, but
further no living thing, except a bird, can get unaided.
Nor is there any other spot where you may pass : this
wall of rock forms a break in your path of, it may be,
a dozen yards or so, and which but for this barrier
would have suffered no interruption.   If you cannot
surmount the obstacle, you must retrace your steps

* Das steinerne Meer ("The ocean of stone") is here,—so called
from the jagged rocks that, rising up one behind the other, and extending on and on, look like the waves of a petrified sea.

Pedro für Amaud in Ketten(?)

for hours, and climb up the other side of the mountain. But to prevent the necessity of this, in such
places bars of iron have been driven into the rock and
left projecting sixteen or eighteen inches. They are
placed slantingly one above another, and by them, as on
the steps of a ladder, the hunter mounts up the steep
face of the rock. He must of course be careful that
his rifle does not swing against it, and that nothing happens which might make him lose his balance while thus
hanging in the air. It is essential too that he should
observe which foot and hand he begins with; for if he
put the wrong one first, he will hardly be able to go on;
the bars being so arranged to receive, as he mounts, this
one the left, that one the right foot, and those above the
grasp of the right and left hand accordingly. To go up
such a place is not quite pleasant, but coming down is
still less so; for in descending you are obliged to look
below to find the projecting piece of iron on which to
place your foot at the next step, and in doing this you
cannot prevent your eye perceiving the terrific depth below; and, as I said before, this is never agreeable. Moreover when coming downward it is somewhat embarrass-
ing to relinquish your hold of one iron bar, in order to
grasp the other below.

There are places in Berchtesgaden where a whole
mountain-ridge has but a single outlet,—one spot only
by which even a chamois can pass out. If therefore this
be stopped up by artificial means, a natural enclosure of
rocks is at once formed, shutting in, like a park-wall,
the game for many miles. This circumstance shows at
once the abruptness of their formation. The stags, that
might otherwise cross the lake by swimming, are prevented from doing so by poles moored in deep water, and
left to float on the surface. When the deer have reached

the poles, their progress is arrested; for, being out of their depth, they are unable to climb over them; and turning, swim back again to the shore.

It was here that Count Arco performed an exploit which hardly the boldest hunter could surpass,—a deed so very perilous that I never think of the several circumstances attending it, without feeling something like giddiness and being ill at ease. Yet there is a strange charm in danger; and as a child will ask for a tale to be repeated which it has already often heard and been frightened at, so I inquired again about his adventure when the other day we were once more together.

" Will you tell me," said I, " the story of your going after the buck you shot near the Königs See,—the terrible place, you know, where in coming back you grew giddy and sat down, and thought you would never be able to get out again ?"

" That was on the Ober See where you mean, just opposite Thal Berg Wand; but I thought you knew the story already."*

" So I do," I replied; " you told it us all a long time ago, one day after dinner; but I don't remember the particulars exactly, and I should like to hear it again."

" Well," said he, " this was how it happened :—I had wounded a chamois, and as usual he climbed up and passed along a wall of rock, where we lost sight of him. We knew that he would not be able to get out further on, for it was a terrible place, I can tell you."

" And very high up, was it not ?" I asked, interrupting him,—" right over the lake."

" Three thousand feet," he replied; " not an inch less, —that I am certain of: it was a perfect wall of rock, and

* The spot itself where this occurred is called Sailer Stütt, and is on the Walch Hütt Wand.

below was the lake. But I do not mean to say that the water was directly at the foot of the rock, though from the great height it looked as if it were so. It was perhaps fifty or sixty feet off, but that did not make much difference. Nor was the wall of rock, though it looked so, as perpendicular as a plummet line; sometimes it receded, and then advanced again, as is always the case. If you had fallen, you might have bounded off from some projecting crag once or twice, but would at last have dropped into the lake, though not quite at the foot of the mountain. Well, we all said that the chamois, if left quiet, would be sure to come down again, and that it was better to leave him now and not follow him. The thing was, I believe, if the truth were told, none of us had any wish to go along that narrow ledge; and we therefore persuaded ourselves the best thing would be not to disturb him. But we first made a fire, to prevent his coming back, and thus had him safe where he was till the morrow."

"This was in the afternoon?"

"Yes, and we then went home. The next day, when out stalking, I looked across with my glass from a mountain opposite to where I thought he must be; and sure enough I saw him on a projecting ledge, leaning against a pine that grew out of a crevice in the rock."

"Was he not dead then?" I asked.

"Yes, he was dead; but he must have expired while leaning against the tree, for he was sitting exactly as if alive; had no tree been there, he would have rolled over, and we should never have seen anything more of him. Well, I then went to see about fetching him out, but they all said it was quite impossible to get along the ledge. However the chamois was there, and I was determined not to lose him, without at least making a trial to reach the place. So I went first, and a young forester and one of the wood-cutters followed."

"How broad was the ledge?" I asked.

"It was nowhere broader than from here to there," he replied, pointing to two lines in the flooring of the room, marking a space of seventeen inches wide; "*broader than that it was nowhere*—of that I am certain; but in many parts it was not larger than this border," pointing to some inlaid woodwork, seven inches wide; "and on one side, rising up above you, the wall of rock, and on the other a depth of three thousand feet down to the lake. We went along some way, when there, right before us, was a gap,—not very broad, it is true, but still too wide to step across, or even for a jump. The cleft was perhaps five and a half feet wide, and below in the chasm it was wild and frightful to look at."

"But how was it possible to pass?"

"We had a tree cut down, and flung the stem across, and went over one after the other. At last we reached the place where the chamois lay. It was a green spot, just large enough for us three to stand upon,—as nearly the size of this round table as may be (forty-two inches in diameter), only it was rather longer at one end, which gave us more room to open and clean the chamois. Now we had to return, and to carry the buck with us; that was the most difficult part of our undertaking."

"It was in going back you grew giddy, was it not?"

"Yes, for the first time in my life. It was not exactly giddiness either, but rather fright,—a feeling that now it was all over with me, and that I should never come out again. But there was no time to lose, or it would really have been all over with me; so pulling out my flask, I took a long draught of the spirit that was in it, and sat down to recover myself."

" But where?—not on the narrow ledge surely?"

" Yes, on the ledge, with my feet hanging over.   I
was obliged to sit down.   I sat there for about a quarter
of an hour.   But then came the getting up,—that was
a difficult piece of work; for as the ledge was narrow, I
could not turn, as I should have done anywhere else;
for, if I had, my shoulder or elbow or head might have
knocked against the rock behind me, and that, causing
me to lose my balance, would have sent me over; so I
was obliged to get first one foot up very carefully, and
then at last the other, and when that was done, all the
rest I managed well enough.   Nothing on earth however
should ever induce me to go that way again."

" How long was the way altogether?" I asked,—" the
ledge that projected from the face of the rock?"

" Altogether about two hundred yards.   But then
you must not think it was everywhere so narrow as this
strip of wood, though often it was not broader; nor was
the rock at our side everywhere quite perpendicular;
but sometimes it sloped back, now more, now less, which
of course made it much easier for us.   If it had been
the whole way so narrow, nobody in the world could
have borne it; and the rock was not everywhere quite
smooth; but here and there, exactly perhaps where the
ledge was narrowest, would be a little roughness or projection, on which we could hold with our fingers; and
that, you know, was quite enough to make the passage
possible.   For example, at the gap across which we flung
the tree; there, rising up from below, was the point of
a rock.   We could just lay hold of it, by stooping down
as we crossed our narrow bridge.   This was a lucky
chance, for without such help we could not possibly have
passed, there being nothing on either side to steady ourselves by: the cleft in the rock went all the way up, and

to walk across that fir-tree like a rope-dancer, three thousand feet high in the air, was no joke. As it was, that chance piece of rock helped us over capitally."

"But the rock, I suppose, rose some height beside you, did it not? for, if not, it must have been very difficult to make an aid of it in crossing."

"No," he replied, "the rock only came up just to about the tree. That was the difficulty: we had to stoop down, almost sitting on the ground, and planting one foot firmly on the ledge, to slide the other forward, till we thought we could manage to reach as far as to the point of rock, without losing our balance. We tried first of course, then stretched out one hand further and further, till at last we had reached it. Once in our hand, it was all right. Then the other foot was to be gently advanced close to the first; and again slided carefully forwards to the opposite ledge; and when it was firmly planted there, and we thought we were well balanced, the bit of rock was let go, and the foot still on the middle of the tree was quickly brought up beside the other. Luckily the rock rose just in the centre of the gap; for if it had been nearer one side or the other we could not have accomplished the passage, as it would then have been impossible to reach and lay hold of the stone, while one foot was still on firm ground."

"When you came back, how did you lift the chamois over the gap?" I inquired. "You surely did not carry him over?"

"No indeed, it was as much as we could do to get over ourselves, without having a dead weight like that at our backs. When we had him so far, we pushed him forwards on the tree, till one of us on the opposite side could lay hold of his fore-legs and pull him over; but we tied him first to a rock: we dared not trust to our being able to hold him; for had he slipped while in our hands, he would have pulled us over too."

"But," said I, "to me it is unintelligible how it is possible to get along a ledge so narrow, when you have a wall close beside you.   Your own shoulder or hip, knocking against it, must make you lose your balance. It is all very well when the face of the rock inclines away from you; but when straight up,—that is what I do not understand."   And I tried to move alongside the wall of the room with my body close against it.

"In that way of course you cannot," said he, watching me.   "For it is an old joke to place a person with one foot close against a wall, parallel with it, and to tell him to lift up the other.   He is unable to do it of course; he loses his balance at once; but move your foot a little, with your toes to the wall, and heel over-hanging the ledge," he continued, and trying the ex-periment himself, while he spoke,—"no, that is not quite enough yet,—a little more,—ah! yes, that will do now.   You see *now* I can lift up the other foot." And turning with his face to the wall, he moved a step in advance.   "And then, as I said before, the wall is seldom quite straight, and one can hold on a little here and there.   But it was not merely ourselves —there was the tree—we had to go back and drag the tree along the ledge."

"I only wonder that you found any one to accom-pany you.   I am surprised that, when the others saw you were determined to venture, they did not let you make the attempt alone."

"No, no," he replied, "they would not do that; first they think that they climb better than any one else; and that, where a gentleman goes, they can also. Beside this, I must say, all those fellows in the mountains never

desert you in time of need : they have a feeling of honour, which I never met with in a like degree elsewhere;
I went, and that was enough; they then would be sure
not to stay behind."

" It is the only time you were giddy : I suppose it is
the ugliest place you ever were in, is it not ?"

" Why yes, I cannot remember having been in any
more dangerous. But what was so disagreeable in this
case, was having to return by the same path : that makes
the matter a thousand times worse. In going the first
time, if you do feel uncomfortable, you have the conso-
lation of knowing that you are leaving the danger behind you, and that every step brings you nearer the accomplishment of your undertaking. Besides, the first
time the difficulties are all new; you are not aware how
great they are, till you are in the very midst of them
and they are half over; and, before you have time to get
ill at ease, they are nearly passed : but in coming back
again the same way, you have a foreknowledge of the
danger to be incurred; you remember what you felt
when in the difficult situation the first time, and have
an unwillingness, a thorough disinclination, to endure
the same once more. All is so fresh in your mind, that
you hang back when called on to do it over again. And
as you proceed, in approaching some ugly place, your
thoughts are occupied with it all the while : instead of
being calm, you are excited, and fancy makes the difficulty greater even than it is. If fear once gets hold of
you under such circumstances, you are almost surely
lost. It was fear, not giddiness, that overcame me, and
made me sit down; for had I been giddy, I could not
have looked, as I did, into the depth below; but it was
a feeling of horror at the place I was in, a shuddering
dread that I could not shake off. What I drank saved

me: without it I should not have been able to free myself from that overwhelming anxiety."

———————

But it is time this last Chapter should come to a close.
In it I have dwelt purposely on the particular sources of
joy for him who follows the game upon the mountain and
in the forest, and the varied excitements that from time
to time will stir up his heart. I have spoken of the feelings which the grand appearances that hourly present
themselves awaken in his soul; of the power which the
stupendous forms that everywhere uprear themselves
around him exercise over his mind. In the others it was
my wish, while describing the art of chamois-hunting, to
give some account of mountain life; to introduce it as a
fitting background, although not absolutely necessary to
bring out the principal objects of the picture.

With regard to the accounts of each day's stalking, it
must be remembered that, except in the Tyrol, I hunted
always in places where the chamois had been harried in
the preceding years, and where consequently scarcely a
head of game was left.   Success therefore was difficult
of attainment, though all the sweeter on that account
than it would have been under more favourable circumstances.   It is perhaps well that it often was so uncertain, for repeated fruitless attempts teach more than the
brightest good-fortune ; and, after all, one learns nothing
really well except by such experience. Be it not thought,
however, that in saying this I mean to exalt myself into
an authority ; I am well aware that, between my experience in chamois-hunting and that of a sportsman like
Count Max Arco, there is about as much difference as
might be found in the military knowledge of a lieute-

nant who had served a campaign, and that of a Wellington or Radetsky. Such as it is, however, the record is a faithful one; in no one instance am I conscious of exaggeration, or that a single assertion may be found which is not truth.

NOTES.

NOTES.

— ♦ —

Note.—Page 50.

ALTHOUGH since 1848 the chase in all parts of Germany has suffered severely, the quantity of game in various parts of the country is still great. In the chase immediately under the supervision of the Crown Ranger (Grand Falconer), were shot in 1854, in the districts Laxenburg, Auhof, and Prater,—

Stags	111	Partridges	7,077
Hinds	260	Snipes	66
Wild-boars	710	Martens	178
Fallow-deer	88	Pole-cats	1,168
Roe-deer	77	Weasels	1,264
Hares	19,637	Eagles	4
Rabbits	2,159	Hawks	1,617
Pheasants	6,258	Sparrow-hawks	393

On the domain of Prince Lichtenstein—in the four districts Eisgrub, Feldsberg, Lundenburg, Rabensburg—were shot, from August 29 to the end of December, 1856,—

Stags (Harts)	47	Pheasants	5,709
Hinds	156	Partridges	2,977
Fallow-calves	131	Quails	42
Roebucks	52	Wild-ducks	857
Hares	13,933		

Note.—Page 85.

ON SCHNADAHÜPFLN.

In the highlands of Bavaria, as is the case in all mountainous districts, the customs and amusements of the inhabitants are as different from those who dwell in the plain, as the pursuits and mode of life of the latter are different from those of the moun-

2 F 2

taineer. Separated, except by occasional intercourse, for many
months in the year from the world below them, the herdsmen
must be content with pleasures simple in themselves and easy of
attainment. Hence that peculiar song, "Jodeln," with which
the lonely milk-maid of the chalet, the woodcutter, or the peasant-boy "drives the lagging hours along," and breaks the awful
silence of mountain solitude. As soon however as a few men
and lassies are assembled, they have not to seek long for amusement. Then begins the merry dance, peculiar to these people,
mingled with song ; and should the number be too small to afford them this their favourite recreation, then the cherished and
dearly-loved cithern is soon upon the table, and accompanying
with its simple, unassuming melody, some equally simple love-
ditty or song of hunting life.

The affection the peasantry bear this instrument is very great:
its tones affect them more than any instrument of greater pretensions would have power to do.

> " Well, 'faith, it is the strangest thing !
>   What's in a cithern's tone ?
> It moves the heart, and makes it sad,
>   As I've heard many own.
> And then it is so sweet and gay,
>   And sounds in merry style ;
> 'Tis just as though you bravely laugh'd,
>   And yet did weep the while."*

But the most peculiar kind of song, and a very favourite pastime of the people throughout Bavaria, particularly in the southern parts, in Suabia, the Tyrol, Upper Austria, and Styria, are
the so-called "Schnadahüpfln." These songs consist of short
verses, not unlike the "Couplets" of the French, and generally
contain some figurative comparison, taken from external nature,
or from the occupations and pleasures of the hunter or the husbandman, and are always of a humorous, gay, or sportive character. By far the greater number have Love for their theme,
and describe the lover or his "dearie," some love adventure or
a lover's grief. The Spanish "Seguidillas" were somewhat like
them : they too were sung to the guitar during the dance, and
were frequently improvised. Seven lines was their usual length,

---

* Kobell's Gedichte.

and their subject a droll simile, or more generally some dalliance with love.*

With regard to the form of the "Schnadahüpfln," it ought, strictly speaking, to consist of not more than four lines, in which a thought, complete in itself, and as was said before, a comparison, should be expressed. Occasionally what is wished to be said is extended to two verses, but more are seldom employed. It is material that the lines should rhyme; and so particular is the singer that his verse should flow musically, that not unfrequently two of the four lines have no reference to the principal thoughts, but are introduced merely for the jingle. These verses are, as may be supposed, extremely simple, but some are very charming; and when sung to music, the cithern is the instrument, more particularly in the mountains, where the freshest songs of this description are to be heard.

When many persons are together, the way of singing them is as follows: one begins, and then the others sing each a "Schnadahüpfl" in succession; but each one ought either to be an answer to that which preceded, or, from an allusion made to something in the foregoing one, to spring as it were from it, and in this way form a connection between the two. These verses are very frequently extempore; and there are some persons who for hours will continue thus singing against each other, till a succession of strophes have arisen, each one separate and complete in itself, yet, like beads on a string, forming part of a whole and having reference to the rest. When such a trial of skill has commenced, he who at last can think of nothing more to say,

---

* The Gipsy songs, such as Borrow describes them in 'The Zincali,' have a still nearer resemblance to the "Schnadahüpfln."

"The Gipsy poetry consists of quartets, or rather couplets, but two rhymes being discernible, and these generally imperfect, the vowels alone agreeing in sound. The thought, anecdote, or adventure described, is seldom carried beyond one stanza, in which anything is expressed which the poet wishes to impart. The musician composes the couplet at the stretch of his voice, whilst his fingers are tugging at the guitar; which style of composition is by no means favourable to a long and connected series of thought. Of course the greatest part of this species of poetry perishes as soon as born. A stanza however is sometimes caught up by the by-standers and committed to memory, and being frequently repeated, makes in time the circuit of the country."

and is consequently unable to sing his Schnadahüpfl in reply, is heartily laughed at by the rest, while shouts of applause reward the other for his ability and wit.

Such verse, being written in a dialect, it is almost impossible to render in another language, and quite so to do it justice. In the original the words are often much abbreviated, and when read or sung, run so much into one another that a line sounds but as a single word.* I give however some specimens in English, beginning with those that tell what are the characteristics of a Schnadahüpfl.

1.

A good Schnadahüpfl
Must be bold and daring ;
Must climb the high mountains,
For no danger caring.

2, 3.

A good Schnadahüpfl
Is a bird in a wood,—
If drooping and moaning,
A sign that's not good.
For a good Schnadahüpfl
Is the dance of a song,
And a sorrowful dance, 'faith,
It does not last long.

4.

And a good Schnadahüpfl
Leads a right merry life,
Like an old wandering fifer
Gladdens all with his fife.

5.

And a good Schnadahüpfl
Is a flower of the field ;
True, 'tis not much heeded,
Yet all like the chield.

---

* For example :—

"A' Tanna is grea',
Is's Jahr aus a Jahr ei',
Und a' freudigi Lieb'
Muass a' bständigi sey'."

6.

I want but a flow'ret,
  No posy want I ;
And a kiss now and then too
  You must not deny.

7.

Now, don't ye refuse me—
  I've only had two!
Come, give me the third kiss—
  'Tis no good to you.

8.

And as true as clouds oft dim
  The blue sky above,
So as true without jealousy
  Never was love.

9.

And love has a language
  That's everywhere known ;
And when that's no more spoken
  The sun will fall down.

10.

If every star there
  Were but a fair lass,
I wish the whole sky then
  Would fall in the grass.

11.

The Turk and the Russian
  Are nothing to me,
If only my Nanny
  And I do agree.

12.

And green is a fir-tree
  Right all the year through:
And a love that is happy
  Must be constant too.

13.

And were there no flowers
  The bees' life were sad ;
And were there no lasses
  The lads would go mad.

14.

And a blossom don't grow
On a dry wither'd stump;
And you can't sing a song
If your heart's a dead lump.

15.

A bore will not often
Do wonders, I ween;
Just in wild dashing waters
The rainbow is seen.

16.

A mind that is happy
Is a sunshiny day;
Around all is brightness,
Look wherever you may.

17.

And a mind not contented
Is rain, fog, and haze;
You see nothing pleasing
Wherever you gaze.

With the exception of the first six verses, the "Schnadahüpfln" are not taken in the order observed in the original; yet in the selection I have endeavoured to make choice of such as, when strung together, would follow each other in the proper order, and have been anxious to give those in which the character of these songs was most decidedly marked. The attentive reader will certainly have observed that in No. 6 the singer has seized on the "flower" mentioned in the preceding verse, as a subject on which to form his stanza; and having introduced something about a kiss, he who follows weaves it, as it were, into his verse, of which he makes it the subject. Nos. 8, 9, 10, 11, 12, and 13 do not so visibly spring one from the other, though the theme is still the same in each. Nos. 14, 15, 16, and 17 refer again to one and the same subject,—the blessing of a happy and contented disposition. The following are strung together at random, taken like the rest from Kobell's book of "Schnadahüpfln."

A tree is not an emperor,
Yet has it a crown,
And the birds and gold-chafers
The jewels thereon.

Though young be the oak, yet
At one glance you see
'Twill be something more than
A poor willow-tree.

And a brook finds its way on
Without much ado ;
And a lad finds his lassie,
If his love's really true.

Fidelity's often
Like a Schnadahüfl—
Before you can look round
'Tis done or gone by.

And often Fidelity's
Like a stag's horn—
Lost quickly, nor soon found
When once it is lorn.

In some parts these "Schnadahüpfln" are sung during the dance. One of the dancers—he generally who leads off the figure —advances then to the music, sings his verse, returns to his place, and the dance is continued as before.

Such then is one of the favourite pastimes of the Bavarian mountaineer. No description however can give an adequate idea of the merry scene, when on a holiday such a party has met together. The youths, with their picturesque dresses, and hats proudly decorated with the feathers of the blackcock, and a tuft of long hair from the back of some sturdy chamois or throat of the noble hart, with a gay posy peeping from among these tro- phies of the chase,—the village maidens, with their boddices of brightest colours, bordered with gold and laced with chains of silver, to which hang medals of the same metal,—their high green hats trimmed with bright flowers, and edelweis, and tasselled cord of gold and green,—their light brown hair in ample braids, show- ing itself beneath the broad rim of the hat,—the shrill cry which from time to time is sent forth in moments of wild hilarity,—the snapping of fingers, with which, castanet-like, they keep time during the dance,—and, heard above all the noise, the cithern's tones, like those of an Æolian harp,—all together tends to form a scene of rural festivity, to which, for picturesqueness of appear- ance, or for good hearty fellowship, it would not be easy to find a parallel.

The following is the melody to which the Schnadahüpfl is sung :—

In Wales, according to Mr. W. Leathart, a similar kind of song, called "Pennillion," still affords a pleasant pastime.   "They originated probably in the Bardism of the ancient Britons, and were chanted to the harp from the earliest recorded period.   This Pennillion consists in singing stanzas, either attached or detached, of various lengths and metre, to any tune which the harper may play; for it is irregular, and in fact not allowable, for any particular one to be chosen.   Two, three, or four bars having been played, the singer takes it up, and this is done according as the Pennil. or stanza, may suit ; he must end precisely with the strain, and he therefore commences in any part he may please.   To the stranger it has the appearance of beginning in the middle of a line or verse, but which is not the case.   Different tunes require a different number of verses to complete it ; sometimes only one.

sometimes four or six, as will be perceived in the directions for singing. It is then taken up by the next, and thus it proceeds through as many as choose to join in the pastime, twice round, and ending with the person that began."

--- --- ---

NOTE.—Page 121.

POISON-EATING.*

For those who have to climb mountains, one essential quality is, not easily to get out of breath. Any means therefore of obtaining such a desideratum will naturally be eagerly sought after, and when found as eagerly employed.

In some districts of Lower Austria and Styria, especially in those parts bordering on Hungary, arsenic is taken for this purpose, as it makes the respiration much easier in ascending mountains. Whenever the individual has to mount a considerable height, a minute morsel of the poison is taken and allowed gra-

---

* These observations on arsenic-eating are condensed from papers which I sent to Chambers' Journal in 1851, 1853, and 1856, and which at the time attracted so much attention that more than thirty-two journals, English, French, Italian, and German, copied them into their pages. From England and Ireland letters reached me, requesting information on the subject. One poor gentleman, imagining, no doubt, I was a physician, wrote to me about the dose he was to take; for he said, " I have almost decided on trying the effect of arsenic on me, as I cannot find anything else to fatten me, and I have scarcely any flesh on my bones, and seem to get thinner every day." I answered his letter according to his request; urgently counselling him however not to think of acquiring the habit, and representing to him the evils attendant on its practice; saying, in short, everything to dissuade him from his intention. My correspondent probably died soon after from consumption, or may-be from an over-dose of self-prescribed arsenic, for my letter was returned to me some months afterwards by the post-office authorities, it never having been called for or claimed by any one. The papers in question were referred to by the 'Times' in connection with a certain " slow poisoning case ;" and at Madeline Smith's trial they were also again alluded to : proofs sufficient that the novel information they contained was found interesting, and an adequate excuse therefore for introducing the subject here.

dually to dissolve. The effect is surprising ; and heights are thus ascended with ease which otherwise could be climbed only with much distress to the chest. The peasantry are much given to this habit. They obtain the arsenic, under the name of *hedri*, from the travelling hucksters and gatherers of herbs, who, on their side, get it from the glass-blowers, quacks, and cow-doctors. But the poison-eaters have sometimes another aim besides that of a freer respiration ; to obtain, namely, a fresh, healthy appearance, and acquire a certain degree of *embonpoint*. On this account, therefore, village lads and lasses employ not unfrequently this dangerous agent in order to become more attractive to each other ; and it is really astonishing with what favourable results their endeavours are attended, for it is just the youthful poison-eaters who are, generally speaking, distinguished by a blooming complexion, and an appearance of exuberant health.

When the dose is suddenly and considerably increased, the effect is fatal ; although the quantity taken at once and innocuously by those long in the habit of poison-eating is quite astounding. Generally the use of arsenic is kept a profound secret by those who indulge in it ; and it is only the confessional or the death-bed that raises the veil from the terrible secret.

There are cases however where it is taken by the educated as a preservative against some besetting evil, as with Mr. F. St. ——, director of the arsenic-mines at ——, who has been accustomed to take daily a small quantity of arsenic in powder on his bread and butter at breakfast for years. He takes it, he asserts, to protect him from the injurious effects arising from the fabrication of arsenic. And the quantity he eats is not weighed : he is guided in the dose solely by the eye, taking it on the tip of his knife as we might a certain quantum of salt. He enjoys the most excellent health ; and his workmen are instructed by him how to proceed in the employment of arsenic, in order to preserve themselves from the hurtful effects caused by its preparation. The quantity daily taken by this gentleman was found, on being weighed, to be nearly four grains.

Some believe it must be taken when the moon is on the increase, and never, except under peculiar circumstances, when it is on the wane.

As with opium-eating, as soon as the habit is discontinued, a painful craving and a derangement of the organs are experienced.

He who was never ill before, grows an invalid ; and the only cure is a return to the customary poison.

It has been discovered lately that among the chamois-hunters of Salzburg as well as those of Styria, the custom of arsenic-eating is very general. All who practise it, however, deny that they do so with the utmost obstinacy : and there is nothing hardly that will make them confess their propensity. It is the same with the opium-eater, of whom there are many more in England than most people suppose.

To give horses, pigs, and cattle arsenic in order to improve their appearance, is a common custom ; and it would not be uninteresting to inquire whether the favourable effect produced on animals by small doses of arsenic, first led men to apply it to themselves, or whether it was tried on the brute after having been found so serviceable in the economy of the human being.

A circumstance has come to my knowledge lately, which is interesting, inasmuch as it shows that the fact of arsenic being taken otherwise than medicinally is known more generally than at first seemed to be the case. I was told by a person of whom I made inquiries concerning the use of arsenic in stable economy, that he remembered long ago to have read that Napoleon was in the habit of taking arsenic, to ensure himself against being poisoned. As I had never heard this report before, I inquired of other persons in quite another sphere of life, and of them too I learned that the tale was not new. Now, whether true or not that Napoleon did take arsenic,—though his known inclination to stoutness, later in life, might seem to lend additional probability to the story,—it is sufficient that such report was *current*, to show that arsenic-eating not only existed, but was *generally known to exist ;* for without such foundation, no one would have ever thought of building up so seemingly improbable a fiction. All popular traditions, if traced back, will be found to derive their strength and vitality from having sprung up in the atmosphere of truth ; although by the time they have come down to us they may be overgrown with the moss of ages, till their outward appearance is changed, and they look wizard-like and unearthly.

For further information see three papers in Nos. 416 and 493, Chambers' Edinburgh Journal, New Series ; and No. 110, Chambers' Journal of Popular Literature.

NOTE.—Page 373.

Kahr, or Karn.—Julius Fröbel, in his 'Journey through the less known Valleys on the northern side of the Pennonian Alps,' remarks: "This word is doubtless of the same stock as the Gaelic *Carr*, rocks, and *Carn* (Cairn), a heap of stones." In the language of the inhabitants of these valleys, many words, as it would seem, are to be found of Celtic origin; and from some peculiar customs common both to these people and those of Wales and the Erinach, or Celtic Irish, the inference is drawn that "Celtic life maintained itself in these valleys more independently than elsewhere, where a Romance language is spoken."

The mode of singing, also alluded to in the Chapter "Pepi's Cottage," where all present stood in a circle taking each other's hands, and moving to and fro with a swaying motion, is similar to a custom of the Highlanders of Scotland, so Mr. W. Leathart relates, "quite peculiar to themselves." "When a song is to be sung, *the parties all round the room take hold of each other's plaids, or if in English dress, they employ their pocket-handkerchiefs for the same purpose.* The song commences; one sings the verse, and all beat time with their plaids or kerchiefs, *rowing, as it were, to and fro;* in the chorus all join, still beating time, and thus the song proceeds. This mode of singing they call *Oran Luathaidh.* Shaw, in his 'Gaelic Analysis,' accounts for it as having originated in the fulling of cloth by the feet, before the improved method was introduced."

This sort of song, as here described, is an exact counterpart of that chanted in my presence at Pepi's cottage on the evening of the *Heimgarten.*

THE END.

PRINTED BY J. E. TAYLOR, LITTLE QUEEN STREET, LINCOLN'S INN FIELDS.

www.ingramcontent.com/pod-product-compliance
Lightning Source LLC
Chambersburg PA
CBHW022009110726
47901CB00006B/1448